Merle Collins grew up in Grenada, and worked there as a teacher and researcher. She was a member of Grenada's National Women's Organisation until 1983. She is currently a member of African Dawn, a group which performs dramatised poetry fused with African music. Her poetry has appeared in a number of anthologies, and her own collection, *Because the Dawn Breaks,* was published by Karia Press in 1985. She co-edited and contributed to *Watchers and Seekers: Creative Writing by Black Women in Britain* (The Women's Press, 1987).

MERLE COLLINS

Angel

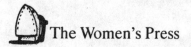
The Women's Press

First published by The Women's Press Limited
A member of the Namara Group
34 Great Sutton Street, London EC1V 0DX

The author gratefully acknowledges use of lyrics from
'Macabee Version' by Willie Lee. Every effort has been made
to trace the copyright holder of this work without success. The
publishers apologise if they have unwittingly infringed the
holder's copyright.

British Library Cataloguing in Publication Data

Collins, Merle
   Angel.
   I.Title
   813 [F]   PR9220.9.C6

   ISBN 0-7043-4082-8

Typeset by Reprotype Ltd, Peterborough
Printed and bound in Great Britain by
Hazell, Watson & Viney Ltd, Aylesbury, Bucks.

Acknowledgments

I am indebted to several people for the valuable gift of time for critical appreciation – in particular to Jacob Ross for constant detailed and nurturing discussion, and to Kwesi Owusu for careful review and commentary. I thank my parents and my nephew Kurt for their inspiration. I would like also to recognise the contribution resulting from the critical comments of Ahmed Sheikh, Cynthia Miller and Rhonda Cobham. One one cocoa full basket. These and other inputs were of tremendous value.

I acknowledge with thanks the assistance of Morgan Dalphinis with the orthography of elements of the Grenadian language. See Glossary at the end for phrases used in the text.

See also Morgan Dalphinis, *African Language Influences in Creoles Lexically Based on Portuguese, English and French, with Special Reference to Casamance Kriol, Gambia Krio and St. Lucia Patwa,* University of London School of Oriental and African Studies, Ph.D 1981 and University Microfilm 1986.

See also *A Handbook for Writing Creole,* prepared by Pearlette Louisy and Paule Turmel-John, with the guidance of Jean Bernabé and Laurence D. Carrington, Research St. Lucia Publications, 1983.

Violence
comes in gentle form sometimes

The river looks calm until rain falls
Then
it vomits old pans, old cans, sticks and stones
a tumbling mass of mud
everything swallowed for years gone by

Sometimes
violence comes in gentle form

One

The yard in front of Paren Comesee's house was full
of restless silence. Quick whispers, staring faces, the sound of an
occasional 'Sh-h-h-h!' Some people stood on straining tiptoe to
see better. Eyes wide open, staring. Eyes narrowed, peeping.
Mouths half-open. A small figure would occasionally make a
quick dart away from an enveloping skirt, only to be pulled back
impatiently by a pouncing hand. Maisie heard a sudden fretful
sound from the baby on her shoulder. She rocked the child
gently. 'Sh-h-h-h! Sh-h-h-h! Hush, baby, hush!'

Heads turned towards them, sharply, released from the elastic
force that had kept them straining to stare ahead. Feet shuffled.
People brushed away the sandflies. You could hear the slap!
slap! against face, feet, the quick brush against skirts. Toes
scratched impatiently against shins; air was whistled in through
teeth. People stamped their feet to send the flies away. They
were so tiny and quick that they were gone by the time you felt
the sting. They made the children fretful. 'Sh-h-h-h! Hush,
baby, hush!'

People glanced about the yard, acknowledging friends with a
twitch of the face, a lift of the eyebrows, a taut smile that just
started to relax the face as the hand came up half-way for a
wave, seemed to forget what it was about to do and stopped
aimlessly. The eyes moved quickly elsewhere. The face turned
quickly to the front again. Another baby took up the fretful cry
from Maisie's. People moved, rearranged themselves, folded
arms, leaned more heavily on sticks. Cutlasses shifted
underarm.

Paren Comesee couldn't be out in the yard. His one leg was

1

giving him a lot of trouble today. He called Joyce. He asked her to take the pancup off the nail and dip some water from the bucket for him. The heat made him thirsty. He gulped, the water dripping down the edges, his hands trembling, his thin face looking relaxed with pleasurable satisfaction. He gave a deep 'ha-a-a' as the thirst buried itself deep inside the water. Paren Comesee asked Joyce to halve the pancup so he could drink again.

Mano, who had climbed the mango tree so that he could get a better view, shouted tensely, 'Look! Look! Allyou look!'

People rushed back to vantage points, heads strained forward, people moved one step forwards, or sideways, or backwards, or stood on tiptoe to see better. Another figure climbed half-way up the mango tree, balancing and peeping eagerly.

'Woy! What is dat, Mano? What take up so now?'

'Is de bukan. It ketch fire from de slide.'

'Look! Look! Look!' someone shouted.

'What?'

'What?'

'Wey?'

'Dey! Look! Ah see people movin!'

'Yes. Yes. Look dem!' Mano held on to another branch, tried to strain forward to see better. He wrinkled his face, squeezing up his eyes to see through the thick smoke that was now turning in their direction.

'Careful, you know!' A face looked up from the branch below him. 'Don fall on me, non.'

'Non. Non. Wait. Ah lookin!' He strained forward. Eyes looked up at him. Heads swivelled, eyes trying to focus on the exact spot that he was looking. 'Ah caan see who it is,' he said. 'Musbe Mr De Lisle an dem dat come back from town. Ah sure is dem. Dose nastiness!'

It looked like the fire was spreading. They could hear a crackling sound, like things splintering. The sounds got louder. People moved. Some had their hands just under their chin. They forgot their mouths half-opened. They stared. Suddenly there was a loud, funny, sort of squelching sound. Maisie shifted the child on her shoulder, heaved the youngster around to settle on her hip. Her mouth went wider in a nervous, excited laugh.

'All you hear dat? Ah sure is me basket o cocoa an dem dat bawling dey.' Her voice cut through the laughter. 'You hear de

2

juice? You hear how it squelchin scroom, scroom, scroom?'

They laughed. Some sucked their teeth. Turned laughing faces in Maisie's direction. They slapped cutlasses against waterboots as they enjoyed the joke.

'Maisie, you could talk too much stupidness!'

No joke non, cocoa. Ah plant you, ah pick you, ah dance in you, but you so damn ungrateful, you don even know you mudder. Dead, you nastiness! You tink ah wounta ketch you?'

'Ho-hoy!'

'Woy!'

'Ah tellyou!'

'Maisie, you don good, non!'

'Ay-Ay!'

'Tongue an teeth doesn laugh at good ting, non!'

People shifted about the yard. Some stooped down laughing. Some just turned around with their backs to the fire for a while, enjoying the fun. The children were getting more fretful. One enterprising young soul escaped, climbed the steps and tried to squeeze past Paren Comesee's chair. The old man leaned across, tried to hold on to the back of the short white vest. His hand slid off a small, bare bottom. Paren Comesee looked around for his grandchild Joyce.

'Joyce! Joyce! Come an ketch hol of dis little one here gimme!'

'Aye! Aye! You little devil!' Joyce rushed forward, but the mother had seen her escaped offspring. She pulled him roughly away.

'Bon Jé, chile, what do you? You want to get me in trouble? Pass you backside here befoh ah . . .'

'Is awright, is awright,' said Paren Comesee. 'He just curious.'

'How the leg, Paren?'

'As the weather changin, you know, it won't let me sleep.'

'Hm. Is de rheumatism. You mus put heat on it in de night. An you see dey where it swell, hot some pepper leaf and tie it down.'

'Yes, dou-dou. I do all dat, yes, an sometime it does give me a little ease.'

'Woy! Allyou look! Look!'

The shout pulled her dashing back down the steps to the crowd, heaving the child to her shoulder as she ran. They

3

pushed forward. Hands went to the shoulders of those in front.

'Lemme see! Jus squeeze up an ben you shoulder lemme see!'

In the distance there was a bright red glow as something else caught fire. The children whimpered, and were shushed. The women pulled the smaller ones closer to them. Some tightened their grip on the sticks they held. The men held their cutlasses firmly. Held up on Doodsie's shoulder, Angel clung round her mother's neck. Mother and child kept their eyes riveted on the fire, Angel wide-eyed, Doodsie suddenly very afraid as she saw the De Lisle plantation houses enveloped in flames, a burning glow in the reddened sky.

Just under the hill from the crowd, Ma Ettie sat down in her house and secured the folds of her headtie. She wrapped it tightly round her head. She looked out of the window at the bright glow in the sky. Her short, squat figure stood framed for a moment against the quiet evening. Then she closed the window again and walked restlessly with both hands behind her back. Pacing. Pacing. Wondering.

Ma Ettie lifted her head and listened. The dog was jumping and greeting someone. Doodsie. Musbe Doodsie dat come. She opened the window.

'Doodsay-y? Doodsie, is you?'

'Yes. Yes, is me, Mammie.'

'What do? What happenin atall?'

'Is the De Lisle estate, Mammie.'

'But, Doodsie . . .'

Doodsie sucked her teeth, impatient. She shifted Angel from one shoulder to the other, frowned.

'Meself ah don know. Ah don know, so don ask me.'

'Ay-Ay! Ay-Ay!'

Ma Ettie watched Doodsie walk up towards her. Her daughter came and stood there, turned her back to the window. The two of them looked across at the plantation houses. Doodsie held Angel close. She glanced up at Ma Ettie and moved closer to the window, suddenly glad that Mammie was there. Ah will stay out here for a while. Ah don want to go inside yet. Ah will jus stay by here still. Above Doodsie's head, Ma Ettie's red and black headtie framed a bewildered face. Her elbows rested against the sill. Her mouth was just slightly open. She looked down at Doodsie and was struck again by how much this child . . . Ma Ettie stopped herself in her thoughts. Child?

4

Qui chile sa? But she really look like me. Smaller, thinner like, but the same same big bottom and big legs. She looked at the thick, black plaits sticking out on either side of Doodsie's head and wondered why these young people never liked to cover their head. Doodsie looked up at her. The strange mixture of fear and acceptance on her daughter's face pulled Ma Ettie's eyes back to the glow from the De Lisle plantation houses.

Doodsie rocked Angel, feeling the fear in the child as she clung to her shoulders. She made a whimpering sound. Doodsie pulled her head back and looked into the small, long face.

'What do? Eh?'

Angel flung her arms round her mother's neck, clung closely. You doh see how you face long! thought Doodsie. She rocked her. You yuh father chile for sure. Nutting like me. She ran her hand all over the hair braided in tiny plaits on Angel's head. De fadder head, too. Not for hell it won grow! She rocked her. The child quietened. She was not asleep but clung there in a wide-eyed silence as tense as the fiery atmosphere.

'Ah goin' inside, Mammie. Time for Angel to sleep!'

'Awright!'

There was a loud crackling sound from the fire. From up the hill came a shout. Doodsie pushed open the door. Lord, ah come back to this Grenada at a bad time. If only they didn lay off Allan, at least we coulda put aside a little more money for the bad times ahead. Is not to say things was dat good in Aruba, non, but was better dan dis. Dey was better dan dis. She lay down, pulled Angel to her, and tried to get the wide-eyed child to close out the flames in her eyes and go to sleep.

Ma Ettie closed down the window, put the stick in the corner, and sank slowly to her knees. She clasped her hands on the bed and bowed her head.

'Lord, let this tribulation pass from us. Let not our enemies triumph over these your children, Lord. Take a thought to the life and salvation of the little children in that burning house, Lord, and to all your children of this world. Lord, if it be thy will, thy will be done . . . thy will be done . . . thy . . .'

The shrill sound of the alarm clock on the washstand pulled her from a deep sleep as the first light of dawn tried to peep through the cracks in the board window.

'Ah forget not to set de alarm,' she mumbled. 'Ah don have to work today, nuh, but ah forget not to set it.' Ma Ettie climbed heavily into bed, muttering, 'Thank you, Jesus, for this day.'

When better can't be done let worse continue

Thoughts struggled to shape themselves in Doodsie's mind as the clip-clop, clip-clop of the donkey's hooves on the road outside penetrated her consciousness. Mano. He goin in de garden early today. Lemme get up. Ah mus write Ezra. Ah jus feel it in me bones dat we shounta come back to dis place. She eased off the bed so as not to awaken Angel, felt around under her pillow for the box of matches. In the living-room, she lit the big lamp.

Doodsie shifted the pen around in her hand, looked across at the bedroom door, looked up at the ceiling. Cobwebs. Must use the straw broom up there. Tomorrow.

Dear Ezra,
I hope this letter reaches you as fine as it leaves me.

Those cobwebs startin to make de place look bad arready!

Over here things not too bad but is real confusion in the land. You should see you boy Leader in form. To tell you the truth, Ezra, the country need a shake up like this, even though I know the kine of person Leader is. I not too sure I like the way they doing things. There is a lot of violence that startin up. I even hear about people that get kill. Is a while now I didn't go down in you area, but I hear that everybody there stout stout behind Leader. Well is what you expect? Is right there self his people from and is like people thinkin he is saviour.

From the opposite wall, Jesus smiled down at Doodsie, gently. His blue eyes watched her every movement. In his hands he held a globe. The world. A globe with a cross at the top.

If we didn't have experience of him over there, who know? I might of even shout for him myself. Girl, I don't know. When that man dress an he stylish, you should see him. People like they goin crazy about him. The other day I hear you cousin-in-

*law saying Oh God the boy nice. He nice he nice, all behin he
head nice. If you hear them you would laugh for so. Well,
Ezra, I don't know where things goin now but it sure is plenty
of confusion. I know we need a change but not in this way. I
don't know where it will end. What is it like over there now?
How are you and Sonny? I hope you all can hold on there for a
long time still because tings not too good here. Everytime I
regret more and more that Allan get laid off. Well is to look on
the bright side and put that behind. Over here work still hard to
get but we tryin. You child Angel there still growin nice. She
look like the father as what. I hope that what old people say is
true and she going to be lucky in truth.*

Jesus was still smiling. People could really do ting, yes. Ah
wonder how dey manage to make dose eyes so dat dey follow
you whichever side you turn in de room!

*Well girl, I wish you all all the best. I went to check on the piece
of land for you and the old man really takin good care of it. He
plant yam and peas and it have a good few corn comin up well.
So you don't have to bother on that score. Sometime when
Allan down by that side, he does take a little look in for you
too. Well girl take care of youself say hello to Sonny and write
soon.*

Doodsie passed her tongue over the flap of the envelope. She
better hol on over there. She know what ah talkin about. Is not
as if she doh know. She better take my advice an hol on over
there if she know what good for her.

She had first met Ezra in Mr Giles De Lisle's kitchen, the
weekend of the big dinner. She couldn't remember if the
governor was there. All the servants kept saying he was coming,
but she couldn't really remember. She must ask Ma Ettie. Ma
Ettie was working for Mr Giles De Lisle's brother Kenneth at
the time, and he had sent her to help with the preparations.
Mammie tail, you call dat. Anytime anybody ask her to go
somewey, so she draggin me behine er.

On the wall near to the door, there were three framed
photographs in a row. Bradman. Doodsie smiled. They had
given Allan that nickname because of his cricket. In the picture
he looked tall and slim. As if he tink he nice! Ezra. Sitting up

7

well straight in the chair, like the man in the studio had told her to do. Doodsie looked at her friend. And me. Me hair was long in dose days. Ah use to have time to take care of meself in dose days.

Angel whimpered, but didn't waken. Doodsie blew out the lamp. The flame had outlasted its usefulness. Looking down at her sleeping daughter, she made the sign of the cross. 'Papa God, jus spare my life let me see her grow up.' She looked at the protective cross over Angel's cradle. 'Let me see her go through school properly an make something of herself. Lord, just spare me let me see her grow up in a proper family, please God.'

Not all skin-teet is good grin!

Two De Lisle plantation houses were burnt that week – the one in Hermitage belonging to Mr Walter De Lisle and Mr Giles De Lisle's house in Dunfermline.

Two

Two tiny bedrooms, a little porch, a sliver of a kitchen opening from the small dining-living-room area, if one could call that an entrance that could barely frame one slim figure an opening.

'What you face set up so for, Doodsie? You don like the kitchen he give you?'

'Cousin Maymay, I don lyin, I feel he coulda do something better dan dat.'

'Well, they say buildin material expensive for so, an anyway, is we family, even though the cousin distant. He won cheat you.'

'Huh!'

'Res youself. Wid you little wall house now, you well settle. Plenty people go be wishing was them.'

'If dey peep inside me pocket, dey go soon see it have nothing to envy.'

'Well they not able to peep so that awright.'

'It not awright non. I wish they coulda see an know that no riches floatin around here. Thank God for the little piece of family land and for dis my mother you see dey. At least we could still get two grain o bluggoe an some nutmeg.'

The spot of land was Doodsie's; a little piece her mother had given her, part of the family plot. They built the house on the spot with money they had both saved up. Allan went to see about the registration. He put it in his name.

'But Allan . . .'

'Why? What happen? Even though it in my name, is obvious it belong to both of us. What is yours is mine. We together. We not separating. So what is the problem?'

'Well then you could have put it on my name. Or if I did go an put it on my name alone, was awright with you?'

'I jus don understand why you makin confusion over this. Is not as if we quarrel or anyting!'

'No. We not in confusion. Forget I ever talk.'

Cousin Maymay was talking now in a low, confidential tone.

'Doodsie, well don talk loud. Ah don know if Cousin Ettie an dem tell you, but tings really bad, you know. Everyting dear, dear, an dose devil an dem takin all you have.'

'So ah hear. So ah hear, yes. They tell me that on the estate down the road they givin spot to worker to make garden an after they done work theyself out clearing up spot an everyting they askin them to plant cocoa in between the crop they growin.'

'Well,' Cousin Maymay adjusted her spectacles, touched Doodsie's shoulder with one hand, 'dat is part of it. But is not that is new ting, you know, is ting dey doin from time. Is jus dat now as if dey treatin us bad in every which way possible. Is all over de place they tramplin us in de groun, yes girl.' Cousin Maymay stood up in the small porch, rested her hand on the banister, ground the heel of her thick shoes into the ground. 'Ay-ay! Huh! Well, it doh easy, non!'

A child walking along the road looked up at the frowning face and sang out, 'Good evenin, Cousin Maymay. Miss Doodsie, ah goin home.'

'Evenin, dear, you goin up? You come out an sell nutmeg for you Mammie? Awright! Walk good, eh!' Cousin Maymay turned her back to the road, folded her arms, and leaned against the banister, facing Doodsie. 'Girl, nutting different. Nutting, nutting, nutting at all. Ay! Is like we have a curse?'

'Huh!' Doodsie was shaking her head from side to side, sitting there on the chair looking at the concrete floor of the porch.

'Well look non, ah pickin up nutmeg for the whole week, an at the end of it ah could barely manage to buy de poun o saltfish, you know! Ay! Is so we have to work out we soul case all the time never to have nutting! Ay!' Cousin Maymay was now walking the length of the little porch, hitting one clenched fist against the palm of her hand. 'Then after you work you piece o ground, put all you labour in it, when the cocoa they ask you to plant in between well in its growth now, they takin away the piece of land from you and give you a new piece to do the same

10

thing. So five to six years later,' she stopped in front of Doodsie, looking intently down at her cousin, as though explaining to her the details that they had both grown up knowing so well; 'five to six years later, when cocoa in that first piece of ground you work in in full bearing, you harvesting it for the boss for one shilling an sixpence a day. Bon Jé!' She cupped her chin with one hand, turned to the road. 'Doodsie, God self see is not so for people to live!'

'Huh!' Doodsie stood up, leaned on the banister next to Cousin Maymay. 'Is the same story all over. Is vyé nèg on the groun an bakra béké on top. We always startin, always in the beginning.'

'Not only dat, non Makomè. Becus when tellin you, if you talk hard an play you vex, they will make you move you house from the estate. Evic you, they callin it. An when you don have a spot of you own, you jus have to play stupid an grin an bear it. Huh! Girl.' Arms akimbo, she looked at Doodsie sideways. 'Youself, what you come back an do here?'

'Well is the only place they caan send you back from. Bad how it is, this is the corner that is ours, so we jus have to make the best of it until!'

'Until what, Makomè? Until the sea push us out, or until we find another corner?'

'Youself, too, Cousin Maymay!' Doodsie looked at her usually easy-going cousin in puzzled surprise. She was the one who usually had to be cooled down by Cousin Maymay. 'Is not you always tellin me to have faith? What do you today? You forget?'

Cousin Maymay took a deep breath. Released it. Relaxed slowly. Stood looking down at the steps. Her shoulders fell back to their customary position. She turned around. Looked at Doodsie.

'Girl,' she shook her head. Looked at Doodsie again. Made the sign of the cross. 'The Lord will provide,' she said.

When Doodsie answered, Cousin Maymay had already pushed aside the low gate and was half-way down the steps.

'Ah goin see you later. I mus pass an see if Paren Comesee awright.'

Doodsie watched Cousin Maymay go up the hill, her body leaning forward as she made the climb, both hands crossed behind her back at the wrists, the palms facing upwards. Her

11

eyes contemplated the changing patterns on the road as she moved.

'Believe me, Papa God,' said Doodsie, 'I don want to be doubting Thomas; but I really hope you provide in truth!'

Above her head, way above the house top, Doodsie could hear the palm tree rustling gently in the breeze as it stood with its top outlined against the sky up there, looking close to where God stayed. When she looked up, the other trees around had started rustling too as the breeze got stronger. She lowered her eyes, left them to their conversation, and went on inside.

Gadé mizè mwen, non!

It was an extra hard year. The talk of strike was all over Hermitage. Regal, Doodsie's brother, was talking all the time about his union. It was a new union started by Leader to fight for the rights of estate workers. Regal was one of its top men.

'Regal, ah see you bringin big long man in me yard, siddown on de grass outside dey talkin seep seep, havin private meetin!' said Ma Ettie quietly from her window. 'Ah don want no quiet confusion brewin in me yard, non!'

Regal made no response.

'He good, girl,' he enthused to Doodsie. 'A real leader in truth. You know, he get three whole thousand pounds compensation for the estate workers down on Dunfermline estate when dey sell the estate and jus did want to kick out people that dey all dey life. When ah tell you dat man good! An he don fraid to talk he mind to them, you know!'

'Uh-huh?'

'But now it look like trouble start again. De goverment sayin dat cocoa price fall, so dey go have to reduce estate workers' pay. Way you ever hear dat? Tings so dear, when for them to put up people pay, dey talkin bout bringin it down.'

'How much allyou gettin now?'

'Well, me, as a driver I gettin a few pence more but what all the ordinary labourers gettin is two shilling an sixpence a day for man an two an two for women. I gettin two an ten.'

'An go an see,' Doodsie emptied the pan of dirty water in the drain at the back of the kitchen, looked at her brother sitting there on the kitchen bench near the door. 'Go an see, those women doin more damn work than allyou self.'

Regal sucked his teeth. 'Dat is not de point. I mean, we know man always get more. But how de hell they could bring down people pay?'

'Ah know. Dese people up there don care a damn bout you an me. Is so it is arready. What to do?' She bent to break off a hand of green bananas. Straightened and stood looking at him. 'But watch it, you know, Regal. Don go an get youself in no trouble. An as for Miss Mary in Dunfermline son, ah don too trus im, you know.'

'Ah, chuts, Doodsie,' he stood up, walked to the door. 'What you know bout the man?'

'That man?' Doodsie put the green bananas down on the dresser. 'Watch youself, you know, Regal. Ah hear you was part o de group dat set fire to dose people plantation. Ah not makin noise. Jus as a sister ah tellin you. Don follow dat man lead too close, you know.' She looked around, found the stained, handleless provision knife and stood leaning against the dresser. Regal said nothing. 'Dat man like a lotta flash. You should o see he weddin in Aruba. Real pappyshow. It was so flashy dey make up a song on it.'

'Well what dat say? Dat don say nutting bout what the man believe in.'

'True.' Doodsie turned to the dresser, broke off a banana, marked along its length with the knife. 'True, but . . .'

'Ah, chuts!' Regal turned, lowered his head to go through the tiny kitchen doorway. 'Is weself we fightin for!'

Doodsie turned her head sideways, speaking to him over her right shoulder as she began removing the skin of the banana. 'It say a lot about what de man believe in.' She raised her voice so that Regal, on his way up the back steps of her house, would be sure to hear. 'I could tell you bout im if you want.'

From the step outside, Jessie, who had been following the conversation, intervened. 'It say a lot, yes. I still have the letter you Doodsie did write to me about that same man doings in Aruba. It dey. You Regal could read it if you want.'

Regal wasn't interested, but later that day Doodsie sat down and undid the string round the package her sister had handed to her.

'Lawd, girl, you don jokin non! How ah write dose letters, so you get dem an tie dem up neat neat as if dey ha to go in exhibition!'

13

'Huh! You tink me is you? Is you dat does take ting an throw vroop, vroop before you turn roun, yes.'

'So ah have time to gather rubbish den?'

'Yes. Dat is me thanks.'

'Non, non, don mine dat. Ah well glad you keep dem.'

'Eh heh!' Doodsie, going through the letters, pulled out one, making two piles so that she could return it to the place where her sister had so carefully kept it according to date of receipt. 'Dis was a long one.' Her eyes moved down the page. 'Was de one ah write de time of de strike?' Her eyes moved slowly along the page. 'Yes.' She laughed, remembering.'Dat was de strike.'

'Oho. Ah remember dat. Was a nice letter. Ah did read it out for Paren Comesee an ah tink Cousin Maymay was dey too. We well enjoy dat.'

Things not too good here. I didnt tell you what was happenin for the las few months but we had a lot of trouble. Well you know I tell you I live on the premises where I work and although those people miserable they not half so bad as those devil I used to work with in Trinidad.

Jessie laughed, her whole body shaking. The heavy silver bracelets her grandmother had given her years before tinkled as she moved. 'All way you meet dem is devil! Some less, some more, but same ting. Poor chance you get a good one.'

... Is the same sort of people but I been a bit more lucky with these here where I work. They have more money too so I suppose that make them not so stingy and stupid . . .

'Dat does help.'

Anyway, someone come to see me one day since last year when I was still pregnant with Angel and said you live on the premises where you work? I said yes, she said, well you better find you skin down the village, we are having a strike tomorrow all you so will get lix.

'Ay!' Jessie was absorbing the letter as though hearing its contents for the first time. 'Well is not so! So dey do it?'

14

The nex morning, there was a strike. The bus entering the gate with the working girls was stopped by the strike leaders. One of them was Miss Mary in Dunfermline son, the one they call Leader ...

'Yes. Gadé bèt-la!'

He and another one from Grenada too. The strike leaders address the crowd and say advantage is being taken of the workers so nobody is to go to work until better arrangement is made for them. And to tell you the truth, Jessie, is true advantage is being taken of the workers ...

'Ah well know!'

... One or two of us might be lucky and work with people that not so bad but we know that on the whole we workin for nutting when you think of all the money they makin in this country off the oil refinery ...

'Pò djab o!'

... An is really we that doing the work. Anyway what we could do. I feel really we should just hush we mouth because all of us from the other islands including Leader who from Grenada just like us and this is Dutch country. The Dutch policemen came forward and said, you come in queen country to make trouble? Bring you passeport ...

Doodsie stopped, leaned back in her chair laughing. 'Those Dutch policemen. Girl, when you hear dey say "You come in queen countr-r-r-y to make t-r-r-r-ouble? Br-r-r-ing you pass-e-port!" ' Doodsie giggled. 'When you hear dey roll dose r an dey shout de pass-e-port, girl was to see people scamper!'

Jessie's laughter was coming in short chuckling outbursts. 'People had to run for dey life, yes. But what dey mean by this queen country?'

'Dey always call it queen country. Ah tink it had someting to do wid how de Dutch always had queen while other people like us de English an so had king, so dey say . . .'

'Oho, I see!'

15

... Well girl is right there the strike end because all of us know that if we get sen home is perhaps not to work at all an is still other people in control and home dont have oil refining. Everybody just run into the bus and to their job. The company layin off people lef and right because they say they dont need so much workers ...

'Well yes, when you glad for de little extra you caan play stupid wid it!'

'Huh!' Doodsie sounded preoccupied with the letter. She continued reading in a lower voice, more to herself now.

I really fraid for Allan because the work he doing in the dining hall, the officers mess, not so important that they go fight to keep him. For me it not so important because I in the house and they still need people doin the domestic work. Anyway, I keepin me fingers cross. Angel is well, so am I too and Allan. Hope all is well with you. Give Mammie my love and say hello to Paren Comesee and Cousin Maymay and everybody else. Remind Mammie that she owing me a letter. I enclose this little change to help out.

'Uh-h-h huh!' She put the pages of the letter in order, replaced it in the pile, started looking through again. 'Ah did write so much letter?' Doodsie paused, her lips moving, her eyes on the letters in front of her. 'Where is the one dat talk about Leader? Was one I write after, becus was after de strike dat . . .'

'Well it dey, it dey somewhere in de package, below where you take out dat one. Ah remember it well, becus you talk about de weddin an me an Cousin Maymay even laugh an enjoy de joke. It dey!'

'Eh – heh – dis . . . oh yes! Look it here!' Doodsie's eyes moved down the page and her finger, moving too, stopped at the spot. 'Yes!' she laughed. 'Look it! You good, girl! Ah mus hol dis to show me good-for-nutting brudder!'

'So he studyin you den? What he have in he head to do is dat e goin to do! You know im arready!'

'How ah don know! Ah could take mud an make a perfect he!'

'Youself does say some ting to make people laugh, yes!' She looked at her sister, intent upon the letter. 'Where de part? Read it, lemme remember.'

They lay off Leader. And he just finish have a elaborate wedding wid that airess from the big family home that he engage an bring up here to married ...

'E eyes big. E aimin high!'

That man is the limit. He so like a show that he had the most biggest wedding possible. They say it had enough shampain to bathe in ...

'Dat sweeten me. Girl dat really sweeten me. Me an Cousin Maymay say "Wee-ee-ee! Imagine all dis people an dem bathin in champagne!" Well dat was fete yes!'

'Girl, was real pappyshow weddin. Dey say there never was a weddin like it an never will there be again!'

... And you know who his best man was? Guess nuh. His boss ...

'Uh huh! Papa Boast!'

That is to tell you. They make up a rime on the wedding that go rum like water, whisky like fire, beer for chaser. Everybody say is weddin poupa ...

Doodsie rocked back in her chair, slapping her hands against the table. 'Weddin poupa is joke, wi! Weddin *gran*poupa!'

The tears were rolling down Jessie's cheeks again as they had when she and Cousin Maymay first read about the grandness of the wedding.

'Ay-ay! Yes. So dat was it.' Doodsie's eyes travelled over the rest of the letter.

'You could show you brudder if you want. Not dat it go make any difference!'

Doodsie was absorbed again, reading quietly to herself.

... We people really stupid. Allan there as usual workin but they layin off people lef right and centre so we still keepin we fingers cross.

Doodsie tied the faded blue string round the pile. Well,

perhaps we fingers din cross tight enough!

'It wasn all good over dey but widdout dat ah don know where ah would have been today.' Jessie looked up, realised that her sister was talking to herself. Age. Is ole people dat does talk to deyself so. De years comin early, girl. Jessie concentrated on her knitting. Doodsie whispered, 'God give Ezra a chance let her stay dey still.'

She remembered how she and Ezra had agreed that father or no father, if anything happened to Doodsie and she wasn't around to see the child grow up, Angel would live with Ezra. After a brief struggle with Allan's Catholic church, Ezra had been duly recognised, by Doodsie, if not by the priest, as Angel's main godmother. Doodsie sucked her teeth now, remembering how even Angel's name had been a problem with which the priest had decided to concern himself. She glanced at Jessie, got to her feet, took a chair out to the porch and sat lost in her memory of those early conversations with Allan about Angel.

Take win but you lose

'The priest say she mus have a saint name, Doodsie.'

'You an dis church awright, yes. Why she mus have a saint name?'

'Well dat is the rule and you know you say you will let her baptise in my church.'

'Yes, although I not too sure why. You say you is Roman Catholic but you don even go to church. In the Anglican church she would at least go with me.'

'But we talk about that already, and you agree that any children will be in my church because you don't want them divide up, with one in this church and one in another.'

'Yes. Yes. So what saint name? Let me look at the church calendar. She born Saint Michael and All Angels Day. We should call her Michelle.'

'But we would still have to find another saint. I don tink it have any saint name Michelle.'

'You know what? Just call her Angel. Is all angels, and the priest caan have anything to say about that.'

'Well . . .'

'Tell you priest is my chile!'

18

So Angel she was.

Ezra was a godmother but because she was an Anglican and therefore unacceptable in the eyes of the Catholic church, she could not be the chief godmother.

'Acceptable how? But look me trouble non! What Father know about who acceptable for my chile?'

'It have to be somebody who could really guide her in the teachings of the church.'

'Like who so? Stupes! So as you is Catholic dey, you for example, you could guide somebody?'

Someone else was main godmother. Anyway, that was the priest's side of it. In reality Ezra would be Nen-nen, Tantie, everything. Would help see Angel through life if anything happened. No church had to tell Ezra what was her duty to Angel. When someone said in front of her that that chile so fair that could never be Allan own, her right hand just went out of its own volition and connected with the man's mouth. Sonny had looked at her as if she had gone mad, but the man was too surprised even to consider reacting. Laughingly recounting the story about Sonny's reaction afterwards, Ezra had told Doodsie, 'E open e big eyes dey an e look at me when de man go an he say, "Ah caan fight non, so when you get youself in you ting, you handlin it for youself, you know!"' Doodsie laughed now. Ezra was always like that. When ah was in school ketchin me tail an stupid stupid was she dat show me how to make a slingshot. Ezra! Don play wid er, non! Allan grinned when he heard the story. He looked over at the little face shaped so like his and said nothing. Doodsie's reaction had been, 'What better god-mother you could want dan dat!'

Doodsie sighed, thought that she should go to prepare Angel's feed. The child would be awake soon. She got slowly to her feet. 'Give dem a chance, Papa God.' she murmured. 'Give dem a chance let dem stay dey still an settle deyself.'

Not all wag-tail is promise not to bite

It was February. Doodsie couldn't remember the dates exactly but Jessie never forgot a date. She said it was the eighteenth of February, in the evening. Doodsie was outside cooking and hoping to God that Allan would come home that evening and say he had found a job. Then she heard Regal shouting in the yard. Jessie, who had the weekend off from her job working with the white people in St George's, was sitting inside sewing, bracelets tinkling occasionally. From the kitchen outside, Doodsie heard her shout.

'Hush you noise dey, boy. Since you small, so you is. You caan do nothing quiet at all, at all.'

'You jokin, wi. Dis is time for shoutin! Strike start in earnest tomorrow!' Regal was talking very quiet now, intense, excited. Doodsie went to the kitchen door.

'Strike?'

'Yes. Dey still talkin bout bringin down pay an so everybody agree to fight it. So no work from tomorrow.'

'Papa God put a hand.' Jessie made the sign of the cross. 'What confusion is this in this land at all?' She shifted on the chair, looked at her brother again. 'So who all workers that goin on strike?'

'Everybody.'

'How you mean everybody?'

'All estate labourers all over the country.'

'But how that possible?'

'It possible. We discuss it arready. They takin from us all de time. We not goin to work. We go hunt for everything we want.'

'Lord ave is mercy!'

We come out in de same crab hole

Mano had decided to ignore the strike that day and was cutting through the cocoa to make a day's work. These days the garden wasn doin too well. He walked with his heart in his hand. The money would help him to stop up a hole. He hoped no one saw him.

'Hold it!'

One foot forward, hand gripping the handle of the cutlass, mouth half-open, he seemed to be thinking about trying to make a dash for it. Glazed with fear, his eyes darted quickly around at the trunks of the cocoa trees. Mano's jaw dropped.

'Maisie! Oh God, Maisie! Is me, Mano!'

'Oh is you?' Maisie moved forward, holding her cutlass. 'Ah

didn really believe was you, non, Mano.'

Mano's eyes slid away from Maisie's stare. He looked backwards. Regal, and a man from Dunfermline, standing with right hands resting on thick sticks taken from the gliricida trees. Mano's neck turned his head slowly, jerkily, to the front again, in the direction he had been travelling. The man whose command had stopped him held a huge rock-stone in each hand. Mano watched. His feet moved uncertainly. The circle came closer, tightened slowly. Mano trembled as he watched them come.

'Allyou know how it is! Is not dat ah don support, non!'

'Wey you goin, Mano?'

'No . . . no . . . nowey. I . . . I . . . ah don going nowey. Ah jus . . .'

'You dirty stinkin dog. Since when dey call Mr De Lisle estate nowey?'

'Me? Ah not . . . ah not . . . ah not . . .'

'You well knot up for true, Mano. You hypocrite dog!'

'Cut out he blasted balls give im!'

'Oh God! Believe me, ah don mean to . . .'

'Don call Papa God name in vain. He don want to hear from nastiness like you! You stand up wid us all de time. Wey you goin now?'

'Is people like you makin tings hard in dis country!'

'Believe me, eh, is only because tings hard for me . . .'

'Ah don waan to hear nutting. You ha to fight jus like us, you good-for-nutting, no-good, stupid, dirty, fool. You is one of us, you ass.'

'God self see . . .'

'You workin for damn nutting an lettin people walk all over you!'

'You don know. You don know. De little girl don well. Oh God, and Mr De Lisle wasn de wors . . .'

'Shut you . . .'

'What do allyou? So we come here to have conference wid Mano, den?'

Regal's cutlass flashed out and one flat side landed with an exploding sound on Mano's backside.

'No. Oh God no!'

'Planass he ass!'

The sticks landed on Mano's back. One of his hands went

over his shoulder to protect his back; the other circled his waist. He twisted his body, screaming with pain. His face contorted.

'Woy! Woy-o-yoy!'

'Shut up! Shut you fuckin mout!'

Hands tore at the worn-out khaki shirt. Mano crouched. A kick sent him sprawling and something hit against the side of his head. He tried to get up, felt something slash at his face. Mano felt the warm blood, tried to shield his face; the feel of blood on his hands frightened him.

'Oh Gawd! Oh Gawd me mudder!'

'You mudder hell! She should shame o you!'

Mano was on his knees crouching away from the hands that reached down to him. Something slashed at him again. Mano screamed. Fell forward. He clawed helplessly. The blood flowed.

'Kill the fool!'

'No. Leave im now. Lewwe don dull we cutlass on dat nasty dog.'

Feet flashed out and kicked angrily at the silent man. He wasn't even moaning now. The branches moved. The green leaves overhead took up their silent whispering again. The departing feet crunched the dried-out leaves.

Sa ki fè'w?

'Well dis is someting.' Doodsie had just rocked Angel to sleep. She looked from the cradle to the cross above it. Jesus' head was bowed beneath the crown of thorns. His palms faced outwards. 'Dis is what you call eatin de bread dat the devil knead. Allan not workin an we don have cent. What de hell we go do? After all the expense with buildin the house and havin to feed Angel, I just don't know what we could do. An dis damn man don look like he even intend to stop de strike. Jesus! Papa God put a hand!'

One day One day congoté!

Throughout the island, estates were going up in flames. The mass meeting that Leader organised in the capital, St George's, was a complete success.

People went down from Hermitage in buses; some went in groups, walking until they found some means of transport. No one asked if a neighbour was going. They just shouted from the streets.

'Makomè, you ready?'

'Woy. Walk on. Walk on, girl. Ah go meet you.'

'Tan Sase! It gettin late! Make it! Make it!'

'Ay, man! Make haste in dey! Make haste!'

'Regal. Rego-o-l! You dey?'

'He not dey, non! He gone since foreday mornin!'

From all over the island, people walked, drove, rode to the city. Shouted. Laughed. Pulled one another along.

'Make it! Make it, Papay-o! Is we day dat come!'

'Come on, Sister Amy! You won fall! The Lord will see to it!'

'Ay-Ay! Miss Mildred? You an all? Wo-o-o-y!'

'Ay! Me name is Mildred Mac Pherson! Me name not An-all non! How you mean me an-all dey? So ah not folks too, den?'

'Yes Makomè, you well right. De foot go bring you!'

'Huh! On a day like dis is only who dead dat inside, yes!'

'Woy. Wopsin, boy ah don know when ah see you!'

People converged from all directions on to the narrow streets around the House of Parliament where the rally was going to be addressed by Leader. The colour and the laughter danced up Market Hill from the direction of the Market Square in the centre of town and up Cemetery Hill, going past the graves behind the Presentation College, up the hill from Lucas Street direction, stopping in at Mr Lazarus' shop to buy a Red Spot to quench the thirst, up along Church Street, past the Anglican church. One woman looked speculatively into the sleepy eyes of Mr Lazarus as he handed her her change. She took a long swallow of Red Spot, put the bottle down on the table as she gave a deep sighing 'a-a-a-ah' and wiped the sweat from her face. She belched. She looked at the woman standing next to her.

'You from down here?' she asked.

'Yes. Jus up de road by Perdmontemps dey!'

'You come in dis shop befoh?'

'Eh-heh!'

'He name is Mr Lazarus for true?'

'Uh-huh!' The woman looked puzzled.

'Well all-you town people don easy! A half-dead man livin not far from de cemetery an he name Mr Lazarus?'

The shop exploded into laughter. Mr Lazarus smiled. The woman put down her empty bottle and went out of the shop, on her way up the hill, still commenting on the 'funniness' of these town people.

Up on the hill, Leader clapped and and sang too as the voices merged in a confident dirge to fast-fading days:

'We shall over co-o-ome
We shall over co-o-ome
We shall overcome
Some day-ay-ay ...'

And as they sang Leader shouted: 'We shall stand together, we shall die together!'

The crowd roared its approval, chanted its approval of this new hope in song:

'We shall never let our leader fall
Cause we love him the best of all!'

Leader's slender form, dressed all in white, moved gracefully on the balcony in front of the Parliament Building.

'Watch im, non! Watch boy, non!' one woman shouted. 'Dat is man!'

Leader held up a clenched fist. He looked at the curtained Parliament building, imagined the governor sitting trembling inside. Leader turned to his people and shouted: 'Fight!' The shouts came back at him and fled past him to hammer insistently against the windows of Parliament. 'Fight! Fight! Fight! Fight!'

Leader held up both hands, a calm gesture demanding silence. His spotless white suit glistened in the sunshine.

'He look like Mr De Lisle, eh!' Maisie whispered to her companion. Is just so Mr De Lisle does dress neat when he playin tennis!'

'Yes. Or when he goin on de golf course. De only ting is he prettier dan Mr De Lisle!'

Gradually, a listening silence covered the crowd. 'My people,' said Leader, 'let us recognise the presence of Our Lord in our efforts today!'

'Thank you, Jesus!'

'Without him, we can do nothing!'

'But the Lord is with us!'

'Amen!'

'Amen, dear Jesus!'

'And the Lord has given us a sign! Last night, my dear people, the rain fell as a blessing, but this morning the Lord brought sunshine to his day!'

'Yea! Yeh! Yes! Praise Jesus!'

Leader held up his hands. Silence fell. 'He brought sunshine to his day so that we could confront Beelzebub in his chamber! And that is how we know that we shall overcome!'

'Thank you, Jesus!'

'We shall overcome!' And the voices made the chant a song:

'We shall overco-o-ome!'

In the crowd, Cousin Maymay took off her hat and fanned her face. She looked up, straining to see her leader. Dat is boy! Dat is boy plus! Dat is de real governor yes!

'Who does the work in this country?'

'Us!'

'Who pick de cocoa?'

'Us!'

'Is we!'

'Who pick up de nutmeg?'

'Is we!'

'We self!'

'Who cutlass an fork an ben dey back an do de task?'

'Us!'

'We!'

'But hear non!' Leader lowered his voice, leaned forward. 'Who makin de money?'

Laughter.

'Who makin de money?'

'Dem!'

'Oho! O-o-o-ho! So dey makin de - ay - ay! So how you go live? Ah say! How we go live?'

Excited murmuring.

'Well, I'll tell you something, you know.' Both hands on the banisters of the balcony, Leader leaned forward. 'If we can't get money for the work we do, we will have to hunt for food, because we must eat!' He turned his head slowly about, eyes focusing on various spots in the listening crowd. 'So I not tellin you to do nutting.' He rubbed his hands together in a washing motion. His eyes moved from one face to another. 'But you have to eat, an if they not payin you, where are you goin to get your food? You have to *hunt!* I say, where you going to get your food?'

'Hunt!'

'Hunt, yes!'

'Hunt!'

'My dear people, this is a great time in our history! We have to take the bull by the horns! We have to move together!' He held up a clenched fist. 'And we can't let each other fall!'

'No-o-o!'

'Ye-e-h-h!'

'We shall never let our leader fall
Cause we love him the best of all!'

'Lewwe sing it all again!'

'We shall never let our leader fall
Cause we lo-o-ove him the be-e-st of all!'

Nutting doesn happen before it time

The government arrested Leader. More buildings were burnt. In Hermitage, Regal kept the strike going. People moved to and fro in the yard, coming to see and talk to Regal. Always meetin somebody, Ma Ettie grumbled. Dis boy go get heself in trouble. Every day is a seep seep in de yard under de window dey. Lord put a hand!

'Doodsie, ah hear how dey sen for police in Trinidad and St Lucia. You tink dat is true?'

26

'Yes. Regal say is true.'

'Ay-ay! Ay-ay! But what ting is dis goin on here at all?'

'Meself ah don know what to say. To tell you de truth me spirit don move good with Leader and sometimes I does feel is only bad mind make him cause all this confusion in the country, but these people treat us so bad for so long that if wasn for the house that not even finish pay for yet an the fact that Angel have to eat, I does feel I would even go and march wid them meself.'

Jessie cleared her throat.

'Huh! Meself that is not me line at all. I don like all this confusion at all at all. I keepin meself well quiet in de corner here.' She paused, sat there with her hand under her chin, looking through the window into the yard outside. Two fowls chased each other in circles, the hen squawking as the cock strutted arrogantly after her. They strutted out of Jessie's range of vision, disappearing behind the kitchen. Jessie turned around on the chair, looked at Doodsie as she stood pounding the heavy iron on Angel's little dress. 'If trouble go come,' said Jessie, 'it have to come an meet me right inside here. Ah have no place to go. When de time come, what have to happen will happen whether ah dey or not!'

Look at de fingers on you hand! All of dem different length!

Ma Ettie put her head outside the window of the little board house next door to Doodsie's and spoke quietly.

'But, Regal, me son, how all you bad so? I hear all you cuttin down people animal straight how dey stand up so in those people land.'

'Is who bad, Mammie? Is us, or is dem that refusin to give us a livin? What you sayin?'

'Bad how it is, Regal, we could always get two grain o bluggoe in the piece o lan behin de house. I mean, I not sayin those people good but you can't go into their land an destroy all the tings they work for. Is theirs, you know. How you would like it if is your lan they pullin apart like dat?'

'You see the way you tinkin? That is just the point, Mammie. Is not my lan an it couldn't be mine, so is no case of how I would like it if. But I know I well work hard on that very lan.'

27

'Oh ho! So is covetous you covetous over what other people have!'

'Mammie, what stupidness youself talkin?'

'Don play man wid me, Regal. Big as you is, ole as you is, I is still you mudder.'

'So what dat have to do wid de price ah flour?'

'Regal! Make you stupidness, but don talk to Mammie like dat. Is what wrong wid you at all?' Jessie was standing on the step now.

'Mammie, lissen. Is not covetous I covetous. The lan couldn't be mine because I too black for one, an is white people that own lan because is them that did have slave in this country. If I was high brown I might ah have white backgroun dat leave lan give me or I might ah be able to get big job, but it din work out so. People like you an me so, the harder we work in people kitchen and in people lan, the more we kill weself out and bring riches, is the poorer we get while we sweat goin in other people pocket. How much time you see Mr De Lisle down workin in de estate?'

'But is he dat buy de lan and is he bussin he brain every night to decide what to be done in de lan nex day.'

'Dat is why they could afford to shut up!' Regal was shouting now, pointing with a stabbing finger at his mother. 'Because they have all fool like you an me to talk the kine of sut you talkin now and make dey argument for them. I does buss me damn brain more than Mr De Lisle about that lan. My granmother an granfather an you buss more blasted brain than Mr De Lisle could ever have. What you sayin? You self, you forget how hard you still working at your age? An what you have to show for it? Some of Mr De Lisle acres?'

'Chile, doh hurt you head. Is de way life is. Look at the fingers on you hand. God make them all different length. We can't all be the same in this worl. It mus have high and low.'

'So you tryin to tell me that God siddown wey he siddown an decide I have to be low while Mr De Lisle stay high? Well if dat true, Mammie, I go really have to start to look for a God of me own, because dat one is theirs for sure.'

'I don't know what this worl is comin to at all,' Ma Ettie pulled her head part way inside and started to close the window. 'Allyou young people mus wait let ting work deyself out. Is God worl; he go fix it.'

'Ah sure you sayin dat since you start to talk, Mammie. Me, I not even sure God lookin!'

His mammie drew her head back inside. Just before her face disappeared behind the window blind, she made the sign of the cross.

'I don want you curse to fall on me,' she said.

She pulled the blind right across the window, pushed her hand out and pulled the window in.

'I wish you well, my son.'

People sat and stood arrested in various positions in the yard. Some had come half-way up the little gap, their attention held by the heat of Regal's voice. They started drifting off. They commented in murmurs.

'You don hear Regal talk to he mudder? What does do dem at all?'

'But you doh hear she self! Ay! Ma Ettie spen she whole life working for dose people, she don want to get out from under dey tail den?'

'But ting does take time, you know.'

'Anyway, dey don gettin away dis time doh!'

'Well dey takin long enough! Is we time dat reach at las! God doh sleepin, non!'

In the yard, Jessie sat on the top step of Doodsie's house, her feet resting on the second step, her skirt bunched up between her legs, shoulders down, hands supporting her head as elbows rested on her knees.

'Regal,' she said, 'we know that the cocoa price fall this year for true. Is not those people fault.'

Like a coiled kwibo waiting for a movement, Regal swung around to face her.

'What the hell I care about cocoa price fall? If cocoa price fall and cocoa is theirs, well they should sell some cow or some house or something an pay us. When cocoa price fall, everybody knowin, but you ever hear dem saying tings good, cocoa price really high, so we go give labourers a big raise? To hell was them! We fightin!'

Three

It was hot. Funny hot; not normal hot. The trees wouldn even rustle. Huggin their breeze to themself selfish selfish and not even movin when people screw up dey face, take off dey hat to fan and look up at the treetops.The dogs whimpered, yawned, and stretched out their necks and squeezed their eyes against the sun, got up, turned around, scratched the dust, gave a mighty shake, and settled down again with a dissatisfied whimper. Ma Ettie loosened her headtie, held the skirts off her body and tried to make a breeze by flapping the wide skirts against her legs. Phew! Woy! A funny, funny kine o heat.

Then all of a sudden Ole Man Evans, who did stay so quiet in he shed for weeks now dat de chilren almost forget de sound of he voice, almost forget how dey use to run out o de road laughin when he come shoutin deep down in he throat 'Ke-e-e-p Ke-e-e-p! Ah lookin for fresh soul today. Only young one! Ke-e-e-e-ep!' Is like Ole Man Evans suddenly wake up. And his voice was on de street again. Ma Ettie heart miss a beat when she hear im. Arms akimbo, she looked towards the road.

'Ay! What is dat at all? Wey he come out all of a sudden?'

You could hear Ole Man Evans' voice shoutin like in the ole time days announcin a death. Two tings was different. He had a bell instead of a bottle of rum. A large bell giving one loud clang each time he lifted and brought down his hand. And he was announcin in broad daylight.

'Jobe Miss Mercifus alé-o-o-o! Father of Minnie an Son-Son and Prannie alé-o-o-o!'

'Ay! Ay!' Ma Ettie sat down in the doorway of her little board

30

house and looked up at Jessie leaning over the banister of Doodsie's house. 'What do Evans at all today? Jobe Miss Mercifus? Ay! Is today Jobe dead den? Ay! Ay!'

'Perhaps e forget. He in another worl!'

'Huh! Or perhaps Jobe spirit din res yet!'

'What youself talkin at all? Is today Jobe den? Is hear ah hear allyou talk about Jobe, you know. All the amount o years ah have on top me head, I never even know Jobe, non!'

'Jobe Miss Mercifus alé-é-é-o-o-o!' The voice was coming nearer.

Gleefully, the children were beginning to fill the street.

'Ay! Evans yes!'

'Allyou come! Come! Look! Evans!'

'Evans?'

'You lie!'

'Well come non!'

From a safe distance, hovering in the doorways of their parents' homes, safe behind a tree, standing safely some yards away along the road, they shouted at him. 'Ke-e-e-p! Ke-e-e-p! Evans! Look a soul!'

The bell clanged. 'Jobe Miss Mercifus alé-o-o-o!'

Ma Ettie laughed. 'Old how I is dey, I never even know Jobe young nuh! When I was still little, helpin you granmother in de kitchen, Jobe was de oldest man working under de cocoa on ole Mr Walter De Lisle estate. Mr De Lisle use to leave everything to him!'

'Ke-e-e-p! Kee-ee-eep!' The children's voices cut across Ma Ettie's story.

'Jobe did so get to know he work that after a while he use was to measure he own task before even Mr De Lisle tell im what an what to do.' Ma Ettie stopped, thinking.

'Jobe Miss Mercifus alé-o-o-o-o!'

'Mr De Lisle use to like dat. He use to say, "Good man, Jobe. That's the spirit!" Even Evans musbe jus hear talk bout Jobe!'

'Yes, Evans not so much older than me, non! He was big boy in school, about to leave when I was in ABC, but is more my age range! Evans doh know nutting bout Jobe!'

'Huh! Jobe!' Ma Ettie made the sign of the cross. 'Deceased Jobe, Papa God rest he soul! What do Evans at all?' Ma Ettie leaned back, picked up a straw hat from the corner near the door and started fanning herself.

31

'When you see dat is go heself goin!'

'Jobe Miss Mercifus alé-o-o-o!' Evans went up the road, not looking to left or right, his head lifted to the heavens. Every so often he stopped, clanging the bell mournfully, his head lifted to the blue sky looking ice-bright in the simmering heat. The dogs howled.

People laughed nervously as Evans passed them in the road, jumped off the road to walk in the drain, looked at others and said with a nervous giggle, 'Ay-ay! What do Evans at all?'

Evans walked right up the road, stopping longer when doors and windows were closed and parts of the street were empty, stopping so that people up the hill or behind the house in their gardens wouldn't fail to get the message.

'Jobe Miss Mercifus alé-é-o-o!'

Evans walked back down the road, clanging his bell, looking mournfully at the sky, making his announcement. He walked across the flat, over the hill, around the corner, back to his shed in the area they called 'Ben-de-corner'.

Hermitage fell silent in the sweltering heat.

Someting in de mortar besides de pestle!

Suddenly, the government released Leader. He held meetings all over the country.

'My dear people,' he explained to the meeting in the old De Lisle plantation yard in Hermitage. 'You should go back to work. Victory is ours. They had to give in. Wages will be wages whatever the price of cocoa. Victory is ours. You will get a fifty percent increase in wages. Not as much as we wanted, but one step at a time. Victory is ours! If you gettin three shillings a day now, this means you will be getting four shillings and sixpence from now on.'

'Leader!'

'We leader!'

'Well dat is boy!'

'If we find in the future that we have to fight again, we shall not hesitate to do it, but for now, from tomorrow, Tuesday, everybody is goin back to work!'

Murmurs.

'Ah fine we shoulda hol out still an make dem leggo who dey arres!'

'Yes. Dat good. We fight it an we win!'

'Well, everyting have good an bad!'

'We well show dem what is what.'

'Well meself ah not so sure . . .'

Leader held up his white cane, the gold of his ring glinting in the sunshine. Faces turned toward him.

'I have promised the governor that this violence will stop. We have been given a satisfactory solution now, so let us go back to work, stop killing the people's animals, stop taking things from the people's fields. We fought for a cause. We won! We know when it is time to stop. We show dem who is boss!'

'Yeh!'

'Don play wid us, non!'

'Leadership, you call dat! Dat is man!'

'But what about who dey arres? An dey don say nutting bout holiday pay?'

'I have never failed you, and I will never fail you! What do we do tomorrow?'

Murmurs. Some half-hearted shouts. Some enthusiastic shouts.

'Let us show these people that we have discipline. We work as a team. We stand together. We shall fight together! Tomorrow we . . .'

'Work!'

'Yes. Yes. Lewwe go back to work!'

'And if you see anyone still interfering with the people's property, come and let me know. Because we cannot let anybody damage our cause. We have to show the governor who has come to this agreement with us that we are responsible people. So if you see anyone trying to destroy all that we are working for, let your Leader know.'

It was Regal who started the tune. The burnt-out ruins of the De Lisle plantation yard were filled with the sound of singing voices.

'We shall never let our Leader fall
Cause we love him the best of all!'

Afterwards, people stood about talking. Some were excited

33

about the victory. Some were subdued. All agreed that if wasn for Leader, tings never could reach this far. Is a true true sayin. When God caan come he does sen. People started moving away. The De Lisle plantation yard fell silent in the heat.

One han caan clap!

'You tink it go rain, Mammie?' Doodsie asked her mother.

She was hoping that she would be able to take the mace off the nutmegs she had just carried down the hill and that the mace would have a chance to dry properly.

'I not sure. It jus funny. It reminin me of a dark day we had when ah was a little girl. In de middle of de day, bright daylight, everything jus get dark, dark, an Papa God cover up he worl. Around feelin jus like dat. De only ting is it more hot now. Ah doh know what it is, but someting funny.'

'They say on the radio hurricane comin.'

Paren Comesee sucked his teeth when Doodsie asked him what he thought. 'Ah chuts! Hurricane what! Ki hurricane sa! Since I know meself in dis Hermitage here – an youself know is not today ah dey here – nearly every year dey sayin hurricane comin an we caan see it yet.'

'But you never know!'

Doodsie was worried. She didn't like the way the clouds behind the mountain kept gathering to whisper silently and frown down at them. She didn't like the sound of the distant rumble that came every so often. It sounded like they were moving about more chairs than usual up there in Papa God's heaven. And then the radio started giving instructions for battening down windows. Doodsie ran up the road to Mr Mirjah's shop and bought two gallons of kerosene for the lamps and a lot of matches and a few candles and some biscuits and cheese. She stopped by Cousin Maymay.

'You better batten up those window, eh! Tings don lookin good!'

'Is de same ting ah saying meself, girl. Make haste an go home, you hear! You hear Evans earlier? He musbe sense someting. The Lord works in mysterious ways.'

As she hurried back down the hill, Doodsie looked back at the mountain and saw that the frown had spread. The face of the

34

mountain was threatening, furrowed. She looked up at the trees along the road. They gave no reassuring rustle in answer to her questing look. She walked quickly, frightened by their strange, silent unfriendliness.

Allan came home early from working on his mother's plot of land in Dunfermline.

'Dey sayin hurricane comin in truth, you know.'

'Bon Jé, ah really hope is not true! Come! Help me nail up some board across de window!'

They carried in some of the things from the kitchen outside.

'We caan leave dis wares an dem here. Dis ting so rickety if you even blow hard it fallin arready!'

Doodsie managed to persuade her mother to move some of her own things into the house. But Ma Ettie decided that she would stay in her own house and go over to the wall house only if things really started getting bad.

'Leave me here still,' she said. 'Ah holin on, still.'

By seven o'clock, the wind was already high and the little house was shaking, shaking. Ma Ettie said quietly, 'Awright, Papa, ah hear you.' She packed some more of her belongings into a little grip, picked up the goblet of water from the washstand, put the white ewe and the washstand itself near to the door. Ah will ask somebody to come an help me bring them over. Ma Ettie looked around the one-roomed house where she had brought up her five children in between going here an there to work. Ah wonder where Hope is today, she thought, her mind suddenly going to her first child. Like he lose! Like he well lose in Panama! She looked around again. Ah din do too bad. Only one o dem dead, full twenty years now. She looked at her Jesus. It was a replica of the picture in Doodsie's house. He, too, held a globe.

'He's got the whole world!' Ma Ettie sang quietly as she took him off the nail and wrapped him in the white cloth that held some of her more treasured belongings. 'In his hands, He's got the whole world!'

Ma Ettie stepped down into the yard and held herself against the wind. She walked over to Doodsie's house, head bowed against the rushing wind. She pushed open the porch gate. There was a whooshing sound of something collapsing behind Doodsie's house. Ma Ettie paused. 'Ay!' she heard Allan shout. 'Is de kitchen, yes.'

Ma Ettie turned to look at her house. 'Ah hope de water don damage de sofa in de corner, yes. Was Ma Grace dat give me dat sofa, an it still strong an good. Well, the Lord knows best.'

You never get more dan you can handle

The storm raged. They sat huddled together inside, wrapped in blankets, looking at the lamp, listening. The flame flickered. Doodsie's eyes travelled around the room.

'Allan, stop up dat little crack dere in de corner by de door. Pass over de scissors for me, Mammie. It on de shelf by you elbow. Lemme make another frill to put roun de lamp shade.'

A loud crash came from the back, somewhere in the area beyond the room. They jumped. Rushed towards the bedroom.

'Woy! What is dat now!'

Doodsie lifted one corner of the extra cloth she had put across the window. She pushed the blind aside. They stood behind her, mouths half-opened, eyes big and staring.

'What? What happen?'

She half-turned towards them.

'Is the tree,' she said in awe. 'De big tree up in the boundary between Uncle James and Paren Comesee.'

Allan came up to the window. Stood trying to peep outside.

'You could see?'

'Wo-o-o-y!'

'Lawd ave is mercy!'

'Ay!'

'Mammie, lemme see!'

'No, chile. Allyou come away from dere. It dangerous to be lookin outside like dat!'

The thunder crashed. They jumped. Allan laughed nervously.

'Bon Jé what is dis at all?'

Ma Ettie couldn't remember a time when that tree hadn't been there. That was the tree she and her sisters used to go and hide in when their mother, Ma Grace, may she rest in peace, was calling them to do something. Ettie jumped. All of a sudden she could hear Ma Grace's voice riding strongly on the wind.

'Ettie! Etta-y-y-y!'

Ettie turned right around in the room, looking. She put her hands up to her ears, pressing the headtie close against her head as the call came again.

'Ettay-y-y! Ettie-o-o!'

'What happen, Mammie, you awright?'

Doodsie had fixed the cloths over the window again and was now holding her mother's arm and looking anxiously at her.

'Yes. Yes. Don't trouble youself.'

Ma Ettie's hands came slowly away from her ears. She stood staring at Doodsie.

'You awright, Mammie?'

'Yes. Come. Come, popo. Come by you grannie.'

She picked up Angel, who was standing there with her blanket trailing, fear sitting wide-eyed on her face. Ma Ettie wrapped her in the folds of her huge skirt and rocked the child gently.

'Hush, dou dou, hush. Is jus de wind dat vex. Don let it frighten you.'

'Try an make the child sleep,' said Allan to Doodsie. 'It go be better if she could sleep.'

'How ah go make er sleep?' Irritably.

'Well, let er lie down at least.'

They folded Angel tightly in her blanket, made up the bed thick in the corner and put her in.

'Mammie,' Angel sat up. 'Ah fraid. Ah want to stay in the hall too.'

A brilliant flash stabbed through the curtains. The child bounded out of the bedding on the floor and over to her mother. Two more quick stabs of lightning. Thunder crashed again, insistently.

'Come on, Angel, behave youself an get back in you bed.' Allan's voice was severe.

'We'll leave the door open. We right here.' Doodsie made the sign of the cross. Another brilliant flash. A deafening growl of thunder.

They huddled together, looking at the lamp, waiting for the storm to ease its grip. Listening. Suddenly there was a pounding at the door.

'Ay. I wonder who that could be?' Allan jumped up, flash-light in hand.

The others followed him to the door, pulled by an invisible

string. Looked at one another. The pounding came again, with torn-away screams flying on the wind. They converged on the door, pulled away the boards across it, dragged away the cloth in the crack.

'Aye! Ay-y-y! In dey!'

'Open de door, Allan!'

'Open it!'

'Bring de lamp!'

'Dammit fut!'

Doodsie lifted the lamp. The flame went out – almost. Flickered. Went out. Doodsie groped for matches. The flashlight's beam sped around the darkness.

'Open de door still! Open it! Dey shoutin!'

Allan's fumbling fingers turned the key. They pulled the door open. Fought with the rushing wind and rain. Stumbled as four people fell against them, pushing to get inside.

'Quick! Quick! Close de door!'

Ma Ettie fumbled with the lock. Allan pushed the cloths back into the cracks. They piled the boards across. Turned frightened eyes and helpful hands to the newcomers, who stood crying, wailing, shivering, trembling. The flame ignored Doodsie's shielding hand and went out.

'It have a breeze somewhere,' she said. 'Bring dose candles. Lewwe keep dem ready!'

They found towels, Vicks vaporub, bay rum.

'Constance, Winnie, what happen?'

'Woy! Wo-o-o-y!'

Constance was shaking her fingers, moving her hands up to her face, holding her body forward and moaning.

'De house. Oy! O-o-o-y!'

'Awright! Awright! Is de shock! Allan, bring me a blanket. Angel, lie down, chile. Mammie, secure Angel dey for me.'

'De house. De-de-de – pillar – jus crumble. We run up by Miss Luck but she house top blow away an ah don know wey Joseph is. He was holding Mark an den I jus don see dem. Oh Gawd, ah don know wey Joseph an Mark go. Oh Gawd!'

'Awright, awright, take it easy, take it easy. Dey musbe safe somewhere. Pass dat piece o cloth, gimme, Allan. Open de trunk in de small room an take out all de res o bedding. Awright, awright. Dey safe some place.'

But Julius, Winnie's man, whispered to Doodsie after a while

38

that he had seen something like a piece of galvanise sheet fly direct at Joseph as he ran with Mark.

'De wind musbe go wid dem,' he said. 'Oh Gawd! Allyou tink it easy outside dey!' He shivered, looked at the door, as though afraid someone would send him back outside. 'Ah sure is a piece o galvanise dat swing across in front me eyes. Lawd God! Papa God! What is dis?'

Jessie made the sign of the cross.

'Thanks be Jesus,' said Doodsie, 'that ah have enough ole clothes and ole bedding in the place so that people could wrap up.'

They put some of the children under the bed, some in the small room with Ma Ettie, who sat there rocking herself on the bed, listening to the wind and murmuring to herself.

'Oh Jesus Chrise! What is dat?'

The children screamed. Everyone looked around, startled. Wide eyes looked from the corner, from the chairs, from the room door, up towards the rafters. James pulled his little girl closer, looked ready to run.

'What it is?'

Doodsie rushed to the room, jumping over those on the floor, peeped through the window over the bed. She scrambled back over bodies and out of the room.

'Open the door. People comin. I believe musbe Miss Cousins galvanise roof that graze de house top.'

It was. Mrs Cousins, Mr Cousins, and the seven children tumbled in. They were wet, bedraggled and frightened. Doodsie and Allan rushed around, looking for the bathpan and the ewe and some cups and the pail and anything that could hold water. The rain started coming in through the holes made in the roof by the Cousins' galvanise.

'Come, come, Doodsie. Put de yo by here. It have a drip comin through in de corner here.'

'You better help Mr Cousins an dem to settle in.'

'Look, put di . . .'

'Non. Don move de pail. Leave it in de middle dey. Dat is wey de galvanise top musbe gash us. De water strong dey. Look!'

'Bring. . .'

'Look, Miss Cousins, you could wrap up de three littlest ones in dis an put dem over by Angel an de oders in de corner dey, half-way under de bed. Dey protected dey. Allan, move de pail a little over!'

'Dry dat little one head. She drippin still. Bad how it is, don let er ketch kol.'

'Miss Cousins, look in dat bag near de trunk in de small room. It have some more beddin.'

'Thanks, you hear, me chile. Lord! Ah don know. . .?'

From the floor in the corner by the table, James watched Miss Cousins move towards the small room. 'Look how dis ting make us one, eh!' he observed. 'Even Miss Cousins wid she high colour an she chabin chilren. . .'

Doodsie looked over to his corner, cutting him short. 'This is not time for dat. In time like dis, God go punish us for bringin bad feelin. Leave dat for after.'

'Yes, is true,' said James irrepressibly. 'Les wait until Papa God put down all dem dangerous weapon he flingin aroun up dey.'

Doodsie cut her eyes at him and he wrapped himself closer in the blanket, holding his sleeping daughter closer to his chest.

The storm spat its rage until about five o'clock the following morning.

Afterwards, Doodsie stood on the step and wondered at the strangeness of the land. The palm tree behind the house had miraculously remained standing, but it looked like a different person now, standing there headless and beardless, silent in the calm. Angel looked up at the tree and kept turning around, frightened. Somehow it looked to her as if the yard had put on its clothes inside out, as if what she knew as the back was now the front, and the palm tree was standing in a different place.

Ma Ettie's house was nowhere in evidence. Not even a bit of board to indicate the spot. It was as if it had never been there. Doodsie turned to her mother, who was standing in the porch murmuring to herself.

'De ole house jus gone, eh, Mammie. But is awright. You have life. You go stay wid me now.'

'Eh?' Ma Ettie looked vague, held up her hand in a listening motion. 'Wait. What is dat they saying at all?'

'What? Who?'

'You don hear dem talking all kine o stupidness?'

'Those people?' Doodsie looked towards the road, cluttered with galvanise and board and mango and coconuts and trees and

40

clothes and people searching and all manner of things. 'They jus lookin for their tings. I hear Sybil little boy dead, an dis musbe de only house in Hermitage dat nutting much din happen to, except for Evans' little shack in the cocoa down the road. I hear it remain standin dere as if no storm din pass. God works in mysterious ways. Even the other wall house up the road lose it top. All how ah quarrel bout de amount o money de builder spen on dis place, he musbe did do something good. It stay standing strong and good.'

'Listen. You hear dem again?' Ma Ettie laughed.

Doodsie looked closely at her mother. 'Who, Mammie? Those people in the road?'

'No. Youself, too. I mean how those others sayin that Ma Grace lookin for us to come inside, non. She well disagreeable when she ready, you know. As if we can't stay out here little while longer.' Ma Ettie paused, looking away at the light, clear, blue sky behind the mountains, and considering. 'That house that you see Paren Comesee stayin in there now, that was Ma Grace house, you know, an it stay wid that side o the family. An my granmother, Miss Augier, you great-granmother, was a pectus, pectus little lady. Everybody did respec er, an she teach all these big ole man an dem an . . . ay-ay!'

Ma Ettie stopped. She lifted her hand. She held her head in a listening motion.

'You hear?'

She looked at Doodsie, away again towards the mountains.

'Ma Grace callin us.' And Ma Ettie laughed, childlike.

Doodsie stood looking at her mother. No! Lawd, no! Ma Ettie kept looking at the mountain.

'Mammie? Mammie, come an res.'

'Ah not tired. Go on. Ah stayin out here still.'

Doodsie left her there on the porch, went inside, and sat down. Jesus smiled at her. Doodsie buried her head in her hands and wept.

That night, she started to feel the belly pains. Just over one week later, the nurse came in response to Allan's urgent call. The child that was just eight weeks old inside of Doodsie decided that it wasn't interes.ted in life after all and dissolved into a bloody mess.

Allan sat there with his mouth stretched out, his right forefinger stroking the corners of his lips in that way she knew

41

he had when he wanted to say something kind and comforting and didn't quite know how to start.

Doodsie closed her eyes. Ah not sorry. God forgive me if is a sin but ah really not sorry. Ah caan tell im dat but ah really couldn't handle it at dis time. Ah not sorry at all! The Lord works in mysterious ways!

Someting boun to turn up!

The little money they had saved was disappearing fast. Doodsie was pregnant again. They decided to open a little shop at the back, in the area they were using as a kitchen since the storm. They built another little shed outside to use as a kitchen. They did not sell many things. Flour, sugar, matches, saltfish, rice, dry peas, sweets, margarine, little cakes, bread, and sometimes Doodsie made fudge and coconut sugar-cake. Just enough to try and multiply the few cents they still had left.

'Good morning, Miss Doodsie.'

'Morning, dear,'

'Mammie aks if you could trus her two ounce of butter please until Saturday and half poun o saltfish.'

'You Mammie didn give you the seventy-five cents she have for me?'

'No, Miss Doodsie. She say she go try to give it to you Saturday please God. She sellin nutmeg down by de pool Friday evening.'

'Awright.'

The shop, thought Doodsie, was a case of spinnin top in mud.

That night, Allan lay there silent for a long time. Doodsie thought he was asleep. Until he spoke.

'Doodsie, I have something to tell you.'

'What?'

'Well, today I hear they asking for people to go to Florida in America, to work pickin oranges.'

Doodsie said nothing. Allan cleared his throat.

'Ah was tinkin ah could try.'

Doodsie could hear Angel beginning to fret in the huge cradle that they had brought back with them from Aruba. She was too big for the cradle now. Doodsie lay looking away into the darkness.

The next morning, she lay turned on her side.

'Allan. Allan, you sleepin?'

'Ah tink so.'

'When it is dey want people to go to Florida?'

'Nex two weeks. They havin a meeting today and who interested have to go.'

'Well ah tink you should go to the meeting.'

Allan said nothing at first.

'You tink you could manage, Doodsie?'

'I will manage.'

'Like ah always travellin somewhere. Ah must ask Jessie what de stars have in store for me.' Doodsie laughed with him. 'Is true ah didn go far in the war, but at least ah reach St Lucia training.'

'You know you glad you din reach further.'

'What happen to you, girl? I was one of the best shots they had, yes.'

Doodsie sucked her teeth.

'So you tink is joke den? No German coulda escape me, non! Ah sure ah woulda get recognition from the Queen if ah did make it to the heart of that war!'

'Eh! Chupes. The Queen sheself wasn dey. An anyway she studyin you so, den?'

'What do you, girl? So you don believe in you boy, den?'

She sighed, turning over, holding him.

Spinnin top in mud

Allan stood, hands in pockets, in the porch. He watched the road. A little boy was zigzagging a roller up the street. The boy had made his roller from old tin cans and sticks. Thick thread had been pulled tightly across from the wheels to the cover at the top which constituted the steering. The boy steered the vehicle expertly, avoiding the bumps in the road. Ah could help out better by goin. Ah caan jus siddown so. Not wid Doodsie pregnant an everyting. Those two little one in St Lucia now. Ah caan sen dem nothing. Ah mus write Martin an tell im to visit them for me sometimes. When they were stationed in St Lucia during the war, Martin used to warn everybody 'not to get their foot tie-up' with the St Lucian women. Allan chuckled. Big

43

mouth! Then he go and get married! So much so that he couldn ever tell de fellas for heself!

Dear Martin,
So how is the family? I hope well. You know they even had police from over there to help out here in the strike? Tell them to keep their police, you hear. We want we own people to lead us. You should see him, black as me you know and talking big with the best in the land. I know you must have heard about the hurricane that hit us, too. I hear youall only get the tail end of it over there. Boy, that was the worse thing we ever experience, but at least all the old cocoa dead and now that make way for a new young healthy crop. So although is not right now we will see the benefit, something good will come out of it in the future. About our situation here, I know you hearing all kinds of stories. The truth is that is a very long time we been waiting for a leader like this one. And one of our own people at that, from down in the area by you father people there. It do my heart really good to see one of our very own black boys fighting for advanc . . .

'Advancement! Advancement, Doodsie! Dat have an "e" in it? Two "e" or one? Ah does never remember.'
'Well, advance have a "e". Don mine. Is a letter. Not a exam.'
'Ah chuts!'
'Look de dictionary on de shelf over you head!'
'Yes. Yes. Is a-d-v-a-n-c-e-m . . .'
'Hip! Hip!'
'Give me a chance, non!'

Well with me personally things are not too good yet because jobs is scarce. I work one or two days on the estate now and then and is thanks to Mammie piece of land and then a piece that Doodsie's mother have otherwise I don't know what we will do. So I decide I have to go somewhere again. I would like you to go and see my two little children over there sometimes. I sorry I don't have nothing to send for them right now but things really hard. If I wasn't so mannish when I was station there during the war I suppose I wouldn't have extra mouth to feed now.

'You mus tell Martin hello for me. Tell him how allyou good-for-nutting frien tiefin all people union money!'

Silence.

'You hear me?'

'Martin don really know im, you know. Martin use to stay moreso by his mother people in St George's an den in Aruba most times he was out in the hospital.'

'Oh! So you know who ah mean?'

Empty crocus bag caan stan up

Doodsie was pregnant with her second child when Allan left. By the time Simon was born things were so bad with her that Doodsie was sometimes afraid that he wouldn't survive.

Allan's first letter arrived one day when she had just come back from picking peas in his mother's little plot of land. She opened the envelope eagerly, thinking that now, with the American dollars, at last she would be able to buy some milk for Simon and treat properly the asthmatic condition that was beginning to trouble him.

Allan wrote that she should take his son to the ball pitch to give him the feeling. He could feel it in his bones. Young Simon would be a good cricketer. He was in Wisconsin, he said. He explained about a compulsory savings scheme. Said they were being paid eighty-five cents an hour for an eight-hour day of picking corn and string beans; their barracks had cold concrete flooring; they had to pay twenty-five dollars a fortnight for their food and upkeep. He hoped that next time he could send some money.

Simon's asthmatic condition got worse. Paren Comesee suggested a little-leaf bush that was good for the wheezing in the chest. Doodsie tried it. Cousin Maymay suggested boiling the bark of the mortelle tree. Doodsie tried it. Someone else suggested letting a lizard jump a few times in a pan of water. Let the lizard go, boil the water and give it to the child to drink. Doodsie wrinkled her face in distaste, but she tried it. Simon remained thin, weak, with a whimpering cough and a constant wailing cry. Doodsie took him to the weekly government health clinic, but felt that she would get better medical attention if she could pay for private attendance.

45

She waited until the day that the doctor would come to the government surgery for his area visit. That, at least, would be free. She went to him there, joining a queue already there at 8 a.m. The doctor came to the area only once a fortnight.

'Ay-Ay! Makomè, is you?' Doodsie leaned across to touch the shoulder of the woman standing two places ahead of her.

'Ay! Doodsie? Ah din see you come non!'

'Yes, ah dey! But what do you eye? De boil still in it?'

'Madam, it did go down. Den is as if every month it comin up. Dis is the third month an den is as if it bus in de right eye; the pus musbe drain inside; ah don know, but Makomè, is so it lancin me, lancin me; ah caan sleep!'

'It don lookin good, non! But ah hope is nothing serious.'

Another woman in the line was shaking her head from side to side.

'Huh! It don lookin good at all at all! Sometimes things like dat could be de sugar, you know. You have sugar?'

'Non! I don know for now, but ah never suffer wid dat. But anyway, ah don worryin; ah dey here an we go see what dey say an pray God for de bes!'

'Amen! An it could be jus a little dirtiness in de blood, you know!'

'Uh-huh! But youself, Doodsie, is you or is de chile?'

'Is Simon dat dey wid dis constant cough, yes! Every minute is a coo-hoo coo-hoo!'

Simon moved, lifted his head slightly off Doodsie's shoulder, obligingly demonstrated the 'coo-hoo, coo-hoo'.

'You hear? You hear him?'

'An you could hear de wheezin on de chest!'

'Uh-huh! All night is dis wheezin wheezin dat wouldn let him sleep!'

'Poor little thing!'

From behind a door marked SURGERY in large red letters, came a peremptory 'Next!'

'Is my turn jus now, yes.'

'An dis doctor doesn like people to keep im waitin, you know, When you hear e shout dis "Next" dey, e want to see people in front o im right away, you know!'

Doodsie's turn came. She reminded Doctor of the earlier visit, said that the child was still ill. Doctor glanced at Simon, pushed up his eyelids, listened to his cough. Simon turned away and clung around Doodsie's neck. He wrote a quick note for her to take to the dispensary for some medicine. He looked at his watch. He shouted for the next patient. Doodsie began hesitantly to explain again about Simon's condition.

'He has a constant wheezing, Doctor. He can't sleep properly. He. . .'

'Okay!'

Doctor pulled a card from his drawer, handed it quickly to her, rose from his seat, said that that was the address of his private office; she could have more time to explain if she visited him there. He lifted his head and raised his voice in the direction of the door.

'Next!'

Allan wrote from another place in Wisconsin. He was still picking corn, now being paid eighty cents. He couldn't send money. He asked her to write to his two children in St Lucia. He couldn't send anything to them either. She should explain. He would write again.

The letter from Florida came on a day when she had had to change her mind about leaving Simon with Cousin Maymay so that she could do a day's work in the house of young Mr Roger De Lisle, Mr Walter's son, the one who had been born just a few months before that big dinner at the house where she had first met Ezra. But she didn't go to the job that day. Simon had been so ill the previous night that she was afraid to leave him. Angel, too, had become a stubborn, whimpering brat. Doodsie beat her so severely that Cousin Maymay took the child away to spend the day with her.

From Florida, Allan wrote that he was now working with other people from the Caribbean; from St Kitts, from Dominica, Antigua. Some worked cutting sugar-cane. His area was fruit and vegetables. The pay was sixty cents an hour. He was picking 1,200 boxes of celery per day. He might be able to send some money the next time. He sounded sad, lonely and worried.

I hope everything all right, Doodsie. I wish you could write me, but we never know where we going to be. I get one letter from you that they forward, but you talk about another one that I never get. How things? I really hope everything all right. We dont see a lot of people besides who we working with.

47

Doodsie fell ill. The doctor at the surgery said that it was an ulcerated stomach. He also said that the children, who were with her, looked malnourished. He told her severely that they should drink more milk. Doodsie stared at him vacantly. The doctor looked at her and his brow furrowed with impatience at the stupidity of some of these people. Doodsie read his impatience.

'You should eat properly,' he repeated slowly. 'Drink some more milk,' he repeated, leaning forward slightly, speaking slowly and clearly, as though trying to make her understand.

Doodsie's lips parted. She could feel the tears of shame tickling somewhere at the back of her nose, but she bit the inside of her top lip and forced them back. I will tell him. I will ask him where the hell I mus get the money. But something seemed to grip her throat and force away the words she wanted to say. Doctor moved some papers on his desk; he removed his stethoscope; he inhaled deeply and let out an audible breath. His face said clearly: Come on, woman! I'm a busy man! Doodsie stared at him. She looked down at Simon in her lap. She looked at Angel standing open-mouthed, staring at the Doctor. Doodsie stared at the doctor again. Her right hand contracted slowly into a clenched fist. No, Doodsie, no! Don hit im! If you watch im you go hit im. Don! Oh Gawd! Oh Gawd! Shaken by the urgency of her need to smash her fist into his face she got hastily to her feet, pulled the children after her, and yanked open the door of the doctor's room. Ah coulda hit im. Why ah din hit im? He think milk is nutmeg. On which tree I would find it? On which tree? Doodsie went home, lay down and slept. Ma Ettie sat on the steps staring vacantly at the road. Cousin Maymay came by and fed the children.

When Mano's cow had the calf, Cousin Maymay and Paren Comesee started taking a bottle of milk every day from him. They told Mano to drop it at Doodsie's house when he was passing down from the garden. Paren Comesee complained to Cousin Maymay about the damn stupid pride that would make Doodsie sit down in the house there and starve instead of coming to the family for something. She musbe learn dat stupidness when she travel, he said.

Privately, some of the family wondered too about the 'Aruba money'. They wondered whether things were really that bad or if it was just that Doodsie didn't want to spend the money. Jessie was so annoyed when she heard this that she told her sister.

Doodsie smiled bitterly.

'Ah know dey tink ah come home with the whole of Lago oilfield because ah stay two three years in Aruba. Still, is family. Is family, an if wasn for them ah might of been dead this day.'

Jessie wished that she could stay with Doodsie for a while, but the only reason she managed to help out at all with some of the medical bills was because she was doing this live-in job in St George's. She had to keep that. She worried about Ma Ettie, too. Day after day she just sat staring. One day, as Jessie approached her, she said, 'Ay, Manotte, is you?' One night she looked up suddenly from her chair in the corner and said, 'Ay! You don know who ah see yesterday? Hope yes! My son Hope! Ah doh know wey he come out all of a sudden!'

Doodsie did one or two days of washing sometimes when Cousin Maymay could stay with the children for her, but it wasn't always easy; she didn't like leaving them. She picked up the few nutmegs under the cocoa and sold them on her mother's book in the nutmeg pool down the road. The money managed to buy just about enough milk for the tea. For her it was all right. She drank soursop leaf tea and spice tea and even the cocoa without milk sometimes; she might even take a little hot water and sweeten it for herself, leaving the bottle of cow's milk and whatever else for the children. Sometimes she went down by Tan Sase, Allan's mother, and got some things off the acre of land there. Thank God, she thought. Thank the Lord for the little piece of land and for the strength ah have so that ah could still plant the two grain o peas and corn, else ah don know how ah would make out.

Doodsie was really glad it was a family yard, especially when she was nursing Simon. Aunt Thomasina would always send down a few cents or a few grains of jacks or something. And from up the hill, Paren Comesee would send a bunch of figs now and then. As funny as they is sometimes, never turn you back on family whatever happen. If wasn for them, me goose done cook.

At long last, a letter came from Allan with something in besides just the notepaper. It was postmarked Milwaukee, Wisconsin.

I am very happy to be able to write and enclose this $20. Since last I wrote to you, we went to Louisiana to work in sugar-cane. Some Antiguans were with us working. Now here in

Wisconsin we are with Barbadians this time. We are harvesting English potatoes and the pay is back up to 90 cents an hour. I have just got my pay and I am writing you immediately enclosing this because I know how hard things is and the pressure on me is not as heavy as when I first came and had to get everything and pay back so much and everything. I know that even this twenty dollars is not much but its the best I can do at the moment. The work is still hard but things going to be a bit better now so I could send you a little regular money. It wont be much but it will help out. How is my son? Is he playing cricket yet? Make sure you oil those feet well good, girl, because that is a future star youre holding. How is Angel? I hope she still growing well. I heard from my sister Carmen. She told me that she visited you and she is thinking of going to England because there is a lot of work and they asking for people there. She write to me about that idea but I dont think I want to go to England now after this experience here especially now that Leader building up the country.

'Pò djab o! Building up the country what?'
'You talkin to me?' Ma Ettie peered from the corner at Doodsie.
'Non!'

. . . Well take care of yourself, and I hope to be able to send some more money soon. I hear that Cristalene and Jeffrey came to visit you too and that Cristalene is pregnant with the fourth one. It looks as if that sister of mine will have about ten children by the time she is twenty-five. Anyway, take care of yourself. I hope you get this money all right. Lots of love.

You make you children
You don make dey mind

Doodsie eventually went down to the estate to look for work. She did it for one week, carrying the heavy cocoa basket and feeling the sticky cocoa sweat mix with hers, tying the cloth tight below her belly to keep the womb in place. Ma Ettie was displeased.

'Why you marry that man, I wonder? Look he leave so long

an gone. Now you under cocoa. We was never dis kine of people. My mother, you granmother, was a decent, neat little lady. She used to sew and teach all those big man you see about the place doing carpenter an mason an everything. Wus a very bright lady, you granmother. I work in people kitchen, yes, but we wus never under the cocoa. Why you marry dis man who caan give you nothing?'

'You mother was pèctus, Mammie, but perhaps you didn like it too much, because you never bother to stay with husban. Me, I stayin. My children go have father, they going to school an . . .'

This was one of Ma Ettie's more lucid days. She looked steadily at her daughter.

'So you trowin word at me now, Madam Elizabeth?'

'No, Mammie. Ah jus saying that is a good thing I not too pèctus otherwise from the time ah small ah could o never survive.'

'Awright. Forget ah say anyting.'

Ma Ettie went out to sit on the steps outside the porch. She stayed there staring at the road. Doodsie watched her anxiously. She wake up good dis morning. It look like ah make er go back into forgetfulness again. But Ma Ettie was remembering.

Ettie had decided, when her then youngest daughter was only ten months old, that there was no joy in life with a husband who was always drunk. She had left his house and gone with her children to live miles away in St David's. Her mother, Ma Grace, had descended in rage upon the one-roomed board house in St David's, chastised Ettie for having no mind, and left with the two older children. A few months later, when Ettie had found a live-in job and needed someone to take care of Jessie while she worked, Ma Grace had visited again and taken away the youngest child. She had looked with contempt at the man she met in Ettie's house.

Ettie could still hear the bitter words. 'So is true! So is true what de people sayin! An other people husban at that! Oh God, Ettie, you doh have no shame? Yes! Yes, Papa God, you make you chilren, you doh make dey mind!'

Ma Grace rejected Doodsie when she was born a few months later. Ever after she spoke with scorn of 'dat fatherless child dat come to spoil the family name'. Through the years, Ettie moved from one job to another. There was always some member of the family to take care of the other children. But never Doodsie. Ma

Grace said that that type of child could bring the curse of God in people house.

Ma Ettie watched the road. She din have it easy. An when she gettin big she din use to want to go an see de father at all. But chilren mus grow up knowin dey father. She was a real little temper, dat Doodsie, all how she did lookin so quiet. All she matité ways come out when she meet that other little one. Was Manotte own. Manotte sister own. What was she name again? What was . . . Ettie closed her eyes. When Doodsie came out to see what she was doing, Ma Ettie was fast asleep on the step.

Make sure you not livin on nobody eyelash so dat when dey wink you fall!

Dear Ezra,
How are you and Sonny? Things are not too bad. I am coping. Thanks for what you send to help out. You dont know how I thank you for that. You say Sonny is thinking of coming back. Girl if you know what good for you, encourage him to stay on a while so that when youall come back you well comfortable. If my foot wasnt tied right now I certainly would get up and go somewhere so dont go and do stupidness with the opportunity God give you. Stay there for a time and get comfortable so that nobody cant walk on you. Is only people walking on people that going on here and I know things not so rosy there but they much better than here. Those there have more so the little they give is a lot. Take it and hush you mouth. We friend Leader reach the top where he was aimin for and he have a lot of support but me, I not supportin him at all. Allan does say is because I just playing big. Ezra, that man Leader just want everything everything for himself. His union is a big thief organisation. On all the estates people have to make purse to give to him regularly. And now he is big hefe too. I feel that what the paymasters do is when they see they have to raise pay they just bought him out by taking him into their company. With the election he become big man in Grenada and some of these very same paymaster kind of people is senators and now when the people get squeeze by the paymasters there is no one to turn to because he Leader is in whisky company with them.

*Anyway is as if people feel that because Leader in power they
in power so things quiet. Between me an you, girl, I never even
bother to vote. I did well want to vote when was the first
election because for the first time everybody could have a say
but to tell the truth I didn even know who to vote for. I not
sorry for the quiet now, but things hard. Things very hard.
Girl, stay over dey as long as youall could manage and dont
hurry to come back. They sayin things lookin up for poor
people now that Leader on top and people have a vote but if
they changin I think they changin for the worse. So make
youself secure while you could manage it. Aruba money does
disappear fast when you see you come back, and it dont have
nothing to do. Say hello to Sonny and take care of youself. As I
always say you are one friend in a thousand.*
Yours
Doodsie.

Not in one thousand, non! In ten thousand. Was a blessed day
ah meet dat girl. At that first meeting in Mr Giles De Lisle's
kitchen, Ma Ettie and Nen Manotte had shouted at them
constantly for rushin in from outside to tramp all over the
people floor wid nasty, dirty feet. Ah hope she make it over dey,
yes. Ah really hope dey make it! It don have nutting here.

Somebody walkin over my grave

During the two years that Allan was away, Doodsie closed down
the little shop she could not afford to keep stocked with goods.
Regal was around at first, organising for the union. Then he and
Leader quarrelled.

One night, during a union dance for which Regal had spent
his own money organising, intending to get back his outlay from
the profits, he said, Leader appeared, stayed a few minutes and
then walked through the door carrying the entire bag of money.
The dance had been a huge success. Regal, standing with a noisy
group of friends, had been watching Leader circulating. He
stared for a few shocked moments at the doorway through which
the elegantly upright back had disappeared. Recovering his
presence of mind, he ran outside to talk to Leader. He took
from his pocket the list of expenses and the receipts for his

purchases. He asked for his money from the total. Leader laughed.

'Man, you not serious.'

'How you mean? I spent my own money. You could see it here. But the dance successful. Even after I get back mine, the union will still make.'

Leader laughed again, placed one hand on Regal's shoulder.

'Man, you're a joker. Look around.'

He took a few steps back. He stood facing the dance hall outlined in the soft moonlight behind Regal. He flung his arms wide.

'Look at how many people there are here, man. You think all of these people would turn out if it weren't for me and my union? Don't get greedy, man.'

Leader grinned. He lifted one hand in a gesture of farewell. Regal stared as though mesmerised at the encircling gold of the ring on the middle finger. He watched the car leave. Behind him the music stopped as the band came to the end of a rousing tune. From inside the hall came shouts and whistles. 'Play dat one again!' The night breeze went suddenly cold. Regal shivered. The shiver came a second time, unexpectedly. Regal muttered, 'Somebody walkin over my grave.'

Keep a eye out for de rain if you know you have clothes outside

Angel was growing nicely. Rude like the devil, too, her mother thought. See er dey? Look how she fumin an frettin if anything displease er! A real little matité. Womanish like hell! You have to watch er! Simon was more angelic, really. He was a quiet, wide-eyed, delicate child. Charmed everyone on the buses when Doodsie went out with him. Winked at the girls when he was still at the tender age of one and a half.

'Ay!' said Doodsie to Jessie. 'Ah don understan! Who teach im dat? Who he see doin dat?'

'Nobody don have to teach im! It in de blood. You forget . . .?' She stopped, turned her head to look at Angel playing in the corner with the little white doll she had bought for her just the week before. 'Little pitcher have long ears.'

Jessie passed her hand across her mouth as though to wipe out the words that still wanted to come, threw the peas shell into the basket on her left and bent down to take another handful from the cocoa basket on her right hand side. She cleared her throat, shuffled her body in the chair as though to put a full stop to the subject. 'But is the strangest thing, you know. The little man. . .'

'Mammie.' Angel came forward, proffering the doll.

'Go an play. Don't interrupt when you see big people talkin!'

Angel drifted back to the corner, sat down singing to her little white doll daughter:

'Do Do petit popo
Maman go in La Bay
Buy cake an sugar p'um
Give popo some. . .'

'He staring at them fix, fix, you know, an making sweet eye.'

'Nobody don have to teach im!' Jessie glanced at Angel. 'Palé Patwa!' she said. 'Se kon sa nonk-li yé. Se kon sa tout nom an famni-a yé. It in de blood, I tell you.'

'Well he better see an wash dat blood well clean, because I don't want no runabout son.'

'Is *dat* one you have to worry about!' Jessie gestured in Angel's direction. 'Simon go take care of heself. He is man.'

'Yes. But when he run about, is not other people little girl that in trouble?'

'Dat is for them to worry about. Youself you like more trouble than what you have arready? Ay-ay. You have one little girl dey to study, dat not enough? You have to take oder people own put on you account. What do you at all?'

Doodsie broke another pod, shelled the fat green peas into her hand.

'I suppose is when those people come aroun an laughin an playin wid him they does teach im all these things!'

Jessie laughed deeply, enjoying it.

'Well girl, you musbe worry mother!'

'Non! Ah mean. . .' Doodsie stopped, giggling suddenly. 'You remember Prince mother across the river when we did growin up? When people complain about she son, she use to say, "Huh! Allyou hol allyou hen! Me cock outside!" '

Jessie chuckled. 'She could o afford to say dat too, because she had five big cock dey. She never had a girl at all, non!'

Doodsie looked across at her daughter as she combed her fingers through the doll's blonde hair. She wondered what Angel would grow up to be. One sure thing if I have anything to do with it, she not going to have my kind of life. She thought of Simon, sleeping quietly inside. He looked so hurt if you ever shouted at him, you just had to shut up after a while. Angel, on the other hand, looked as though she wanted to find out how long you could go on shouting for. She wouldn't take no for an answer when she decided she wanted something. The most annoying thing was the way she would just stand up there and look at you as though she want to see who will give in first. The child turned suddenly and came to her, holding the doll's head in the palm of one small hand, the body in the other.

'Mammie, it break.'

'Yes. Well, satisfy. You finish it now.'

Doodsie continued shelling the peas. Angel stood, holding out the doll. Doodsie grabbed the parts, pushed the head down on to the gaping hole at the neck. Angel stood rubbing one eye with a grubby hand. Doodsie looked at her, pushed the doll's head back into place, suddenly flung the doll back into the corner where Angel had been playing.

'Go. Go. Give me some peace. You doll fix. Go back an break it up!'

Jessie shook with silent laughter. 'Girl you really rough! Always heatin up youself over everyting! You go dead before you time!'

'Ah won do dat at all! Whenever ah go is me time dat reach!'

Jessie smiled and said nothing.

Allyou blow shell! Stranger in de place!

Doodsie turned away from the window. She bent down to the bucket of water and rinsed out the cloth. Pulling a chair, she looked up at the top panes and prepared to climb. Her five foot two was not exactly designed for this sort of work, she thought tiredly. A car stopped outside. One foot up on the chair, Doodsie listened. No further sound. It must be for her aunt next door, or perhaps for those Cousins across the road. She climbed on to the chair. Since Simon's birth, and in spite of the hard times, she hadn't really lost some of that baby fat. Perhaps is not really fat. Me body musbe just change. There was a rattle at the gate of the little porch. She got down from the chair. Someone pushed the door open. Allan, pushing a suitcase before him. Doodsie stood, open-mouthed. Simon looked up from the floor, staring at this strange presence in the doorway. Then he rushed to the door. As Allan was about to step inside, Simon opened his feet as far as they could go across the doorway. He stretched both arms out wide to keep out this stranger. Allan laughed and scooped the struggling figure into his arms.

'My son! My son! So you keepin me out den?'

Doodsie moved her right foot forward.

'I guess he figure one man in the house is enough.'

Allan smiled as he pulled her close. Angel stood at the room door, unsmiling, just awakened from her nap.

'Hello, Angel.'

He squatted in front of her.

'That's your daddy, Angel. Say hello to Daddy!'

Doodsie was laughing and crying, saying over and over again, 'Ay-ay! Ay-ay! Well jus so!' Allan alternately hugged her and Simon, grinning uncontrollably himself.

'Ma Ettie!' he shouted. 'Ma Ettay-y-y! Jessie!'

'Jessie not here. She in town. Mammie somewey in de back.

Angel stared fixedly at him. Allan cleared his throat, stood up, touched his daughter lightly on the head.

'So how tings, Doodsie? Tell me, non!'

Doodsie shrugged, laughed. Just started laughing and couldn't stop. Allan pulled her close; they stood there holding each other tightly. Through her laugh-cry, Doodsie kept repeating shakily, 'All you oy-y-y! Look stranger! Stranger in de place!'

Four

Everyone said that Angel was a real bright little star. Doodsie bought her an ABC card and a slate with the figures on it. People shouted from the street: 'Doodsie, who is dat you have inside dey countin loud so? Not you little Angel?'

'Is Angel self, girl!'

'Ay-ay! Like she ready for school arready! How ole she is?'

'She not quite four yet.'

'What! Dat chile go be bright as a new shilling! Musbe a doctor you have dey for us, girl!'

Doodsie laughed.

'Roy, you hear? You little cousin jus three, you know! You hear how she readin? Study youself, you know! Take out you han in you mout, boy, an stop doing like a chupid-i!'

Angel was not quite four years old when Doodsie took her to school for the first time. She had hesitated, thinking her much too young, but Teacher Bertha said that she would take her in the little pre-primary school that she kept under her house. She ran the school on her own, teaching, counting, doing sums. The school flooring was the hard brown dirt underneath Teacher Bertha's house. The children sat on benches nailed across from pillar to pillar. Sometimes they went out under the tree. And during the day, if mammies and aunties and cousins and sisters and brothers or even daddies were passing by up the hill to go to do some work in the garden or to go home, they could hear the children shouting. Sometimes they heard A is for Apple, B is for Bat. And Teacher Bertha would shout, 'G is for . . .? And the shout would come, 'Gun, Teacher Bertha.'

'You, Jonathan. G is for?'

Jonathan never knew, and the thick strap that they said Teacher Bertha soaked every night in strong pee to give it more sting would come slashing across his shoulders. Or sometimes it was the pesee, a long flexible cane which Uncle Regal helped by cutting for her from the tree in the yard. The pesee was a real whistler and all the children lived in constant fear of it.

On her first day, Angel did not want to stay. Her eyes were big with apprehension, and the tears fell quietly at first. Doodsie turned back, looked at the crumpled face, and started walking back to her.

'She's too little. Perhaps I shouldn't . . .'

'No. Leave her, Doodsie. They always act like that at first, but she will soon settle down. Leave her.'

Angel was bawling by the time Doodsie started walking down the stony road. Angel looked around at the two dozen or so interested eyes around her and the tears came even faster, even though she saw her three cousins and James from across the road. Teacher Bertha intervened.

'Now, now, Angel. Little girls don't cry like that in my school, you know.'

Angel howled.

'You see this strap here, Angel? It hits little girls very hard, you know. Especially when they cry like that for nothing.'

Angel gurgled, sniffed, sobbed quietly. A giggle came from somewhere on the back bench. All heads swivelled round. Angel's face puckered again. The tears started coming faster. Teacher Bertha moved slowly to the centre of the room and fixed her eyes on the back bench.

'Mr Thomas, there seems to be a joke behind there somewhere? It must be in your head, that's why you are a grandfather in ABC.'

Teacher Bertha stood there looking at Thomas, now squirming on his seat. The heads moved slowly back to face her, fastening on the face carved at the top of her six-foot frame. Thomas cringed. Teacher Bertha released him from her eyes and walked along to Angel's side of the front bench. Angel had stopped crying when the class turned its attention to Thomas.

'Good girl.'

Angel looked out from under her brows at the others and muttered her ABC, sniffing, drawing her hand across under her nose, putting out her tongue to lick the sticky wetness, ducking her head when a frown fell on her from the direction of Teacher Bertha.

Some children sat in the corner doing sums, others were out under the tree. Teacher Bertha moved from one group to the other, giving work, taking up work, shouting here, explaining there, swishing an occasional pesee there. There was a constant buzz of ABC and 'One and one is two' and hushed whispers as fingers went to lips one after the other trying to work out problems like three from ten, throwaway three, four, five . . .

After the first week of strangeness, Angel lived for school. She chattered constantly about Roy and Dick and Maria and Cynthia and was forever counting and reading and spelling. Simon looked at her, twisting the end of his too-short white vest in his hands and biting the inside of his mouth.

'Mammie, I wan go to school with Angel.'

'You'll go nex year. You not big enough yet.'

'Simon, ah go bring Dick an Maria to play wid you.'

Jesus. Trouble start. Ah not so sure I want dis mal levee little Dick an Maria running all over me house arready. Dick? Dick. . . Oh yes. Dick is Mynoe little boy an she does let him do jus what he please. An de Maria an Cynthia self is Constance two does be runnin wile wile all over the place.

Martin came over from St Lucia to visit.

'Allan, how you do, boy? Lord, Doodsie, Angel really get dark, yes, girl.'

'Uh-huh! No doubt bout who the father is, right?'

'An she look like him too. She go lucky like hell, wi, Allan.'

Allan laughed.

'One thing, though. She name did suit her better when she was a baby.'

'How you mean?'

'She was a real little angel then. Pink and white, white, an really cute.'

'So she not cute now?'

'Yes, but she too dark for angel now. Where you ever see black angel?'

'Well she is the first one. An who say God don have some little black angel sittin by him up dere?' Doodsie wasn't pleased. 'Youself too, Doodsie. . .'

'But wait. Listen.' Allan interrupted in that way he had when he felt he was going to say something important. 'Listen. St

60

Martin de Porres. Was a black man, you know.'

'Who?' Martin was not too versed on this saint business and he had never heard of this important namesake.

'St Martin. A black saint.'

'In the Catholic church?' He considered the answering nods. 'Well, I don know too much about that but in all those books an ting I know it never have no black angel.'

'Yes, is true.' Allan gave a little awed, wondering sort of half-laugh, thinking about it for the first time. 'But you musn take too much for granted. St Martin was a black man.'

'All I know,' Doodsie interrupted, pulling Simon away from the board he was trying to remove from across the opening of the back door so that he could get outside. 'Move befoh you bus you tail, chile. All I know, is that for sure it have at least one black angel who making it to heaven.'

'Awright, awright,' Martin laughed, 'she go well lonely up there wid all dem white people God have roun im but awright. Ah not fighting.'

Martin was laughing and holding up his hands to fend her off and looking like his namesake without the cross.

'When all you havin the nex one? Ah could do wid a christening.'

Doodsie cut her eyes at him. 'Tell us when you havin yours.'

Martin grinned, turned towards the door. Turned back and looked about as though he had misplaced something.

'By the way, Doodsie, er, ah . . . when Angel reach in heaven wid all those white people, what she go do? Domestic?'

He ducked through the door, laughing, as she reached for the cutlass.

Never trouble trouble until trouble trouble you!
But if trouble attack fend for youself

Angel was five years old. Teacher Bertha suggested that she move to the big school three or four miles away.

'It's a good, Catholic school, and Angel doin so well it will be good for her.'

But Doodsie hesitated. 'She's so little and anyway ent you does teach them up to second and third standard? Angel could stay with you still.'

'Yes, but she's doing very well. She's way ahead of the others her age and in the big school they could do more for her, I think.'

'I think I'll leave her with you still. And anyway she will be company for Simon. He settlin down better because Angel there with him.'

'Okay. That's true, although he would manage, you know, if she's not around. It's just that I was thinking it might be good to expose her to the big school. Anyway, she will be going to Standard One, and most of the children there are already seven.'

Angel moved to the group in the far corner, the group that went outside under the tree most times, doing addition and subtraction. She held the slate so that Roy could see because he couldn't do them very well. Her cousin Roy was seven. When Angel had just started at Teacher Bertha's he would call for her in the morning and hold her hand for the short walk up the hill.

'Mornin, Cousin Doodsie. Angie ready?'

'I jus puttin on her ribbon. Wait a minute.'

'Ba-bye, Simon.'

A watery stare, Simon's teeth biting the inside of his mouth, his eyes looking distant.

'Say bye to Angel, Simon.'

'Ba-bye.'

Once Simon was four, he went too. In the afternoons, at two o'clock when they were going home Angel held Simon's hand and pulled him to walk in the drain at the side of the road when the big boys came running and tumbling and shouting down the middle of the road.

'Come, Simon, walk here.'

'Hey, boy, gimme you slate.'

'Come, Simon.'

'Hey, little boy, ah say gimme you slate befoh ah bus you head.'

Angel held tight to Simon's hand. The other little boy moved closer; Angel let go of Simon and closed her right hand over the top of her own slate, which lay in the cloth bag hanging from her left shoulder.

'Touch im you go see how ah mash up you face.'

'Ay! What do dat girl? Who fraid you? You tink you could beat me? Ay, boy! Gimme you slate.'

Angel pulled out her slate, pulled away the frame, and held it like a huge, square cutlass. Out of the corner of her eye, she saw two others, a boy and a girl, coming slowly, waiting for the fight. Angel's eyes darted to the little board house at the side of the street. A hand flashed out, making a grab at Simon, and Angel jumped forward, slate slashing. The boy jumped back. Angel pulled off her bag, dropped it to the ground.

'Stay on the side, Simon. Come, non! Come if you bad! You tink ah fraid you?'

'Angel. Mammie say we musn fight.'

'Stay on the side, Simon.'

'Angel, Mammie say if she hear we fight in the road, she go half-kill us.'

Angel stepped back, looked at the house again.

'Miss Maisie!'

'Woy! Who dat? Somebody callin?'

The board window creaked open and a white headtie appeared, came up slowly. Miss Maisie's crinkled face appeared right in the corner of the window frame.

'Ah did jus taking a little res, chile. You goin down?'

'Yes, Miss Maisie.'

Angel looked quickly over her shoulder, but the three had disappeared. She put a hand up to the trailing ribbon, picked up her bag and pushed the slate and frame inside.

'Ah jus sayin good evening, Miss Maisie. Me and Simon goin down.'

'Yes, chile. Tell you Mammie good evenin for me, eh. How you do, Simon?'

'Ah well tanks, Miss Maisie.'

'Wait lemme see if ah have a ripe sugar-apple dey.'

'No tanks, Miss Maisie.'

'Take it, Simon.'

'Okay, den. Walk good, eh.'

'Yes, Miss Maisie. Tanks, Miss Maisie. We goin down.'

Afterwards, Simon said, 'Angel, ent Mammie say we musn take ting from people?'

'She don mean Miss Maisie. Miss Maisie different. An to besides, we go bring it home.'

Angel glanced around quickly to see if the three were in sight, held tight to Simon's hand and walked as fast as she could, forcing him almost to run down the road until they got home.

Simon appealed to Angel's wisdom for most things.

'Angel, what is an apple?'

'Ent you know is de ting in de ABC card!'

'You could eat it?'

'Yes, is like a mango.'

'So A is for mango too?'

'No. A is for apple. If you want, you could aks Mammie to buy an apple for you.'

'Ah aks her arready. She say it too dear.'

Sometimes you have to take de worse an call it de best

Soon after Allan came back, he found a job as a driver on the Dunfermline estate. With that and what they got from the piece of land near to the house, they managed to make ends meet.

Doodsie was under the cocoa picking up nutmegs in the little piece of family land the day she heard the story for the first time. Down there, too, under the trees, was Cousin Maymay, cutting two young bluggoe just on the other side of the lime tree, over the boundary line. Cousin Maymay liked the young bluggoe because, she said, they were softer on the chest. The inside wasn't too good, she said, and when the bluggoe was too full, it formed a hard knot and stayed riding on the chest; for days she felt unwell.

'Doodsie, oy, ah din want to talk to you about dis, non, but ah feel you should know.'

Something rustled in the cocoa tree nearby, and a dried twig broke off somewhere and fell gently on to the moist leaves. Doodsie pushed off a congaree with a twig and picked up two more nutmegs.

'Eh heh? What?'

'Well, you know Cousin Mayrotte youngest daughter dey, de one dat have chilren for Samson?'

'Yes. Em . . . dat one is Geraldine.'

'Yes. Well, I . . . Lord, ah don even know if ah should tell you.'

And immediately Doodsie knew. The cat that had skipped daintily down under the cocoa and now sat fastidiously licking her paws and washing herself high up on the stone on the other side of the drain blinked and meowed. Doodsie looked at it savagely. I can't stand cats. Always looking so superior, slinking about and brushing themself against you foot when you not even thinkin about them and comin up behind you quiet quiet an standin up there staring and meowing.

'Well, you should tell me. If is something ah should know, is better you tell me, however bad it go make me feel.'

'Yes. Dat is what ah tell meself too. Is jus dat . . .'

'Tell me, Cousin Maymay. Ah could take it.'

'Well, girl, God self know I only tellin you because I tink is wrong an unfair to you.' Pause. 'Something goin on between Allan and Geraldine.'

The cocoa tree rustled again, as if it had stayed silent only to listen.

'Look, eh, in de beginning when ah hear it, I say is not true, I say people only want to cause trouble, an den Geraldine frien sheself tell me how dey does meet in the driver quarters on de estate. An everybody else talkin about it. Is only you that don know. Since Allan get to be driver and he getting little more money, dose woman an dem like dat. You caan really blame dem too. Tings hard.'

Doodsie walked slowly up the hill. Lifted the little bunch of figs from her head and put it down in the corner of the kitchen outside, put the cutlass in the corner, emptied the bag of nutmegs close to the step where Ma Ettie sat.

'Ma, take out the mace for me.'

'Hm. You get a good few.'

'Yes. I guess is because de little rain come.'

'Wey de children?'

'They playin inside.'

'How they quiet so? What they doin? Angel! Simon! What y'all doing?'

'We sittin down, Mammie. I just showin Simon some pictures in my Royal Reader book.'

Doodsie stood on the top step and looked suspiciously at them. They were too quiet. What had they been doing? She took the heavy boots off her feet and stepped inside. Looked inside the bedroom closest to the door. Turned towards the door of the little shop which once again had a few things like sweets, coconut fudge, sugar-cake, sugar and a little saltfish. She sniffed as she stood at the little doorway leading from the back of the hall into the shop. Then she saw the smoke rising slowly from behind the straw broom in the corner.

'Jesus Christ!'

Doodsie lifted the smouldering broom into the sink and opened the pipe. Checked around the shop rapidly and turned raging towards the door. She walked towards the two wide-eyed children and demanded: 'What happen out there? Eh? What y'all been doin in the shop? What, ka dammit?'

'Me an Simon did want to take a fudge, so I climb up on de stool.'

'You had no right! You want to fall an bus you face an give me hospital bill? Ent ah give y'all fudge befoh ah leave here? You go find out!' Pulling a strap from off the chair, 'Now! Tell me how de fudge burn the broom.'

'No, Mammie. Is not the fudge alone. When ah climb up, ah see the matches an Simon say let us light it an . . .'

'Ka dammit fut, youall want to put me in trouble?'

Even before the strap landed, the neighbourhood was filled with screams. It was difficult to hit out too often at Simon, crouching, crying pitifully in the corner, repeating 'Won do it again,' his face all crumpled up and hurt and sorry, but a jumping, screaming Angel, pulling at the strap and stomping about Doodsie's legs, fed her rage and fuelled her anger.

'Awright, awright, don kill them.'

Ma Ettie moved to stop her, pulled Simon to her, protecting him, crooning, singing to him. Angel subsided at last into the corner, whimpering, trying to stifle her sobs.

When Allan came in, he sat down and yawned tiredly. Simon came forward timidly, holding out for inspection a little car that his auntie had given him. Allan gestured impatiently.

'Go an sit down now.'

Simon wandered away. Doodsie came in with the hot bowl of soup. She sat down opposite with a plate and began chipping the coconuts to make tomorrow's batch of sugar-cake. He ate. As he picked up another spoonful, she asked quietly, 'How is Geraldine?'

The spoon went back down to his plate. Her eyes remained fixed on the coconut in her hand, but Doodsie could see him put another spoonful to his mouth, chew slowly.

'What you talkin about?'

'Geraldine, I say.'

His chair scraped back. He took the piece of meat in his hand and walked out to the porch.

Angel said, 'Mammie.'

'Leave me alone, ka dammit! Go outside an play, you an Simon. Get outside, ah say.'

'Come on, Angel.'

'Don go outside in the road, now. Stay in the yard.'

'Yes, Mammie.'

They started to be really watchful of each other. Sometimes they were so tense it was like a pin drop could cause an explosion. When Allan came home these days, he looked at her carefully from under lowered brows. Ah sure he wondering if ah hear something. She went about her work, put his food on the table. So what e watchin me under e eye so for? You see im? Underneath like de devil! If Angel or Simon came close to her in times like these, she would shout 'Gimme some peace, ka dammit!' Doll, car, old milk tin, whatever they held out to her would be flung through the door. Allan would look up briefly, adjust himself on the chair, and begin to eat. Doodsie went about her work silently.

Every comment or question from a neighbour began to hold in her eyes some hidden meaning that she tried to decipher.

'Ay-ay, Makomè, how tings? How de chilren? Allan awright?'

'Uh-huh! We dey. Everybody awright.'

'Yesterday self ah meet Allan goin down to work. He lookin well, Ma.'

'Uh-huh!'

So what she ha to tell me he lookin well for? Ah caan see?

One day, Doodsie confronted him with a story she had heard about yet another woman. Allan sucked his teeth and started walking towards the door. Doodsie seized the heavy bowl from the table near her and flung it with all her force against the doorjamb. It just missed Allan's ear. He ducked, his left hand going up protectively. The bowl crashed into the door in front of him. Allan swung around.

'Ay-ay! Ay-ay! You crazy or someting?'

He pushed a chair out of the way as he reached around the table for her. 'What's wrong wid you at all? So you want to fight?' Doodsie backed against the wall. Allan advanced. 'Well les fight non!'

'You good-for-nutting!' she screamed at him. 'All dese nasty dirty woman you runnin behind!' She struggled against his grasp, kicking at him.

'What make dem nasty an dirty, eh? What you tink make dem nasty an dirty?' He swung her around, pushed her roughly away from him.

'All of allyou together is one dirty band of nastiness dey under the cocoa. Go! Go an meet dem! You doh deserve nothing better!'

'You hear you? Is dis same hefe attitude you have make you don like Leader! Damn stupid attitude!'

'Damn stupid attitude hell!' She faced him with both hands clenched, eyes on fire. 'Ah not talkin about Leader now. I talkin about something else! Don try to . . .'

'Well I talkin about dat too!' he shouted, interrupting her. He pushed the dining table against the wall and walked heavily towards the room door. He yanked the curtain as though he were going to enter the room, released it and turned back to face her.

'You jus fine you too damn high an mighty, dat is what!'

'Well if you want to drag Leader into it, drag im in, non! Ah don fraid! Ah could handle dat nastiness too! Dat is Leader too? Dat is not my Leader! Dat is stupid people Leader!'

'Yes, ah know! Your leader is those hefe an dem down in town! You want to see white people rulin us for ever!'

'If dey doin it better let dem do it, yes! Who want anybody dat don know what dey doin rulin over dem! A ole dunce jackass dat could only spell e name little better dan ah could spell mine!'

'You stupid fool!' Allan moved towards her with such threatening rage in his face that she took an involuntary pace backwards. Ay-ay! thought Doodsie, like he more vex about dat dan when ah talk bout he stupid ooman an dem! 'The man need every bit o support he could get from people like you an me an de res of us dat here ketchin we nenen to make ends meet! He black like us, you damn ass!' He shouted, leaning forward to drive his point home, his face almost touching hers. 'When he reach somewey, is we dat reach somewey! Is we he fightin for!'

'Is you dat is de damn ass!' She moved sideways, moved in a

semi-circular motion around him. Allan turned, watching her. 'When he reach way e reach, is he dat reach! Me don reach nowey! He *say* he did fightin for us an damn fool like you you believe im! When e voosh pass in e car now, siddown far far back in de corner so dat de road dust wouldn touch im, is he alone dat passin, not me an he, not you an he! Me?' Doodsie's forefinger stabbed into her chest; her lips curled; her eyes opened big with the question flung at him. 'I don reach no damn place!'

'Sometimes ah could jus . . .!' He lifted his hand as though to strike her. Doodsie pushed out her chest, stood her ground.

'Yes! Hit me! You, he, all you ole woman and dem, all o you is one band of nastiness!'

'You wan fight?'

'Is you dat want fight! Allan!' Doodsie screamed as he grabbed her. 'Don touch me!'

'Eh! What do you, eh?' He pushed her away.

'Ka dammit fut!' Doodsie seized the cup off the table. She flung it at him. He grabbed her again. Doodsie kicked at him. She tried to slap his face. He held her hand fast. She pulled and twisted and manoeuvred her hand free. She dug as deep as she could into his face with her nails, wishing that they were longer.

'Ay-ay! Ay-ay! So you really want to fight?'

He cuffed her. Doodsie sobbed with anger. She bit him. He flung her away from him. Doodsie fell against the wall, crying not so much because of physical hurt as from anger. Allan stormed out of the house. The door banged behind him. Doodsie sobbed. Moments later, she looked up. Angel's wide eyes were peeping from behind the curtain of the small room.

Sometimes the rumours were untrue. Once, after a particularly bitter fight, Doodsie discovered that the woman referred to was really the girlfriend of their friend Martin. But soon, Geraldine was pregnant with Allan's child. They fought. Doodsie pushed him so violently against the wall that Allan hit his head and collapsed, stunned. He stayed away from home for three days. Cousin Maymay whispered to her that he was in Dunfermline at his mother's house.

As long as you have life you could turn you han to someting

'Is only dis mornin ah sayin is a little while ah din hear from Ezra an look now a letter come. She gon live long!'

'Praise de Lord!'

'Ay! Is not she usual length! It well short dis time!'

'She musbe busy over dey!'

Doodsie's eyes travelled quickly down the page.

'Ay! Wi papa! Jessie, well look trouble!'

'What is dat?'

'Listen:

Before I say anything else, let me tell you that they start layin off people again and bringin in more and more local people to work, and this time Sonny get his share.

To tell you the truth we dont really mind because we been thinkin of coming home and building a little house and seeing about the land and so on. We more or less make up our minds to use the money we going to get now that we laid off to open up a little shop, a kind of store to sell material and shirts and things as well as sugar and flour and other goods for the home.'

'That is not a bad idea. Look how well Miss Antoine doin since she come back an set up!'

'Uh-huh! Is not a bad idea, an in dat area, people will buy, because it go save a lot of people going quite in La Bay to make dey little message.' Doodsie looked down at the letter. 'An dey put by a little bit, she say here.

We have something to start with so it shouldnt be too bad. To tell you the truth, I get tired having people ordering me about and me cleaning their house and saying yes Maam all the time. So I am not so sorry really. We should be home in a few weeks time.'

Hol you hen . . .

Angel had been sent to the shop. She walked and skipped down the road, her hulahoop slippers flip-flopping with her, the short print dress with one band missing and the other swishing at her side, moving up and down as she danced down the road. She liked the smell of the trees after the early morning rain or dew or whatever; she jumped and splashed at the leaves; she laughed as she felt the dew-wet sprinkle fall about her. She ran a little way down the hill, stopped; started skipping. She jumped hop-scotch on one leg. One! Two! Three! She held her right fist closed tight so that the money wouldn't drop out; she stretched out her right and left forefingers and sang softly:

'Two little blackbirds sittin on a wall
One name Peter
One name Paul . . .'

Lifting the right hand over the right shoulder, she chanted:

'Fly away, Peter!'

Left hand over left shoulder:

'Fly away, Paul!'

And both hands danced down again as Angel skipped off down the road to her chant of:

'Come back, Peter
Come back, Paul!'

She stopped, turned right round in the road, spinning, spinning, began to get giddy; she steadied herself; she tried to remember clearly what was she going to buy. In a low voice, to the flip-flop of her slippers, she repeated: 'two poun o flour, quarter poun o butter, five penny bread, two poun o flour, eh-m, eh-m, quarter p . . .' A protesting penny coin sped out of her fist and straight across the road to the shallow drain at the other side. Angel raced after it. Stooping, she was just retrieving it from near the dried mango seed when she sensed a presence and looked up.

Tommy frowned. He stood there, hands in pockets, his stocky

71

five foot three assuming giant proportions to the stooping child.

'Wey you goin?'

'In de shop.'

Tommy stood back a pace; Angel stood up. She climbed out of the drain. She started down the road again, walking quickly, watching him. Tommy kept pace alongside. When they got to the little track that cut across through the cocoa to the road below, he stopped.

'In Nen K shop you goin?'

'Yes.'

'Les pass here. It shorter.'

'Mammie tell me go straight an come back.'

'Well here straighter. You go reach back faster.'

Angel looked doubtful, but when Tommy held out his hand to help her across the drain, she jumped over and walked with him down through the short cut. Tommy kept his head down, hands in pockets. In the dark, under the cocoa, he looked up. Looked over his shoulder. Looked around at the cocoa trees. He cleared his throat. Angel walked quickly, anxious to get away from the dark cocoa and back out into the road. She pulled at the dew-wet leaves. Tommy spoke quietly.

'You want to pull down you pantie?'

Angel looked at him. Something slithery passed close to her feet. Angel jumped, brushed at her legs.

'You frighten?'

'Non. Ah thought was a snake dat pass dey. Musbe a lizard or someting.'

'You want to pull down you pantie?'

They were still walking. Tommy had slowed down the pace.

'No.'

'Why?'

'Mammie don like me to pull down my pantie in the road. She tell me if even ah want to pee-pee, ah mus wait until ah reach home.'

'She won know.'

Angel shook her head, watching him, suddenly afraid. Tommy had been to their yard, had stopped sometimes to talk to her uncle, to her cousins. He had never talked to her like this before.

'Is nutting to fraid. Come!' He moved closer to her, his hand outstretched. 'If you don tell er, she won know.'

72

'No!' Angel backed away. 'No! No! No!'

Angel was suddenly shouting, backing away, her right hand holding up the bag threateningly. Her mother's severe, warning face was clear in her mind.

'Sh-h-h! Hush!' Tommy looked around quickly. This was Ole Man Nono's land. The old man could be anywhere about.

'Is awright,' he said in a hurried, hushed voice. 'Is nutting. Don make no noise!'

Sensing his uncertainty, emboldened by it, the child shouted again, 'No!'

'Sh-h-h!' Tommy glanced around nervously.

Turning away from him, Angel ran the short distance to the top of the hill. Tommy shouted after her.

'Don tell anybody you pass under the cocoa, you know!' he called in a low, urgent voice. 'Because you mudder go beat you.'

Angel disappeared over the hill and ran down into the road below.

The child found herself peeping constantly through the window to see if Tommy was passing along the road. She made sure he was not around before she went out to play, before she went out to go to school . . .

Then one day, before she even realised that she was going to say it, she heard her voice saying quietly to Doodsie: 'Mammie, you remember the other day when you sen me down de road in de shop?'

'Eh heh?'

'Tommy did make me pass under the cocoa.'

'What?'

Doodsie looked up, her attention totally drawn from the pot of soup.

'Why?'

'Nutting.'

'What? What he do? What he tell you?'

Angel hesitated. Now that she had started, she didn't know how to continue. Doodsie stood like a statue, her hand on the spoon still in the pot, watching her. She let go of the spoon, walked toward the child. She tried to speak calmly.

'He tell you anyting? He do anyting?'

'He did want me to pull down my pantie.'

Doodsie stared at her daughter. She managed to speak

73

conversationally. 'An what happen?'

'Ah tell im you say ah musn pull down my pantie in de road.'

'An den what happen?'

'Nutting. I run.'

Doodsie was down on her knees, looking anxiously at the child's face.

'You sure dat is all, Angel? He didn touch you?'

'No, Mammie. He din touch me at all because I did start to get fraid and I run.'

'Why you pass under de cocoa?'

'I don know. He say les pass an I jus jump across an I go.'

'Never, never go down through there wid anybody at all excep me an Auntie Jessie. You hear me?'

'Yes, Mammie.'

'Angel, sometimes men could do wicked things to little girls, so you musn go wid dem when dey call you. You hear me?'

'Yes, Mammie.'

That evening, Doodsie went up the road to Tommy's house, in the yard facing Miss Maisie.

'Cousin Kame!'

Cousin Kame looked out. Doodsie went up close to the window. She stood there talking. Miss Maisie, looking out from her window on the other side, wondered what the problem was; she could see Cousin Kame put her hand up to her mouth in horror.

'Bon Jé! Well de boy doh good! He only here wid me for a little while, but ah caan make it. Ah go have to make im go back an meet he mudder. Bon Jé! Dese chilren could make people shame, wi! Tommy! Tommy!'

Tommy came from the yard behind the house. Paused in his stride when he saw Doodsie.

'Tommy, why you interfere wid Angel?' his grandmother looked as if she hoped there was a miracle explanation.

'I din do her nutting, non, Ma.' Eighteen-year-old Tommy looked half his age as he looked at his grandmother. 'I din do er nutting,' he repeated.

'An you better bless you stars you didn't.' Doodsie cut in. 'Because if was one time ah din fraid to take jail, it woulda been now. Ah woulda murder you so-an-so!'

Doodsie had walked up the road with her cutlass, as she usually did if she was going to the garden up the hill. Now she

74

suddenly scraped the blade across the stone in the yard.

'Ah not lying! So help me God! An remember dat. De day you interfere wid er, is de day ah cut out you blasted neck!'

The cutlass scraped across the stone again. This time what it formed was the sign of the cross. Over on the other side, the white headtie moved up and down in emphatic approval. Miss Maisie pulled the blind back across the window. She sank back to rest on the sofa under the window.

We ha to hol one another up

'Doodsie! Jessie! Miss Ettay!'

'Woy!'

'How it have noise inside dey so? Allyou goin up de road by de saracca later?'

'Yes. Yes. Cousin Maymay! Come inside a bit, non!'

'Ah don have much time, non, because ah tryin to fix up tings so that later . . . Ay! Girl is you? Bon Jé! Well dat is a surprise! Doodsie tell me allyou was comin, but ah din know was so soon! Sonny, how you do? Ezra, allyou lookin well, man.'

'Yes, girl! We back in de land, yes.'

'Ah should know is people like allyou dat dey here have Allan an Doodsie laughin so!'

'So how you mean? They doesn laugh den? Eh? Allan, the lady say you an Doodsie doesn laugh, non!'

Allan chuckled. 'Have another drink, Sonny!'

'He givin me drink to hush me mout, yes. Ay-ay!'

'Well is a real good breeze dat blow dis way! Is a good ting ah call out!'

'But look at how dis chile get big, eh!' Ezra was looking at Angel, saying the words for at least the tenth time.

Doodsie laughed. 'Martin say she not angel again, yes.'

'How she not angel dey? She too black now?'

'Uh-huh! He say she go ha to work domestic in heaven.'

'Trust Martin!'

'An suppose she get a boss like . . . what is she name again? You frien dey, Doodsie.' Sonny looked from Doodsie to Ezra.

'Oho! Mrs Smithson!'

'Woy o yoy!' Ezra was laughing her belly-shaking laugh. 'Well dat was devil, yes.'

'Somebody allyou work with in Aruba?'

'Trinidad, yes, Cousin Maymay. Was Doodsie dat work wid her. Trinidad wasn easy non! You doin donkey work for de madam for nothin. Ah mean, de money was big compared to what you was gettin in Grenada at the time, but nothing, non, for livin in Trinidad. You busin you backside jus to sen a little bit home every month and then to try an put by a little for a rainy day.'

'Ah tell you, the worse ting is, after dat ketch hell, the Trinidadian workers hatin us, yes, because dey say we doin donkey work for thanks. Ah suppose it make tings harder for dem, but pò jab us. Wasn easy, non!'

'Girl! Ah remember when we did leavin Grenada, Nen Manotte say "wey allyou goin? Allyou doing de little work in de De Lisle kitchen here, gettin a little change well comfortable, wey allyou goin? Ah never see two little ooman wid more hot foot dan allyou." Sometimes when you see me an Doodsie ketchin we tail in Trinidad dey, ah rememberin dat, eh! Ah tell you!'

'Wey you mother now?'

'Nen Manotte? Me aunt! She dead a few years now, when ah first reach Aruba!'

'Eh heh? Manotte dead?'

'Mammie, ent you know dat?'

'Leave er, Doodsie,' Ezra said quietly. 'She don remember. Yes, Ma Ettie. She gone, yes.'

'Well tell us about Mrs Smithson, non.' Allan prodded.

Doodsie laughed. 'You hear dat howmuch time!'

'But Cousin Maymay don hear it!'

'An meself . . .' began Sonny.

'Ah chuts!' Ezra interrupted him. 'You lie like what!'

'Mrs Smithson! Was a white family in St Ann's I work with. The little boy was ten at the time. Well one day he want me to take his shorts out of the drawer an he fin ah doin it slow. Ay-ay! De gentleman jus walk up an slap me, yes!'

'What!'

'Well dat little devil din know who he dealin wid! Ah jus turn me han on he face an ah give im pye! He eye full up of water! He lucky! He get off light!'

Sonny chuckled.

'Ah say, "Never you do dat again! You little devil!" He look

76

at me an say "I will tell my mother."''

'Ay-ay!'

'I say to him, "You better tell her how you slap me." Ay-ay!
The mister man shout out, "You're not supposed to slap me
back. I'll tell my Mummy! Blackie! You're not nice! I'll tell my
Mummy!"''

'Blackie, eh!'

'He did want another slap.' Cousin Maymay decided.

'Well allyou in dis family don easy! Ezra, you don hear Cousin
Maymay?'

'You did say worse dan dat.'

'When Mrs Smithson return from her dinner party the evening, Mark, the little boy, he tell her. Ah tell you, de woman turn
purple. So ah say, "What he didn say, Ma'am, is that he slapped
me first."''

'Eh heh!'

'Eh heh what! De madam tell me, "But girl, don't you
understand that he's a child?"''

'Child? Ki chile sa?'

'Well she din want to hear nutting, non. She tell me if she din
have a good heart she fire me on the spot. But because she heart
good, she go only take one week wages because she caan have
dis savage behaviour in the house. In the vexation, she stretch
out she neck long, long an she telling me, "You'd better watch
yourself Elizabeth."''

Elizabeth King was the name on Doodsie's birth certificate.
Ma Ettie had called. her first Dou Dou and then Doodsie.

'Elizabeth!' said Ma Ettie now. Doodsie glanced at her.

'Ah know de only reason she ain fire me is because she know
she won get nobody else in a hurry to do donkey work for nex to
nothing!'

Ezra laughed. 'So de madam fire sheself, wi! She jus lan up by
me de day. Ah say well, oh God, Doodsie, you don even have
papers in dis Trinidad here. You shoulda stick it out! What we
go do now? Den when ah study de slap, eh, all ah coulda do was
laugh. Because all dose girl an dem dat work in dat house befoh
say how the little boy is real donkey, so ah know he bounce wid
de right one!'

'Ah was like a fish out o water. Thanks to Ezra, yes. She say,
"Girl, it always have ting. Wey it is, we go fine it! We go start
lookin tomorrow!"''

'Another time she workin for a lady an she come an say, "Oh God, Ezra, dis one now is de devil incarnate!" Woy! You tink it was easy in dose place an dem?'

'Dat one did want me to work miracle wid two loaves an if ah caan do it she searchin all up me nose-hole to see if ah tief she ting!'

'Well meself ah was lucky at firs in Trinidad because de work wasn hard and was de nicest set o people ah work wid. But then de little boy was reachin school age, so everyting change up and they din need me any more. But however we meet it, de ting was dat we dere to get a little livin so we jus do it an play we stupid.'

'Yes. Well is like dat. Den Ezra frien Josefa come an set up tings for her to go in Aruba an den sheself sen for me.'

'Josefa was a good person, yes. That is one person ah caan forget at all at all. She fix everyting, get the work, get the madam to sign the papers, everyting!'

'An then is the same ting youself come an do for me!'

'Well is so it is!' Cousin Maymay said. 'We caan let one another sink. Is you, is me. We ha to hol one another up!'

Tim Tim

At the saracca, Doodsie looked around the circle of food spread out on the bluggoe and fig leaves. She found a spot where she could sit with the two children.

'Mammie,' Angel pulled at her hand. She pointed to another spot. 'Lewwe go over by de drum.'

'No. We stayin in dis end by here so.'

'Mammie . . .'

'Sh-h-h! Keep youself quiet! Look all dose Maria an de others here! Wey you goin over dey goin?'

'Ay-ay!' came a voice. 'Allyou listen to dis!'

Allan chuckled. He knew that once Jeremiah started to talk, you could expect some funniness.

'Hear dis, non. Allyou doh hear de latest bout Nono?'

'Non. What? What he do again?'

'Who? Papa Nono? Wha e do?'

'What? What happen?'

The voices came back at Jeremiah from all sides. People were already laughing in anticipation of a good story. Carmen was laughing so much in anticipation of the joke that Roy pushed

78

her away from the circle. She ended up rolling on the ground behind them, howling with laughter.

'Eh! Well what do er so?'

'Doh study er! So she stupid!'

'Ay! Well ah caan even give me story in peace. Dis one so sweeten up arready dat she won even listen.'

'Doh study er, non, Jeremiah. What Nono do? Tell us, non.'

'Yes. Tell us. Move you skin, lemme siddown by you, girl!'

'Well keep youself quiet, non!'

'Well,' Jeremiah looked around at them, 'ah hear Papa Nono walkin de oder day go up in de garden, an dis big white man stop in one of dem flashy car . . .'

'In a donkey cart?' The young questioner stood biting on a blade of grass, looking straight at Jeremiah.

'Look, boy!' Threateningly.

'Shut you mout, boy!'

The young tormentor had anticipated the reactions. He straightened his short, tattered khaki trousers, scratched at his bare round belly. 'Well, as he say Papa Nono ah tought was a flashy donkey cart dat woulda stop!'

'Fitzroy, if you don't behave youself, I senin you right back home quick sharp. You hear me?'

'Yes, Auntie.'

Allan chuckled quietly. He leaned across and whispered to Doodsie.

'Dat is Selma little boy. Real devil, you know.'

Doodsie laughed. Caught in her hand the meat Simon spat out after he had chewed it up. She focused her attention on the story again.

'Yes. Well, when dis flashy car stop, it turn out to be de big man on de estate. He know dat Nono going up in he garden to plant cocoa in between he crop, so for some reason he get it into he head to give Papa Nono a lif.'

Chuckles round the circle.

'Ay-ay! Well, me dear, when de man say, "Er . . . Nono, wouldn't you like a lift?" Papa Nono say, "Is awright, sah. I walkin, sah, is awright, boss." But boss now determine he go give Nono dis lif whether Nono want to take lif or not. He musbe tink to heself that he ha to do someting for dis Nono who help him out, you know, an who always tell im who tief little bluggoe an ting.'

79

'Huh!'

'Is true, yes.'

'He mout fas too much!'

'So anyway, Boss insis dat Papa Nono taking de lif. Papa Nono twis roun he hat in he han. He stumble over de words. He say, "Well, sah. W-w-we-well, b-b-boss . . ." "Oh, come on!" Boss lean over.' Jeremiah leaned back over an imaginary car seat. 'He open de door in de back over on the other side.' Jeremiah opened the door. Turned around and put his hands back on the steering wheel.'Papa Nono cross de road. As he passin behin de car to get in, he study say, well it raining, an he boots full up ah mud.' Jeremiah considered his feet. 'He feelin well shame to dirty up boss car. So me man . . .' Jeremiah reached down, held on to his imaginary boots, 'pull out he boots . . .' Jeremiah pulled, 'quick behin de car. He put dem down togedder in de bush behind de car on de side o de road an he sneak in easy easy an siddown dey in de back o de car. Boss close he door. He put back he pipe in he mouth. He drive off wid Nono sittin down little little in de corner. Ay! Me frien!'

By this time, everyone was laughing openly in anticipation of the end.

'Woy!'

'Woy o yoy! Me belly!'

'Oh Gawd! Ah want to pee!'

'Bon Jé! Woy-y-y!'

'But allyou doh hear de story yet. Ay!' Jeremiah's brows rose dramatically. 'Well, Papa Nono drop out o car when he reach an he wave little wave for boss. An as boss drive off so, Papa Nono look down at he foot . . .' Jeremiah looked long and hard at his feet. 'He look up at de nutmeg tree . . .' Jeremiah threw back his head and stared up into the spreading branches of the frangipani tree. 'He look down at de cocoa leaf . . .' Jeremiah looked hard at the ground next to him. 'E look, e look at de cocoa leaf on de groun. He look across at de big drain . . .' Jeremiah looked around at the laughing faces in the circle. 'He look up in de hog-plum tree, den he say . . .'

The laughter rushed up to meet the rustling trees. The shouts of delight brought those who were around doing other things closer to the circle.

'Woy! Oh God, Oh Gawd! Ah caan take it!'

'Lawd, ah gon dead!'

'Papa Nono say, "I goin for me boot!"'

'Ha! Ha! Ha! Ha! Ha!'

'Woy!'

'Woy o yoy!'

Angel clapped her hands. She and Maria held hands and jumped around in a circle. Their faces were one big grin. Seeing Doodsie absorbed, Angel joined the other children rolling around on the ground. Simon jumped up and down. With his rice-and-peas hand, he tried to help Doodsie wipe away the laughter tears on her cheeks.

'So,' continued Jeremiah gravely, 'Papa Nono walk all de way back down de road. He put on his boots; he walk back up to de garden to plant boss cocoa and boss never had to take out no mud from inside he pretty car.'

'Ha! Ha! Ha!'

'Oh God me mudder!'

A laughing voice cut in. 'Jeremiah you too damn lie!'

'Ay-ay! Girl, when you reach here?'

'Ezra! Sonny! Allyou come an siddown by here. Ah didn know you woulda finish by Paren Comesee so quick.'

'Miss Ezra, ah only hearin all you in de country, yes, but is de first time ah lay eyes on you. Allyou looking well!'

'Yes, she looking good eh!'

'All you so absorb listenin to Jeremiah make up story, you don even see us come!'

'Sonny, youself know is true!'

'Me? What ah know bout Nono?'

'Is true, Miss Ezra?'

'Me, ah don know. Ah hear Sonny an Jeremiah talkin dey ting but dey always on about Nono. He caan stupid so. All stupid ting dey hear about dey sayin is Nono.'

'What! Ezra, youself, you playing you don know Nono?'

'But he stupid in truth, you know. I remember one night, eh...'

'You see? You see de same ting? Youself know . . .'

Doodsie laughed. This was just what Ezra liked. Although she had lived with her Aunt Manotte since she was small, after her mother died, she was usually in her grandmother's house with fifteen or sixteen cousins. Sometimes Ma Ettie and Nen Manotte had left the two of them together with Manotte's mother. Doodsie used to enjoy that. Ezra spent hours telling an enthralled Doodsie about things the sixteen had seen, done and heard. Ezra even had an older cousin, one of the sixteen, who was a teacher. They called him 'plus one' behind his back. He was far bigger than the others and often shouted at them.

Doodsie hadn't been following Ezra's story. Someone was shouting now.

'Oh God, Ezra! Not true. He couldn really stupid so.'

'Ah tell you. His people use to live right by me father dey, so ah know.'

'Not true, Miss Ezra!'

Ezra laughed. 'Ah tell you!'

Ezra's father. A quiet, gentle man who lived by himself in a little house some distance away from her grandmother. He visited her often and sometimes took her away to spend an afternoon with him when her grandmother would allow it. Ezra would have liked to stay with him. 'He tell me no,' she had said to Doodsie. 'He say is better if I stay for me granmother to bring me up properly.' 'If you go you go miss dem res,' Doodsie had said, not understanding how Ezra could want to leave a house full of exciting people to go and live with one father. 'Even self ah stayin wid im, ah go go by me granmother all the time,' Ezra had explained. But it was not to be. Sometimes when her cousins were away with their family or romped with their sisters and brothers, Ezra would suddenly get sulky and sit quietly in a corner. 'Dey tink is only dem dat have father and mudder,' she said to Doodsie. 'Yes,' Doodsie said then, 'don study dem.' But that was only sometimes. Usually Ezra was like she was now, with a stock of jokes and stories that had some connection with the life of one or all of the sixteen. It had been good to have her around in Aruba. It was good to have her around again now. Already she could laugh with Ezra about Allan. She looked from him to Ezra to Sonny. All three were concentrating again on one of Jeremiah's stories.

The drums became louder. The flambo with the long yellow flames flickering in the cool darkness pushed the drummers to greater heights. The drums crashed.

The voices crescendoed.

'Manman-o-o!
Mwen wivé.
Pwangad waya piké mwen!'

82

The rum flowed more freely. People threw back their heads, knocked backed the flaming white mountain dew, smacked their lips with an 'ah-a-a' which gave vent to their satisfaction and at the same time let a little cool air in. One by one, Angel, Simon, Dick, Maria and the other children started falling asleep on the grass. Mothers pulled half-asleep youngsters by the hand, shouldered some, started drifting away.

The voices of the happy spirits awakened by the saracca drifted after them on the breeze. A burst of laughter. A snatch of song. The branches moved and the leaves murmured gently, sleepily.

You have to make a move to help youself! You caan siddown dey like de livin dead

'You know, some people jus don like to see black people strive. For so much years, eh, it was de white man on top; dem votin, dem passin rules, dem decidin who to pay an who not to pay, who mus work an who mus not work. Now ting change an we have we own leader, you know it even have black people self that cursin im an doh want to see im dey!'

The dog lying on the floor at his feet, thin, scrawny, its black coat ashy-grey with dust, lifted its head and yawned sleepily.

'Well don go too far. Ent you own wife is one of dem?'

'Chupes. Ah don know. Sometimes ah doesn too understan Doodsie, you know!'

'Me, I understan er too well. She jus want to play big. Because Leader is for poor people, she figure she don want to be in dat bracket.'

'Uh! What youself saying! Don talk stupidness. What bracket? Same bracket I in is same bracket she in.'

The dog whined, shook one ear to dislodge a flea.

'Yes. I expec you to jump to defend er. Ent is you wife?'

'But Cristalene, youself too know dat dis bracket ting you talkin about have nutting to do wid it.'

'It have everything to do wid it. Because dey fine Leader too low class and too black, dey don want to see im strive.'

'Yes. I agree. Dat is de way some people tink, but not Doodsie.'

'Eh heh? Well what den?'

'Gi me a glass o water dey.'

'Celia, bring a glass of water for you uncle.'

'Cristalene, you havin dem so fas ah lose count of which is which. When ah was in America, was number four. So . . .'

'You own business not so brown, me brudder.'

'Hm! How Mammie doin?'

'You didn pass and see er? She did sayin only de oder day that she want to see you. Pass by there if you get a chance.'

'Yes. Ah go see. But today ah have to pass an see Mr Peter.'

'Ah hear he wasn doin too well.'

'He have a cough dat does take im sometimes, but otherwise he not too bad.'

'Dem people so doesn like to drink bush, but a good dose of coraile would a do im well!'

'You might be right!'

Cristalene passed a hand across the table, flicking away imaginary specks of dust. The cracked wooden table was always as clean as the floor. She musbe does scrub dem mornin and evenin, Doodsie always said. The table, she said, was so clean you could drink soup straight off it without thinkin twice.

'You doesn tell me you business, but I hear dey givin you big job.'

The dog yawned; stood up; shook itself.

'Dat dog don smellin too good, Cristalene.'

'Yesterday dose chilren bathe it. It musbe roll in some nastiness. Get outside! Outside, Rover!'

Rover looked resentfully from one to the other of them, walked slowly to the doorway and jumped down into the yard beneath. Cristalene got to her feet, took the bamboo broom from the corner by the door, swept the spot where Rover had lain. She took a damp cloth from the corner and wiped the spot. Allan watched her. Cristalene sat down again.

'How you mean ah doesn tell you me business? The man jus mention something to me but is nothing definite yet. An way you hear dat arready?'

'Never you mind. Bush have ears. Dey does talk sense.'

'Well dis time dey even know befoh me.' Allan stood up. 'Anyway, ah mus go befoh he go out.'

Cristalene picked up the empty glass from the table.

'Celia, come an wash dat glass an put it back in the cabinet befoh allyou break it!'

She walked to the door with her brother.

'Okay, den. Doh forget to pass an see Mammie. She musbe want to give you some corn too.'

'Hm-hm!'

'Ah hope you get de work, me brudder. Den you go be able to give me a little help out an perhaps take one o dose chilren to stay wid you.'

'What happen to you? You forget ah have family too?'

'Uh-hm!' In the yard, Cristalene pulled a long stalk of grass, started cleaning her teeth with it. 'An especially as you have more family dan you family even know about!'

Allan sucked his teeth dismissively. He walked away from the one-roomed, spotlessly clean board house where his younger sister lived with her five children.

Doodsie was pleased about the job. But in that strange way that Allan didn't understand sometimes, she was very annoyed because the Madam had given him a few little cards for Angel.

'I tell you arready ah don like to hear no talk about Madam. Madam hell. She is Peter Madam. She not mine; she not yours.'

'Ay! Well what all dat for? The lady jus bein nice.'

'Nice what! Tell er keep she niceness. Angel tell er she want card? She cleaning out she house so she figure she mus dirty mine wid all stupid little Christmas card people sen for her? Card for Angel, hell!'

Allan said nothing more. He knew that even though the argument went on, when she did decide to stop, she would simply say, 'Awright, take win, but you lose,' and leave him with a sense of really having lost.

85

Five

       Doodsie hated the big estate house with its one huge bedroom. All the rooms were massive. But she couldn't understand why there was only this one huge bedroom, one outsize drawing-room which could make three little houses the size her mother's used to be, then a big dining-room and kitchen. She made up her mind that some time in the future, if they stayed in this place, she would divide up the place better and get at least two bedrooms out of it. She couldn't help thinking that those long time hefes used to live very strange. The only good thing, she thought, is that it easier to bring up you chilren the way you want them because this place was far away from everybody.

       Allan loved the house. He loved the land around. He was totally pleased. Angel and Simon opened big, watchful eyes at the overhanging cocoa trees, moaned quietly the loss of their friends, and turned despondently to each other for companionship. Soon they were making coconut bats and picking gospos to play cricket in the big yard. Ma Ettie hated the place. Everything about it. She hated the big yard with nobody in it. Nobody to sit on the steps and talk. Nobody to shout to. Nobody passing along the road. 'What kind of place is this?' she muttered. And more and more she talked and laughed to herself and answered eagerly when Ma Grace called.

       Ma Ettie started disappearing from the house for hours on end. Once they had to call the police. She was eventually found about thirteen miles away, sitting under a coconut tree, resting before she continued her walk back to Hermitage. The coconut tree was just opposite the entrance to one of the big houses where Doodsie remembered staying in the servants' quarters while Ma Ettie worked. They brought her back, muttering about Ma Grace and her grandmother and great-grandmother and the tree. In the house, her dislike seemed to centre on Allan, Angel and the radio. She didn't like the noise of the radio. Once, as the music stopped and a voice began an announcement, Ma Ettie flung her hand dismissively at the radio. She walked to the kitchen, came back with a glass of water. Angel looked up from her book just in time to see water flung full in the face of the radio. 'De damn man inside dey only talkin, talkin,' Ma Ettie mumbled. Sometimes she would try to encourage Simon to go for walks with her, but now he preferred to stay and play cricket in the yard with Angel. Ma Ettie didn't walk for long after they moved to Delicia. She sat down, withered away. She muttered more to herself. Was more irritated with Angel. Angel stuck her tongue out and made monkey-tricks at her when Doodsie wasn't looking.

Ma Ettie got on better with Simon. One day, both she and Simon disappeared. Doodsie came out of the kitchen and saw Angel sitting on the step trying to blow a tune on the mouth-organ Nen Ezra had given her. Hearing the sound of the mouth-organ from the kitchen, Doodsie had assumed that both children were playing with it. Now she saw that Angel was alone.

'Angel, where is Simon?'

'Hm?'

'Wey you brother?'

'Ah don know, Mammie.'

'How you mean you don know, Mammie? Wey Grannie?'

'Ah don know, Mammie.' Irritated, Angel frowned, began to blow on the mouth-organ again.

'Stop dat blasted noise dey, girl!' Doodsie pulled away the offending instrument. 'Listen to me when ah talking! Wey Grannie an Simon?'

'Ah don know!' Angel stamped her foot. She moved quickly away as Doodsie's hand reached out to slap her. 'Ah don know, Mammie,' said Angel, more quietly now. 'Ah believe ah did see dem go down de step by dey so.' She pointed towards the gap leading down from the house to the road below.

'Mercy!' Wiping her hands on her dress, Doodsie moved quickly towards the gap. 'Simon! Simon! Mammie! Papa? Simo-o-n!' She moved quickly, almost running, looking left and right. At the end of the gap, by the hog-plum tree where the road forked, she looked in all directions, standing there undecided where to go, shouting. 'Mam-a-a-y!' Doodsie thought she heard voices. She walked straight ahead in the direction from which she thought she could hear the sounds. A little way down, under an incline, Ma Ettie and Simon sat under a tree, talking.

'Mammie!' Doodsie called.

They looked up. Ma Ettie got to her knees, struggled to her feet. She held out a hand to Simon as Doodsie came running towards them.

'I looking all about for allyou. What allyou doin here, Mammie? Ent ah tell you you musn walk off like dat?'

'Me an Papa just siddown dey talkin,' said Ma Ettie vaguely, lifting her shoulders dismissively. 'Eh, Papa?'

'Wey you come out, Simon?'

'Ah come out in de garden. Ah come out an tie de goat!'

'Goat? Which goat?' These days Simon was always talking about goats, sheep, cows. Doodsie sucked her teeth. Lifted the child to her shoulders. 'Look here, boy! Mammie, ah tell you not to wander off like dat!'

'Awright! Awright! You always grumblin, grumblin!'

Doodsie could no longer depend on Ma Ettie for any assistance. Most times, she seemed completely out of touch with her surroundings. She often sat in a corner on the floor muttering to herself. Sometimes she called, 'Papa, go up dey in de yard an tell Ma Grace we down here by de tree!' Sometimes Simon simply continued what he was doing; sometimes he said 'Okay' and turned away as though going to find Ma Grace. If Doodsie were around, she would say, 'Come here, boy!' and Simon would look at her and smile as though it were all a huge joke that he understood perfectly.

Doodsie was constantly running from the kitchen to make sure that her mother hadn't disappeared again. By the time Allan came in from the fields, she was tired and irritable. She took Ma Ettie to the doctor. He wrote a prescription. Told Doodsie there was nothing he could do. It was just old age, he said. Did Doodsie want her put away?

'Away?'

'In the mental home.'

'But she's not mad.'

'No. But she can't take care of herself. And you . . .' He looked closely at her. 'Do you have any children?'

'Yes.'

'Can you take care of her?'

'Yes. Yes. It's awright.'

Ma Ettie ate very little now. She sat in a corner on her bed, muttering constantly. One morning, when she didn't get up at her usual time, Doodsie pushed aside the blind in the corner of the big drawing room where she slept.

'Mammie?'

Ma Ettie was lying with her hands crossed on her chest. She was smiling a peaceful, triumphant smile. She had apparently died quietly in her sleep. Doodsie rushed out of the room, shouted for Allan.

Doodsie cried quietly, kept repeating, as though explaining to someone,'But it better dis way. Oy-y! Oh! Oy-o-yoy! Uh! But it better so. Is all to de good. It better dis way!'

She took the body back to Hermitage and buried Ma Ettie in the graveyard by the Anglican church, not far from where Ma Grace, the pèctus one, had been buried. Hermitage turned out in force to moan her passing. They sang:

'When the ro-o-oll is called up yonder
When the ro-o-oll is called up yonder
When the roll is called up yonder
I'll be there!'

If wasn for de chilren, eh! . . .

In the kitchen one day, Doodsie said quietly to Allan, 'So ah hear you start you nastiness again?'

Allan said nothing.

'Me, ah coulda do it too, you know. An if wasn for dose chilren ah would do it too. Is jus dat ah know what ah go through an ah don want dat for dem.'

'Ah know you could do it. Ah know you wasn no saint when ah meet you.'

'What you mean by dat? What de hell you mean by dat? I know well it don have not one damn ting you could reproach me wid!' And she pushed him away from where she stood drying the dishes.

'Ay-ay! What wrong wid you at all?'

89

'Don ask me what wrong wid me. Ka dammit fut, move out o me eyesight if you know what good for you eh!'

They were fighting constantly again. Suddenly, one day, Simon flung his young body between them and started pummelling his father.

'Leave her!' he shouted. 'Leave my mother alone! Go wey you come out. Leave er alone!'

Startled, holding him off, both Allan and Doodsie were arrested by the sight of Angel in the doorway, the hammer held tightly in her hand as she stared with intense hatred at her father.

'No,' said Doodsie, moving towards her, her mind flying back to the thought of herself perhaps just a little older, flinging a sharp stone that sliced into the cheek of a man with whom her mother had been fighting. 'Jesus Chrise, no!' She knelt down and held the child close to her. Angel's clenched hand relaxed and she pulled away from her mother. Allan quietly picked up the hammer and put it on the shelf. He looked down at his daughter, and felt awkward, suddenly remembering that day when he had returned to Hermitage from America.

This time, he did not leave the house after the quarrel. After the children had gone to bed, Allan and Doodsie sat and talked way into the night. During the years that followed, the children often heard them angry and impatient with each other, often witnessed tense, angry discussions. But they never saw them fight again.

Ah have nutting to leave for you when ah dead all ah have is in you head so make de best of it!

At seven, Angel was going to a 'big school' for the first time. Doodsie was proud. Teacher Bertha had done a good job. Angel was in Standard III. The youngest in her class. She didn't like it at first. The children kept shouting 'country-bookie' and telling her to speak properly. Simon was ill, adjusting to the cooler atmosphere of Delicia and fighting off constant colds. He looked sad and frail and delicate. Doodsie felt it was like those early days again. De sickness stay in he bones. Poor ting. God good. He go through dat. He go make it! At least, bad how tings is, dis one ah carryin inside me dey now won go through what dese oder two had to pass through! God good! When Simon went to school, they teased him too. Every afternoon after school, the two would rush quickly outside and run the two miles down the hill and inside to the refuge of their home hidden away inside the bush in Delicia. Angel told one of her young tormentors that she came from Aruba.

'Liar!'

'Is true! Is why ah caan speak so proper.'

'Say something in Aruban.'

'Pappia doto.'

'What is dat?'

'It means, "Ah have to go".'

Maria was impressed. 'Say something again.'

'Mammie say I mus talk English all the time now so as I could learn quick,' said Angel, trying hard to keep in her mind what she had said, so that she could say the same thing again if asked to say 'I have to go' in Aruban.

'I feel if was me I woulda talk a lotta Aruban.'

'Ah don know. Ah tink . . .'

'We always tellin you not to say "Ah don know". It soun real country. Why you caan say, "Me en know"?'

Angel asked Doodsie to teach her Aruban. Doodsie brushed her aside, impatiently.

'In Aruba we used to talk English same as here and a little bit o Pappiamentu.'

'Ah don even know Patwa. Allyou does only talk Patwa for us not to understand.'

'What you have to study is you book, not stupidness. Go an do you homework!'

Soon Angel and Simon were staying in to play after school and walking home much later than Doodsie considered safe. When their baby brother was born, they at first rushed home early to sit and watch, to play with him, say 'tc-tc-tc-tc-tc' over his cradle and watch him smile. But the novelty soon wore off.

The cocoa trees along the Delicia road shut out the skylight quite early and the road was a mass of criss-cross, eerie shadows. Simon whispered about spirits, Angel gave details of lougarou, and Doodsie said, 'Ah chuts! The dead is you friend.

Is the livin you have to fraid!' The children considered this long and deeply, but it was really the thought of the dead that made them call out sometimes to Louise who lived half-way down the hill. Louise would quarrel with them about staying so late and then send someone with a masanto to guide them part of the way home.

Doodsie kept saying that hefe or no hefe, this was the worst place to live. It reminded her, she told Allan, of a story she had read long ago that started, 'In a bush where beasts can talk.'

Very often, Angel, on her way from scholarship lessons, or sometimes from just playing and forgetting the time, although she had to say it was scholarship lessons to avoid punishment, would walk with her heart in her mouth or somewhere around her throat. Her eyes darted from side to side through the trees on the dark road. She repeated over and over in her head, 'In a bush, in a bush, in a bush where beasts can talk.' And then she would imagine she could hear a drum beating in time to the words. But as she walked faster and the drums kept pace, the sound inside her head moving together with her darting eyes frightened her so much that she would close off the words, take her mind's hands away from the drumskins, make the sign of the cross three times and say instead, 'God is good, God is good, God is good!' Then she would feel a little better.

But after she had gone past the last houses on the hill with the little lamp-light showing pale and flickering through the window curtains, all words were a hammering hurt in her head. For the next mile or so, there would be only darkness and cocoa trees and sharp stones pressing through the eaten-away soles of the soft-walk shoes. She walked quickly under the stinking-toe tree, covering her nose against the pungent smell of the fruit, down to the bend right after the river. Every time she stayed late and got to that point, Angel was a living shiver of fear. She walked counting: one, two, three, one, two, three, holding the cloth schoolbag close to her body with both hands, her eyes moving quickly from one side of the road to the other.

God! God! God! Make me reach home safe, please! Don't make nothing happen to me, please, an I promise I won stay late again an play an say is lessons! God! God! God! Papa God help me please!

That corner guarding the river at the bottom of the hill was the dreaded corner. Everybody in Delicia and the area around said that the bush on the right-hand side with the huge stone walls coming out of it was the home of spirits. The children told how one night the Sunday-school teacher was passing there with a candle and the moment she got to the corner, the candle went out; something or somebody pulled her hand; and for a few hours the teacher was completely bazoodee, unaware of her surroundings. Angel never got to hear what happened afterwards or how she got away. She looked at the Sunday-school teacher with a distant awe. So she clung to the left-hand corner of the road and tried not to look at the right as she pounded home on jelly feet.

Doodsie, at home, would look outside at the coming darkness and listen out for Angel. She finished washing up the wares; she started the ironing. Lord, keep dis chile safe for me, please! Wey she is at dis hour? Dey could keep dem for lessons late so? She glanced at the clock. Seven o'clock; it dark arready. Ah caan ask Allan to go an meet er because he go just get vex. An sometimes de little devil don even have lessons, you know. She musbe stay an play. Doodsie sucked her teeth, softly. She folded the shirt, passed the iron on the collar again, glanced at the clock. Non, it too late; she caan walk dis dark road alone.

'Allan, ah goin down the road to meet Angel.'

'Hm-m-m!' Allan was listening to the radio.

'Simon, start spreadin out you bed!'

'Mammie, huh!' Simon stood at the room door, rubbing the toes of his right foot against the back of the left.

'Boy don bodder me, eh! Take de small lamp off de table in de dining-room. An don make noise now, to wake up you brudder. When you finish, get ready for bed an say you prayers.'

'Mammie!'

'Don bodder me!' said Doodsie in a fierce whisper. 'Tell you fadder to come an keep you company!'

Simon subsided. Doodsie set out to meet Angel.

Angel would dimly see the approaching figure and at first sink into the drain at the side of the road, her sinking feet afraid of snakes but more afraid of this shadowy figure. The half-moon hovered dimly overhead, peeping through the tall tops of the almond trees. An almond dropped almost on top of Angel's head. She jumped. Recognising her mother as she drew closer, she ran to her.

'Mammie!'

'Angel! Chile, why you so late?'

'I had lessons, Mammie.'

'You sure, Angel? Well I must see Mr Grant and ask him not to keep you so late because you have far to walk. Not like those other chilren who livin near.'

'No, Mammie. If you tell him, those other children might still get extra lessons an den I could lose out.'

'Angel. Yesterday I meet Andrea mother and she tell me that Andrea didn't have lessons Monday because Mr Grant was sick. So how come Monday you reach home so late sayin you have lessons?'

'Well . . .'

'Eh, Angel?'

But Angel had no words.

'All you chilren could make people go in jail, you know. You stay and play, Angel?'

'Yes, Mammie.'

'Well, Angel, you is devil? I workin out me soul case, you know I can't tell you fadder come out dis hour an meet you. Is me dat have to do all me work an den come out because bad as it is, I caan leave you outside in de dark an you still takin you own way and stay an play?'

Angel walked holding on to her mother's dress, fear largely forgotten, shame a silent weight inside her.

'If ah tell you fadder dis, you know is half kill he go half kill you.'

'Yes, Mammie. Don tell im, Mammie. Ah won't do it again, Mammie.'

'De only reason why ah not tellin im is because ah caan tell im. He won only half kill you, he sure to say you caan stay to lessons ever again an den dat is de end of you. You big enough to understand, Angel.'

'Yes, Mammie.'

'Ka dammit fut! Yes Mammie, yes Mammie, an den you doin de same damn ting again nex time . . .'

'No, Mammie.'

'Shut up, ka dammit! Ah won beat you tonight only because ah caan beat you without him knowin but tomorrow is Saturday an when he leave de hoouse ah go dékatjé you little tail gi you!'

94

In a bush, in a bush
In a bush where beasts can talk

The rain fell. It was as if someone up there just pulled back the curtain of sky and kept emptying out all the water behind it. It tumbled down. Angel had closed all of the board louvres except one. She peeped in at her baby brother; to her annoyance, he was doing the only thing he seemed to be good for – sleeping. She stood at the open louvre feeling the splash of the water against her, her hands up against the louvres, her chin resting on the board, her nose wrinkled against the splash of the water and the rainy smell from the grass outside. In the distance she could barely see the tops of the houses in St Paul's. The dog Bingo, his unusual black and white tail curled in a round O which she, to Bingo's irritation, often tried to stretch out, ran wetly through the tall grass in the big yard, going to the kitchen on the other side. He must have jumped against the door, crying to get in, because Doodsie's voice rang out a moment later.

'Stay outside, ka dammit. You wet an dirty as ever. Go an shelter in de coals room.'

Bingo usually did as told then, looking cold and sad as he trotted across to the little outhouse with its old, old walls, sinking down immediately into the coal dust and lying there.

The rain poured. Doodsie came through to the living-room.

'But what you doin standing there gettin all wet, Angel? Den tonight you coughing coo-hoo, coo-hoo an expectin me to get up an see after you as if I not tired enough? Look, girl!'

Angel pushed up the louvres, moved away. Sat down. Simon was spending the weekend in Hermitage with their cousins. There was no one to play with. Angel longed for Hermitage. She put her head down on her knees, feeling sorry for herself. She longed for next week, when she would be going up to spend one week of the holidays with Nenen Ezra. She looked forward to filling the one-pound paper bags, knocking them against the counter, and then putting them on the scales to check the weight.

'Mammie, ah could go by Andrea dis evening?'

'What! Wid all dis rain outside?'

'The rain might stop.'

'If even self de rain stop now, you goin swim to go at Andrea?'

'Me ent like Delicia. Me ent have nobody to play wid self.'

'Tell you father.'

Doodsie went back out to the kitchen. Angel went to get her books. The adventures of Marco Polo didn't hold her interest for long. She put the book down and moved to the other window, one ear open for Doodsie's approach. She pulled down the louvres a little bit, quietly, not letting them bang down. The overgrown garden, a few white roses coming through, a few red roses; the morning glory folded on the side, the sunflower looking dejected, a tangled mass of fern. Angel looked sideways at the cocoa trees, her tongue out to catch the spray from the rain. Straight ahead, at the back, the guava tree looked so wet she felt like bringing it a raincoat. The gospo tree which provided gospos for juice and for when she and Simon played cricket in the yard, looked washed and waiting. Below, in front of the garden, was the tall grass where a lawn might have been if they had the money.

'Angel!'

She jumped, pushed up the louvres; turned around. She had forgotten that Allan was asleep inside.

'You want to ketch you death of cold?'

He moved out to the kitchen. Angel took up her book. The rain thundered down.

Vini ou kai vini, ou kai wè!

One morning in late August, Angel got up early. She just couldn't sleep. She stayed quiet for a while so that Mammie wouldn't know she was awake and call her to go and feed the fowls. She turned, crept over to the other side of the room, peeped into Simon's face. He was fast asleep, left cheek resting on his open palm. She eased up and pushed lightly at the open door of the bedroom. There was only Rupert, surrounded by pillows and bedding to keep him from falling off her parents' bed. That meant both Mammie and Daddy were up already. The next moment she heard the sound of the kitchen window being flung open and Mammie's voice calling out to the fowls.

'Ke-e-e-ep! Ke-e-e-ep! Ke-e-p! Phew-oo Phew-oo Phew-oo!

Come! Come!'

Angel shook Simon, trying to waken him.

'Simon, Simon!'

'Hm-m?'

'Get up!'

Simon stretched, his face crumpled like an old cocoa pod; his outstretched hand hit the partition behind him. They were sleeping on the floor in what used to be Ma Ettie's room, a spot curtained off at the end of the drawing-room. Now it was a real room, because Doodsie had encouraged Allan to build a real partition. The bed was unused, but they had left it because Doodsie said Auntie Jessie might come for a few days, might arrive after they were asleep. She hadn't come that night. Angel waited for Simon to wake up properly. Her eyes met those of Simon's Gentle Jesus picture, smiling down at her. Simon sucked his teeth, pulled up his legs again, turned over on to his right side, and sank back to sleep.

'Angel!' Doodsie's voice from the kitchen. She must have heard the movement.

'Angel?'

Angel moved quietly back to her bedding in the other corner and lay down, eyes closed.

'Angel! Come on, ka dammit. I know you not asleep. Come out here an go an sweep the house.'

Angel washed, took off her nightie and put on a home dress. She went to the kitchen.

'Good morning. Mammie. Simon won wake up, Mammie.'

'Good morning. Leave im. Simon is man. You is little girl. You say you prayers?'

Angel pretended that she hadn't heard.

'Ah say, Madam! You say you prayers?'

Angel frowned, fretted, pulled up the drooping sleeve of her dress.

'Look girl, go an say you prayers befoh ah bus you head, eh!'

Angel went out of the kitchen.

'Say it in the drawing-room there quick an come here an help me.'

Angel knelt down, leaning on a drawing-room chair.

'In de name of the father and of de son and of de holy ghost, amen! Our fadder who art in eaven allowed be dy name dy kingdom come dy will be done on eart as it is in eaven give us dis

97

day our daily bread an forgiveusourtrespasses as we forgive-
demdattrespassagainstus and lead us . . .' she paused, remembering that the quicker she finished, the quicker she would be
out in the kitchen helping her mother.

She looked up, her eyes moving around the drawing-room.
She looked at the sign over the door: 'Christ is the Head of this
House, The Unseen Guest . . .' She looked quickly away,
looked at the pictures of Auntie Ezra and her mother and father
hanging in the corner by the sewing-machine. She looked across
at the bedroom door and wondered if Simon were awake now.

'Angel?'

Angel didn't answer. The only time people were allowed not
to answer one another in the house was when they were at
prayer.

'. . . lead us not into temptation, but deliver us – from –
evil, Amen.'

'Angel? You praying for ever dis mornin?'

Angel's eyes focused on Christ with the globe. 'Glory be to
the father and to the son and to the holy ghost, as it was in the
beginning,' Christ smiled down at her, 'is now an ever shall be,
world without end, Amen!'

Angel went out to the kitchen.

'Go an tidy the rooms an sweep dem out. Sweep out the
dining-room an fix the table for breakfast. Simon will sweep the
yard when he wake up.'

Angel moved off, grumbling, making sure to keep well out of
Doodsie's reach. She knew that a hand could reach out from
nowhere and land none too gently on her. By the time Allan had
come back in from feeding the cows, they were all ready with
breakfast and Simon had swept the yard.

'So today is the great day!' Doodsie sat down and pulled the
bowl of callaloo towards her.

'You mean the exam results?' asked Allan. 'She better pass.'

'She better had. Huh! She better had! Anyway, she do it
arready an we jus have to let God do the res an hope for the
best.'

So nex year is your turn, young man.' Allan looked meaning-
fully at Simon, who looked at his plate. 'Pass de pear for me,
Doodsie.'

Doodsie handed him the avocado.

'These pears really big, yes, an dey sweet too. Which tree dey come out in? De one at the top of the hill?'

'Hm-hm! Is a good crop.' He glanced at Simon, who looked as though he hoped he might have been forgotten. 'Look, your turn is nex year, you know! An ah lookin out for you! You better be sure you know what you doin!'

'Ye-e-s,' said Doodsie slowly. 'And Angel have another chance at it again nex year if she don pass. She young still. But if they don't pass we will have to try an see how it possible to pay for their schoolin.'

'They better pass! A whole eighty children in the country gettin free high school if they pass an we talkin about if they don't pass? They better pass!'

Two flies buzzed together across the table, settled on the avocado.

'Mu dey, fly!' Angel flapped her hands at them.

'Use de cloth, Angel!' said Doodsie. 'Cover the plate.'

'Mu dey, fly?' said Allan. 'That is any way for people going to school every day to talk? When for you to correct us, youself sayin "Mu dey, fly"?'

Simon giggled. Angel cut her eyes at him.

'If youall finish, bring you plate in de kitchen,' advised Doodsie, 'an stop sitting down dey breakin allyou neck as if somebody give you a jail sentence!'

Angel stood washing up the wares in the kitchen. She could hear her mother talking quietly with her father. He agreed that if the worst came to the worst, he would have to find money to send Simon to high school.

'And Angel?' Doodsie asked.

'Huh! Look, that's a different thing, you know. We might have to choose. We mightn be able to send both of them, and Angel is a girl. They grow up and before you know it is confusion, they don even finish school or they finish, get married, their name not even yours again and somebody else get the praise.'

Is true, thought Doodsie, but she goin still! She threw some scraps through the window. The clean-neck hen rushed to the spot, picked up the piece of bread quickly. From across the yard, the big deep-brown cock saw her and came rushing forward, his wings kicking out. The fowl squawked and ran off. The cock gave chase.

Throughout that morning, out in the field, measuring the

task, cracking the cocoa, Allan kept stopping to rest on the handle of his cutlass stuck in the ground, thinking of what he wanted for his children. Simon should be a doctor, not to catch hell in this land like he was doing, killing out his soul case for little or no money. Simon should be a doctor. He would be so proud. Angel should be a nurse or something. If I ever see her with any little man, he thought, I break she tail. He thought of his sister, of how suddenly one day she had stopped being his playmate and was carrying her first child at the age of twelve. He had felt strangely betrayed. And the same had happened with his other sisters, one after the other. And Cristalene, he thought, look at Cristalene state today! His mother always said that girl children were too difficult. He spat between his teeth and shouted to the workers to hurry. I would break her blasted neck, he thought angrily.

Throughout that morning, Doodsie was very quiet. Every time Angel tried to say something to her, she would suck her teeth in irritation and brush her away. Angel stood in the kitchen helping her to peel the provision for lunch and watching Simon through the window as he stood in the yard heaving up limes and hitting them with the coconut bat as they fell back down. Doodsie was silent for a while. Angel sang quietly:

'All day all night Mary Ann
Down by the seaside siftin sand . . .'

'Angel, what stupid ole calypso you singing dey?'
'Dat is not a calypso, non, Mammie!'
'What it is, den?'
'Is a calypso, yes,' shouted Simon from outside.
'Hush you mout, boy. You don know nutting!'
Simon stretched out his tongue at her. Angel took a handful of water and flung it at him. Simon skipped away. 'Ay-y! Boo-oo!' he laughed. He started singing, the words unclear:

'All day all night Mary Ann
Ya ya ya ya ya ya ya ya!'

'Ay! Mammie! Hear what Simon sayin!'

100

'Ay! What do dat girl? What ah sayin?'

'What he sayin? Both of us hear de same ting, so if you hear more than me, is something you know arready!'

Angel said nothing. Doodsie stood at the back door of the kitchen looking up into the damp gloom under the cocoa trees. The air was quite still. She go get de bes if even ah have to scrub floor to give er. She won be like me. By the time I was her age, ah go to six different school arready. Every time Mammie move to another work, so meself behin er. Never could have time to learn nutting. Always like a big chupid-i in de class. As if it were yesterday, Doodsie could see the ring of children around her, small waists jerking this way and that, hands beating to the musical tempo of the taunt. Duncie Duncie Mama Palavi, Duncie Duncie.

'Look, you big for ten years. You body develop arready an you look more than you age. I tell you arready be careful. Any day now you could expect that ting I tell you about.'

Angel frowned. She hated it when these conversations started. She remembered the day she had pulled up her bodice to show a little boy in the yard her chest. Doodsie had seen her. She had almost half-killed her with licks. She didn't like it when her mother started talking about things like this.

'Anybody interfere with you on the street come an tell me. An study you head. Nobody does expec good out of little girl an all those you tink is you frien just waitin to see you fall for them to laugh. They not interested in you. Any time you see man smilin for you, is because they want to drag you down with them. So study you head. Learn you lesson an don grin grin wid nobody, because the moment you turn you back is laugh they laughing to see how they fool you. You see me in de kitchen here is bluggoe I peeling day in day out an is all for somebody else pocket. I could never have a cent because ah workin without thanks, without pay. You big enough now to know that you father have other children, other people to mind, that he never have enough for us, that the more I work inside is the more he have to give outside.'

The rain had started to drizzle.

'Bon Jé, an ah did mean to wash today, yes! Simon, if ah doh tell you to come in out of the rain, you doh know!'

Simon dashed to the kitchen door. 'De rain only drizzlin, Mammie. Watch de mountain! It won come!'

'Go an siddown inside an if it stop you could go back out!' She pushed open the kitchen door for him to enter. 'Go an see what you brother doin! He wake up an eat, but ah think he musbe sleepin again!'

'Ah never see a boy could sleep so!'

Simon rushed off inside. Doodsie looked at Angel. 'So study you head. Nobody could be more interested in you than you is in youself. You see for youself dat if ah doh have drawers to put on an ah ask for a dollar for one is confusion.' She looked at Angel.'Put a little bit o salt in de pot!' Angel stretched behind the coalpot to get the pan of salt off the shelf. 'Study youself. Ah don't want that for you. If you get you own education, nobody is you boss. Ah want the best for Simon too, but he is man, so he start off . . .'

'Mammie,' Simon shouted from the drawing-room, 'ah could go back outside?'

Doodsie looked outside. Glanced up at the mountain. 'Yes. It look like it was just a passing cloud. Simon, now, because he is man, he start off as boss arready. You have to work for it. Study youself!'

Angel said nothing. For some reason she felt like crying. From outside, Simon shouted.

'Mammie! Mammie! Watch!'

He had perfected the skill of hitting the lime the moment it reached eye level. The bat flashed out. Lime centred. Simon looked eagerly up at his mother.

'Good. Bravo! Do it again!'

'Eh!' Angel sucked her teeth. 'I could do that too. That not hard. Dat is someting den?'

'Hush you mout an peel de bluggoe, girl.'

They worked in silence. Doodsie looked thoughtful. Angel was irritable, moving her head to keep off the sandflies, stamping her feet, sucking her teeth. The flies buzzed and worried. The sandflies looked for bare skin and stung.

'Ay! Mammie! Look Rupert!'

'Ay, papa! You wake up? How Mammie baby? You wet! Come lemme change you!' She picked up Rupert and went out of the kitchen.

Angel swept the kitchen. She thought about the scholarship exam. It hadn't been really hard, except that stupid general knowledge paper. Doodsie came back out to the kitchen.

Rupert toddled quietly behind her, looking sleepy. She peeled a banana, handed it to him.

'Sit down dey, papa. Look! Pass the callaloo for me, Angel!'

Angel picked up the bunch of leafy green callaloo, handed it to her mother.

'Come, les siddown in de dining-room here and get dat ready!'

Angel sat down. 'Simon now, things different for him. He is man. He growin up to be in charge. You father say Simon education sure if even he don pass scholarship. I say that even if I have to go back on me knees and scrub floor in white people house an leave dis job here dat not payin, yours go be sure, too. But notice what ah tellin you. You not stupid. You could understand. Tings easier for man. Don shame youself an me. Show dem dat nobody could pull you down. You hear me?'

Angel didn't answer.

'You hear me, Angel?'

'Yes, Mammie,' quietly, with tears sounding at the back of her throat.

'The results go announce on radio tonight. You tink you pass?'

'Yes, Mammie.'

'You sure?'

'Is only the general knowledge ah didn do too good an ah don know how much marks dat carry, but ah tink ah do de arithmetic good an ah know the English was good, so ah tink ah pass.'

'I hope so, chile. Ah really hope so. All you teachers say you very young an you have another chance still but ah would be glad if we could pass de hurdle. You wastin de callaloo, Angel. Just peel off the threads, don throw away dese big junk!' Doodsie took the big junk out of the pan, peeled off the thin thread, put the callaloo into the bowl. 'Ah warning you to study you head. Don take on no little boy that tryin to pull you down, because dat is where confusion start an you life mash up an ah don want dat for you. You hearin me?'

'Yes, Mammie.'

That night, they were all grouped around the radio, waiting for the seven o'clock news. Doodsie's knitting was on her lap. Allan was in a good mood, talking about his cricket days. He used to be the best batsman in the team, he said, had scored a century more than once.

'Is true, Mammie?'

'So he say!'

'Eh! Youself, Doodsie, you know is true.'

Doodsie laughed.

'Dey say he good in truth, although not as good as he sayin.'

'You could still bat good, Daddy?'

Angel and Simon leaned against him. Rupert looked up from the corner where he sat absorbed, using shoes for building. Whatever he found, he used for building. He was always building something, putting shoe upon shoe upon shoe, book upon book upon book, standing back and looking with joy at the result.

'Eh, what do you? None of these fellahs caan touch me, you know. Ask you mudder how dey use to call me.'

Doodsie laughed. 'Bradman!'

'Who is Bradman?' asked Simon and Angel in unison.

'One hell of a cricketer!' Allan leaned back in his seat, ready for the story.

'Uh! Papa Boast.'

'This is the Windward Islands Broadcasting Service. Here is the news read by . . .'

Angel settled down on the floor.

'The British government today announced . . .'

Doodsie said, 'Lemme put dis chile to bed,' picked up Rupert and went towards the room door. Angel started whispering to Simon.

'Hush youall mout an let people listen to the news,' said Allan. 'Youall children jus don listen to news!'

Angel and Simon fidgeted. Tried to look as if they were listening. Heard nothing until: 'The results of this year's scholarships examination were announced today. The following are the names of those who passed the examination. First: Mark Antoine, St George's RC Boys.'

'Uh-huh! RC get first again! Dat school good, you know!'

'Uh-huh!'

'Ay-ay! Second, third, fourth – and fifth too! wo-o-o-y!' Allan laughed excitedly. 'Nobody caan touch dem, non!'

'Is de belt dat talking dey, you know! Ole Man Henson makin dem understand. Is his pass more dan dose chilren own, yes!'

'Ay! Mammie! Andrea! Andrea come eighth, Mammie!'

'What! Miss Barnes mus be laughin!'

'Woy!'

They fell silent, listening. Angel started to think of the general knowledge paper. Twenty-second. Still no Angel. Simon looked at his sister. He saw the tears start to gather in her eyes. He started tearing the bits of paper in his hand into small pieces, biting his lips and bending over to stare at his feet. He glanced at his father's face. Allan cleared his throat. Doodsie sighed.

'Twenty-fifth: Angel McAllister, St Paul's Government.'

The room exploded. Doodsie was laughing and shouting, Allan looking quietly pleased, Angel crying, Simon on the floor somersaulting.

'Well, we make it, we make it, eh, girl.' Doodsie hugged her, an unusual treat.

'Yes,' said Allan 'you make the McAllister name call. Dat good.'

'Meself,' said Doodsie, 'I don have name, but we make it.'

The announcer was now saying that those who had passed should visit the school of their choice with their parents during the coming week.

It had been decided long before that the convent would be the best for her, since the children and Allan were Catholics; and, anyway, Doodsie felt that the convent gave girls just the sheltered, good type of education that was best. Allan agreed. He trusted Doodsie's judgement in things like this.

Six

Angel felt very stupid that Monday morning. She stayed close to her mammie as she walked into the big school and looked up at the pink walls of the Convent High School. A statue of the Virgin Mary was just inside of the gate. A little way up, at the top of the steps, stood another statue of Mary. The Catholic cathedral was right next door. Doodsie had ordered Angel to make the sign of the cross in front of the church like everyone else was doing. Angel pulled gently at her hand.

'Why, Mammie?' she whispered. 'Why they doin dat?'

'Jus do it, ka dammit.'

They had stopped in the church for a minute to kneel down and say a short prayer before coming up here to the convent. Doodsie didn't much like the Catholic church but she always said that God was God and since this was where he and Angel were going to meet, she sort of felt that she needed to talk to him on home ground.

Angel looked around for other children from the St Paul's Government, but she didn't see anyone. Andrea was of the Pentecostal religion and her mother didn't like the convent, so she was going to the Anglican High School. Besides, the nuns gave first preference for places to the Catholic children. Angel was sorry. She missed Andrea already.

Doodsie and Angel went into a little room with smaller statues of the Virgin Mary. Angel looked at Doodsie and the nun talking about the good opportunities for young girls at the establishment, about books, ties, uniforms, regulations. She had the strange feeling that she was eavesdropping. It was as if it wasn't her affair.

They were talking about things concerning some other little girl whom she hadn't yet met. She felt more at ease then. She sank down into the big armchair, fixed her eyes on the downcast head of the Virgin Mary and was soon half drifting off to sleep.

Suffer the little children . . .

It was during her second year at the convent that Angel discovered how serious things were with her soul. She discovered also that the souls of Doodsie, Allan, Simon, Rupert and even the baby who was just born and didn't have a name yet, were also in serious trouble.

Every morning the first subject they did was religious knowledge. At this time, the non-Catholics sat together in another room and studied something else under supervision. As Angel began more and more to understand how fortunate she was to be a Catholic, she felt very sorry for those non-Catholics and wondered how best to help save those who were her friends.

Every mid-morning breaktime, the Catholic students, with nuns and teachers, went to the church for a short prayer, putting on short while veils. Every first Friday, they wore white skirts to school and had a school Mass, dressed all in white with only the dark grey ties a stark contrast against the whiteness.

Angel joined the Legion of Mary. She went to meetings every week and sometimes visited old people to pray with them because they were 'less fortunate'. Now that she knew that missing church on Sundays was a mortal sin for which she could burn for ever in hell fire, Angel got up every Sunday morning very early and walked up the hill the two miles to church. Sometimes, if she got there early, she tried to sit towards the front, just behind the pews where the Josephs sat. The Josephs always sat together like a neat, proper family, because whatever time they arrived, they had a paid pew waiting for them. Once Angel asked Doodsie about getting a paid pew. At first Doodsie only looked at her and sucked her teeth. When Angel insisted, she finally demanded:

'You go sit down in it alone for the whole year? De seat go stay empty until Christmas when you father go to church with you an Simon?'

Responding to Angel's pensive silence, she had added after a while: 'Chile, you don need to travel first class to go nowhere, especially not in God house. The important ting is dat you reach where you goin.'

Sitting in front, Angel could follow the priest's actions closely. Sometimes she asked God to make sure that if by chance she missed Mass for some strange reason, she would not die before being able to confess to the priest all about it. Sometimes in church she remembered the time she had let a boy hold her hand and kiss her. When she thought about the warnings of Doodsie and the nuns, she really felt frightened. She talked to the priest about it.

And then one day, during the religious knowledge class in second form, Angel had a rude shock. Mother Superior said that not only was living together without being married a mortal sin, but if a Catholic got married in a non-Catholic church, then that was no marriage and the person and the whole family was living in sin until there was a confession and repentance and a real marriage in a Catholic church. When Angel got home that day, Doodsie confirmed her fears. Angel went quietly to her room and wept her disappointment.

Later, she pleaded with Doodsie to get married to her father again, in the Roman Catholic church. Doodsie laughed.

'You an you nuns damn awright, you hear. Me an God going to sort it out when ah reach up there.'

Angel told Doodsie about mortal sin and hell. Doodsie told her to discuss it with her father. For weeks, Angel tried miserably to persuade her.

'Look, chile, you doin you bes. God caan vex wid you once you try, so you won't burn for dat. God goin to be really unreasonable if he let you burn too even after you try so hard.'

Angel still looked worried. Doodsie tried to settle it.

'As for me is awright. I always talkin to God. We have an understanding.'

'An Simon an Rupert an de baby?'

'Well dis God of allyou own really drastic. Even Simon an you baby brother an Rupert who barely could say e name yet in problem too because I din married in you church? If he dat drastic, I not so sure I want to know dat kind o God.'

Angel thought that perhaps God would understand. She considered talking to Simon about it, but decided it would be be better if he didn't even know.

'Please God,' she pleaded, on a breaktime visit to the church next day, 'don't let me or Mammie or Daddy or Simon or Rupert or Baby or anybody else close to me burn in hell, please. Is not because I don't love you I not tellin Simon, Lord, and Mammie don't really understand, but don't let none of them burn in hell, please, God.'

And she made the sign of the cross intensely once, twice, surreptitiously three times. She didn't want anyone else to know that she always did this three times when she was particularly anxious for something to work.

Once in a blue moon

Uncle Regal suddenly appeared for a visit. Angel and Simon could barely remember him. He came one night, dead drunk, and said that he would stay the night. What impressed the children most about the visit was their uncle's story about how he had seen spirits by the hog-plum tree. They had tried to follow him, he said, and had only turned back after he stopped and cursed them thoroughly, walking backwards away from them.

'What you tell dem, Uncle Regal? What you tell dem?' asked Simon.

'Never you mine,' said Doodsie. 'He cuss dem an that settle it.'

'Eh, Uncle Regal?' Simon prodded in a lower voice. Doodsie cut her eyes at him. He somersaulted away, laughing.

Simon soon forgot the story as he romped and joked with Uncle Regal. When Angel went with her mother into the kitchen to tidy up, she asked in a low voice whether Doodsie thought Uncle Regal had really seen spirits.

'Yes,' said Doodsie shortly, 'an if I was drunk like im, me eyes woulda certainly make spirit too. He have every right to see spirit.'

Angel said nothing more about the subject, but, after that, every time she passed the crossroads by the hog-plum tree, especially if it was late at night, she made the sign of the cross three times and kept a wary eye on the tree as she hurried past.

Don play de ooman wid me

One of the women working on the estate whispered to Simon and Angel that there was going to be a mawun that weekend. That was why, she said, she was at the grinding-stone sharpening her cutlass at the end of the day's work. Julien's cane was ready, so they were going to have a mawun to cut it. Angel and Simon danced with glee.

'Dat's why we hear people askin Miss Dinah in de shop up de road for kerosene tin!'

'Yes, dat is for de food.'

'An you boilin de rum, Victoria?'

'Look, girl, you want to get me in trouble? You does see me boilin rum? Ay! Ay! What do dis chile at all?'

'Yes, Miss Queen, you does boil rum!' was Simon's assured contribution.

Some people called her Victoria; some, Queen. Victoria had explained to Doodsie that she had been christened Victoria after Queen Victoria, but her mother had always called her Queen. Victoria had only been used when she started going to school.

'Look here, boy,' said Queen now; 'Ah bet you ah cut out you ...!' Queen raised her cutlass as if to bring it down on them. The children ran a little way off, laughing.

'It goin have a lot o people in de mawun, Miss Queen?'

'Well, you caan know before, but ah expec so, because Julien does always help people when dey have work. Now is his turn, a good few should turn out! One han caan clap, you know.'

'Lemme see?' Angel held up her right hand, started pretending to hit it hard against nothingness. 'Ay!' she said, 'how ah caan hear no noise? Ay!'

'Chile you too stupid! Ah don know how Miss McAllister could put up wid you!'

'Ah going to mawun! Ah going in mawun!' sang Simon.

'Huh!' Victoria poured some more water on the point of the cutlass, and put her right hand down on the flat side as she rubbed the edge against the stone. 'Huh! you know you mudder won let you go.'

'Ay! Yes, wi! She go let us go, wi.' said Angel. 'We use to go to saracca an mawun in Hermitage, yes.'

'Ask er, den.'

Doodsie said no.

'But, Mammie! Is Julien cane, you know. An dey go have a lot a lot ah people an chilren dey and dey go be tellin stories an.' Simon stopped suddenly at 'an', as he so often did when he seemed to feel that it was obvious what the rest of the sentence would be.

'No. We does tell enough stories right here. No.'

'But, Mammie!'

'Don "But Mammie" me, ka dammit fut. No.'

'Ent we use to go in Hermitage? An now here . . .' Angel joined the attack.

'In Hermitage we did know the people and the situation was different. I not lettin you go jumpin all over the place in no mawun.'

'But, Mammie, you could come too.'

'No, caraho. An dat is final.'

Simon sulked. Angel stomped off, muttering. 'Me ent like dis damn place.'

'What! What is dat you say, Angel?'

'Nutting, Mammie.'

'Come here, Madam.'

'I didn say nutting, Mammie.'

'She din say damn non, Mammie.'

'You shut you mout! . . . So you smellin youself, Madam? Come here let me show you who is woman.'

'Woy! Woy! Don beat me, Mammie! Ah din mean it, Mammie!'

Doodsie took the peas whip from the corner. For the next few seconds, the hurt of missing the mawun disappeared in the much more immediate hurt of a stinging peas whip across bony shoulders and small backside outlined in a thin cotton dress.

'Oh, Gawd! Oh, God, Mammie it burnin!'

'Shut you mout, ka dammit!'

Angel had recently learnt from her schoolfriends that putting cloth at the back of your panties when expecting a whipping always helped, but since she rarely had advance warning of the whipping, the advice had so far not proved helpful.

'Now siddown in de corner dey an take you book an don let me hear a word out o you. An you, Mister, go an clean up de fowl run.'

Doodsie marched off to the kitchen. As soon as her back was turned, Angel pushed the book angrily away, sobbing quietly.

She heard a sound, glanced at the door, pulled the book back, rumpled its pages in sobbing frustration. One page came away, crumpled. Hastily, Angel glanced at the door, smoothed the page, tried to fit it properly into the book, turned quickly to another smooth page. She began to read the poem about the birds all singing to welcome the light of spring.

> Get up, little sister
> The morning is bright
> And the birds are all singing
> To welcome the light . . .

Make de most of you young days, chile!
You doh know how lucky you is! Dey won come back again!

Dreams and visions often came to Angel as she sat at Sunday service. She sat staring at the priest and the altar, mesmerised by the stylised movements. The droning sound of the Latin soothed her and made her want to sleep. All sorts of stories about faraway places came to her. In her mind, she went off sometimes by boat, sometimes by plane. She enjoyed these journeys. She never arrived anywhere in these daydreams; but she was often travelling. A nice boat with a lot of people in long gowns and the men wore jackets and there was music and people sipping from glasses and lookin relaxed and the women, always beautifully dressed and with long hair, smiling up into a handsome man's face. She often returned just in time to see the priest holding up the white bread which was at that moment being transformed into the body and blood of Christ. She looked around a little guiltily but didn't feel too badly because she had still been to church and done her Sunday duty. The danger of everlasting fire was kept at bay.

The school library was filled with Enid Blyton adventures. Angel devoured these. Her friends also brought in love stories, Mills and Boon paperbacks which they traded under desks and in corners. At night, sometimes, when Angel sat down to do her homework, she just stared at the maths book, seeing upon its dull pages herself transformed into one of the ladies in some love story, long blonde hair flying in the unruly wind, blue eyes sparkling, laughing up at some dark-haired young man of indeterminate colour. Or sometimes she dreamt that she was in fact really the child of some queen in a distant country, that she had been given a drug to change the colour of her skin so that her kidnappers could keep her hidden without being suspected, that one day the whole affair would be exposed. But she could never get to the end of that particular story, for even while she saw herself transformed, Angel could never resolve the problem of having Doodsie and Allan exposed as evil kidnappers.

At school, her love of drama remained Angel's embarrassing secret. She enjoyed the school operetta about gondoliers and fair maidens and things. But she felt small and strange in the face of this distant beauty. The school songs enthralled her:

Spring's the time of all the year
No o-ther sea-son can compare
The Spring – is here – agai-ai-n!
Refreshed by A-pril ra-a-ai-n!
So now we sing of the spring!

She felt all the joy of the season of spring. The Christmas plays she also loved, and would have liked to be an angel in one, but angels were white, or at least very fair and she would not even dare whisper the idea to her closest friend. Still, she loved them and wished she looked more like the girls who could participate in them. They might laugh at me, she thought, but ah woulda really like to be an angel. I mean, she corrected herself in her thoughts, I would really have liked to be an angel. She remembered always that day during her first year at school, when one of the nuns who took a deep interest in her welfare told her that she should ask her mother to have her hair ironed or straightened so that it would look decent. Angel had held her head down, her hands had fingered her tie, she had muttered some answer of assent, then slithered along the wall of the corridor around the corner to the noticeboard. She stood staring up at it through her tears, feeling untidy and stupid, rolling and unrolling the grey tie around her neck.

113

Going home that day, every time someone seemed to be staring at her, Angel felt sure that they were saying that although the child's uniform looked good, her hair was really a mess. When she thought no one was looking, she would put up her hand quickly and try to scrape back the rolled-up 'cousins' at the front of her head or try to unravel the little ones at the back just under the ribbon.

When she told Doodsie about the ironing of the hair, her mother just sucked her teeth. She didn't want Angel to start getting cold in the head. She would get a good, strong brush and really scrape the hair back properly so that the cousins wouldn't roll up so much. Angel felt more miserable each day. She looked at those of her friends who had mothers who could understand better, who were more adventurous, more modern and pressed their daughters' hair. Angel felt resentful. She had the kidnapping vision more often now. They will be sorry. They goin to understand then. She noticed how the girls who had long ponytails, fair skins and no cousins rolled up around their heads, tossed their heads, laughed a lot and looked pretty and confident in the streets, just like the ones in all the books. Angel felt sorry for herself.

And when she walked in the streets with her unglamorous mother who didn't go to the beach often for picnics as all the best mothers did in books and essays, who didn't frequent the cinema, whose fingernails were stained from peeling provision and looked nothing like those of the pretty mothers in all the books, who never wore one of those frilly white aprons which made kitchen work look so inviting, whose kitchen looked nothing like the beautiful ones in books, Angel felt ashamed. She walked a little ahead or a little behind. Look at er, thought Doodsie, she don want to walk wid me. Sometimes she shouted at her to walk alongside. Sometimes she just held her head high, kept the work-stained fingernails pressed into her palm, and kept her head high so that the hurt would pass without tears having to come.

One day, when she was in her second year at the convent, Angel told Doodsie that she thought some of the nuns looked at her with scorn because her head looked so scruffy and bad.

'An, Mammie, today Margaret laugh at me an say dat me hair hard hard an picky an how ah always lookin scruffy!'

'Chupes!'

'Mammie is me dat does feel bad, you know.'

'Is not de same Margaret dat use to want to teach you to talk proper in the St Paul's school? She is de princess or what?'

'No, Mammie, dat was Maria. Is Margaret sister. But, Mammie, when I gone to school an dem laughin, you doesn know, you know.'

'Angel, how you talkin bad so? What you takin in in school? Is so convent girl does talk?'

'Mammie, press my hair for me please, non, Mammie!'

'She say non, Mammie, so she don want you to do it!' shouted Simon from the dining-room table where he was seated doing his homework.

'Boy, hush you mout eh! Somebody talking to you?'

'He hey!' laughed Simon.

'Eh, Mammie? Please, Mammie?'

Doodsie looked at the tears in her daughter's eyes and relented.

'Ah caan let her look de worst.'

Monday morning found Angel with ironed hair and a tiny ponytail. The rubber band pulled every bit of hair tightly together at the back, and a ribbon tied in the shape of a white butterfly, perched precariously at the very tip of the ponytail, gave the illusion of even greater length. Angel was happy.

Ann was Angel's best friend. Together, the two laughed at the fair-skinned girls who tossed their heads, giggled a lot and looked over their heads. Angel and Ann would walk out to the convent playground, turn up their noses whenever one of the 'high-ups' passed by them, and mutter something uncomplimentary.

When Ann and Angel were together, the world was easy to live in. Together they could confront people, talk positively, express opinions, condemn people without fear. When either was alone, she shrivelled, became silent and gloomy.

Angel stayed one magic weekend at Ann's house. She had been afraid until the end that Doodsie would not let her go, but after she had not pouted or shrugged her shoulders or been late home for two whole weeks, had washed wares and cleaned the house without having to be asked, Doodsie had without comment taken out her Sunday dress and two good home dresses, told her to put together her toothbrush, shoes and one or two other little things, not forgetting her underwear, warned her to behave herself in people place and help with the work in the house, given her a bus fare, and told her to have a good weekend. Even then Angel was afraid she would do something she wasn't supposed to, and almost tiptoed out of Doodsie's presence. She tink ah don notice she crossin her finger. Doodsie tried not to smile as an unusually meek daughter said, 'Ah going, Mammie.' 'Awright, remember to behave youself, now.' Only when Angel was down the gap and safely on her way did she hold the bag by one hand and swing it around high in the air above her head, shouting, 'We-e-e-e-! Ah going away for de weekend! We-e-e!' The bag handle snapped.

Angel danced and skipped along the road on her way to Paradise. Paradise was the village where Ann lived. There were lots of houses around and some of the children whom she saw in other classes at school passed along the road sometimes. Each time Angel saw someone she knew, she called out to Ann.

'Ay-ay! Dat girl livin up here?'

'Yes,' Ann would answer. 'Dat is Miss May-May daughter. Dey livin up de road.'

Or: 'Dat is Cousin Sintin second chile. Dey livin in de cocoa.'

Or: 'No, but ah tink dat is Carla cousin. She musbe spenin de weekend.'

Angel went to church with Ann that weekend. The Pentecostal church, she discovered, was much more lively than the Catholic church. They clapped their hands and sang and answered the preacher, 'Amen. Lord! Thank you, Lord Jesus! Amen!' One part of Angel enjoyed it. Another part felt ashamed and a little bit disgusted at all this show of emotion. Besides, she felt guilty about going to a non-Catholic church. In Bible Knowledge classes, Mother Superior always warned them about the sinfulness of this. Angel kept her head down in the church, shifted uncomfortably from one foot to the other, wondered whether it would have been best to tell Ann she couldn't accompany her to church. She frowned because Ann was shouting and clapping too. Angel wished she were somewhere else. Mother Superior always told them about the importance of self-discipline. Ann was so indisciplined, shouting like that. Angel remembered how, in Bible Knowledge class, when they had to write about which qualities they found it easiest to develop, she had written about self-discipline as Number One. She held her head high, pressed her lips together and did not join in the singing and clapping.

Ann went to spend the weekend with Angel. They played cricket with Simon in the yard.

'Angel, go over by the fowl run an fiel! She does hit de ball hard. No. Go over more! Right! Stay dey!'

'Ay, boy! You caan bowl? What kine o ball is dat?'

'Ketch de ball! Ketch de ball!'

'Give up! You out! You out!'

On Sunday morning, Ann went to church only because Doodsie insisted. She went with Doodsie to the Anglican, walking across to meet Angel afterwards, because, she said to Angel, 'That church really borin, girl. Ah caan take it. Anglican little bit better.' Angel said nothing, only hoping that one day she would be able to convert her friend. Doodsie told Allan that it was so dead in that bush, they should allow Angel and her friend to go out if they wanted to. Angel could hardly believe it when Allan gave them all money to go down to Regal cinema in town to see an Elvis Presley movie. Ann enjoyed the weekend, especially because on Monday she and Angel could nonchalantly join the group talking about how 'scrumptious' Elvis Presley was. But about Delicia she was unenthusiastic.

'Lord, Angel, you don get lonely? No oder house around at all?'

Angel shrugged. After losing Andrea, Ann was the first person Angel had invited to her home. The two were better friends after those initial visits. Ann often had a rough time at school. The other children said she was ugly. They called her Hottentot; the Hottentots, Angel knew, were some of the strange African people they read about in their history books. She didn't laugh when Ann was teased; she didn't think Ann was that ugly.

The first time that Angel got her periods at school, it was Ann who told her to take the toilet paper in the bathroom and use it as a pad. It helped a little, but that afternoon, Angel could feel the back of her skirt wet and sticky as she sat on the bus. When she got out, she climbed down carefully, stood at the bus stop with her back to the wall, letting the other people go away. Then she looked back surreptitiously, pulling the skirt around to see if it was dirty. There was a dark stain on the blue. She did as Ann had advised her to do if this happened; pulled the skirt around, easing it so that no one would realise what she was doing, and

117

when the back was now in front of her, held her bag in front and walked slowly. The long walk down the hill was very uncomfortable and Angel was not able to read as she walked that day. She was glad that she hadn't waited for Simon to come from his boys' college that afternoon, because she knew he would be impatient and would either laugh or run down the hill and leave her to walk alone.

Angel never got up the confidence to think really seriously of trying to get the part of an angel in a school play. She and Simon each had hanging up in their room, a picture of Jesus which they called their Gentle Jesus. In Angel's picture, Christ held up his thumb and forefinger, supporting what looked to her like a globe. He looked mild and imposing. He stared straight at Angel each time she entered the room; when she was in primary school and still used to sleep on the floor in her parents' room, the picture used to hang there. Once, Angel had gone into the room on tiptoe to search in her father's pocket to see if she could find ten cents to buy a snow-ice; she happened to look up just as she pushed her hand in. Christ was staring straight at her. Angel froze; she looked quickly over her shoulder, looked again at Christ. She frowned, pulled her hand out of the pocket and walked back towards the door. At the door she looked back at him. She thought he looked pleased that she hadn't stolen. It made up a little for missing the snow-ice. In Simon's picture, Christ looked very meek, his head slightly lowered, one hand resting on his chest close to a bleeding heart. The spot was red. It was Simon's Gentle Jesus of the Sacred Heart. In between the two pictures on the wall, was a picture of Christ's angels, beautiful, winged, white, floating figures. Now, Rupert, sleeping on the floor in his parents' room, had his own Gentle Jesus picture. Their baby brother Carl only had a tiny picture of the Virgin Mary which Angel had brought home for him. Rupert, a quiet, intense four-year-old going to a nearby pre-primary school asked his sister for – he held up two fingers – four of the pretty pictures.

'That is two finger, boy! What you want four for?'

'De usual ting, non!' said Simon with a grin. 'He want to build. Ah never see a boy so!'

If they handed Rupert a bat, he looked for a second one to put on top of the first; if he was given a banana, before he ate it, he looked for something to stick into it to make it higher.

'That one is the architect!' said Allan with a knowing smile. 'No question about dat!'

By the end of her fifth year at the convent, Angel was beginning to be less particular about Sunday Mass. She even felt a strange kind of bravado when she dared to miss. She still confessed these absences to the priest, but now more with a dull sort of uneasy resentment that she had to if her soul was to have a future in everlasting life. And sometimes now her wandering spirit refused to be controlled, staying outside of the Mass even during the transformation of the holy bread into the body and blood of Christ, returning only as Angel got up to shuffle her way back outside into the clean, uncluttered air. Still, she did her duty and tried to encourage Simon to go to church more often than he did.

'Eh, who studyin you? You tink ah don know why you reach home so late from church las Sunday?'

Angel frowned. 'Wha you talkin about?'

'Dat is for me to know an for you to fine out!'

He turned away.

'Simon!' she pulled at his hand. 'What . . .?'

'Ay!' Simon pushed her hand off. 'Behave youself, non! You only dey playin goody-goody. When you stan up a whole hour on de church step talkin to Canute after church, who tell you anyting?'

'Ay!' Angel lowered her voice. 'So what wrong wid dat?'

'Ask Mammie an she go tell you!'

'You better don tell nothing about me, because ah know a lot about you too!'

'Don't be stupid, girl. You tink I in little children tell-tale stupidness? You tink is Rupert you talkin to? Jus don come an pretend you tellin me nutting bout church, dat is all!'

The nuns were generally unimpressed with Angel's academic work. The Principal voiced real surprise when she passed her O-level examination.

'And surprisingly, I must say, Angel McAllister passed all of her subjects.'

Angel, Ann and Janice giggled. Angel and Ann sank lower in their seats and kept their heads down as Sister turned questioning eyes towards them. Janice kept her head up and stared questioningly at Sister. Janice always walked out with a defiant pride when called out on the bad side for the monthly House

119

Notes. Students were called out on the right side for being good and on the left for being bad. Janice was always among those on the bad side who got a lecture. Angel admired Janice, although she wondered how Janice could be a good Catholic who went to church every Sunday and still do the things that she did, or that everyone said she did. The others whispered that Janice had two boyfriends, that she went to the beach with them and many whispered about Janice's imaginary exploits.

One day, Angel said to Janice: 'Girl, how you could bole so wid dem nuns an do all dem ting? You don fraid dey expel you?'

Janice sucked her teeth.

'You, Angel, you awright, yes. Siddown dey an let dem nuns mess up you head.' Janice was leaning against a statue of the Virgin Mary; the Virgin wore a blue and white cape. Her hands were held half-way out; she looked protectively down upon Janice. 'My mudder tell me take in de education but don forget what real life is all about. My mother say that all twelve of she children go go to high school an nobody won mess up none o dem mind. You, Angel, huh! Siddown dey!'

Angel, standing opposite her at the bottom of the steps, looked at Janice standing in the shadow of the Virgin: behind her were the imposing walls of the convent which had recently been painted a brilliant white. Angel said nothing; she wondered whether Janice's mother was one of those 'misguided parents' the nuns talked about. Still, though, she often wished she could handle things with Janice's confidence and uncaring attitude. Once, when they had a difficult Latin assignment, they were all feverishly comparing notes on the morning before the lesson started. Janice sat unconcernedly reading a Mills and Boon.

'Janice! You do de homework?'

'Uh-huh!'

'Girl, de translation did hard, eh!'

'So-so!'

'Wey yours? Lemme see it, non!'

Without taking her eyes off the book, Janice felt around in her schoolbag. She located an exercise book, glanced at it to make sure it was her Latin copybook. She found the correct page, handed it across to the group.

'Janice, wey de homework?'

Janice looked up. 'Dat is it you lookin at. De page ah give you!'

'Girl you mad! You caan give up dat!'
'Ay, how you mean?'
'Lemme see?'
'What? What she do?'
'Lemme see! Lemme see!'
'Janice, girl, you mad! You don mad give up dat?'
In place of her assignment, Janice had written:

Latin is a language
As dead as dead can be!
It killed the ancient Romans
But it won't kill me!

'Girl, you crazy!'
'You could never give up dat!'
Janice handed it in. She got nought for the assignment and
three marks against conduct. At the end of the month, she
walked out on the bad side. She had to be told to remove the
gum from her mouth and was given three more marks against
conduct. Angel admired her, but wondered, as her mother
would, what kine o ting dey take an make dat girl.

It was not until the end of the sixth form that God and Angel
had their first serious row. Her interest in him had been
gradually failing, but during her A-level exams, for which she
did her usual lackadaisical preparation, things came to a head.
Now the results were due. And she was still worried about the
history. The Tudors and Stuarts had gone quite well. Angel had
been sure it would. If dey ask me anyting at all about Henry VII,
she thought, ah eatin it up. Dey caan touch me on Wolsey
either; ah know Cromwell good; Charles I is a breeze; Mary, dat
awright, too. Up to Charles II, she decided, turning the pages of
her history book, I cool. But is de damn West Indian history ah
worried about. Dem stupid long passage on education an dose
long slave reports well borin! Who could study dat? Ah sure to
fail dat paper. The West Indian history paper had been as bad as
expected. Angel tried to imagine herself correcting the papers
and felt that she would certainly fail that history paper.

In those days before the exam results came, Doodsie and
Angel had constant quarrels. Angel roamed the town with
Janice, even defying Doodsie's orders and going to dances. One

night she stayed out until about 3 a.m. Doodsie and Allan, lying there and worrying, could hear a car coming slowly along the stony road. The car stayed outside for some time, Angel apparently saying goodbye to whoever had taken her home. Doodsie, pacing the living-room, could hear a man's voice saying the final goodnight. She could hear Angel's laugh. Doodsie frowned. She big. She feel she big now. She smell woman. Angel opened the door. She stepped inside. Doodsie was waiting for her.

'Madam, if you father fraid you, is me self dat go give you what you deservin dis night. Don mind how big you tink you is.'

Angel fumed. Her first thought was to keep the noise down. Partitions had been shifted in the large house and now Simon and Rupert shared a room. Carl still slept on the floor in his parents' room. I don want dem to hear dis confusion, thought Angel.

Doodsie advanced.

'Don touch me, you know. Don touch me, ah say!'

'Is awright,' said Allan. 'Leave her to me.'

'Believe me to God, ah say if is a chair ah have to stand up on to reach her tonight . . .'

From the room on the right, in between her room at the end of the drawing-room and her parents' room, came the sound of someone scrambling around. Angel glanced that way. Ah sure dat is Rupert getting up. Rupert slept at the bottom of the bunk bed. At eight, he was always poking his nose into everything.

'Allyou better don touch me, you know!' Angel's rage was almost spilling over in tears now.

Allan's belt hit out at her again. Angel didn't see the room door squeak slightly open; but she did see Doodsie pull it firmly shut and stand with her back to it.

'You tink you big, eh?' said Allan. 'So you tink you big?'

'Don touch me! Oh God! Don touch me!'

And finally Angel just stood there crying and letting him hit out at her until he decided to stop. And through the shaking tears in her voice, she spoke over and over to Doodsie.

'You make im beat me. You stand up there and you make im beat me. You! You an you husband . . .'

And Angel put her hands up to her face and sobbed shakingly; Doodsie and Allan went back to their room. Doodsie was muttering. ▾

122

'You so big now, you smell youself! Any damn ting could happen to you.'

Ah give as much as ah could, chile, an den you on you own!

Angel talked to God. Oh God, ah know ah din study, but don make me fail, non. Ah won fail dose others. But de history! Lord, lemme get even a E in it, jus to pass, an ah could get a scholarship. God, please. De English okay, an dose other subjects not bad but de history. De West Indian history! Please help me to pass it! She suddenly remembered her grandmother saying to have respect with God. Please, Papa God, lemme pass! She talked to him in proper English, too. From now on, I will always study hard. Please, Lord! The picture she talked to was the same one she had had from childhood. She hadn't really looked at it for some time, but now she picked him up from under the bed in her room, stared at him, tried to get her seventeen-year-old mind to renew acquaintance with this stranger, and somewhat shamefacedly made tremendous promises. The exam results came. Angel had done brilliantly in the other subjects, had failed West Indian history.

Doodsie was in the living-room knitting when she told her the news. Rupert was sitting on the steps with some bricks. He was putting up a building. He built a solid wall, and was now trying to remove one brick so that he could find space for a window. The only pictures on the wall now were the ones of Ezra, Allan and Doodsie which had been newly and more fashionably framed. Both Angel and Simon said that the Jesus pictures were better in the rooms. Allan and Doodsie had agreed. They had also agreed that there shouldn't be too many photos on the living room partition. Auntie Ezra had given Doodsie an outline of the map of Grenada framed in mahogany; that was right next to the glass-covered words proclaiming Christ the Head of the House. Angel looked at the words. She told Doodsie the news of her results with an impassive, indifferent face.

Rupert looked in from the steps. 'You glad?' he asked, watching his sister's face.

Angel did not answer him. She went to her room and closed the door. Rupert looked consideringly at his building. Looked

123

up at the bird chirping merrily on the grapefruit tree. He pushed at the building with his foot; a few bricks tumbled to the ground beneath.

Mouth open, head thrown back, Angel screamed soundlessly inside her room. She raged that this meant she would not get a scholarship to go to university. She raged at God. She told him that she would never ask him for anything again. Who are you, anyway? If you can do anything, why couldn't you do a little thing like that for me? She ripped him away from the brown string which had once more held him to the nail on the wall after he had been promoted from the floor under her bed. She dropped to her knees and pushed the picture far under the bed once more.

We lookin to you young ones to raise we nose

Sister Teresa, who had been Mother Teresa when Angel had been in Form I and II before the nuns started to be called Sister instead of Mother, told her that she was a graduate of whom the St Joseph's Convent was proud. She was a bit lazy, said Sister Teresa, and should work at overcoming that. She was capable, said Sister, sensible and religious. Sister Teresa had remained her mentor since those days in first form. She had guided Angel to the pressing of her hair. She tried now to encourage Angel to remain in school another year. Young, she said, chances of a scholarship were still there. But Angel wanted to work. Doodsie said it was up to her. She would like her to study further, so Angel should do whatever she felt would give her the best chance for that. 'When youall was small ah ketch me tail trying to make ends meet. Tings not bright, but dey one hundred per cent better now. You have de chance to decide what you want to do.' And Doodsie said to herself, ah won mine at all if she start workin, though, an find a few cents for herself an put by a little bit for the future.

Doodsie talked to her about trying for loans, about trying for any sort of help possible.

'Try,' said Doodsie. 'Take the chance ah never get. Don let no chance pass you. Education is everything in dis day. Try, me chile. Save as much as you could for you education. Ah willin, but you know ah don have university money. Try you best.'

Angel taught for one year at the Catholic primary. She guided the young ones in distinguishing right from wrong and in the rudiments of religious knowledge. Then she got a small government loan. She had barely enough to pay her first year's fees and her passage to Jamaica. Doodsie wanted her to go to a place close by, like Trinidad, she said, which would be cheaper.

'Ent dey have university dey? Why you mus go quite in Jamaica?'

'If ah go Trinidad, is like ah don go nowey! Ah jus want to go far!' Angel leaned against the doorjamb, looked past the grapefruit tree, out to the horizon in the distance. She looked up at the clear, blue sky. Suddenly sympathising with the poet, she forgot Doodsie standing next to her and repeated in her mind:

Season of mists and mellow fruitfulness
Close bosom friend of the maturing sun . . .

'Jamaica expensive, Angel. How you go live? Go somewhere closer. Somewhere you can afford!'

'How you go manage?' repeated Allan from the drawing-room behind them, where he was seated.

'One of our dollars is only about forty cents there, you say. Forty cents, you know! Dat is madness! Wey you ever hear dat! If ah scrape an sen you twenty dollars sometimes, you still won have nutting much. How much is twenty dollars?'

'A hundred is about forty!'

'A hundred!'

Allan chuckled.

'She don even talkin in terms of twenty dollars, non! One whole hundred is forty! Huh! You don see dat is madness?'

'Is dey ah want to go!'

'Well . . .'

They stood there in silence. The dog Bingo, old, scrawny, half-blind, looked squintingly up at them. His round O of a tail still stood tightly at the base of his spine. The sunflower smiled a brilliant yellow at the bottom of the steps. Doodsie looked beyond it to the cocoa trees.

'It look like you gon get a good cocoa crop dis year, Allan. De ones around here lookin good.'

'Uh-huh! It look so, you know. Ah thought they was getting the thrips, you know, but since after the sprayin, they doin well! We could expec a good crop, an ah hear de price goin up dis year!'

Angel sighed.

'You Aunt Ezra say she willin to help how she could. But is not long demself move to the Virgin Islands and dey not really settled yet, so we caan ask for no big loan. Huh! Go somewey nearer and cheaper, Angel!'

'I want to know about somewhere further away. You always tellin me to try. Ah tryin!'

Allan cleared his throat. 'So what you intend to do for money after de first year? You tink is so? You tink life easy? Huh! Allyou children don know trouble non!'

'Ah would find out. Ent dat is what life about?'

'Well,' said Doodsie, 'meself ah could only advise. But when youall get big, is for you to decide.' She stood with both hands behind her back, looking towards the horizon.

'Mammie!'

'Carl! What you doin here? Ah tought ah give you you lunch an sen you back to school ages ago!'

'Mammie,' Carl looked tearful, the small cloth bag with his slate in it looked like it was weighing down his small shoulders. 'Ah caan pass, Mammie!'

'How you mean you caan pass?'

'Is de cow, Mammie. Daddy big big big cow standin up dey under de road and it watchin me bad eye!' Carl started to cry.

Allan came to the door. They burst out laughing.

'Ay!' laughed Allan. 'What do dis boy at all? Quite wey de cow is dey?'

'But when de cow watch im bad eye, is danger e see dey, you know!' Doodsie giggled. 'Well dat is de bes one ah hear for a long time.'

Carl howled.

'Awright,' said Angel, going down to meet him. 'Les go, eh papa! Ah go pass by de cow with you. Awright? Dry you eyes, now.' Holding her brother's hand, she walked down the gap.

Angel had no idea what she really wanted to study. She decided to continue with the English she had done with such success at A-level, throwing in for good measure some courses in history, the subject she had repeated and passed during her year of working.

'Ah don even know what ah want to do when ah finish, but, well, dat in front.'

'Uh huh!' agreed Doodsie. 'Cross you bridges when you come to dem.'

Seven

Bishop's Hall felt as strange as the convent had felt on that first visit with Doodsie. She stood with her suitcases round her at the end of the long concrete walkway near to the porter's lodge. She wanted to go home.

They called the long walkway the Spine. It ambled along from the porters' lodge right up to Block G, sprawled there looking remote and distant if you tried to gaze at it from the other end. You could stand at the porter's lodge and shout to someone standing or sitting half-way up the Spine, outside Block B, perhaps.

'Ay! Moira! Shout Roopsingh dey for me, non! Tell im is overseas and he have to take it down here!'

'Eh?'

'Overseas for Roopsingh!'

And Moira would walk a little further up the corridor and shout to John, Roopsingh's room-mate.

'Ay! John! Jo-o-hn! Tell Roop to run down fast to the porter's lodge for a overseas!'

The Spine would be impassive and unflinching under Roop-singh's pounding feet as he sped past the other men's blocks, down past the women's blocks, C, B and A, down the three steps past the dining-room on the right, to converge in a flurry into the tiny porter's lodge and speak breathlessly and off-handedly to the porter on duty as he picked up the phone.

'Tanks, man. But de damn phone on de block dey for e looks, man! It never workin!'

And other students liming about outside the porter's lodge would drift down to the bench by the noticeboard, to give some measure of privacy to Roopsingh as he tried to answer his mother's anxious queries from Trinidad.

They lounged near the water cooler, and thought of the hills in Dominica; they sat down on the Spine, gazed at the riotous bougainvillaea cheeky pink along the walls and thought of the noise of Frederick Street, Port of Spain, Trinidad. If you want to meet anybody under the sun who you don see for a long time, jus go down Frederick Street. They looked at the big tree outside Block B where people sometimes sat down to beat books when the walls of the room pressed in too much and thought of the damp under the cocoa trees and of the plum trees that once upon a time they used to stone. They stood with their backs to the porter's lodge and looked at the outside gate, as they called it, the gate that led to a different life outside the university. They did not know much about that other Jamaica. The university was their home for a while. They wondered if anything was wrong with Roop's mother in Trinidad. She called often and they knew that calling from Trinidad was no joke.

Later, the Spine would feel the quiet returning tread of Roopsingh's brown sandals. Ah wish you wouldn call so, thought Roop. Ah know she worried an ting, an ting hard an ting, but dat jus making matters worse, man!

That night, Roopsingh and Sivanan sat on the concrete with their backs against the wooden post. Roopsingh hugged his knees; Sivanan sat with one foot down on the ground. Then Sivanan sprawled out, lying flat back on the concrete, looking up at the sky.

'Dis damn place col, man!' said Sivanan. 'Ah here a whole year an ah caan get accustom to it at all! Is like you in North America, man!'

'Well it ain too far, you know. An dis col here is joke compare to what we hear about America, man! Is only because is October. Dat goin jus now!'

Sivanan sucked his teeth.

'You remember de fella dat come from de States an use to share wid me? It col like hell, de boy fannin an openin door, yes! Dat was horrors, boy!'

Roopsingh laughed. 'Dem dread, boy!'

A frog hopped across the grass, paused. Sivanan moved his foot. The frog hurried away, squeezed itself down a hole close to the base of the Spine.

'De ole lady havin it hard, man!' said Roopsingh. 'Since de ole man dead, tings jus get worse. She say de shop ain makin nutting, man. Tings hard like boli!'

'Huh!'

'Sometimes ah feel to give up de damn scholarship! At least den ah could earn some money.'

Sivanan sat up. 'Don do dat, man! You jokin or what? Dis is you chance! Hol on! She go make it. If you hol on now, is pressure for she but is she an all de res go benefit too in de end! Hol on, man!'

They fell silent. Roopsingh picked up a dry stick from the ground. He looked up at a moon of the palest butter yellow, just barely visible in glimpses between floating grey clouds.

'Ay!' Rikki shouted up the Spine at Roopsingh's back. 'Roop! Push in me back door dey for me, non! It look like it go rain!'

'Cool!'

Roopsingh broke the stick, flung the pieces on the ground, watched them.

'If ah did get de livin allowance arready, ah woulda sen someting home for dem now but . . .'

'You ain get dat yet? Mine's come trough las week, you know!'

'Yours is university, man! Mine is trough govament an dem never hurry!'

'Why you ent tell me, man?'

'No. I cool, you know. Ah could manage. Is jus now because ah want to sen something home.'

'Well, ah could len you a little ting, man!'

'You sure you could do dat?'

'Yeh, man! How you mean? You know is so we ha to move! Ay! So you not stranger, you know! Wha you diggin, man?'

'Dat go be heavy, man! Real cool! Ah go give you back when mine come trough!'

'Cool. We go fix it up tomorrow!'

'Ay! Roop! You close me back door?'

'You want it close from de dark or from de rain? No damn rain ain comin, man!'

In her darkened room on Block A, Angel heard the voices. She sat on the pillow at one corner of the bed, feet up on the blue bedspread, arms folded just above her knees, head down, face hidden. She wanted to go down to dinner, but the thought of going out on to the Spine filled her with dread. She listened. There was no sound of laughter now from outside Block A. Just the constant movement of feet down to the dining-room. She listened. She could hear feet jump off the Spine, just after getting past Block A, just close to her back door. Angel cringed. Her head came up, eyes watching the door. She pulled the blanket closer around her feet. The feet whispered across the grass, going down towards the dining-room. Angel's eyes travelled over the bare white walls of her room. Her chin went down to her knees; her hands relaxed.

'I could pass there,' she thought. 'I could open de back door an go down to the dinin room across the grass.'

She considered it. Inside, they would be all lined up with their trays, waiting, moving slowly towards the kitchen door. She remembered her second night, three nights ago, when someone had shouted from one of the long tables.

'Freshette!'

Angel had ignored her, not realising that the shout was for her.

'Freshette!'

Three commanding voices now, and Angel had realised, with a shock, that all eyes were focused in her direction. A lanky young man standing just in front of her had turned fully towards her, distant laughter in his eyes. He spoke.

'Freshette, the young lady calling you, Freshette. When a senior calls, you jump, Freshette!'

'I . . .I . . .' Angel looked confused.

'You what, Freshette?'

'Listen, Freshette.' the voice that had spoken first came again, closer to her now; the slim body, leaning against a table just opposite the place in the queue where Angel's plump eighteen-year-old body would be in a few moments as the line shuffled slowly forwards, seemed to have all its energy focused in Angel's direction.

'Listen, Freshette, you have me move from where ah sitting, to come all dis way to address you! So you important, Freshette?'

'Ay-ay!' The lanky youth in front turned around and shuffled up as the queue moved. He turned to Angel again. 'Dis freshette have a senior movin towards her for her attention, yes! This freshette is the queen of . . .!' His eyes moved to her sweater, to the place at the left where they had told her the tag should be. 'Where you from, Freshette?'

And irate voices had shouted *'Where is your badge, Freshette?'*

'The freshette not wearin her badge?'

'Well wait, non! Like dis one take over!'

'De freshette is de queen o Grenada, man! She in control!'

'Dat is wey she from?'

'Yeh, man, dat is Grenada queen!'

'Ay, Moses! What wrong wid you countrywoman, boy?'

'So. Freshette, you defying the orders of you seniors? Where is your tag, Freshette?' Lanky was leaning against a table now, looking quizzically at her.

'It's lost!' There was dawning anger in Angel's eyes.

'It's lost! It's lost, *sir!*' he corrected. 'So we on de same level, then? What is dis at all! You didn listen to de rules we read out last night, Freshette?'

Angel gave a barely audible 'Huh!' and ignored him, moving forward in the queue, remembering the elaborate ceremony of the previous evening when they had all sat assembled in the large dining hall, dressed in their red gowns, to hear the seniors read out to freshers a list of 'Thou shalt nots' for the two-week initiation period. Angel hadn't been sure of just how serious all of this was, but the ceremony had seemed frighteningly authentic.

The slim one, or 'the dry one', as Angel was now thinking of her, moved up as the queue moved.

'Freshette,' she said quietly, 'go and get your tag, but get me a glass of water from the cooler first.' She pointed. 'Look the glasses over there, and the cooler outside that door. When you finish, you'll find a new place at the back of the queue, because of course you know you caan break the line in front of all these people!'

Angel looked at her. Looked from the top of the dry one's afro head, down past her chunky blue hall sweater to the toes of her jim-booted feet. Angel folded her arms, pressed her lips together, and looked ahead again. The dining room exploded:

'Woy-y-y! This freshette bad, boy! Ba-a-a-d!'

'Woy! You ain't see that freshette eyes, boy!'

'Dat freshette dangerous, you know!'

Three more women joined the dry one now. A Chinese-looking one whom Angel had heard the others call Marva said quietly, 'Move, Freshette! Do as you're told!' Her voice sounded Trinidadian, like that of the dry one.

Three men ambled up, placed their empty trays on the rack. They waited. One of them was smiling. One just stood looking fixedly at Angel as at some new species of curious animal. Angel looked at the smiling one. She remembered Alice in Wonderland. That, she thought, is a Cheshire cat grin. You Cheshire cat! she said in her mind to Smiley. The other man was lighting his cigarette and leaning against the table; he looked into the distance beyond the open door; he seemed to have no immediate interest in the proceedings. Angel recognised him as the one who had presided as chairman at the previous night's ceremony.

'Freshette, you ain really got no choice, you know,' came Lanky's Barbadian voice. 'Because you might force us to lif you up an bring you to your room to fine dat tag an dat would be reaa-lly bad, Freshette,' – with a smile of anticipated delight – 'because you won't have a easy time for de res of the week!' He grinned. 'Is up to you, Freshette!'

The queue moved up. Angel didn't. A knot was tightening not only inside of her but also around her. Some sniggering, others looking bored, some freshers trying to look into the distance and appear unconcerned, people from behind moved around Angel and joined the moving queue. Lanky spoke.

'You know, Freshette, ah hungry! Ah will have to join the line again, so hurry up!'

One youth pushed up the sleeves of his sweater, moved closer. They all, women and men, moved in.

'You goin, Freshette?'

Angel frowned. She muttered.

'Yes, Lemme pass.'

'Yes? Lemme pass?'

'Yes.' She eyed him, looked at the others. 'Yes, sir.'

The knot around her loosened reluctantly. Inside her, the knot tightened. Angel moved towards the door, blinded by tears. Ah caan stan dem! Ah want to go blasted home! One good ting, though, dey din see me cry!'

'No bodder stay up dey, Freshette, cause we comin for you,' said a voice that Angel later learned to recognise as from Honduras, from Belize City, they said. As she walked towards the door, a giggling freshette was accosted by a senior.

'What you laughin at, Freshette?'

The freshette ostentatiously wiped the smile off; she replied accommodatingly. 'Nothing, sir! Sorry, sir!' She smiled broadly to his answering, 'Smart, Freshette!'

Damn ass, thought Angel.

In the queue, the freshers moved forward, arms folded, respectful, some careful to avoid the eyes of the seniors. Angel had heard that some of the freshmen had walked into their rooms to find bed and floor soaked, that some had had to sleep on the corridor in the unfamiliar cold of an October night in Jamaica. Angel walked up the Spine. One senior with an American accent came up behind her, turned with her through the downstairs doors of Block A.

'Don't take it so hard,' she said. 'It's all a joke, really. Just go along an you'll be okay. Relax and try to enjoy it!'

'I don't like it.' Angel was tentative, not sure if this senior would really accept conversation.

'I didn't either when I first came. I still don't. But . . .' she shrugged, 'you'll survive and possibly enjoy it in retrospect. Relax! I'm Connie, by the way. I'm from the Bahamas. I'm on this block. Will probably see you around.'

Angel had done as she was told. She found the tag, returned to the dining room, got the water, joined the queue at the back. Remembering it all now, she slid down under the covers. She decided to skip supper.

Two days later, Angel skipped both lunch and supper. She was lying on her bed with the bedside lamp on and shaded. She tensed to the sound of a timid knock on the door. She listened. Closed the love story and pushed it under her pillow. Listened. The knock came again.

'Angel?' It was not a voice she recognised. 'Angel, it's me. Could you open, please?'

Me? Who the hell is me? she wondered, none too pleased. She got off the bed and opened the door a crack.

'Yes?'

Standing on the corridor, smiling apologetically, was a young woman whom Angel knew only as 'European Freshette'. She remembered her because she had thought from the beginning that she looked like Ann. Her skin was blue-black. A broad nose settled comfortably under wide-spaced eyes in a longish face. Not very long, not like what Doodsie called her cutlass-face. More like Ann's. But Ann had been unpopular because of her looks. Here it was already obvious that people found European Freshette attractive. Life really funny, thought Angel. European Freshette always walked in a way that Angel thought annoyingly dainty. She hadn't decided what to make of her. She didn't really like the way European Freshette's voice sounded like it should belong to the nuns.

'Hello,' said European Freshette. 'I notice you didn't come down to dinner. We had bananas for dessert so I brought mine up in case you wanted it.'

Angel looked at her blankly. She didn't quite know what to say. Now why on earth would she do that?

'Oh!' She was uncertain. She opened the door a crack wider. She looked at European Freshette's apologetic smile and thought suddenly: Me ain tink ah want no damn banana anyway. European Freshette continued to smile. Angel felt ashamed. She opened the door right out. 'Do you want to come in?'

'Yes. For just a minute.'

Angel flicked on the light. She pointed European Freshette to the room's one armchair. She turned on the tiny pocket radio that Aunt Jessie had given her when she was leaving home. The reggae music filtered slowly into the room.

By the rivers of Ba-by-lon
There we sat down
And there we sta-a-a-a-yed
While we remembered Zi-i-on!

'I can see you're hating it here. So am I.' European Freshette smiled. 'But it will soon be over.'

Angel nodded.

'Last night's march wasn't too bad.' continued European Freshette. 'I quite enjoyed the exercise and the singing.'

Angel thought about this. She smiled. 'Yes,' she said, sounding surprised. Come to think of it, she had enjoyed it too. 'Yes. That was okay. And I think we even outsang Livingstone Hall.'

'Yes, we did!' European Freshette laughed. 'They really take this thing seriously, don't they? Giving us all this talk about

135

having to do Bishop's Hall proud and outdo the other halls!'

'It's something else. I never know when they're serious or not!'

They sat in silence for a few moments, each lost in her thoughts.

'You're from Grenada, aren't you?'

'Yes.' Angel tried hard to remember what European Freshette's real name was. 'Where are you from?'

'I'm Jamaican!'

'Jamaican!' Angel looked at her in surprise.

'Yes. We went to England when I was only two years old and we also lived in France for a while. My mother used to work as housekeeper for a very wealthy German family who lived in England. We only came back two years ago.'

'Oh-h!' Angel's sense of fun was beginning to return. She pulled apart the curtain across her closed back door, to let the light in. 'That's why you talk so funny!'

'Now don't you start! I'm trying, but it will take time. Give me some time!' she laughed.

'Yeh, but try, eh! Because dat accent too kine o staishey an lifeless!'

Angel turned the radio higher.

'How come you on campus?'

'They take in some Jamaicans, you know; and I'm from way, way out in the countryside, a place called Jericho. It's beautiful, but very far away.'

A sudden shaking at the back door startled them both back to campus reality. A commanding voice was shouting.

'Freshette! On to the Spine! Freshette! Hurry up, Freshette!'

They had both tensed.

'Open up, Freshette! On to the Spine, I say! All freshers out! Block A!'

The voice moved on along the row of doors. European Freshette got to her feet. In a stage whisper, she said, 'I'd better go up to my room.' She moved to the door. Stopped and looked back. 'I don't think I need anything there, really. Why not let's go out together? You want the banana?'

Angel nodded, gulped it down, offering some to her new friend. Together they walked out on to the sprawling Spine.

'Freshette Joy Happiness! You ready for some enjoyment tonight? We goin on a outin to the pool. You like dat?' one senior shouted at European Freshette.

That's it! Joy! Joy Hapworth!

Angel didn't think the ribbing was too bad that night; perhaps because for the first time she was able to throw an occasional giggle at Joy and have a quick private joke at some senior's expense. She doesn't hear very quickly, thought Angel, after she had to repeat a joke for European Freshette's benefit. It takes her a while to pick up things, but she can be okay, I guess.

Well yes, wi! You live an learn!

Angel's decision to keep at her studies from the beginning lasted one complete half of the first term. In addition to her own general arts classes, she even went to sociology classes with Joy once or twice.

'I not so sure dis studyin ting is for me, non! I fine is such a flipping waste o time.' Angel was feeling the pressure of preparing for end of term papers.

'Girl, don start, because I can't stop wondering why I'm here doing sociology. Sociology! What do I do with that afterwards? I'm fed up. I guess it's just the sociology. I don't know!'

'Girl, is de place, not the sociology!'

'Hm! Is a hell of a ting, yes.'

Angel looked at her friend. 'Anyway, you comin on, you know.'

'How you mean?'

'De language. It improvin.'

Joy sucked her teeth, laughing. 'Leave me alone!'

Joy became very involved in campaigning for the election of Student Union representatives.

'Well how you so caught up in dis ting? You barely here a year an you thick thick in the business as if is part of you life?'

'Is only three or four years we here for, you know. And we should have a say in who will run the union and ensure that things are okay, that hall conditions are what we want, that we have access to loans, etcetera.' Joy plugged in her percolator. Sat down on the chair next to her desk. Behind her on the wall, a large poster proclaimed in thick black letters: 'We shall struggle on!'

'You don't hear what happen when they try to expel three

students last year just because a damn stupid professor say how they tried to destroy the Sociology Department premises? If there wasn't a strong union, anything could happen.'

'Hm!'

'We should follow up these meetings, girl!'

Angel walked to the table. 'Where you cups?'

'Look below there, in the cupboard.'

'You mean *you* should follow them up. Me ain studyin allyou, non!'

'So you won go an vote for hall rep?'

'They could put who dey want. Is all the same to me!'

Angel handed Joy her cup of coffee.

'Let's at least go to the meeting.'

The outgoing union president talked about the student struggles during the past two years. He outlined what the union had done to try to ensure that the Jamaican government did not expel Caribbean nationals indiscriminately from the country.

'As students of a regional university, we have to ensure that the backward political machinations of neo-colonial governments do not prove detrimental to regional unity and rob us of the opportunity for learning from some of the region's most informed and brilliant minds. It is to the lasting shame of the government that there could even be the thought of expelling from the university and the country Caribbean nationals who are making a tremendous contribution to the black struggle. Their aim is to intimidate our most brilliant minds, so that neo-colonialism will triumph. As you know, they did manage last year to expel from the country two of our Caribbean nationals. By our involvement, by bringing the issues to the attention of the student body and to the Jamaican public, we have aroused people's consciousness of the fact that this is a regional institution; we have made Caribbean governments aware that they cannot make decisions without taking student opinion into account. The university students have to continue to play an active role in the political understanding of the region!'

'That one sitting at the end is who I supporting for Bishop's Hall rep next year!'

'How you so know who is who?'

'Because I have been attending meetings.'

'Hm! He didn't sound too bad, but they could really talk!' She yawned.

Angel went to a few meetings with Joy. She bit her lip when Joy greeted her favourite speakers with a raised, clenched fist. 'I used to have a friend at school called Ann,' she told her. 'Youall could have been sisters.'

Joy wasn't really listening. 'Raise your hand, girl!'

Angel sucked her teeth.

'Joy,' she asked, 'who you supportin for Jamaica elections?'

'You jokin?'

'Hm! I guess it has to be the opposition!'

'And they will win, because for one thing, Jamaican politics is always like that. One party two terms in, two terms out.'

'So why waste the money or time on elections? They could just stand aside let the other one take a turn.'

'True. We should tell them. Let's form a delegation.' Her friend laughed. 'But, seriously, they're sure to win. Even around here, where I understand there used to be strong support for the government before, everyone will tell you how much worse things are now for the few years since this party is in power! Cost of living gone up, jobs more scarce, everything!'

Angel yawned. 'You believe a change of government will make a difference?'

'Well, the others talking about socialism, and if they're serious, things could change.'

They sat looking at people moving back and forth along the Spine. They were sitting outside Angel's back door, enjoying the sunshine, their eyes on the Spine along which flowed so much of the life of Bishop's Hall.

'Well, I hope it will mean a change, but as my mother would say, is usually six o one, half a dozen o de other.'

Edward, a senior from King's Hall, invited Angel to a fête on his block. Angel had met Edward at student union meetings; he had come to one of Bishop's Hall parties with Yvette whom she always thought of now as 'the dry one'. She had referred to her like this in the presence of Joy; Joy looked shocked.

'That's unkind, Angel. She's not bad, really.'

'She's not? You don fine she look really dry and hard?'

'Oh, Angel, you're really awful!'

Angel was irritated. 'Why you so English and goody-goody?'

'If you feel like takin out you bad mood on somebody, you better look somewhere else.'

139

Joy had pulled the faded red rose out of her vase and flung it with obvious annoyance towards the basket.

'Wow! Dat healthy! You could get vex! If somebody else did tell me ah woulda say dey lie!'

'Anyway, Yvette won't be too pleased with you for the way you were dancing with Edward at the block fête. That's her beau!'

'You jokin! True?'

'Haven't you seen them walking across campus together?'

'You know I never notice these things.'

When Edward invited her to the King's Hall party, Angel remembered how he had scoffed at the idea of her coming 'all the way to university in Jamaica to do an *arts* course.' Angel hesitated. She thought of how hurt 'the dry one' would be. She accepted his invitation.

The speaker blasted out the sounds.

By the rivers of Babylon
There we sat down
And there we stay-ay-ayed
While we remembered Zion

And the room shouted above the music

'For the wicked!'

and the voices toned down again:

'Who carry us away cap-ti-vi-ty
Require of us a song
How can we sing the Lord's song . . .'

Voices rose above the sound of the music to:

'In a stra-a-a-nge land?'

One foot forward, one back, hands sometimes near parallel to

140

the floor, sometimes moving loosely at the sides, bodies moved far, far back, almost touching the floor behind. They came forward, leaned forward to the rhythm. The music made its own motions. The tune came to an end. Everyone shouted 'Version! Version!' The DJ played the flipside with its pounding bass; Angel's face was one lasting grin of enjoyment.

Bring back Macabee Version
It belong to – de black man!

Give back King James Version
Dat belong to – de white man!

'Come! Lewwe dance dat!' she pulled Edward to his feet. 'We caan siddown for dat.'

They left the party early. 'Why did you choose to do arts?' Edward asked. They were drinking coffee in his room. There were no pictures on his walls, Angel noticed. Not even a poster, self, she thought, her eyes going over the entirely bare walls.

'Because that's what I liked.'

'But it's so pointless, really. What are you going to do with it? Teach?' The coffee was bitter.

'No idea. Perhaps. Why did you choose to do medicine?'

'Felt it was something I could get my teeth into.'

'May I have some more sugar? Thanks. How much longer do you have?'

'This is only my third year, and I had to do pre-med. So I still have four, five more years!'

Three years and not one poster? Perhaps they were rolled up inside the cupboard. Jesus! Those books have to look so neat on de shelf?

'I thought I could get my teeth into English, too.'

'Yes.' He smiled indulgently.

The coffee was tasteless. Angel frowned. She looked quickly away from him.

'Let's go back to the party,' she put down the cup of coffee.

'No. Let's stay for a while and relax.'

Irritated, she looked at the long slim shape relaxed on the arm of the chair, considered the high forehead, the firm mouth, the strong black face.

'Let's go back to the party.'

'I'll take you back to Bishop's.'

'Why?'

'I'm not going back to the party. Come! I'll take you back.'

They moved off the walkway of Livingstone Hall, on to the grass. They walked under the trees. I don't like Livingstone Hall, Angel reflected. No Spine. She smiled at the way she was now claiming Bishop's Hall Spine. Livingstone Hall too piece up, piece up, one block here, one there, and nothing joining them up. Edward put an arm around her shoulders. And Angel thought, 'To hell with the dry one!' She stood still.

'I'm going back to the party. I'll find my own way back.'

Edward shrugged. He walked away from her, back to his block. Arms akimbo, Angel stared at his retreating back. She leaned slightly forward, pushed out her bottom; she stuck her tongue out before moving back towards the sound of the music.

Examinations came around. The university chapel attracted a trickle of extra souls; the trickle did not become a flow. A calm, unobtrusive cream-coloured building, the chapel stood on the edge of the campus, a Garden of Eden waiting to be explored. Outside, the bougainvillaea, in a red as deep as the bleeding heart of Christ, reigned in riotous colour. Below, the shame bush crept bashfully along the walls, covering crevices, growing, growing; if you came too close and touched it, the bush curled in on itself, sank into a deep and immediate sleep; slowly, cautiously, it would open up again.

Inside the church, at the end of a long corridor, Christ, too, remained in apparent sleep upon the cross. Head bowed, hands and feet nailed, the figure looked lonely. One hour a week, sometimes two, a trickle of students went to keep him company.

My shepherd is the Lord
There is nothing I shall want!

The singing did not reach the many who, wanting, remained outside. As exams came closer, Angel said some surreptitious prayers. She avoided the university chapel. She did go to a service once during the year, stopped to touch the shame bush and watch it curl away from her. What stayed with her was the memory of the bougainvillaea and the shame bush and the quiet of the church. Her next visits were in the early mornings, for walks in the gardens around the church, to steal a rose from the well-kept gardens and to try and force conversation from the shame bush.

The University Arts Centre was more crowded than the chapel during those exam days. Angel, like many other students, sometimes just sat on the broad steps of the centre, enjoying the June sunshine and watching people go by. Angel found it very restful at the centre. She listened to poetry readings. She listened to discussions. More than anything else, it was the picture of the Arts Centre, the steps outside the Arts Centre where one could feel at peace for hours on end, that she took home with her for the long August vacation.

What is joke for schoolchilren is death for krapo

Rupert had taken his scholarship exams for entrance to secondary school. The results were due during the long August holidays.

'You tink you pass?' his sister wanted to know.

Rupert put a record on the small record-player, lifted the needle on to the album. He shrugged. 'Peraps,' he said.

Angel looked at her mother, seated at the sewing-machine darning something. Doodsie had apparently not heard. Angel looked around her at the living-room walls. Aunt Ezra's mahogany carving, a framed outline of a boat made out of thread, which someone had given to Simon, Christ is the Head of this House, and a large clock in the shape of a star. All photos had been removed to the bedroom. Angel remembered a conversation she and Simon had had with Doodsie once about not wanting photographs in the living-room. She had replied sharply that they should not put any in their living-rooms when they got their own houses; now the photographs were in her room. Angel smiled. Had Doodsie heard Rupert?

'So you son do scholarship?'

'Uh-huh! Ah hear im sayin "peraps" he pass!'

'Oh so you hear!'

'Ah hear yes! Who studyin im?'

Angel laughed. 'Ay! Boy you lucky! After one time is two

time yes!'

'Angel!' Rupert called, 'Angel, you like dat tune? Listen to dis!'

Doodsie sucked her teeth. 'Since he godfather give im dat stupid record-player, we have not a moment's peace in dis house. One o dese days ah would jus fling it outside! Is jus a noise noise noise!'

'Hey!' Rupert ignored that. He was singing along with the voice:

'The Egg Nog!
The Egg Nog!
Yesterday I got a letter
From a friend
Fighting in the Egg Nog!'

'What! What is dat, Rupert? What you sayin?'

'Eh?' Rupert looked at her blankly.

'Say what you sayin again, lemme hear?' Angel was on her feet, watching him, a half-smile on her face. 'Say it, non!'

'What? The Egg Nog!?'

'Boy you mad! Mammie . . .' Angel's laughter now reminded Doodsie of Ezra. 'He-He-e-y!' Doodsie and Rupert were laughing also, although they didn't quite know why. 'Mammie, you know what dat song sayin? It talking about Vi-et-nam, you know! The war in Vietnam! Rupert singing about The Egg Nog? Ay! What do dat boy?'

Doodsie chuckled. 'Well, he not responsible. He din write it! He din stan for it in church!'

Rupert sucked his teeth. 'Girl no, girl! Is not dat!'

'An he tellin me is not dat, you know! Ask you friends, let dem laugh at you!'

'Uh! So dey better off dan Rupert, den?'

'Well allyou in a bad way, boy!'

'Well,' said Rupert, rubbing his hands together and changing the record. 'The war quite wey it is, who know anything bout dat!'

Angel found a holiday 'hold-on' at the post office. She was bored. It reminded her of church. She put the post office stamp

144

on letters going to the USA, London, Trinidad, Aruba, and got lost in thoughts of these places. She always travelled to them by boat, watching the silver-blue glitter of the sea as she stamped the mail. The one redeeming factor about the post office was that Janice worked there as well.

'How's the love life?' she asked Angel.

Angel looked through the open window of the post office. Right along the wharf, the boats were lined up waiting to load goods or passengers for St Lucia or Carriacou or Trinidad. In the distance, anchored a little off-shore, was a huge tourist boat that had just arrived.

'The boat in,' she said. 'Is race for bus dis evenin because all of dem goin an transport tourist!'

'Uh-huh! As I was sayin,' Janice positioned herself with her back to the window, blocking Angel's view. 'How's the love life?'

'Chupes. Wha dat? Wha dey call so?'

'Girl you really stupid! You don know what you missin!'

'Uh huh? Married life so sweet?'

'Non! Not married life. Ah mean, ah missin a lot since ah married, but jus man life generally!'

'Ah just din lookin for you dey, you know! You real surprise me!'

'Me? Girl what do you? I never hide . . . !'

'Non! Ah mean de married ting, non! Ah din looking for you dey in a hurry at all!'

'Oho! Well, yeh! Well . . .' Janice considered this. 'Well, you know dey say is three time for de church really! Christenin, married an dead! Ah jus figure if ah get through two fas, ah go have more time to play wid before de third one come!'

'Uh-huh! Dat make sense.'

'So you . . .'

'Well dere is dis guy who kin o cute!' Angel looked at the fly which seemed determined to share her lunch-time sandwich. She brushed it away. Ah might as well talk about him, she thought. It ain really have nutting dey, but if everybody want to hear about somebody, might as well be he. She kept her eyes on the fly which insisted on returning. 'But is only one ting he after.'

'So what wrong wid dat? You jus go after de same ting too an den nobody lose nutting!' Janice drained her Coca-cola.

'Huh!'

'Girl you musbe should be a nun!'

'You want de convent to close?'

'Well I ain know what wrong wid you. Dis guy, what he like?'

Angel watched the fly. She tried to focus her mind on her room in Block A, on Aaron, dropping by for a quick visit. 'Tall, fattish, I suppose, but he sleepin wid everybody, I tink . . .' She bit into the sandwich, foiling the fly's latest attempt. 'Except me, so far.'

'So dat is a achievement for you?'

'Perhaps.' Sometimes I really want the company, she thought, sometimes I'm just bored. She knew Janice would howl with laughter if she said that too obvious attempts just to get into her bed and be done with it insulted her. 'Is a question of what you want,' Janice had told her once. 'Me, I cool wid dat,' she had said; 'if is not dat ah want from somebody, ah not cool wid it, so is up to you to decide.'

'Girl, you drink jays!' was Janice's verdict now.

Man proposes; God disposes

The doctors said it was heart trouble. Ann's mother said to Angel, 'Dey sayin is heart but ah know better. When Ann take in de mornin, she jus start to vomit vomit an is a set of blood! By the time ah run out an hire Mr James car to take her to de doctor, de chile collapse.'

'Ay-ay!'

'Angel, dey poison me chile! Dey give er ting to drink or to eat or someting. Ah don know how dey do it, who dey send it by, but is poison dey poison my chile. Is jealous an envy make it happen! She get job in de Civil Service, you see. Woy!'

'Don take on so. Is awright.'

The rocking-chair squeaked as Ann's mother rocked back and forth, eyes closed, her memory a continuous groan of pain. Over her head was a picture of Christ in a garden. He wore flowing white robes and his form was in profile as he strode away across the garden. The picture seemed very alive, covered with a glass which gave an impression of depth and realism to the green of the garden.

'Is awright,' said Angel again. 'Sometime is not nobody dat do anyting. Ann used to jus stay so an get sick sometime. You

146

remember? Don take on so.'

'Angel, as God is me witness, ah sure dey poison me chile. An ah know who do it too! But dey go meet it. Dey go meet it. Dey go meet it, yes. Papa God don sleepin.'

'Okay, awright, Auntie.' She wondered what to say to soothe Ann's mother. 'You know, sometimes tings don't always turn out the way we want. We well plan things and then . . .' Angel stopped. What the hell am I saying, she wondered.

'Yes, yes, me chile. Ah know. Man proposes, yeh! But God disposes! What to do?'

Angel looked at Christ. He seemed to pause in his stride across the garden, his profiled face more intent on their conversation. She called out to Ann's young brother. He was about ten, about the same age as Rupert.

'Make up de bed, let you Mammie lie down little bit.'

'Janice,' Angel asked her friend later, 'you tink dey poison Ann in truth?'

'Girl, meself ah don know! You remember Ann use to jus stay so sometimes an fall down in school nobody don know what do er? The doctor an dem jus use to look wise an give two tablet but de girl coulda been sick wid she heart all de time in truth. Who know!'

'An de vomitin?'

'Girl, ah don know! Me ain no doctor! Man proposes . . .' Janice lifted her shoulders.

'Ah believe God does kine o propose more in countries wid less medical care an ting.'

'She use to say she would be a doctor! She always use to say she would be a doctor!'

Angel said nothing.

'I have a picture of her, Angel, I will give you.'

Angel wanted to say that she didn't want any picture. She said nothing.

Ann's photograph went with Angel to campus. On the back of it, Janice, always a part of any teasing, had scrawled in her schoolgirl hand, 'Hottentot'. Angel showed the photograph to Joy.

'That's my friend. She died during the holidays. I think she looked like you.'

'True. The mouth. The nose, little bit. What was wrong with her?'

'Heart, I think.'

Joy turned the photo over.

'Hottentot?'

'Uh-huh! They used to call her that.'

'Hottentot? Why?'

'They said she looked like an African.'

'Jesus! So Hottentot was a tease?'

'Uh-huh!'

'Mercy! But you people were not joking! So they thought she was ugly?'

'Uh-huh!'

Joy looked at the photo of the attractive black girl and shook her head in disbelief.

'Your school was different?' Angel asked her.

'Jesus no! It was worse!'

One one cocoa full basket

Angel stood for thirty-five minutes in the queue. Every student seemed to have some business to settle at the registry. The queue shuffled up; it wandered up; it sighed up. Students looked bored, busy, patient, impatient. The desk came slowly closer.

'Yes?'

Angel leaned across the desk, her voice confidentially low. 'I'm checking to see if my student loan has . . .'

'Could you speak a little louder, please? I can't hear what you're saying.'

'Oh!' Angel cleared her throat. She felt like she had felt that day at the end of the previous school year when she went to see the Bishop's Hall warden. He had agreed to sign the form recommending her for a university loan. He hoped, he said, that she would not disappoint him. Some students never repaid the loan.

Angel stated her mission again.

'When did you apply?'

'Last year.'

'Did you submit all the required information?'

'Yes.'

'Your file says that you have been asked for an affidavit. Did you submit that?

'Yes.'

Her father had had to swear that his sudden inability to continue paying for his daughter's education was due to unforeseen financial demands that had been made upon his property, that if his daughter failed to repay the loan, he would honour the debt.

'Affidavit is serious ting, you know,' he had said. 'Dis two acre me mother have there not really property dat could pay for university, you know. You mus make sure an pay back that money after you leave university.'

'Yes, ah go pay it back.'

'She go pay it back, yes. If we don sign dis, how else she go keep on goin?' She looked at Angel. 'Don forget all o dis sacrifices, you know.'

Angel had frowned. 'Yeh, ah go pay it back.'

'Oh yes,' said the registry clerk at last. 'It has come through.'

She walked from the files back to the desk. 'What do you want to do? Pay it towards your fees or . . .?'

'Yes. Most of it. I also have a government loan. If that has come through . . .'

'Grenada, isn't it?'

'Yes.'

Angel tried to change her smile. Tautened her face so that the smile wouldn't look too full of gratitude. How did one look at times like this, really?

'No. If you check back next Monday, perhaps. Would you like me to put all of this towards your fees, meanwhile?'

'Er . . . all except a hundred dollars.'

'Okay. You can cash that at the bursar's. I'll give you a receipt and a note.'

Angel smiled the awkward smile.

Elizabeth and Helen, who had been in the sixth form with Angel, went to live in Bishop's Hall during her second year. Their room doors always stayed open. Someone was usually relaxing in one or other of the rooms whether the permanent occupant was there or not. The three often studied together. They drank coffee to stay awake and study; they stayed awake and talked. Elizabeth, from Dominica, had kept their sixth form alive with stocks of stories about her family of sixteen.

'Sixteen!' they had exclaimed.

'Is allyou dat doh know how to have family! Two an three children is family too?'

Elizabeth always wore a chain with a pendant carrying a picture of the Virgin Mary encased in glass.

'I never take it off,' she had told them. 'Never ever. I'm dedicated to her.'

'How you mean?'

'Well when ah was small, ah disappear one day.' Elizabeth, sitting on a desk in the middle of the sixth form, was studying her nails. Ten pairs of eyes were focused on her.

'How you mean disappear? Dat is ting all children does do!'

'Was when I was baby, just start to talk. Mammie leave me upstairs in me bed an when she go up dey couldn fine me nowey.'

The others gaped. Their eyes remained riveted on Elizabeth's face. Elizabeth gazed at her nails.

'Huh!' Unimpressed, Dolly had folded her arms and leaned against her desk. 'Is long you have own way!'

Elizabeth laughed. 'If youall don want to hear, what you askin me for?'

'Non! Non! we want to hear. Don study Dolly.'

'Well, they search the whole house. I wasn nowey. Dey look outside, in de bush . . .'

'Not the same ting ah say! Own way, you call dat!'

'Dolly hush you mout!'

'We wus livin in a lonely place far far back. Me big brother – he was about fifteen at the time – say he go all different place searchin wid de others. He and the others stand up under a bois canot tree not far from the house – it still dey – and they shout. Although I don know what they shoutin for because ah couldn't even talk yet.'

'Ay-ay! What kine o ting dat?'

'Girl don touch me, you han cold! Talk, non, Elizabeth!'

'They look all about. Afterwards, when me brother passin back . . .'

'The fifteen-year-old one?'

'Uh-huh!'

'Hush you mout, non, girl! What it matter if he fifteen or sixteen? So what happen?'

'When he comin back, he just fine me sittin down under the

bois canot tree right by wey dey been standin up. I siddown dey in the road, jus looking up at de tree an pointing up in the branches.'

'What!'

'Woy!'

'You lie!'

'So what you figure happen?'

'I don't know.' Elizabeth laughed.

'So then what happen?'

'After that, for two years I jus couldn talk again. Not until I was nearly three. Doctors say they couldn't understand the case. They couldn't do anything for me. I just kept on gettting thinner and thinner.'

'That child in Form Three!' said Dolly. 'The skinny, skinny one! Allyou figure she did disappear too?'

They sucked their teeth. Ignored her.

'So what happen?'

'Go on, non!'

'Go on!'

'The priest told Mammie I would die unless she dedicate me to the Virgin Mary.'

'Transcendental!' exclaimed one eager listener. The sixth form literature course included some discussion of the trans- cendental philosphers.

'So how dey do dis dedication?'

'Holy Water and ting in de church wid de priest. So . . .' Elizabeth stood up. 'My mother always reminds me that I am alive today because of that. It's since then I have the pendant.'

Helen had said then, 'I always hear allyou Catholic church full of obeah.'

Relaxing now in Elizabeth's room on campus, Angel thought that Elizabeth was a bit like Janice. She didn't let her belief in the church let her close herself from the joys of life that the church frowned upon. With physics, English, sociology and French books opened and flung about in various positions about the room, the friends were relaxing. Elizabeth lay flat on her back, staring at the ceiling. Helen was sitting at the desk, chin on the back of her right hand, turning a knife about in her hand; Joy lay on her side on the floor. Angel sat sprawled in the armchair, eyes closed.

'Study somewey else tomorrow night,' Elizabeth advised the

ceiling. 'Dean staying over.'

Angel cleared her throat.

'What you bawlin ehem ehem for? Aaron doesn stay over? You playin de ass!'

Angel's eyes remained closed. She said nothing. Her friends chuckled.

One day, Aaron picked up the iron comb from near Angel's hotplate. He asked her why she needed it.'Is just to soften it. When I don press it, you should see how hard it is.'

'So what wrong wid hard hair? By now, it spoil wid pressin. Stop pressin it, watch it break an look bad for a while, and then your natural, hard, beautiful hair will come through.'

Angel lifted her eyebrows; she looked unconvinced.

'An afro is really sexy.' he pronounced. 'Feels good under your fingers.'

He smiled. Angel shrugged.

Aaron visited her the next day. Angel was pressing her just-washed hair.

'I should have known I had said jus de ting to make you go on pressin it!'

They walked back together from a fête that night. It had rained. The wet grass felt as cold as a dog's nose as it tickled their feet through the sandals. The wind was chilly.

Angel pulled her back door shut and sank into the armchair. Aaron flopped on the bed. They sat looking at the thoughtful face of the little rasta boy whose picture dominated the wall over Angel's desk. Next to him was the profile of a woman done in oils, red, green, gold. It had been done by one of Angel's friends.

'She's good,' said Aaron, looking at the drawing.

'Hm-m-m!'

'I'm staying the night.'

Angel looked at him. She thought of Joy. He had visited Joy regularly the previous year. Then he stopped. Angel didn't know why. She just knew that Joy hadn't got over the hurt. There were lots of others who hadn't got over the hurt of missing him.

'Come here.' Aaron stretched out his hand towards her.

'I'm tired. I'd like you to leave.'

His hand dropped. His eyes moved to the ceiling, then to the painting. He put both hands behind his head. His eyes moved to

152

stare straight ahead at the yellow curtains across the door behind her.

That's just how I expected him to react, she thought. He would either decide that dammit to hell, I sleeping wid him whether I like it or not or he would jus watch me with scorn an leave. Aaron swung his feet off the bed. He put on his sandals. Stood up. He straightened his clothes. He walked to her closet, glanced into the mirror at the face which he continually told her was 'pure, beautiful African'. He passed the afro comb through his hair, ran a hand over his beard. He was out of the door before Angel had decided whether she should speak again.

Say it aloud!
I'm Black and I'm proud!

Helen was the first of the group to cut her hair. She touched it constantly. You would watch her walking up the Spine and each few steps, her right hand would go up and gently pat all over her head. Joy already had an afro hair cut when she first arrived on campus. Carl, the lanky one, had cut Helen's hair. The day Angel got her haircut, there was a large group on the Spine. Carl laughed at her apprehensive face.

'Youall ever hear bout de lamb being led to the slaughter?' he shouted. 'Look this way for a demonstration!'

It was after she cut her hair that Angel auditioned for a play with the hall drama group and got the part. In the play, she was a woman trying to escape from prison. She stood on one side of the wall, tapped constantly, and waited for tapping responses from her friends on the other side. Sometimes they rehearsed at the Arts Centre. Outside on the steps, they practised moving along an invisible wall. One hand up, feet moving cautiously forward, the other hand pressed against the wall, they inched forward, eyes searching, looking up, ears stretched for the sound that could give them some key to an escape route from the enclosing wall.

They started a group called Search. Search met often in Livingstone Hall. They were seven when they met for the first time. Kamau, Joy, Kai, Angel, Corina, Edward and Martina. They talked about conditions in hall, about student loans, about the food, about the old women who came to the dining rooms to collect the food they left on their trays while they grumbled about the constant white rice. They talked about living conditions in the villages around, about lack of student knowledge concerning the surrounding communities. Angel maintained a sort of detached interest.

'If we organise a strike like the one last month, about bad food, it will be successful,' said Martina, 'but if we call a meeting to discuss the shooting last week of those two rasta youth, watch how many people would come.'

They talked about conditions in West Kingston, about housing, about the Beverly Hills houses poised over the shacks below the hill.

'And our new reggae stars are buying houses up there now. They movin up into the hills,' said Joy. 'Perhaps that's good.'

'Good?' Kai looked up at the map of Africa dominating the wall. 'One person move up and so what bout de res? Dat ain solve nothing.'

From the radio, the singer advised:

Give back King James Version
It belo-o-ngs to the white man!

Edward frowned at the radio. 'Switch off that damn ting! How we go talk wid dat racket?'

Angel chuckled. She could see Ma Ettie assaulting the radio with a glass of water. Kai was looking at the mabouya on the wall. Angel's eyes followed his. She shivered. The lizard-like creature clung there, unmoving, as if someone had pasted it to the wall. If dose ting stick on you, dey just stayin, Doodsie used to say. Dose sticky-lizard would cling to you like a vice. Angel watched them clinging to walls and shivered at the idea of them clinging to her skin.

'So what do we do about moving up into the hills?' Edward frowned, indicating the radio again. 'It's the way capitalism operates. Somebody switch off dat ting, non!'

'Is a good tune, rasta! Turn it low, but let de tune finish.' Kai closed his eyes, feeling the rhythm.

Black man get up stan up on you feet!

154

'When we get out of here,' Edward continued, 'we too will have the potential to do what we call "move up". So what? We say no thanks, we waitin for the rest? Are you telling me that I should not take big money from my patients because that would put me up on the hill?'

Angel looked at Edward. Looked from Edward to the others in the room. She remembered a story her mother had told her. 'When youall children was small,' she had said, 'an you father was in America, ah eat de bread dat de devil knead. Ah could never forget dis doctor who siddown on he throne an look down at me as if is mud alone he seein! Huh!' Doodsie had looked at her, 'chile study you head. When people reach wey dey reach dey does tink everybody under dem is dirt! Ah coulda kill dat doctor clean!' Would there be someone somewhere wanting to kill Edward clean? Maybe not. He understood. Joy was talking now, screwing up her face in that curious way she had, as though she couldn't exactly pinpoint in what part of her body the pain was. The sticky-lizard was still clinging to the wall.

'You know it not that simplistic. We have to live in the society and we live in a capitalist society. But we know it don benefit de majority and that we're on our way to reaping benefits that the women who come in to eat our left-overs are not likely to see.'

The women always came just before the end of the meal, before the cooks came to take the final trays to dump the left-overs in the garbage cans. They came with paper bags; mostly old women, walking slowly. They did not talk or look at the students. They picked up the trays, emptied their contents into the paper bags. The students ate hurriedly, sharing quick jokes and confidences. They were eager to get back to closed rooms to continue study for their exams – studying sociology, politics, chemistry, biology. The women filled their bags and crept out.

Joy was still talking. Over her head, the sticky-lizard still clung to the wall. 'It is because we see the unfairness that we would want to be involved in trying to change that even while we know it would mean individual losses for us . . . at least initially.'

'So! You're saying we should wait!'

Kai switched off the radio.

'No,' Joy was answering Edward. 'We not turnin back de clock. We jus not gettin high an mighty an we know what we workin towards!'

The room fell silent. Like an angel passing. The sticky-lizard had disappeared. She looked quickly at the top of Joy's head. It wasn't there. Angel looked around in consternation. Where had it got to? She looked up at the wall again.

'What happen? You lose something?'

'No. No . . . No.' Angel glanced quickly at the wall. The sticky-lizard had not returned.

They talked about the black struggle in the United States, about the marches.

'That was one hell of an experience,' said Joy. 'I was there on one of those marches.'

'Yeh?'

'Black people in the US know what suffering is. They go through it first-hand.'

'So do we. Only it's so well disguised that we tink it's okay cause we're all black.'

'I remember something one American friend told me. She said her mother had been to Ghana in the fifties, and got this fire to fight for black independence. She herself had visited Jamaica and the thing that really made an impact on her was being in a country where black people were leading. Can you imagine that!'

'What part o de US she from? Washington?'

'Iowa.'

'Jesus! Well dat mus impress her, I suppose. I hope you showed her the contradictions.'

'But really,' Corina was venturing a comment for the first time. 'I think we here in the Caribbean might be importing a way of thinking that has nothing to do with our experience. Black Power has its place in the US because black people there go through a lot. They feel racism from the white population and it's a constant struggle. For us here it's different. We don't have that.' She looked at the door with its large portrait of Mary Seacole and a poster stating 'THE SPIRIT OF NANNY LIVES.' Corina shrugged. 'Not in the same way!'

Joy's long fingers framed her face. She leaned forward. Her eyes always lookin like somebody jus beat er up an she rememberin it, thought Angel. She glanced quickly at the wall again as Joy began to speak. 'I grew up in Europe, and perhaps because of the experience there I totally empathise with the black American struggle. But I feel it's the same for us in the Caribbean, really, even though we don't see it sometimes. The system that made black people suffer was built on racism and is still being supported by it.'

Kamau's coal-black eyes looked out from beneath his rasta locks. Dat boy eyes nice, Angel decided for the umpteenth time. 'As long as we know dat even when we have black people in control in these parts, is really roast breadfruit we dealin wid. Is other people outside control dem. De profits not stayin here. De blackness is only someting de eye feel it see! It don go deep! The struggle is de same here as there.'

'But I don't agree,' Corina insisted.

'No,' agreed Edward. 'I don't think I agree. It's different. Their experiences are different. We don't go through here what they go through.'

'It not different. Perhaps it a little more subtle, dat is all.'

'But here in the Caribbean we have Black Power.'

'But it not doin us no damn good,' said Angel suddenly. 'Look at Leader!'

'Exactly!' Kai went on talking, but Angel didn't hear what he said. I actually said that! she marvelled. It was a line borrowed straight from Doodsie in answer to arguments about Leader's control of the country. Jesus, thought Angel! I said that! She focused more intently on the conversation.

'We have a few black people in power, which is an entirely different thing. They workin for white profit!'

'So what we sayin is dat we want black people to have the profit.'

'All black people,' Kai put in, 'not just a few at the top.'

'True,' agreed Angel. 'True.' She was thinking of the story of Leader's rise, of what she had heard of his disappearing with the money from Uncle Regal's dance.

'What we sayin,' continued Kai, his eyes moving round the circle, holding his audience, 'is dat we don want dis system at all. Things have to be different so that we don't have things like – like . . .' he lifted his hand, looking for examples. 'Like those people coming in to beg from us the cash we ourselves don't even have, or eating our left-overs, or their children not being allowed to have a good education because they have no money. Or look at us! How many of us woulda been here if we din get through in the dog eat dog competition in schools!'

'Aha!' Edward laughed. 'You're preaching revolution, my man.'

'Of course! What else?'

The answer startled Angel. She looked at the map of Africa. They talked on. It was becoming quite dark. No one seemed anxious to leave. Kamau sat on the chair near the desk, his back to the table. Corina sat on the desk, legs drawn up, chin on her knees, her eyes boring into the dimness of the room; Martina lay back, the upper part of her body supported by elbows resting on the floor, left cheek resting sideways on left shoulder. She was looking consideringly at the ceiling. Had she seen the sticky-lizard too? Kai stood leaning near the back door, hands in pockets, eyes on the floor, lips twisted sideways, teeth apparently biting the inner side of his left cheek. Edward was flat on his stomach, right cheek on crossed arms, eyes closed. Joy sat on the bed, face looking pained, right elbow on her thigh, right forefinger and thumb stroking her chin consideringly; Angel sat on the floor, feet stretched out in front of her, head down until she looked up and her eyes followed Martina's. She leaned across. Whispered.

'Did you see a sticky-lizard on the wall at the top over Joy's head earlier?'

Martina smiled. 'Uh-huh! Then it disappear.' She looked up to where the ceiling met the walls at the corners. 'I think it must have gone in the crevice. In these old buildings they always find some corner to hide.'

Angel sat back. Yes. In the old estate house, they appeared sometimes, then disappeared into crevices to come out again later.

'We should meet again,' Kai's voice broke into their thoughts. 'Arrange a definite time for our next meeting, prepare an agenda and invite other people.'

It became a regular Sunday affair. By the second meeting, the group had grown to sixteen.

Open up you head an take in what dey teachin you!
But don get grand grand an do as if you foot caan touch de groun! Dat is wey you ha to walk!

Many of the members of Search spent the next long vacation on campus. Some had said they couldn't afford it. Those from outside Jamaica argued that they wouldn't be able to find jobs.

'Rubbish,' said Kai to Angel. 'Learn to survive. Squat.'

'If they catch me, I have no place to fall back on.'

'You're joking. There'll be heaps of squatters. If you have a problem, squat somewhere else. We have a right to squat, you know. Only rich people could afford to pay for all that time. You rich?'

Angel and Kai enjoyed each other's company. Together they went to see as many plays as they could manage to get to with their student passes. They saw *Missing Steps,* in which a young plant was the only fragile symbol of hope in the midst of poverty and deprivation. The old man in the play, Mr Panny, reminded Angel of Ma Ettie. He was forced to leave his rickety old home and settle with his children in a beautiful, fancy new house. Before the removal, Mr Panny had been vocal, quarrelsome even. He had strong opinions on all issues. He always boasted that he had never been sick one day in all of his eighty-nine years. After the move, he became very quiet, vague, uncertain of things. One night, they found him lying dead in his bed, a triumphant smile on his face.

'But still, in a way, the move was a step forward.' Angel decided.

'If you want it. It's somebody else's step forward if you don't.'

Angel didn't comment. She was thinking of Ma Ettie. Doodsie always said that the move killed her. Kai didn't seem to notice her silence. He, too, was always restless and thoughtful after the plays they went to see.

They went to hear rasta drumming, poetry readings, political discussions. Angel went, sometimes with Joy, sometimes with Kai, to political meetings, but these remained somewhere on the uncomfortable fringe of her consciousness. She didn't like going by herself. Helen and Elizabeth refused her invitation to go along to listen to the electoral speeches.

'If you don like to go alone, sit you backside down,' was Helen's advice. 'Why you caan do like everybody an keep you tail on campus? I not going nowey. Ah have me books to beat.'

During that vacation, Search decided on a project that would take them down to West Kingston to talk to poor families at least once a week. Kai and Angel didn't too like the idea. Is like high-up people trying to find out bout who low down, they argued.

'How else we will make the links that we must make and know exactly what we're fighting for?'

'I know already.'

'An what you doin wid de knowledge? Huggin it an feelin good you have it? If you don know what side you on, you go just get bury.'

'Ah won get bury, Joy. Ah won get bury at all.'

For six weeks, Search visited families in West Kingston. They cooked. They laughed. They talked.

'Nyam de ital, young bway! Is how you a push de yellow yam roun you plate like you fraid for touch it?'

'Non, man! I accustom eatin yam!'

'Eh heh? An is how it look to me like it strange to you?'

'Oonoo young people up a university ha fo study what oonoo a take in . . .'

'An what oonoo a put out!'

'Yes, dread! Cos most times oonoo dis a chat chat an na a say much!'

'An we know dat oonoo a come, nyam up de ital, reason wid we good good an den move back up a palace fe continue de nice life! Is like ting different for oonoo, see?'

At the end of six weeks, not one member of the group had missed a week. Kai often stayed overnight at Angel's room after these visits. He was at his quietest then, staring for long periods at her wall poster of the little boy with rasta locks. Gradually, he seemed to withdraw to some silent place where she found it more and more difficult to reach him.

During the final two weeks of the long vacation, Angel went to Jericho for a few days with Joy. Joy's mother lived in a small two-bedroomed board house way up in the hills of Jericho, a full day's journey from campus. They got to it up a bumpy, stony road until Joy's cousin said that he would drive no further because he didn't trust the sharp stones with his tyres. They walked the rest. Treading carefully across two slippery boards positioned across a small stream, they reached the steps of the house.

'Well,' said Joy gleefully, 'this is it.' She looked up at the murmuring leaves of the mango tree, passed her hand along the brown trunk. Smiled up at the banana trees on the hill.

Angel thought of the Delicia cocoa trees. 'Awright. Stop lookin so please with yourself.'

'Even I,' said Kamau, also Joy's guest, 'born into more palatial circumstances, can occasionally enjoy such beauty.'

They walked up the steps. Joy's mother was saying, 'Welcome, welcome. Feel at home. Feel at home.'

Christ is the Head of this House! The heart-shaped plaque above the entrance opposite, a doorway with a red cotton blind, a doorway which probably led to the dining room or kitchen. Immediately Angel felt at home. Christ is the Head of this House! The Hermitage house! The Delicia house! Joy's house in Jericho!

Kamau sat with ostentatious care on the edge of a chair. His eyes went from the Christ plaque to the wood carving of Jamaica, to the pictures on the wall. Joy laughed.

'You know it's true, Angel? The scamp comes from a real honest-to-goodness middle-class family!'

'Middle!' Kamau shook his head. 'My father would be most unappreciative of your reticence! Upper, thank you! Upper-upper!' He pulled up his shirt-collar, sat up. '"Michael"' he said, assuming his father's voice. He looked around at his audience. 'That's me,' he informed. 'Was me. "Michael, is that any way for you to keep your hair? What's that? The immorality of wealth? My dear boy."' Kamau got to his feet, folded his arms, walked back and forth across the room. Their laughter encouraged the act. '"Without my wealth, my boy, you wouldn't be where you are today! And you remember that when you are running around with your ragamuffin friends!"'

'That's us!' shouted Joy.

Aunt Minnie, Joy's mother, came through the doorway above which the plaque proclaimed Christ the Head of the House. Through the doorway, Angel got a flash of a picture of what looked like the Sacred Heart.

'Come in here,' said Aunt Minnie. 'Come over into the dining room here and eat!' Aunt Minnie was tall and thin, with a very long face. She pulled aside the curtain. They walked through the dining room dominated by a picture of Simon's Gentle Jesus!

Aunt Minnie put a plate of yellow yam on the table. She put down a plate of fried fish and tapped Kamau lightly on the knuckles with the knife as his hand reached out towards it.

'Leave it alone. Wait you turn.'

'Greedy.'

Minnie walked the few steps to the kitchen tucked away behind a curtain at the side of the dining room.

In the middle of the meal, while they were leaning across for more yam, more rice, more fish, Minnie said suddenly, as though continuing a conversation, 'You children trying to solve the problems of the world in one flash.' She glanced at Kamau. 'Your father tried his best for you, so you must understand. You young people should have some faith.'

'Oh, Mammie! Faith!'

Aunt Minnie walked out to the kitchen.

'So who fraid faith?' Angel laughed at Joy. 'If you come home with me through the islands on the boat next year, you'll meet one amount of faith at my house!'

'True?'

'What! I can't think what she'll say when I get home next year!' Angel looked up at Gentle Jesus pointing towards his sacred heart. She grinned, winked at him. 'Last time I was home, I had hardly changed at all and she was already saying that she didn't like my new ideas.'

Kamau licked his fingers, belched, said quickly as Minnie came back into the room, 'Lord, excuse me, Auntie Minnie. Is jus . . .!'

'You father would disown you.' Kamau ignored Joy and belched loudly again.

'He do it once already!'

'Leave the man alone!'

'You mus come an cook for us on campus, Auntie Minnie.'

'I know. You want me to be forever cooking for oonoo high-up people! Why you don learn to cook for youself?'

'Wo-o-o-o-y!' They greeted this in unison. Kamau slumped back in his chair, head to one side, hand limply on his chest in the region of the heart.

'Blows! Blows!'

We have to take night an make day!

Three weeks before final exams, Angel panicked. She sat on her bed and wondered how to cram three terms' work into three weeks. At about one o'clock one morning, she walked over to Elizabeth's room on Block B and knocked at the door. The light was on; there was no answer. Elizabeth must be asleep; or perhaps she didn't want visitors. Angel went upstairs to Helen's room. Her friend was awake, studying.

'What's up?'

'I can't get to sleep. I want to take a rest and do some work later because I've been studying since early yesterday afternoon and . . .'

'Since . . .?'

'I want to rest; I just can't get to sleep.'

'Whappen? You worried about something? Exams?'

'No. I okay. I have a lot of work but I okay.'

'Is not Kai?'

Angel considered this. 'No. No. I dealin with dat. I think he really sick, an that . . . But I dealin wid dat. I awright.'

'I know how you stupid wid coffee arready when you decide to study. You drink coffee?'

'Uh-huh!' Angel shrugged.

'How much?'

Angel sucked her teeth. Helen, understanding, sucked her own teeth in annoyance.

'How much cup you drink?'

'One. Only one.'

'Eh-heh! An how much coffee you put in it?'

'Girl, musbe dat in trut, yes. I did want to stay up, so ah put about five teaspoon.'

'Look, girl, go out o me room, eh. I never see a ass like you! You go put five heap teaspoon o coffee in a teacup an den come tellin me you caan sleep? What you want me to do? Pump it outa you nose?'

Angel leaned against the door. Looked past Helen into the room. It was peaceful, really. The only thing on the wall was a copy of the Desiderata. 'Go slowly amidst the noise and haste . . . Avoid loud and aggressive persons; they are vexations to the spirit!'

'Why you must be so damn stupid? How coffee go help you learn what you ain do for a whole damn year? Girl go back in you room!'

Angel followed her into the room. She sat down on the bed. Helen sat down at her desk and was soon lost in the wonders of biochemistry. Angel lay staring at the ceiling. Her eyes moved around the walls. There was no sticky-lizard. The Desiderata.

Remember what peace there may be in silence! The Delicia house had sticky-lizards. Ah wonda what they doin now! Ah shoulda never come to dis damn place! Angel lay there, eyes wide open, staring at the ceiling where a sticky-lizard could have been. Helen glanced over her shoulder occasionally. Once, she brought over a glass of orange juice. Angel lay and looked at it. About 2.30, Elizabeth knocked.

'Thought you asked me to wake you up.'

'I got up earlier. I'll study until six and then go to bed for a while.'

Elizabeth walked into the room.

'What's her problem?' The dimple in Elizabeth's chin appeared.

'Coffee.'

The dimple deepened. She slid to the floor near to the bed. 'When I was small, Mamido use to come an pray by me sick bed to take out de bazoodee in me. You want me to pray for you?'

Elizabeth leaned forward, looked into Angel's face. 'Ah believe she dyin! De eyes have a whitish look!'

She was ignored.

'Did you knock earlier?'

Angel nodded.

'I heard. Couldn't take you on just then. I had visitors.'

Angel gave her a withering look. Elizabeth laughed.

'You jus jealous.'

'Les go for a little walk,' suggested Helen.

They walked along the Spine. It snaked, as usual, quiet and sturdy, through the centre of the building. They walked down to the porter's lodge. They walked back up, half-way along to the men's block. There they joined a small subdued-looking group on break also from the books. The group sat silently, the cool night air soothing their faces. A frog squeaked somewhere nearby. Someone joined the group, muttering, 'Ah takin a break from beatin de books.' The frog croaked. Someone left the group, muttering, 'Ah goin back and beat some book.' The breeze blew against their faces. The frog croaked. Two Trinidadians, one Dominican, one Bahamian, three Jamaicans, one Guyanese, three Grenadians, one Vincentian, many coming and going, they relaxed uneasily on the Spine. Each thought about the future. Angel thought of the picture of Jesus with the globe in his hands. Of Doodsie's last letter. 'Do you bes, chile. De

164

future in you hands. You have to take night an make day.'

Twenty minutes later, they were back in Helen's room, feeling somehow more subdued. Elizabeth, standing near the door, said, 'I'll bring up my books and study for a while.'

'No, thanks,' said Helen firmly. 'You does snore too hard when you studyin in people room. Stay in you room.'

Elizabeth's dimple appeared. 'Ah might come back.' She pulled the door closed behind her.

Helen went back to her books. Angel stared at the ceiling. At about 5.30, when Helen glanced at her, Angel was at last turned on her side, hands under her left cheek, knees drawn up. Helen shook her head.

'Girl, you jokin, yes. You got de devil wid you.'

'I don tink is only de coffee,' Angel opened her eyes and looked at Helen with interest. You got de devil wid you was a Ma Ettie saying. 'I think is everyting.'

'You better break that damn bottle o coffee if you know what good for you.'

Angel chuckled. Thought of something else that had had to be chucked away at one exam time.

'And put it under the bed?'

Helen frowned and looked blankly at her. But Angel was suddenly deeply asleep. Helen looked at her Desiderata and turned back to her books.

You of age to see after youself now! So pull up you socks!

Dear Janice,

Girl, imagine that it's almost over here! I can't believe the three years really gone! Yes. I know. It's a long time since I've written to you. What's been going on? Well, we're in the middle of exams and as usual I have a heap of work because I've left it all to the end. I've given up hope of ever working any other way.

I guess I'll come home right after exams because really there's no work here and I can't afford to be without a job for any length of time. I have enough loans to pay back as it is.

Girl, this place is something else. You think I came to it too soon after the convent? I imagine you're saying it's not jus the

*place but the person, because if you had come to it straight
from the convent, you woulda handle youself different. Awright! Awright! Ah get the point. But girl, is something else! I
suppose some people grow up more quickly than others. Stop
looking so please with yourself. But Janice! If at the tender age
of twenty-one I've just begun to grow up, then Jesus! I'll be
forty before I'm of age. Of age to do what, she asks? No, that's
done, but I don't feel any different. I'm almost sort of sorry
campus life is coming to an end because I believe I was just
beginning to learn. Not from the books, but other things. The
books? Well, I can't see myself going into this study thing
again. I understand some people become professional students
and sort of never leave campus, but for me, kaput! Done!
Fullstop! Which isn't to say I think you shouldn't do what you
planned. Get the degree if you want to. It will help you along.
You know, it's amazing how it's easy to stay on campus and
never know a thing about the country. You could go out to the
shops or to a show or whatever, come back inside and never
know what's going on outside the gates. I hardly know
anything about Jamaica outside there, and yet I know much
more than a lot of people. It's crazy!*

*So how's Grenada politically and otherwise? I hear your
Premier is still saying he is the country's one and only Black
Power. Sounds to me like he's playing with fire. Not wid those
kind of people that around today! If things at home are as
confused as I hear they are, am I going to get a job, you think?
I've already written to two or three schools. Yes, you've
guessed it. One of them is the old Alma Mater. Frankly, I'm
quite enthusiastic about coming home. If the idea of the US
interested me, I might try that, but right now, all I want is to
come home and sleep for three or four years . . . yes, years . . .
while I decide what the hell to do. Sounds like the idle rich,
doesn't it?*

*This letter didn't get finished before, so now, four days later,
I'm starting it up again. I'm feeling pretty much down in the
dumps at the moment, but I suppose it's partly exams and
partly just Jamaica. I don't know, Janice, it's probably because
I have more time now that I see so much more and probably
because I listen more. I don't know. But I get so really angry
about all of this poverty all around. It just have to be immoral*

166

that some have so much and others could barely drink hot water. And all of this study! And I get angry when I think about church, and about school and everything. I wonder how you have managed to keep going to church still. I'm just feeling depressed, I guess.

Remember Kai, who I told you about? Well, I hadn't seen him for a while and then two weeks ago he just walked through the door of my room, which I had left open. He came in, didn't even look at me, sat in the chair, put his head back and seemed to be asleep. Stayed for about half an hour like that, then got up and walked out. I suppose I should have said something, but you know me. I feel that if people want their silence, they maybe need it. Yesterday he came back, came in as before. Then he took some paper and pencil off my desk, sat down and was doodling. After about fifteen minutes, I went to see what he was doing. The paper was covered in a series of drawings of boats, planes, clouds, and then just little round things like balls of – well, fire, I suppose, although they weren't coloured. Then he looked up at me and when I said, 'Are you okay, Kai?' Janice, he just started to cry. Just sat there looking up at me sobbing with tears running down his face and saying, 'I want to go home. Angel, I think I want to go home.' Well, to cut a long story short, he went to the doctor a few days ago and he's been given some treatment. Exhaustion, they say, exam pressure, etc. so I don't think he'll be able to do the exam. But it's not just exam pressure, you know, Janice, it's life pressure. Kai is brilliant. He doesn't freak out about exams either. He tells me he's wondering why he's doing a degree in English. He talked about doing sociology, but after going to a few classes with his friend Derek, he decided he didn't want to do that either. He just cries and cries, saying that nothing makes sense. He seems much calmer now, but it's frightening, really. Because you see, Janice, I think it's true. Why are we really doing all of this? Is there really any sense in it? Well, I guess those of us who have got the opportunity can afford to talk, right? Anyway, besides that, things are fine, really. Just an occasional low patch. Kai, by the way, is the first really beautiful man I've met.

How's the love life? Hope it's bright and promising. Say hi to all of the others, and give my respects when you pass near to Ann's people. Take care of yourself and write soon.

167

Eight

There was a tall, skinny man standing on deck, looking over into the blue waters. He was First Mate, or something like that.

'It have an animal like him. What it is again?' Angel and Joy stood a little way along the deck, looking over into the sea, too.

'What animal?'

'One of those animals in books.'

Joy looked at the man, at his cheeks continually moving, chewing, chewing. She looked at the peanut shell floating from his hands down into the sea.

'Squirrel?'

'Uh-huh! Is dem dat does eat nuts, ent? It look like that is all he does eat.'

He looked over at them. Waved.

'He kinda cool, though.'

'Uh-huh!'

They were enjoying this trip down the islands. Helen, Elizabeth, and quite a few others were on the boat, people staying off in their home islands at every port of call. Some were going for the trip to Trinidad, and waiting to stop off home on the way back.

'It's like a tourist trip,' said Angel.

'You don know the right kind of tourist.' Helen had been vomiting constantly ever since the boat left Kingston. 'Who tourist sleepin in bunkbed like that on a rockin boat?'

'Poor you.'

Conditions were far from excellent, but the rest of them were enjoying the trip.

'It's the end of the road!' said Angel. They had returned from a fête at a club in St Vincent. Even Helen had forgotten all about the peace of Desiderata and been as loud as everyone else.

'Stop moaning.' Joy looked gloomy herself. 'Armed with our education, it's the beginning of the road. Do you think you've passed?'

'Yes. I haven't done brilliantly, but I've passed, I expect.'

'Yes. I think I have too.'

'So! A full-of-shit three years is over!'

'Ah! Come on! That's not true, Angel. We learnt a lot!'

'Yeh!' The ship rocked heavily. The waves lashed against the sides. 'I'm just feeling dread, I guess.'

'Me too!'

They sat on deck. Feeling the rocking of the boat. Squirrel came by and gave them two packets of nuts. They stood at the railings, watching the brown shells drift down to be lost in the churning waters of the Caribbean sea.

They dozed. It was early morning when an excited Helen shouted.

'Land, allyou! Land!'

'Awright, Columbus! Who dere already could go to hell! Is who comin dat matter!' Joy leaned with the others against the railings, peering into the distance.

They looked at the outline of brown against the horizon. They looked at the rocks which seemed to guard the entrance to the island's waters. Overhead, a white bird hovered. Angel remembered something her mother had told her about understanding the tourist's point of view for the first time when she saw the birds as the boat came in from Aruba.

'What do you name the island, Chief!' asked Joy quietly.

'Conception. Later on, if it looks more like the landscape back home, I might decide on something like Granada, but for now, Conception.'

Some potato jus doesn follow de vine

Ezra and Sonny were living in the Virgin Islands now. They said the money was better there. Aunt Ezra, as Angel now called her

godmother, went to Grenada on holiday. Doodsie poured out
her disappointments to both Ezra and Jessie.

'Meself, Ezra ah don know. Ah woulda give the last piece o
rag off me back to see dat chile get an education. An de way
how she turn out, it hurt me heart.'

Aunt Ezra adjusted her hat. She looked into the mirror to
make sure it was all right. Decided she didn't want the hat but
would walk with a mantilla in her bag. Jessie peeped into the
mirror too. The black hat sat sedately on the shining black wig
that her Cousin Emma had sent her from America. A small bit
of net peeped over the left side of the hat.

'Is that okay?'

'Yes. Jus pass you hand under you left eye. It have a mark
there. It look like powder.'

'Oh! Dat okay now?'

'Uh-huh!' Doodsie passed a hand over her hair. 'I don know if
is because ah press de hair las night late, but it didn take de
curlers good at all. How it lookin?'

'Lemme see! It okay. Nothing don wrong wid it.' Jessie
walked towards the door. 'Ah goin an finish dress in de other
room.'

Ezra passed the powder puff over her nose.

'Girl don stay dey an trouble you head about Angel. She not
the worse, you know. Ah mean, she do awright in the university
although I never understand why you let er go an do something
like English. She could have studied to be a doctor, a nurse, an
economist or something like that. It just sound wrong for her to
study English.' The powder bowl went over the edge of the
dressing table, rolled along the floor. 'Oh! Oh-h! Look how ah
messin up you place, non!'

'Non, is awright, is a good ting I did jus cover it down. Is
awright.' Doodsie retrieved the cardboard bowl from under the
bed.

'Or even if she did study maths or biology or something! But
English! That don make sense to me at all!'

'Well, meself ah don know about that. Me, is not me to make
the choice for them. Is what she like an she always good at that
sort of thing and she like the debating and the drama and things
like that. Ah caan judge. But she do well in whatever she choose
and I thank the Lord for that.' Doodsie looked towards her
bedhead, where Christ, the globe in his hands, looked benevo-

170

lent. 'God be praised. But is the manner she come back with, Ezra. The chile that come back to me is not the chile that go. She vex, vex with the world. You have to beg her to put on a decent piece of clothes. Is like she see nothing to please her at all. No. No I don't understand. I mean, if somebody put me siddown an explain this ting to me, ah willin to listen, because ah really caan understand.'

She took up the pail from the side of the bed furthest away from them, went out to the toilet with it.

'Don bother about it, Doodsie. She reach dis far, she go make it, girl. You might as well not take the problem so hard. Is the ideas that they get, the things they study and are exposed to that make them so bitter.' She turned around from the mirror. 'Where is my prayer book? Where you put it?'

'Look it over by the bedhead dey, under the Jesus picture.'

'Right. Open de window, non! It so hot in here!'

Doodsie pushed up the window, throwing up the white cotton window curtains with the lacy pattern at the bottom. Ezra sat down on the bed.

'Look, eh, Norril have a little one that does visit you cousin Emma there in America. She as rebellious as anything, and Norril say that back here in Grenada she used to be the mildest person imaginable.'

'Well we better make sure an keep them here then, if jus leaving the country make them so stupid.'

'Some of them stay right here in jookootoo Grenada an get their ideas.' Ezra shrugged. 'Girl, we see too much in life arready to let ting so worry us! Don study that. Is the way people think and what they want out of life!'

'Well believe me, eh, if I had another girl, she so wouldn see no university.' Doodsie lifted the lamp, dusted the shelf. Put back the lamp. The same one that had seen her through the hurricane. 'If is that that does happen to them when they go . . .'

'Sh-h-h-h!' Jessie put her head in through the doorway, finger on her lips. She withdrew quickly and went out to the kitchen.

There was the sound of a key being turned in the drawing-room door from outside. They heard the door squeak open. Doodsie pushed up the other window. Angel's voice came through the open door of the bedroom.

'Mam!'

'Yes. I in here.'

'Morning.'

'Angel?'

'Ay-ay!' Angel came to the bedroom door. 'Auntie Ezra? I din know you here! How you do?'

'I dey here yes, girl. I came down last night for a few days.' Angel walked towards her. Kissed her lightly on the cheek. 'I'm leaving on Sunday.' Ezra sank down onto the bed. 'So I'll spend the rest of the time here with Mammie before I go. You all right?'

'Yes. Tings okay. Ah mess up you powder? You goin to church?'

'Yes. Come, les go, non!'

'Me?'

'How you mean me?' Doodsie turned around from arranging things on the top of the big trunk that they had packed things in to come from Aruba on the boat. 'What's wrong with . . . Look, ah better hush me mout, you hear, before ah say something ah shouldn't!'

'Leave the girl alone! She tired!'

'Chupes.' Doodsie picked up two books from the trunk, knocked them together hard enough to dislodge the dust of centuries. Angel leaned against the partition.

'Mammie like the nuns. She prefer ah go an sit down on the church bench an sleep rather than lie down in me bed.'

'But when you sit down talkin nonsense wid you friends an dem, when you sit down on the side of the road talkin to the string band you always have with you, when you go to party an jerk out you waist, you doesn fall asleep?'

'No. How people could fall asleep while dey jerkin dey wais out?'

'Youself, Angel, you lookin for confusion! You mother upset! She would like to see you do the things she like!'

'Well, Auntie Ezra, it have things I like too, you know.'

'How the teachin?'

'It not bad. The school different to the convent, at least to the convent how it was when I was there. Everybody not so polite an fraidy fraidy. That better. But is still a lot o backward history we have to teach.'

'What do allyou at all? So it have backward history an forward history then?'

'Uh-huh! The backward history tell us, for example, that

172

Europeans discover the Caribbean an act as if the Arawaks an them was nobody. How you would feel if you livin in you house good good an ah come take it say ah discover it?'

Ezra laughed. 'Is true those Europeans do jus what they like wid us, yes.'

'Only they talkin a set o nonsense.'

Doodsie looked at her daughter. 'You don't feel it right, Angel, to go to church and say a prayer? Give thanks to God for where he have you today? You don tink it right to listen to what the priest have to say?'

'No, Mammie. De pries boring, you see. An to besides, he does never have anything to say to me.' Angel sat down on the bed near her aunt. 'He never have nutting interesting to say.' She lay back, looking at the ceiling. 'Ay! Mammie, look a mabouya up dey!'

'Girl, don tell me no damn nonsense, eh!' Doodsie was suddenly shouting. 'After people kill deyself out to give you a education, you siddown dey lookin drab, drab like a big ole dunce. You wouldn even go to church. Look, move out o me eyesight before ah do something dangerous dat ah caan answer for, eh!'

Angel pushed herself from the bed. 'Why de hell ah mus go to church, eh?' Tensely, she stood facing her mother.

'Angel! Youall stop dis, non!'

'Why de france I mus go an siddown an hear some blasted pries stan up in he ivory tower shoutin stupidness bout ting he don know nutting about? Even de Christ allyou talkin about was fightin against people like dat same blasted pries who tink he so great!'

'Ay-ay! Ay-ay! What is dis at all!' Jessie had come running to the room. She moved forward and put a hand on Angel's shoulder. 'Chile you musn say dese tings! God go punish you!'

'Leave me alone! Leave me alone! De pries know what people life like? He know what people sufferin? Everybody goin an give im dey little twopence dey work hard for so heself could live comfortable an tell dem dey go get dey reward in heaven. So help me God if Christ come tomorrow sayin he is king of poor people and talkin revolution, all like you pries so is de firs one to mark he door wid X to make sure dey kill im! What you tellin me bout church?'

'Bon Jé but what is dis at all?' Hand up to her mouth, Jessie

173

looked from Doodsie to Ezra. Doodsie stood, breathing hard, mouth slightly open, eyes swimming with angry tears.

'Angel. Angel, chile.' Ezra's face never lost its calm. 'Even if you have a difference of opinion wid you mother, is not so to behave.'

Angel breathed deeply, turned away from her mother, walked towards the door. The others stood listening to the silence. Angel walked to stand looking at the picture of Christ over her mother's bed. She spoke calmly. 'Christ inside us dey say, you know. An every time ah tink of a white man wid a globe floatin aroun somewhere inside me, eh, I want to go the doctor.'

Ezra laughed, put her hand up to her mouth to stifle the giggles. 'Bon Jé, what do dis chile at all? She don good, Doodsie?' Then the shout of laughter got the better of her and she collapsed on to the bed. Jessie moved her hands helplessly and left the room.

'You hear her? You hear the blasphemy? You hear how she ungrateful? If wasn for those nuns, my bright and beautiful child, you wouldn't be where you are today. They teach you everything you know, you damn fool.'

Angel turned, sat down on the bed. Looked at her mother.

'Yes. They tell us that too, you know. When I was in Form I an Irish nun tell us that she had come all the way from Ireland to take us out of the scum of the earth. Because I din know nutting about Irish history then and even less about my own history, I was really grateful. Yes. They teach me everything I know. Perhaps that is why I have so many questions now.' Angel's voice went higher. 'That is just why I am a damn fool.'

'Okay. Okay.' Ezra looked at her watch. 'Stop quarrelling. We'll be late if youall two don stop this. Let us go, Doodsie!'

But Doodsie wasn't finished. She put on the white shoes with the little heels.

'Every time ah look at you, eh, it hurt me heart. Look at you! Look at that big, baggy, shapeless dress. Look at you head! Like it don't see a comb in years. What is that? Black power? Black dirtiness! With the education you have in you head, when for you to make youself look nice an move about in a way to make people respect you, look at you! I not lyin, chile, you spoil de way for any other girl chilren I have after you. So is a good thing I don have none. Because no way dem would smell university an certainly not Jamaica. Not when I see what it do to you.'

'Look, I doh have time wid all dis talk, non!' Angel moved towards the room door.

'No. Because after allyou get the little piece of education, everybody else stupid an is you alone that have sense. I might be stupid, but when you was growin up an I killin me soul case after you, I wasn't stupid then. Is not so I was, you see, is so I come.'

'You hear?' This kind of argument always got Angel angry. 'Hear what you sayin now! As if ah feel I so big an great an . . .'

'Is that, yes. Believe me to God, chile, not me be so stupid again.'

'Awright. Awright.' Jessie's voice came through the doorway. 'Youself don sen up you pressure so nuh.'

'But you have two more comin up there, Mammie, an they might want to go to university. What about them? Their sister spoil their way?'

'That different. Is boys. They could take the chafin. But you, my one girl, I not lyin, it hurt me heart to see you.'

'Yes. Well, I tryin to find out how to take the chafin too.' Her voice was low. These arguments left her drained, angry, sad, puzzled.

'Come on, non, Doodsie, we go be late, you know.'

Angel walked out of the room. Ezra looked at her friend's tight face. 'Take it easy, girl. Simmer down.' Doodsie moved silently about the room. Ezra laughed. 'Dose chilren could give you heart attack if you take dem on, yes, but between me an you, girl, she don lose road, you know.'

'Youself, Ezra, ah was never like dat.'

'Who say? You jokin! So ah don know you, den?'

Doodsie stood at the window looking out at the whispering cocoa trees.

'Allan goin to come an drop us to the church? Is such a long walk.'

'Heself, when you see he disappear in the bush like dat early in the morning, we might not see him again for a while. Ask you god-daughter. He does let er drive de ole car.'

Angel returned from taking her mother, godmother and aunt to church. She sat for a long time on the bed with her head in her hands. She looked up at the picture of the little rasta boy which hung on the door opposite the bed. She stared at him unseeingly for a long time, moved her eyes from him to the postcard-sized picture of the little black girl stuck over the bed. The little girl had wide-open eyes and a pensive finger in her mouth. Angel dropped her head into her hands.

'Jesus, make me understand.'

The mud dey take an make you dey, dey throw it away when dey finish

Ezra, I don know where I did get that chile from. Simon not like that at all. He settle down, he look like he intend to married soon to the same girl you meet when you were here. A proper girl, you know. She is an excellent cook and know what she is doing in a home. Simon would not want for anything. I hope they make it together. In that department, Angel self like she not thinking that side at all. A young man came home with her the last time and the boy look like his intentions are good but Angel acting sometimes like he not even there. Afterwards when I asked her about it she told me he's boring and she think he looking for a cook and helper. I tell her already that she so choosy that she will find the world gone an leave her before she know it an she collecting dust on the shelf. You know what she say to me? That the way things going, the kind of people she see she meetin an the attention they want from woman, the shelf startin to look well attractive. She say she don intend to lose in nobody kitchen. You could tell me what kind of chile is that? I tell her already that no matter how she see life, no matter the fact that those men don good in truth, for the sake of the future security sometimes you have to take the worse and call it the best. She tell me yes, she understand that but is when she come to try to put it into practice that the problem start. She even tell me that she might marry but divorce quick. Imagine that eh! How could you start off thinking that you go divorce? Is what the world come to, I guess. But Cousin Dickson always tell me that the way this girl goin after book there, she wouldn't get married. Well, is jus to wait an see, but I really wouldn't mind havin a few grandchildren. An de little good-for-nothing tell me she could give me dat some time but it have nothing to do wid marriage. I tell her already dat I don want no pattern-book for er.

Doodsie lifted her head. She sat looking through the window at the big copper in the yard. Ah must clean it, she thought. That look like green mossy ting on the side over there. Ah mus clean it.

I gettin old now and I would like to settle down and see the next generation. The most hurtful thing she tell me the other day, though, was that if she have to get married to live man life for them like me, she think she better off alone. Then when I tell the ungrateful wretch that I only stay because of them and particularly her, you know what she say? The madam tell me, you wrong, Mammie. You should have leave. What I suppose to do as you stay because of me? That was really hurtful when I know all the sacrifices I make. You boy Rupert all right. He is a big man now, startin to think about O-level in a year or two. Believe me, those chilren grow so fast they does frighten me. Rupert a little bit more wild than the other two was at that age. I think his father spoilin him too. He lucky. It not easy for me to help he and Carl in school as with the other two, especially with the sums, because these days everything different. You know that in subtraction we always know that when you borrow you mus pay back? Well these days that is not the rule. I try to help Carl with some sums the other day an when I telling him about paying back, he don know nothin about that. The sums right in line with what goin on. Is a kind of grant-in-aid subtraction, jus like the grant-in-aid government always talkin about. I don't understand it. So these two have to fight for theyself. When Angel and Simon around, they does help because they understand the grant-in-aid, but otherwise they on their own.

Anyway, what about youself? Say hello to Jeremy's chilren for me. I hope I see them one day. Take very bes care of youself and write soon.

Is not everything everything you could believe but some dream trying to tell you something!

'I just don like the way Angel get on with her father. I mean, is true she an Simon almost not livin here any more but any time they in this house they treat Allan like he is a stranger. Both a dem. But especially Angel. Now she teachin in that school way out there it mus be a good ting becus it mean that she not around much. But each time she come near this house is a confusion.'

Doodsie stopped talking, sucked her teeth, waved her hand at the fowl that jumped onto the kitchen windowsill.

'Caraho, fowl, move you tail, dammit fut!'

The hen jumped off the sill, back into the yard.

'Chupes.' Doodsie pulled in the window. 'I don like to keep de window close but dese fowl so damn disgustin!'

Jessie laughed. 'Which one is dat? De clean neck one? Dat is de one ah caan stan at all!'

'An Allan pay a set o money dat e don have for dem, you know. Buy dem from the farm down the road, say is special high-breed fowl wid good yield.'

'Huh!' Jessie chuckled, the pink gums showing at the front where two teeth were missing. 'Musbe high breed, in truth. Not so dey disgustin? Like people, like fowl!'

'Ay!' Doodsie moved to the little screen door she had put up between the kitchen and dining-room. She pushed it open. Stood peeping in at Jessie as she sat there taking the mace off the nutmegs. 'Ay-ay! But you don know! Lemme make a little piece of hypocrite.' She moved closer, sat on the chair facing her sister. 'He tell me he thinkin of gettin one o dose big Alsatian kine o dog dey, asking me what ah tink!'

'What! Ay! Dat is white people dog, man! Expensive to feed like what an always fierce fierce looking like dey ready to spring on you!'

'You askin me! That is one thought dat go stay right dey in he head an dead right wey it born. Ah not feeding no dog dat want more food than human. So ah crazy den?' Hands flat on the table, she pushed herself to her feet. 'Me? Ah well satisfy wid me common breed dat ah could shout at an chuck de bluggoe give when ah don have meat. Me keep dog dat go grab me han when ah caan feed it? Now dat poor Bingo gone, if we caan get another one like him, den we could do without.'

'Ay! Well what he want dog so for?' Jessie threw the mace into the basket on the floor, turned slightly, sat with her hand on the back of the chair, looking questioningly at her sister.

'Huh!' Doodsie moved back to the kitchen. 'Meself ah doh know. Hefe ideas, non!' She turned on the pipe. 'You know how he like hefe style arready!'

For a few moments there were no voices. Just the sound of running water, knocking plates, pieces of cutlery knocking against one another. In the yard, a dog barked. Jessie cleared her throat.

'But you know,' said Doodsie from the kitchen, 'is the shoutin an de confusion each time dose chilren here dat ah caan stand. And then the higher Allan climb wid his vexation, is the more Angel self feel she mus go higher, so sometimes this house feel like it on the verge of explodin. Huh! Dat chile self is something else, yes. You doesn watch she face sometimes when she in she temper an dem? Real devil, yes. Ah don know wey she get dat from at all at all!'

The water sprayed over the dirty plates. Jessie cleared her throat.

'Is fadder dat could say is not theirs. Mother business dey for de worl to see.'

She took the small basket of nutmegs, walked stiffly to the outside door of the kitchen, emptied the basket into the big barrel outside the door. 'God! The limbs stiff, stiff. It don easy, non!'

'Well is not younger you gettin!'

'Ah could feel it!' She walked back to the table in the dining-room.

From the kitchen came the sound of muttering. Doodsie saying something to herself in a low voice. Low singing. More muttering. Jessie, listening from the dining-room, smiled. Doodsie started singing in a louder voice.

'The Lord is my shepherd!
I shall not want!
He ma-a-akes me down to lie!
In pa-a-astures green
He lea-ea-deth me
The qui-i-et wa-a-a-ters by!'

The two started humming the next verse quietly. Stopped at the same time, as though one spirit reached out to the other and wrote silence into the script.

Doodsie spoke after a while. 'Lord, after de way I work in life

179

arready, you would imagine that by now I could relax and have a little peace.'

'Youself, Doodsie. I always tellin you you worryin too much. The whole time you stan up there in the kitchen washin the wares you only talkin talkin to youself, worrying about dis, worryin about dat, worryin about Allan, about Angel, worryin about everybody except youself.'

Jessie straightened the tablecloth, rearranged herself on the dining-room chair. She turned to the safe behind her back, pulled her chair away so that she could open the door properly. 'Ah takin piece of dis jelly here to sweeten me mouth. You want some?'

'No thanks.'

'Uh. Dat is good jelly. It jus de right texture. It taste like Ma Grace jelly dis time. Ah get it jus right.'

Doodsie sighed.

'Ah don know what do youself, non. They go sort things out. Think about youself for a change.'

Doodsie was silent. Jessie smacked her lips. Suddenly she laughed. 'You never look at her when she really vex an she stretch dat mout at the fadder? Is de exac exac picture of him, you know!'

'Girl!' Doodsie came to the door. 'Is as if somebody take dat and stamp it dey like a picture. An de worse ting is dat in a lot o ways dey very alike, too, you know.'

'Uh-huh! Is why dey caan stan each other!'

Doodsie went back to the work in the kitchen. Each remained lost in her thoughts.

'I had a dream last night,' said Jessie. She moved her elbows from where they rested on the table, straightened the tablecloth again. She got up, pulled the connecting door open wider and stood leaning against the doorjamb, one hand on the top of the small screen door.

'I had a . . . ay-ay!' Jessie's hand was at her waist, her face distorted with pain. 'Ay-ay! What is dat at all! Doodsie, oh!'

Doodsie turned, flung the skin of the green bananas toward the tin behind her.

'What do?' She looked at Jessie's face, at her half-opened mouth, at the left hand squeezing against her right side. 'What do? Is you side again?'

'Uh-huh! An dis time not only de wais, non! It feel like if is de whole side. De whole right leg by here so!' She sucked in air through her teeth, making a whistling sound.

Doodsie walked over to her, shaking the water from her hands.

'It still bad? You awright?'

'It passin now! It jus grab me sudden so, but . . . it . . . it look like it passin!'

Slowly Jessie straightened. Her eyes on her sister's face, Doodsie moved back to the sink.

'Awright?'

'Yeh. Sometimes it jus hit suddenly so when I move. Right above the leg there, right here so, right in the joining there. I don know what it is.' Slowly she relaxed. 'It gone now, but is always a sudden kin of grip an then . . .' Jessie paused, as though waiting, listening to the signals from her body.

'You should check with the doctor, you know.'

'Yes. But is ole cart arready. All kine of parts does need mendin. Perhaps nex weekend if it continue, but you have to pay so much just so that they could look at you face. And then is another whole heap for the medicine. Ah will wait an see what is happening.'

Jessie moved her body around slowly, testing the pain. She pushed the screen door wide, pulled a chair to keep it open. She sat down on the floor in the doorway, her bottom on the dining-room floor, feet resting down on the kitchen floor, one level lower.

'Yes, ah was tellin you. This dream. It was as though right on the hill there behind the house, up there so,' she pointed beyond the kitchen door, where the cocoa trees shaded the anthuriums that Doodsie had planted. 'Right up there in the area between the grapefruit tree and those cocoa tree over dey, a set of dirty dirty water rollin down faster and faster, and we standin right here in the kitchen lookin out. And Angel on the other side out there, in the drain behind the cocoa trees, watchin it and youself shouting to her trying to tell her to pass around it. You know,' Jessie struggled to her feet, pointing, 'is as if you tellin her to go up more behin de cocoa an come down through the nutmeg on de other side of the anthuriums and come inside, to get out of this water . . .'

'Eh heh? Well ah don like to place too much trust in dream, but dat not soundin good . . .'

'Well, is not everything everything you could believe but some dream tryin to tell you something and meself, ah know for sure, that most times when ah dream, they does come true in one way or the other.' Jessie walked to the kitchen door, opened it, walked down the two steps at the back, cleared her throat, spat into the yard. 'And this dirty water thing is not good.' She turned back to the kitchen.

'Man is lo-o-o-nely by birth
Man is o-o-only a pilgrim on earth!'

'Ay! How is dat hymn you singin dey? Ah don tink dat is a Anglican hymn!'

Doodsie laughed. 'Musbe Angel ah take dat from. Even in dese godless days of hers dat is one hymn ah does hear er still singin!'

Jessie grinned, tying up the bush broom tight, beginning to sweep the yard. 'She musbe like dat one!' She stood up, looking at Doodsie through the kitchen window. 'But how it is she mean she don goin to church at all, she don havin nothing to do with dose procession an dem she use to spen she life in dey?'

'Girl ah don know non. Ah don know at all. Musbe some Jezebel style she pick up in de university.'

'She does pray, non?'

Doodsie sucked her teeth. 'What question you askin me dey? Everytime ah ben me knees ah does say one for er, so ah hope Papa God accept dat for de present until she self decide to turn back to im!'

'But what does get inside those chilren head at all when dey get big nowadays?'

'Ah don know, non!'

'Mornin, Miss Doodsie!'

'Mornin.' Jessie walked towards the front yard. She looked up at Doodsie's face in the window.

'Is two little children. Look as if dey come for water.'

'Mornin, Miss Doodsie. We could tek some water in de pipe, Miss Doodsie?'

'Mornin. Whose children is dis?'

'Miss Clementina up on de hill over dey.' The bigger girl, about nine, a straw hat on her head, pointed in the direction away behind the cocoa trees on the hill. 'We in de garden down de road cuttin cane, an Mammie tell us to come an ask you for some water, please.'

'Try de pipe but ah not sure if it have, non, chile. Jus now dey it did start the stupid gurgling, so it musbe gone arready.'

The child put down her bucket, and opened the pipe. The smaller one, about four, stood sucking her thumb, scratching away the sandflies that bit at the legs exposed by the short dress.

'No, Miss Doodsie. It don have non.'

'Is for drinking?'

'No, Miss Doodsie. We cookin!'

'Well if you go boil it, you could use what in de copper if you want. Is rain water an we wash out de copper yesterday, so it awright.'

The two children walked towards the copper. The bigger one bent over. Her reflection danced back at her, looking for a moment like the figures of the workers who used to dance on the cocoa in this copper to give a shine to Massa's cocoa. She dipped the bucket in the copper, filled it. Lifted it with a powerful swing to her head. Steadied it.

'Les go, Marian. Thanks, Miss Doodsie. We goin, Miss Doodsie.'

'Okay, chile.'

Jessie stood watching them go. 'You don see how she balancin de bucket on she head like nobody business?'

'Huh! Dose chilren accustom seein for deyself, you know. Is mine here dat grow up havin me doin everything for them, but dese chilren aroun here growin like how we grow! My chilren tink dey know trouble but they had it well easy, yes! Huh!'

'Is true!'

'Look.' Doodsie passed a basket of provision skin through the window to Jessie. 'Put dat in the garbage outside dey give me. You remember how one time when Angel was about twelve, she come tellin me she want six dresses?'

Jessie threw back her head, sending her laughter to the tops of the grapefruit tree at the back.

'Ay-ay! Ah tell you! De madam siddown talkin she stupidness wid she convent frien an dem; she work out how much dress she need an she present me wid the number!'

Jessie chuckled.

'An she decide she not takin no for a answer, you know.

"Mammie, ah want it!" she tell me. Dat time meself caan even buy drawers to put. Pò djab me, if ah stand up somewey on a high hill an de wind blow me frock ah have to hide me face from de worl! She self askin me for six dresses!'

Jessie laughed deep down in her throat, pulled the kitchen door close behind her. She rushed to the stove. 'Bon Jé, Doodsie, youself don see de milk boilin over here?'

'Ah chuts! Look! Look! Look a cloth! Ah jus look at de stupid ting, you know.' The milk swelled protestingly, spilled over the sides spitefully just as Jessie lifted it off the stove. 'It wait until ah turn away to boil over.'

The milk settled slowly, frothing sulkily.

'Put it down by here so!'

Doodsie looked angrily at the pan of milk. It puffed out defiant wisps of smoke. Jessie laughed, and moved back to her chair in the dining room.

'Is anyone there?' A voice came from the front of the house. 'Why does this house look so deserted? Hello-o-ow!?'

'Wait, non!' Jessie was startled out of her seat, shuffling her feet into the soft slippers. 'Who voice dat?'

Doodsie laughed; she looked around the kitchen door. 'If ah not mistaken, that soun like the dirty water you been talkin bout!' She giggled, straining now to look out of the kitchen window. She raised her voice. 'Hello-o-ow?' In a lower voice, she said, 'Ah caan see nobody through here, Jessie. Check the front door. Ah hope is nobody special because all me clothes stain up with this provision ah forever peelin.'

Jessie went out to the drawing-room. She pulled the door open, laughed, shouted.

'Woy! Father Christmas, yes! I thought this was November? He early dis year!' She dropped her voice. 'How you do? Come in, come! We by the kitchen. Doodsie o-o-oy! Your dear brother!'

'I thought so!' Doodsie advanced to meet him in the dining-room, drying her hands on a kitchen towel. 'Well blow shell! Which kine of dear you talkin about? D, double E, R?'

Regal laughed. 'Come on, Doodsie. That's no way to greet a brother.'

'True. Have a seat, brother mine. Look at you! Spotless and regal as ever. Come, come lemme give you a kiss. How tings?'

'Well, as usual. You know how it is. When Regal walks, the

184

heavens open.'

'That is what being Regal is all about, I suppose.'

Jessie laughed merrily. 'Yes. You mother, God rest her, always use to say that when you born, it was because heaven smiled at her at last and give her a king.'

'Yes. Lemme siddown by you here. The king dat never even visit her for years befor she dead and didn't even bother to come to the funeral. That is king fadder! Visit once after dat an den disappear for good in Trinidad! King plus!'

'Doodsie, let's not go over that again. You know how badly I feel about that. And is only because of circumstances that happened. If as a small islander you in Trinidad without papers, trying to make a living you can't make here, there's no way you can move in and out. I had to wait until I had things organised. You think I feel good about it?'

'Yes. Yes. I was just teasing. But joke they making. After twelve or howmuch years, you own part of the damn country. And then I suppose with not lettin you move in an out they break you han too and put it in plaster paris so you couldn't write. Poor you. Don tell me stupes, is poor you, yes. But how tings really, boy? You manage to meet the people you told us a few weeks ago you were anxious to meet?'

'Yeh! Dey tryin to encourage me to get into politics in de opposition, but ah tink really my days with that kind of ting gone!'

'Man that don even want they finger stain wid mandarin.'

'Girl you remember nonsense.'

'You remember, Jessie? Ah did tell you? He come here once an ah give him a mandarin. He say,' Doodsie sat stiffly on the chair, flicked her fingers, ' "Yes, thank you, but I don't want to dirty my fingers. Er . . .'' and he holdin up he hand so . . . '
Doodsie splayed the fingers of her right hand, sat back, tapping her fingers on the table. Jessie roared with laughter. ' " Would you peel it for me, please?'' ' Doodsie collapsed into giggles, slapping her hand against the table top. Regal sucked his teeth. 'Ah don believe he did really remember who he talkin to!'

'Huh!' Regal joined in their laughter. 'Where you toilet, Doodsie?'

'Through there. Same place.'

He turned to the door behind him. 'You change up here, Doodsie?'

'Yes. Ah cut a passage behin de room so we could have something dat look like a decent bathroom. But dis big ole estate house an dem really ugly ugly an wasteful. Dis big ole stone bath they have there, you could scrub it for life an it still lookin like it never see a cleanin. As long as ah live in dis place, ah caan get to like it.'

'You daughter say she like it. De problem is that you have to have money to keep up place like this.'

'Wait eh! Ah comin! Lemme go by de toilet!'

'Ay-ay!' Jessie smiled. 'Ah wonder what good breeze blow im by here?'

'Doodsie o-o-oy! Any water?'

'Oho! Hol on, lemme get a bucket from the copper for you! One of the joys of this place!'

Doodsie offered Regal a drink of cider, reminding him of that time some fifteen years ago when she had offered him the same out of the one bottle she usually kept for ages, just to give a visitor a small glass. To her horror, he had consumed two tumblers full. Regal laughed, said he would only drink one now, and did.

'You haven't changed much, you know. I realised that the moment I came back. Jessie still delicate and complaining, and you, Doodsie, still straightening out everybody.'

'Ay. Well what do all you at all? Ah caan really help it if I'm not well.'

'No.' Doodsie passed her hands across the plastic tablecloth, the gold wedding ring a coppery colour against the red. 'And from morning you could afford to be so whereas I couldn't. Mammie always act like if because you complexion little bit fair, you delicate and people mus always be bringing ting up in Hermitage for you. I not sayin you not sick in truth,' she added hastily, as she saw the storm clouds gathering on Jessie's face. 'But that is how it start. You just never had to deal with it. And then because you always been sick and I was always the stronger one, I just had to do more running about. So I get accustomed to working things out for myself. Especially because of how tings was with me. You see what ah mean?'

'Uh-huh!' Jessie was a little bit mollified, the wind taken out of her billowing sails. Her cheeks relaxed. 'Well I caan help that, you know.'

Regal laughed, a bit of gold glinting between teeth at the right side.

'An youself,' said Doodsie, 'no less a devil than you always was, because you always been king.'

'You not goin to blame me for not being born a woman?'

'No, my dear.' The ring struck against the red tablecloth. 'I just congratulating you.'

Jessie laughed quietly. 'Mammie did always like boys. Is the same way she did like Simon, Doodsie.'

'Ah tell you! After a while, she an Angel couldn't get on at all, partly because Angel so stubborn. She used to call her that ole crooked foot girl. Because you know how Angel foot like she fadder own!'

Their merry laughter was cut off by a voice demanding: 'Who foot like dey fadder own?'

'Ay-ay! When dis one come?'

'Who dat? Angel?'

'Talk about de devil!'

'Well allyou, blow shell! Look who in de house!' Angel hugged her uncle. 'What good breeze blow you dis way? Is you dat have everybody so happy an laughin? People could go wid de house, allyou won know!'

Uncle Regal and Angel got on excellently. She was always laughing at him, always reminding him of the time, years ago, when she and Simon were still at school and he had come on a visit from some country, Trinidad perhaps, complete with walking stick and Yankee accent. He had rented a car, picked them up at school. Angel could vividly remember the conversation as he stopped to greet a friend on Church Street.

'Hey, ma-a-an! How you doin, man?'

The man had answered something quite mild, stammering slightly, intimidated by this opulent stranger-friend. Then Uncle Regal: 'Just visitin, ma-a-a-an! Keep well, huh? Walk on the right si-i-de, ma-a-an!' And he had rolled along in the car, leaving the man looking bewildered. Angel never tired of telling the story. Uncle Regal never tired of hearing it.

'How long you stayin, Angel?'

'Weekend. I have to go up to the school in Sauteurs to do some classes next week.'

Doodsie went out to the kitchen to check on her pot. Angel went through the living-room to her room. Stopped on her way through and shouted suddenly.

'Wait non! What dis picture doin out here?'

Doodsie came quietly out of the kitchen, exchanged a look with Jessie. Jessie smiled. Doodsie returned swiftly to the kitchen. Regal lifted his brows.

'Mammie! What dis picture doin hangin on the wall out here?' Angel was almost in tears with anger, back now in the dining-room. From the kitchen there was the sound of running water. Jessie tightened the lid on the jelly bottle. Regal passed his hand across the tablecloth, making a swishing sound. Doodsie came to the door. She leaned forward slightly, one foot on the dining-room floorboards.

'Is you father, chile. He put it up there.'

'And you let him put it?'

'How you mean if I let him put it? Is the man house, you know. When dey cut up de estate an dey sellin out to who want lan, is he dat had money to buy piece wid house on it, not me!'

'How you mean is the man house? You not livin in it? Is the man sweat an blood alone that keepin this house goin? Mammie, for thing you tell me, ah don understand you.' She walked swiftly back to the living-room, looked up at Leader smiling placidly from near to Nen Ezra's mahogany plaque. Above his head there was the proclamation: Christ is the Head of this House. 'Mammie, how you could have dat picture *dey*?'

Regal got up, went to look at the offending photograph.

'Uh oh-h-h!' he exclaimed quietly. 'Uh-h-h huh!' He leaned against the doorjamb, facing the dining-room, head down, hands in pockets. He listened to Angel's rage.

'Ah mean, dammit to hell! It upsetting enough having the man ruling the country and so many asses supportin him! But how you could have his picture up on the wall in you house?'

Doodsie walked towards Angel. Lifted her hand as if to put it on her daughter's shoulder. Frowning, Angel stepped away.

'Listen, chile. You know dat left to me I would be wipin me foot all over dat picture.' She paused, looking up at Leader's serene face. Regal turned, confronted Leader again. He smiled, walked back to his chair. Doodsie sighed, turned away, walking back to the dining-room. 'But is not my house for one thing. And,' she turned back to look at Angel, 'the asses you talkin about, watch you mouth, because you father is one o de supporters. So jus relax an behave youself.'

'I don understan that. No. I just don understan that at all.'

Angel turned towards the dining-room, turned back. She walked towards the shelf where the radio stood. Switched on the radio. Switched it off. Marched back to the watching silence in the dining-room.

The door slammed. Carl, in his new college school uniform, burst into the dining-room. 'Good evenin, Mammie. Evenin. Auntie.' He looked around, the schoolbag held in both hands. He moved slowly into the dining-room. 'Evenin, Uncle Regal.'

Regal nodded, smiled, looked up, cleared his throat, put out a hand. 'Evening, Carl. How are you?'

Carl looked around. 'Evening, Angel.' He lowered his eyes from her frowning face. Squeezed past behind her to get to the kitchen. 'Mammie . . .'

Doodsie frowned. Gestured. Pointing towards his room inside. Carl went through the passage behind the room to the bathroom.

'For how much hundred years you inside here workin, not gettin no payment youself always say, an you go tell me you caan take a decision about what picture could hang in you drawing-room. Well, I ain see why you married. You could have been the manservant. At leas he would o pay you a few cents so you could buy a little shack of you own an hang up what picture you want in it.'

'Angel!' Jessie didn't like to interfere, but she knew how much this would be hurting Doodsie. 'Ay-ay! Well how? Is you mother you talkin to, you know!'

'But what dat picture doing hangin up *dey*?'

'Yes.' Doodsie's voice was quiet. 'I could have been the manservant, but the man didn't say he want a servant, you see. At the time was a wife he say he want.'

'You mean he realise dat it didn make sense payin servant when wife mean de same ting an you don have to pay it.'

'Ay-ay! Angel! Well what kine o ting is dis at all? But how? Is not so!' Jessie's bracelets knocked against the edge of the table. She shifted in the chair. Her eyes widened.

Regal pulled the bottle of jam towards him, tightened the cover, pushed it away. From his pocket he pulled a spotless white handkerchief. Shook it out. Refolded it, passing his thumb along the crease. Put it back into his pocket.

'Come on, now, Angel, that is no way to talk to your mother.'

'Angel chile, calm down. Jus calm down.' Doodsie walked to

the kitchen, picked up a towel. Slapped it at the fowl. It jumped squawking into the yard below. She closed the window. Walked slowly out to the living-room where Angel now stood leaning against the partition, head down, arms folded. Doodsie looked at her daughter. Ah coulda been de manservant, she tell me. Ah make sure she don have a life like mine. Ah remember how Mammie use to force me to go an see dis father wid he wife and chilren. She din use to treat me bad but dose little devil an dem use to really hate me an make me do dey work an shout at me to go at me mudder. Ah coulda been de manservant, she tell me.

'If ah did take on a servant work without the wedding ring, Angel, ah still might of end up gettin no money and youall might still have been there without the respectability. Bad as it is, ah manage to give youall an education. So climb down. Leave de man picture where it is an know what you believe to youself. You jus passin. Ah here wid it all day an you know how ah hate dat character.' Doodsie paused, her hand pointing towards Leader, eyes on his framed face. 'But you have to learn to swallow vinegar an pretend is honey.'

'Why? Why?' Angel was actually in tears now. 'I actually hear that man at a meeting in town, eh.' She walked to the dining-room, blocking Carl's view as she stood in front of the passage, talking to all of them directly, emphasising her points with the stabbing forefinger of her right hand. 'Tellin people that if they look an see that is the educated people who study in university abroad that causin the trouble in the country now, they would realise that educating they chilren ain make no sense.' She stopped. Picked up the screwdriver from the shelf in the dining-room where Allan always kept it. Hit it against the partition between the dining-room and living-room. Dropped it back on the shelf. Jessie moved her hands from underneath her chin. Looked briefly at Angel's face. Looked away. Put out her hand and pulled the louvres open wider. 'An meanwhile he own children in university abroad, you know! But nobody ain think to ask him why. So he could talk that stupidness an spend no money on education for the country.' She went out to the drawing-room. Stood staring at Leader. Swung back to them in the dining-room. 'An Daddy heself know how he drainin the estates dry to have his private parties; everytime he come from a trip he on the radio talkin a whole set o . . . o . . . sh . . . stupidness . . . about . . . about what he eat an what great hotel he stay, nothin about how his trip goin to help poor people forward an people still talkin nonsense about how is he get them enough money to wear shoes, he first get money for them to buy pantie an a whole set of ignorance.'

'But in a way is true, Angel,' interrupted Regal. 'An that is what you have to realise before you could do anything about what goin on in this country.'

'You too?' Arms akimbo, Angel faced her uncle.

Regal's chair scraped back. He stood up.

'Wait! Wait!' He took a step forward, holding up his hands. 'I don't support the man. I can't stand the best bone in him. Is through him I turn me back on anything to do with politics, but we have to understand that in his time, when people needed support an direction, he was the only one that come forward an lead an fight for workers on the estates. The problem is that he jus use dat to push himself forward and then get worse than the res, but people still livin in the past and thinking of him as a black saviour.' Regal moved back to his seat. Sat down slowly. 'An he did do a lot of good.' He got up again, walked towards Angel at the entrance to the living-room. 'A lot of good.'

Angel put her hands to her head. Moved restlessly. Looked at the photograph. Leader looked confidently back. Above him, Christ is the Head of this House, its only Inspiration. The white lace curtains on both sides of the wall hangings fluttered gently in the breeze as the wind poked its fingers through the louvres. In the dining-room, Jessie sighed. Peeped outside, lifting her bottom slightly off the seat as she leaned forward.

'Ah don tink it gon rain today,' she said.

Suddenly Angel took up the scissors which rested on the machine near the window and flung them at the smug face in the photograph. The glass splintered. There was a silence inside. Outside, the wind rustled in the grapefruit tree. Jessie didn't move. Continued looking outside, hand under her chin, right forefinger curved over her top lip. Doodsie and Regal walked slowly to the living-room. Looked up at the photograph. The broken glass curved across Leader's mouth. His eyes, out in the open now, stared back at them. Angel pushed past them, went out to the kitchen, returned with the broom and dustpan. Jessie continued looking outside. Doodsie and Regal watched Angel sweep the bits clean.

'Get a wet cloth,' advised Doodsie.

191

Angel went to the bathroom for a cloth. She wiped the floor clean, ensuring that no bits remained to get into bare feet. As they watched, she reached up and removed the picture. She took it to her parents' room, pushed it under the bed. Is a good ting Rupert not around today, thought Doodsie. He woulda make things worse by supportin Angel. Rupert was the most vocal critic of Leader in the house. Is a good thing he not here. Doodsie moved back to the kitchen. God works in mysterious ways!

Simon came by with his girlfriend when Angel was in her room. He heard some of the story from Aunt Jessie, laughed, pushed open the door of Angel's room.

'Ay! You dey?'

'Uh-huh!' Angel looked up from sorting exercise books on the bed.

'What you break de man picture for?'

Angel pressed her lips together. A vein or something jerked in her cheek. Simon laughed.

'You playin you like confusion! Ah mean, ah glad it break ...' he chuckled. 'But you know what ting you do dey?'

Angel sucked her teeth.

Simon chuckled. 'You tink you bad?' He kicked at the door of her clothes closet. 'What happen to dat? It caan close?'

'It just stupid sometimes. Is de lock on de inside.'

'Hm-m-m!' Simon let the door swing.

'Anyway, girl, I ain't stayin, non. Ah don want to be aroun when bottle start to fly. Ah goin an see if Mammie have meat in de pot dey.' He pulled the door of the tiny room which, years ago when Ma Ettie was still alive, Doodsie had cut out of the drawing-room. He looked back at his sister. 'You don jokin, girl. Mammie always use to say you does buy confusion cash. Dis one good, though.' He went through the door laughing.

In the kitchen, Simon leaned over the pot.

'Look!' Doodsie indicated with the pot spoon. 'Take dat piece dey. Is a good-size piece an you not stayin!'

'Ah mean,' Simon stopped, flared his lips, opening and closing his mouth to let in some air to cool the hot meat. 'Oh gawd, Mammie, dat ting hot.'

'Is what you expec if you take something from a cookin pot. Ah don know how to cook on ice.'

He pulled in air through his mouth. 'Ah mean, eh, Mammie, I

wouldn do it. Ah just wouldn even see the picture, but really, it couldn stay there. We really couldn live here then or bring anybody here. But I better miss dis showdown, you hear.' He stepped into the dining-room. 'Uncle Regal!' He rested his hand on his uncle's shoulder. Laughed. Started again to tease his uncle as he had done when he first came in. 'What's happenin, ma-a-a-a-an?' Regal and Jessie laughed. 'I gone, you hear. I'll see youall when things quieter around here.'

Doodsie went back to dishing out the food. Angel stayed in her room.

Regal said quietly, 'Is a damn hard thing to have a face like that on the wall in you own drawing-room, you know.'

'Youself, you better hush you mouth. If he didn run away with all you dance money and the union money and take it for heself when you were his union boss up in the north, you mighta still been together.'

'Oh no!' Regal shook his head. 'No, Jessie. That is one hell of a "if". Because dat was only one of the things that show what the man was all about.' He pulled open the screen door to get Doodsie's attention. Got up and stood at the entrance to the kitchen. 'But he really did start off as though he wanted to do something for poor people and that is what Angel and her friends' generation have to realise.'

'Chupes. For poor people what! He did only fightin for he pocket.' Jessie bunched her fingers together, made a movement as though pushing something in the pocket of her skirt. 'He did just want to take all what he get shove inside he pocket. He din concern with people.'

'That is how it turn out to be.'

Doodsie looked sideways at him. 'Ah did tell you dat is how it was!'

'Yes, dat is true. Ah not doubtin that. But it had more of me than you, more like me who take the ting at face value and want a change. Ay! Youself too, girl! You forget what hell we did ketchin? De man bad, is true, but you have to put the ting in some kine o . . . some kine o . . . framework. If you jus keep sayin de damn asses supportin him, then they go just keep supportin him because of what they remember an because you jus lookin down you nose at what you not even tryin to understand.'

'Meself ah don know.' Jessie moved her eyes to the table.

193

Smoothed the plastic. Her bracelets tinkled.

'Food ready. So make sure the table clear.'

Just as they were all seated and had started eating, there was the sound of Allan clearing his throat in the yard. They ate. From outside came the sound of nutmegs being emptied into a basket. Allan stood at the back door of the kitchen, removing his boots and clearing his throat.

'Dammit!' Doodsie pushed back her chair. 'Jus as ah start to eat.'

'He know where the pot is,' said Angel. 'All he have to do is take out some food for himself.'

'An that kine o ting you always doin could give you indigestion, make the stomach sour,' Jessie chewed on the peas she had cooked separately without salt.

'Ay-ay! What!' Allan laughed as he entered the dining-room. He shook Regal's hand.

'Bradman, boy!'

'Ay!' Jessie laughed. 'Is long time since ah hear dat name!'

'So what good breeze blow you dis side, boy?'

Doodsie went out to the kitchen. She listened to the talk and laughter coming from inside.

Allan went to the bathroom, moved around in the bedroom a bit, came back just as Doodsie was moving her own plate from his spot on the table, replacing it with his, moving hers closer to Jessie's end of the table.

'How thing, Angel?'

'Not bad.'

Allan pushed up the louvres. Leaned forward, looking outside.

'Ah don like how de mountain lookin, non. Ah don want dis cocoa wet at all. It almost time to bag now!'

Doodsie looked up. 'Ah don tink it will come. It look like a passin cloud.'

'I hope you right.'

They talked and laughed throughout the meal. Everyone enjoyed Regal's jokes about his life, his affairs, his encounters with family members. Carl, subdued after the scene which he had observed from the door of his room, kept his eyes on his plate. Tense scenes always left him curled inside himself. Allan looked at his son.

'How was school today?'

194

Carl frowned. Mumbled 'Okay'. Then, 'Ah tell you arready ah don like dat question!'

Allan laughed. Doodsie always marvelled at the way Carl could say almost anything to his father. Angel looked at her brother and smiled.

'Ay-ay!' Regal was getting down into a story. 'Well one day – one Tuesday evening – I cruisin down Frederick Street.' Uncle Regal rubbed his nose, shifted on his chair.

Carl grinned. He enjoyed this. He looked at his father. Allan laughed back at his son.

'Yes, that is all you fit for. You could give dis boy story for breakfast, lunch and dinner.'

'Dat time ting bad. Two weeks ah lose me job on de building site an nutting doing! Ah putting two nail in me pocket to get the jinglé.' Regal shook his pockets. There was a jingling sound.

'Is de nail you have dey now, Uncle Regal?'

'Sit quiet, boy!' Doodsie chuckled.

'You arready dat never know to put someting by for a rainy day,' said Jessie.

'Well,' Regal cleared his throat. Looked around at the faces. 'You boy belly empty like nutting. If wind blow hard ah fallin! But ah well deck off! Black bell-bottoms wid de crease neat . . .!' Regal lifted himself half-way off the seat, straightened the creases of imaginary bell-bottomed trousers.

'Ah tell you!'

'Razor-sharp! If you pass you finger too hard it cuttin!'

'Uh-huh!'

'So you boy movin down Frederick Street.' Regal pushed back the chair. Pushed it away to give him more room. Head held high, hands just lightly touching the tops of his pockets, he demonstrated the walk.

'Saga-boy!'

'Ah jus hear dis voice say: "Ay-ay! Regal?" Ah ain look. Ah say to meself, ah wonder who dat now?' Regal sat down. His eyes widened. 'Then from the other side of the road over dey,' moving his hands, 'ah hear a shoutin now ' "Regal! Regal! Wo-o-y! Regal!" Ah say Bon Jé!'

Doodsie chuckled. Allan sat back in his chair, laughing. Angel and Carl kept their eyes on their uncle's face, smiling, waiting for the rest. Jessie chuckled.

Regal looked from one side of the room to the other. Shook

his collar as though to lessen the heat. 'Ah say Bon Jé! Who dat come to make me shame on Frederick Street in dis Trinidad here shoutin out me name loud loud? Ah start to walk fas!'

'Oh God, Uncle Regal! You bad!'

'Ah hear a shout "Ay! Regal! Boyo!" Ah say to meself woy-o-yoy! So ah walkin fast now an after a while ah ain hear de shout again. Ah still fraid to look back, but ah slowin down now an same time dis han grab me . . .' Regal's right hand went across to grab his left shoulder.

'It good for you!'

'Who it was, Uncle Regal?'

' . . . grab me right on me shoulder. Swing me roun, you know. Ah mean, really swing me roun!' He dropped his hand on Allan's shoulder to demonstrate.

'Ay, man! You breakin me shoulder!'

'Ri-i-i-ight!'

Sucking at the chicken bone, cracking it with her teeth, Doodsie chuckled.

'Nex ting is, "Ay ay! You is not Ma Grace grandson Regal, Miss Ettie boy dey?" Ah look at de face. Me ain know de woman from Adam, you know. An a ole man come up behin er now breathin hard, like he been runnin to catch up. And now de two o dem talkin, an me in the middle. "Look, Josephus! Dat is not Ma Grace gran? You not Regal?" An now he grab me shoulder pee-ee-eerin in me face!'

'Ay-ay! Dat is joke, yes!'

'Well when ah eventually get a word in, it turn out dat is Cousin May-May husban family from up the hill in the cocoa. But me ain know dem people! Well ay-ay! In de middle o Frederick Street, you know! An when you see we establish de relation is huggin an kissin an ting for dey cousin, you know.'

'Eh-heh!'

'Oy!'

Regal sat forward in his chair, smoothing the tablecloth. 'A whole half hour before ah get away from dem. An by dis time you boy more hungry dan ever!'

'Oh-h-ho!' Jessie suddenly exclaimed. 'Ah know who dat!'

Doodsie giggled, knocking her hand against the table.

'Ay-y! Watch Mammie!'

'Ah know dat, you know. Ah was jus waitin. If Jessie doh know dem, dey not family in truth, regardless how far away dey

196

say de connection is.'

'But ah know in truth!'

'Who?'

'Josephus is Cousin May-May uncle-in-law and Clementine
... is not Clementine she name, Regal?'

Regal pounded his fists on the table with delight. 'Girl, you
good in truth. I couldn even remember the name. Yeh, is
Clementine.'

'Well Clementine is his wife an she come out down in La
Fillette area by Ezra people dey, Doodsie.'

'Uh-huh! How dey call me again?' Doodsie grinned.

'Dat's right! By those people dat don know dey name!'
Jessie chuckled.

'What is dat?' Allan was grinning even as he asked the
question.

'Yeh, ah tink ah know dat story.' Regal nodded.

'Allan know it too. He jus forget.'

'Who people, Mammie?' Angel, always last with the chicken
bone, and looking around for bones not properly dealt with,
reached across to her mother's plate.

'Move you han, girl! Ah tell you dat story arready, chuts!'

'Ah caan remember!'

'Tell us non, Mammie.'

'Well is Myson dat married to Comesoon.'

'Myson an Comesoon?' Carl giggled.

'Myson an Comesoon was really Joseph and Mercy Husbands.
Mister and Mistress Husbands.' Doodsie cleared her throat.
'Dey use to live right opposite to Ezra granmother dey, Nen
Dill.'

'Uh-huh!'

'Oh gosh! Those children in dat house din jokin non! If win
pass, they tease!'

'Well, dis day, a white gentleman an lady hear about a piece
of land dat sellin dat dey say Myson an Mercy in charge of. Ah
tink it was Bouchen, those fair skin people dey, de las son, that
go in England leave Myson takin care of dis land an then stay
over dey an decide to sell!'

'Uh-huh!'

'So he sen dese people to see the land! So Comesoon outside
in de back an Myson out on de step. The man say,' Doodsie
lifted her hand, waving. "Hello! We've been directed to this

197

house. Er . . . we've been told to contact you by Mr George Bouchen." He stretch out his hand, taking Myson hand in his. He say, "I am John Roderick, and this is my wife Joanna." So he introduce heself an he waitin now, you know, to get a return. So Myson shakin he head up and down, up and down. He say: "Yes sah!"

'Uh! So why he mus say yes sah?' Carl looked disgusted.

"Morning, sah. My name is . . ." he stop. Look roun.' Doodsie looked over her shoulder.

Angel grinned. Jessie laughed.

Carl leaned across and whispered to his sister. 'You fine he mus say yes sah, Angel?'

'Is so dey did have us stupid thinkin dem was God. Is dem dat train us so! Dat is why everyting good white! Dat changin!'

Carl nodded.

'He say, "My name, my-my-name . . ." He look back over he shoulder again. Scratch e head wid e lef hand, thinking. Then he shout . . .' Doodsie looked towards the mountains.

'Wo-o-y!'

'Papa-mèt, well that is stupid, yeh!'

'Real fool-fool!'

'Dey stupid too much. All dey siddown dey doin was watchin people lan!'

'"Comesoon o-o-o-oy! What is me name again?"'

The dining-room was filled with laughter.

'Well yes wi!'

'Comesoon come runnin up; she say in a low voice, "Oh God, Myson, you name is Mr Joseph Husbands; suppose Ezra an dem hear you now?"'

'Well dat is a good one!'

'So dey hear im, Mammie?'

'Well how you tink you hearin de story now?'

'Ah sure Ezra an dem use to make up some o those stories about Myson an Comesoon. People caan stupid so!'

'Tell us another one, Mammie.'

'Don bother me, boy!'

'Meself ah wish ah could stay, but I have to go now.' Regal pushed back his chair.

'Stay longer, non, Uncle Regal.'

'Non, girl.' Uncle Regal kissed his niece's cheek. 'Ah have a lot of rounds to make.'

After Regal had left, Allan was sitting alone in the living-room with his customary small glass of mountain-dew. Carl went to sit on the copper outside, stirring the water with a stick from the gliricida tree. Allan tossed back his mountain-dew. It was then that he noticed the space on the wall where Leader's picture should have been. His eyes moved to other spots on the wall. He sat still. He looked at the mahogany plaque. He looked at the framed picture of a boat made out of thread. Looked at the radio on the shelf. He stood up.

'Where is this picture that was on the wall here?'

No answer.

'Well that is strange. Doodsie, where is the picture that . . .?'

'It was broken.' Angel intervened from her position on the dining-room chair, exercise books splayed out in front of her as she went through her students' work with a red pen. She didn't look up.

Outside, Carl stopped stirring the water. Dropped the stick in. Sat staring at his reflection. Listening for sounds from inside.

'Broken?'

'Uh-huh!'

'How that happen?'

'Fell.'

A gospo fell from the branch of the tree, knocked against the old galvanise of the fowl run, fell into the copper with a splash. Carl moved his head as the water splashed. His reflection broke up.

'Where is it?'

'Under your bed.'

Allan laughed mirthlessly. Went into the bedroom. Came back out with the picture in his hand, the broken bits of glass still holding to the frame, the Prime Minister's face calm beneath the piece which now sliced his nose.

'Well I don't understand this. The picture not only fall an break, it walk to sit down below the bed too?'

Jessie moved on her chair, put out her hand and opened the window, laced her fingers together under her chin and sat there looking outside.

'No.' Angel didn't look up. 'I put it under the bed.'

'But why?' Allan stood sideways at the door between the living-room and dining-room. His eyelids moved rapidly up and down.

Carl sat up on the copper, his back to the water.

'Because I fin it lookin well stupid hangin up in the drawing-room.'

Allan laughed the mirthless laugh, paced restlessly back to the drawing-room, stood with one hand in his pocket, the other holding the photograph in its frame with the broken glass sticking out of it.

Carl slapped at the sandflies attacking his feet.

'Well this is someting! In my own house, ah can't put up what picture ah want on the wall? No.' Suddenly flinging the picture on to a chair. Some more glass fell out, enraging him further. 'This is damn nonsense. Ay-ay! Ay-ay!'

He paced back and forth. Went to the dining-room. Stood looking down at Angel. Carl slapped at the sandflies.

'In your own room in my house, you put up all ugly picture you want of little rasta boy, other picture of one face with about five heads all around it, all sort of beads an stupidness. Ah never tell you nothing, now I put up my own picture, you breakin it an throwin it down?'

'Daddy, that picture on the wall will make me feel ashamed. I could never bring no friends here.'

'Why? Why not?'

'Because it's stupid, that's why.' Angel's voice was rising.

Carl got up from the copper, went to sit on a stone in the middle of the yard. There was the sound of voices as people walked along the pathway below. A dog barked.

'A man who have the country in such a mess, we have him up on the wall like a hero. They would think everybody in this house stupid.'

'Meaning I am stupid, I suppose?'

'I didn't say that.' And then, in a barely discernible mutter, 'So if you want to say it, well . . .'

'Jessie, you want to help me shell this peas?' Doodsie passed the bowl of peas to Jessie through the kitchen door, returned to her work in the kitchen. 'Carl, you better feed the pigs now, before you settle down to do you homework!'

'Well, well, well! You and you friends, I don understand youall. Talkin about black people havin power and a whole lot of nonsense. An when black people really have the power now, you still looking for high brown people who still don have you interest at heart to give the power to. You don even know what you want! You learn so much stupidness in Jamaica an now a set o black power nonsense full up you head!'

'So because you Prime Minister skin black, you figure he interested in black people? Look how much he have for heself and watch who his friends are!'

'You're the one who stupid! Because what hurtin the high brown people you supportin is the fact that they always been Grenada white an it hurt to see a black man have something.'

'Someting that he sharing with you? And this ting about who high brown an who black is nonsense. All of us black, and if you fightin something an you honest about it an you know what you fightin for an what you fightin against is to all poor people benefit.'

'That is what you think, that is the communist nonsense they tellin you.'

'Carl, look! Take the pan o food ah put outside de door dey an go an feed the pig!'

'Communist nonsense hell!!'

'Angel! Who you talkin to?' Doodsie went to the dining-room door.

'Is awright. Leave er. That is what she learn.'

'No. Ah does vex for stupidness like . . . for . . . for . . . for dat kine o ting. All you life you hear that communism bad. Years ago, you, me too in the convent, all of us, say endless prayers for merciful God to kill Castro and leave Cuba in the hands of beautiful America. But explain to me in detail what you know communism is.'

'So you defending it?'

'You opposing it. I want to know if you know what it is you opposing or if you opposing it because all you masters tell you to oppose it.'

'Who masters?'

'The newspapers, the radio, all those that Britain an America leadin that have the correct line from America an the rest.'

'Ah chuts, stop dat now!' Doodsie fretted from the dining-room. 'De communism oh, de what ism, who want to know, all we want is for ting to go good.'

Carl picked up the pan and walked towards the pigpen.

'Jessie, pass dat towel in de corner over dey for me, please.'

Allan walked heavily to the living-room door. Pulled it open. Stood looking beyond the guava tree at the sea outlined in the distance. He came back to confront Angel.

'Ah don know what nonsense you talkin.' His eyelids were moving rapidly up and down. 'Every man have a sense of right and wrong.'

'An you born with it, right? All the things you tellin me now you could have told me since you had two years?'

'Look, I not gettin into all of that. I know you feel you educated, you have all the sense in the world and I stupid. The point is, I want that picture there, and it going back up. When you ready to decide what picture to hang up, find you house.'

Allan marched back through the living-room to the step outside.

'You damn right.' Angel pulled her books together. 'Ah blasted well know is not me house!'

'Angel!' Doodsie put a hand on her daughter's shoulder.

Carl came racing back with the empty bucket, dropped it with a clatter on the stone outside.

Angel sucked her teeth. 'Look, is you dat married an you feel you have to work an give all support to stupidness, so good luck.'

'Angel! Well what is dis at all?' Jessie asked, getting half-way to her feet, sitting down again. 'Bon Jé!' she tried to steady the glass at her elbow. It crashed to the floor. Sucking her teeth, Jessie walked to the kitchen for the broom. Spoke to Carl standing at the back door. 'Pass the ole piece o cloth out dey for me, chile, lemme clean up dis mess.'

In her room, Angel pulled a few things together, slammed the door, said a general 'See you all' and was gone. Doodsie followed her to the steps outside, watched her retreating back, threw up her hands in the air and went back inside. Carl stood near the grapefruit tree looking down at the road below.

Allan removed the remaining bits of glass from the frame, muttered 'Damn nonsense now'. He found a nail in the kitchen and put the framed photograph back up, putting two extra nails and turning them over to keep the picture in place until he could replace the glass.

Jessie opened the window wider. She looked up at the mountain with the clouds now bunching together. 'De rain go come,' she said. She started shelling the peas again. 'My dreams always mean someting. The dirty water, and Angel on one side.'

Allan sat down on the wall outside, right foot up, right hand resting on his right knee. He spewed a thin stream of saliva through the gap between his top front teeth and brushed the sandflies from his face with his left hand. He looked across the palm tree into the distance over the cocoa trees. Dammit to hell, that child come into the world only yesterday. What she know about what we go through? She figure she is boss in this house?

He was proud of her, in a way, but he hated the silent way she came and went in the house, never talking to him, acting like he wasn't there, even looking annoyed when he stopped her sometimes to ask or say something. Once, when he mentioned it to Doodsie, she had sucked her teeth. 'Oh it hurtin?' she asked him. 'I didn know it could hurt. Is same kind of ting I get from you all the time. Is you daughter. Blood will tell.'

Sometimes we have to drink vinegar an pretend we think is honey!

Angel was driving much too fast along the stony road. She would have to pass by and tell Moonshine that he wouldn't be able to get a lift with her on Monday morning because she wasn't staying down here for the weekend as planned. Dammit to hell! I'm not going back to that blasted house. How come he could never see things? He feel so lucky to be where he is that he's jus a bow head, house slave. Like me, the thought suddenly flashed across her mind as she remembered her fears and uncertainties in Jamaica. 'No need to look like a lamb being brought to the slaughter!' someone had said once. She frowned. The old car lurched drunkenly forward as she pressed down on the gas. Mammie is something else, yes, jus lettin him do what he want. But still, she different. Uh-huh! She different.

She remembered the story her mother had told her about that little boy in Trinidad. Angel sat back, smiling. Doodsie had been working with a Scottish lady in Point Fortin. Angel chuckled. She could hear again Doodsie's voice describing the lady as 'like a wasp, very disagreeable and ready to look at you as a thief. I open the fridge for a drink of water, she appear immediately and ask, "What do you want?" So I handed her the glass and said "a drink of water please." Angel had asked, 'And den what happen?'

'Well, she jus give me the water, non, lookin as if she feel wasn't that I want. She was a real devil. I couldn't even wash my clothes as I had to give account of every minute in every day. A friend came to take some of my clothes to help me wash. The lady saw her going with the parcel, she called out to ask, "What is this she taking away?" I had to call her to open the parcel so she can see.'

The fourteen-year-old Angel had almost overturned the bowl of peas as she knocked the peas shell down angrily.

'So why you din jus leave an go?'

'Huh! Allyou chilren don know trouble. Sometimes you have to drink vinegar an look like you tink is honey. That is why ah tryin to give you a education now, to make sure you don have to go through what I go through, so open up you head.'

Angel had sucked her teeth, incensed by the way her mother had been treated, impatient with the shelling of the peas.

'Huh!' Jessie had cut in. 'Allyou tink those people easy? An it still have people goin through dat, you know.'

'Of course,' Doodsie had agreed. 'Now things little better with us, so we not goin through dat.' She shelled the shiny green peas into her hand. 'An den perhaps those devil an dem smarter now so they not so blatant and open with it. People not takin as much stupidness as before. But de same ting going on.'

Angel had remained quiet for a while, thinking. She remembered going with Aunt Jessie to the house where she worked. Staying in the room sometimes; towards evening, she would walk timidly to the big kitchen door to help Jessie clean up. And sometimes the lady came, saw her, and patted her on the head. But Jessie didn't want her to be seen too often.

'Aunt Jessie,' she had said then, 'the lady you workin for now, she does treat you like that?'

'No. This one not so bad. Is just that the work hard an sometimes ah can't leave de kitchen before all eight, half past eight in the night. Wid de last one, I use to leave earlier but she was a real devil, use to watch me like a hawk – and de man hand did fast too.'

'How you mean?'

'Uh-huh!' Jessie had said. 'You want to know too much, now.'

'Eh? How you mean?'

'Dammit fut, stop botherin people.' Doodsie had put an end to the conversation.

204

Angel was furious again by the time she drove away from Moonshine's house. She thought of the quarrel with her father, of details from her mother's life.

Doodsie had told them that she quit the job with that woman in Point Fortin and found something else. Then one day she met the lady's six-year-old son out walking with the new person who had taken her place.

'The lady used to call me Betty, because she said she liked that for short.'

'But Elizabeth not that long.'

'Anyway, she use to call me Betty. So the new person said "Johnnie, that's your maid Betty, do you remember her?" He said, "Yes, I do! I don't like her" and he step towards me and kicked me. Ay!' Doodsie, remembering, dropped the peas shell and stood up to act the story. 'Well, meself, I was on the alert. I din wait to think. I just handed him a kick in return.' Her right foot went out, kicking. Her face was full of remembered fury; her hand clenched.

'Woy!' Angel and Simon had giggled, enjoying. Jessie chuckled.

'Allyou mother din easy, you know.'

'These people!' Doodsie sat down. 'They treat you like dirt so all that came to me is you got to defend yourself. Fight back.'

Angel remembered the scene, focusing on every detail. Simon had leaned forward to take one of the peapods that she, Angel, had placed next to her. She had slapped his hand soundly. Simon jumped to his feet, ready for a fight.

'Angel!'

'But, Mammie, Simon could ben down an take up the peas in the basket for heself.'

'Look, girl . . .'

'But, Mammie,' Angel had muttered, drawing to the far end where Doodsie couldn't reach her. 'You got to defend youself.'

Jessie chuckled; then the laughter sound started coming through her nose like a hiss. Simon frowned.

'You go see what ah go do you, eh! Come outside!'

'Boy what do you? Like you don know who is me mother?'

And this time Angel had had to dash away from the table as Doodsie's hand shot out towards her.

She drove fast as her mind wandered back over the years. Is like Daddy was hardly ever there. Ah see im laughin wid Rupert an especially Carl these days an Carl goin out with him in de land! After one time is two time in trut! He was always out in de land somewey an we jus use to lissen for im clearin he throat so we could go where he wouldn see us. He's lonely now, though, she thought suddenly. Is only Carl he really have – sometimes.

Me? I always in de middle like a maypole, an both sides pullin!

Allan came and went in the house like a stranger. Whenever he had a difference of opinion with the children, he pulled further away from Doodsie. She responded by folding her lips, holding back the words she wanted to shout at him.

Dear Ezra,
How are you? I hope fine . . .

Doodsie paused, looking at what she had written. She thought of what the children always said to her when they saw her begin a letter. All of them, even Carl now, laughed and said, 'Mammie dat look like school book ting. Write as if you know er, non!' She wished the others would make more of an effort to keep Carl's head on his exams, but . . . she sighed. Dat is the wild one, she thought. She turned the page. Started again.

Dear Ezra,
How's tings, girl? Over here is as if they gettin worse. The
country is in a total mess. As you know, we had independence
earlier this year so we no longer British. I know you please
about that but sometime I really wonder what difference it
make. The only thing I really glad about is that I wouldn have
to dress up no chilren again to go an burn whole day in the sun
for Queens Birthday parade. Anyway they all big now so I
wouldn have to dress them so is just as well. I even hear some
people sayin we will still have queens birthday but I find that
will be real stupid. Anyway that is those politishan an those at
the top business. I know you not in favour of these young boys
who now leadin demonstrashion all over the place, but girl,
they talkin a lot of sense and they have a lot of support. The
hospital in a mess, if you get a nail juke, you afraid to go there

because they might give you a wrong injection, so I agree that is thing to demonstrate about. But you know the big boy cant stan to know nobody oppose him. He prompin up his gang of bad boys and everybody talkin about how the gang beatin up people. I warn all of mine not to get involve but all of dem excep for Simon head an head wid those demonstrashion. Carl all right. He doing well in school. I think I tell you before that Rupert jus leave school an didn bother to go ahead wid the A-levels. Now he jus walkin de streets an lookin for work! I had it easy wid the firs two compare to how these las two have own way. An Rupert as silent as usual. Sometimes I watch him an wonder what he thinkin. But they all right. The boys sayin they not fightin election, they just want people to see the evil but they talkin sense, so if they in election, they have my vote. For years now was a half dead opposition we have so we been waitin on somebody who would do something to oppose that devil so perhaps the Lord send them. People sayin they dont believe in God and things like that. I dont know but whether they realise or not it certainly look as if they are Gods instrument an he workin through them. The strikes going on, and things scarce in truth but you dont have to bother to send barrel of food as you said. Whatever people tell you we are not starving. It not easy to starve in Grenada with so much bluggoe an fig an peas an yam there. It might be harder to buy meat and a little bit harder for town people, so if you want to send a extra dollar especially for you family living right in town, that is good. But we not dyin, and sometimes you have to get a little hardship so people could see the evil. Last month those boys get such a beatin in Grenville was a shame. I have to try to check on the little piece of land you tell me about up in Tivoli. It look like everything all right. Say hello to Sonny and tell him things are okay for the time being. You talk about comin for a while but I know if allyou come at all is just for holiday. Youall doesn stay in one place long. Is a good thing Sonny just like you in that way otherwise you would have been in problems. Take care and write soon.

Never damn de bridge you cross

Angel hadn't been home for weeks. But now that she and

Rupert had installed a telephone, she called occasionally during the day, when she knew that Doodsie was likely to be alone or with Carl. Doodsie had said that the phone wasn't really necessary but with the children away so much, she was glad to have it. One day, about three months after what the family, following Jessie's lead, referred to as 'the incident', Angel telephoned her mother.

'When you coming down, Angel?'

'Ah not sure. You mus come up and see me. The place I rentin not bad. It have enough room. I could pick you up one day.'

'You mus come home. You father didn say anything but I notice he move the picture. Even though he not talkin about it, I know that is a concession to you. You mus come home.'

Angel said nothing for a moment. Doodsie looked up at the spot dominated by Christ is the Head of this House.

'Okay. Next weekend.'

Angel put down the phone slowly. She looked up at her picture of the little rasta boy. She looked across at the framed drawing of a woman's clenched fist. She thought about her father. She didn't feel victorious. In fact, she felt a little ashamed. When she went home, her eyes strayed to the empty space on the wall. Allan was at home, reading his newspaper, *The Voyager*. On the arm of the chair was a small glass of mountain-dew.

'Good evening, Daddy.'

'Good evening.' Glancing up from his paper.

Angel went through to the kitchen to talk to her mother.

Nine

The people gathered early. Some joined the procession along the way. No traffic could move through the small town as the people walked four abreast, some ten thousand of them, a tenth of the island's population, singing, shouting, clapping, drumming. They paused in front of the policemen standing at the gap leading up to Leader's house on the hill. They walked slowly past, singing more slowly, more clearly, more loudly.

'We shall overco-o-ome
We shall overco-o-ome
We shall overcome
Some day-ay-ay-y!

I say deep in my soul
I do belie-eve
We shall overcome some day!'

From the windows overlooking the streets, people waved red handkerchiefs, white handkerchiefs with a nutmeg embroidered in brown and red, white cloths with a cocoa pod embroidered in deep brown. People craned their necks, squeezed their faces between shoulders on narrow balconies, looking down at the blaze of colour and sound on the streets.

Two men who seemed to be in their late fifties held up a banner made from what looked like a white sheet. The bold black letters proclaimed: MASSA DAY DEAD! WE KILL IT IN '51! One young man had on his back the sign LEAD-ER! He was holding one end of a string, the other end of which was tied round the neck of a young girl who pretended to be choking as he led her. From the windows above, the people could see an old man moving along on crutches, keeping to the side of the road. Every so often, he stopped and shouted something, throwing his head well back. The windows and balconies close to him caught the shout thrown up at them. *'We fightin today! We go fight tomorrow! As long as we fightin for someting!'*

Someone on stilts wore a placard stating: AH NOT KEEPIN ME FACE IN THE DUST! AH REACHIN FOR THE STARS! The students in their uniforms, church schools, government schools from all over the country, started a chant:

> 'Run Leader Run!
> The people's on your way!
> Run Leader Run
> For a spot in an open ba-a-ay!
> You got to drown youself dey
> Hide youself wey
> Lewwe pull we country straight!
>
> Run Leader Run ...'

The tune spread throughout the crowd. People knocked bottles, picked up sticks, knocked them together, blew the tune on bamboo flutes. Two steelbands had come on the march. The women and men flashed their pan-sticks, picking out the tune.

A man dressed all in white looked around for an open space. Ran to the centre of the space. Pushed his arms forward, simulating a dive. Someone appeared as if from nowhere with a bucket of water. Was just held back from splashing it all over the actor.

In one section of the winding procession, the tune was different.

'Oh Law-aw-d! The bucket have a hole.'

One group answered: 'In the centre!'

'An i-i-if you tink ah tellin lie!'

'Push you finger!'

Three women had come prepared with a bucket of cocoa. One carried the bucket. Another poured cocoa from a container. The cocoa streamed out of the hole at the bottom centre of the bucket; it was caught in another container by the third woman.

'Leader-o-o-oy-y!
Me bucket have a hole
In de centre!
An i-i-i-if you tink ah tellin lie!
Push you finger!
Leado-o-oy!
Me rooftop have a hole
In de centre!
An i-i-if you tink ah tellin lie
Spen a night dey!'

The crowd danced along the streets. Greens, blues, whites, reds, danced and sang their rage. People stopped off on the sidewalks, fanning themselves with handkerchiefs, with hats, with hands.

'Come come! Buy a snowcone, chile! Cool down de heat!'

'Make noise! Make noise let im hear us! De house jus up de hill dey! He boun to hear us!'

Doodsie laughed. She bought a snowcone. This was one demonstration she just couldn't miss. She looked up the hill. Ah sure he up dey peepin out from behind e curtain an frighten like hell.

'You tink he hearin us for true?' someone wanted to know.

'He hearin us, wi. Me cousin daughter workin up dey and dey say when you see ting frighten im so, he does go in de little room where he feel safe, you know, de one wid de crucifix.'

'Eh heh? He musbe does stan up dey an sprinkle de holy water roun im! Pò djab he! Dat caan save im now! Come lewwe sing a funeral song for he an he crucifix!'

They stood facing the road leading up to the house on the hill. They sang:

'Now de roll is called up yonder
Now the roll is called up yonder
Now the roll is called up yonder
And you'll be there.'

'Let im siddown up dey wid he eternal flame an he crucifix!'
The singing went on.

'Olé Olé O
Djab Djab
Olé Olé O'

Singing the song of the carnival bands Leader had banned
from the streets the year before, the bands in which people
covered themselves completely in black grease and paint, clat-
tered through the streets with cans, pans, horns, celebrating like
their African ancestors had celebrated emancipation, parading
the blackness that gave so much fear and making sure it left its
mark on anything white.

'Olé Olé O
Djab Djab'

From the windows and balconies, people looked down past
the raised clenched fists on to plaits, curls, hats, moving bodies.
The people marched in front of the Parliament building on their
way down the hill. Some kept their fists raised a few seconds
longer as they aimed them at the closed windows of Parliament.
The crowd slowed and then stopped in front of the building.
Those behind up on the hill wondered why the lines weren't
moving. The news went back. We stoppin for a while. People
settled down to act out their protest. A truck carrying steelpans
came slowly along from the back. The players concentrated,
heads down, some with red T-shirts tied around their necks, hat
hanging from an elastic band around the neck.

'We will always let our leaders fall!
When dey treat us de worst of all!'

The truck eased through, stopped somewhere inside the
crowd. The band was playing.

'We will always let our leaders fa-a-all!

When they treat us
Like shit an all!'

A babble of sound; hats fanning faces.

'Woo-oo! It hot, girl!'

'Look Miss Joyce sellin snowcone in de corner over dey!'

'Look! Buy one gimme!'

'You want shave ice or you want syrup in it?'

'Non. Not syrup. Jus de shave ice.'

'Look. Buy one for me too! A snowcone. Ah want syrup.'

'How much han you tink ah have?'

'Ay-ay! Justin! You here?'

'How you mean if ah here? So we could watch Leader kill people an don lif foot den? We ain dead yet!'

'Ay! You don hear how he beat up dose boy an dem?'

'Push dey head in toilet an all ting, yes. What he figure it is at all?'

'You doh see people, girl?'

Angel looked up at the church and remembered the first day that she made the sign of the cross in front here before going up to the convent.

She threw back her head. 'Ay! Papa God! you watchin?'

Her friend poked her in the ribs. 'Don do dat, girl! What do you? You want you curse to take me?'

Angel grinned. 'Les go! We moving!'

The crowd walked on down the hill to hold their rally in front of the Union house. The rally was organised by the movement calling itself Horizon. Chief and the others of Horizon walked singing and chanting with the crowd to the Union house.

Pli mal. More worse!

Downtown, the clouds were just beginning to bunch slowly together: the sea crashed against the retaining wall in the city, sending salt spray flicking across the faces of people walking along the road. The sea roared, splashed; people scampered away. Angel walked away from the sea. She stood on the sidewalk opposite the market square. The market square was empty of vendors. Not one person remained selling; only two lonely boxes upturned in the middle of the market. Angel looked at the sidewalk opposite, near The People's Stores. The building had been closed for weeks. When Leader had started to act out his threat to 'answer fire with fire', the business people closed their shops and stores. *Stop the violence,* they warned him. Stop beating up people, or we'll close down the country. You mean, he had asked one shopowner with a smile, you people will try to force my hand? The beautiful black face had glinted a smile above the snow-white suit.

Now the group people called Leader's 'Rabies Gang' was on a rampage through the town. They smashed show windows. Shattered the windows of The People's Stores.

'Open! Open! We want to buy!'

Earlier that day, Angel was in the middle of the demonstration. She was standing outside the Union building. They called it the People's Parliament. The Rabies Gang had come jumping up like a shortney band at carnival, singing:

'Horizon, Horizon
Go far away ah say!
Lose youself in de ocean boy!
We go murder you today!'

'Woo-oo-oo! Horizon Horizon! . . .'

Feet high, heads low, swinging around with the shortney jump, only the bells were missing. There was the glint of knives and bottles. A hand lifted. Bottles crashed to the ground.

'Horizon Horizon
Wu! Wu!
Horizon Horizon
Go far away ah say!
Horizon place
is out dey in space!
We don want you here ah say!'

Bottles crashed to the ground. At some point they stopped crashing around the dancing gang and started to explode inside the crowd. Suddenly the gang was rushing towards the demonstrators. The people, forced to stop their meeting, had been

214

standing quietly, watching the display. The gang charged. Children screamed. School uniforms flew every which way in fluttering disarray.

'Woy-o-yoy! Dey shootin!'

Angel felt her friend pull her towards the alleyway.

'Oh Gawd, Patience! Dey couldn be shootin! Wasn a gun! Was a gun?'

'Oh Gawd walk fars, Angel!'

'Yeh! Yeh!'

'Oh Gawd! Look! Dey comin up here.'

'Come on! Come on, Patience!'

'Non! Walk slow! Dammit, Angel,' Patience hissed. 'Walk slow as if you home. Don let dem see us runnin!'

Angel turned to look with wide eyes at the face of her friend. A mask fell across Patience's face. She yawned. Looked up at the sky. Leaned against the door of the house on her right in the alleyway. She knocked. 'Mammie?' she called. 'Mammie, you dey?' Angel found her voice as the pounding footsteps came nearer. Beyond Patience she could see two men running. Hands. Revolvers. 'Mammie, open de door, non!' she called. The men approached them running. 'Ay!' said Patience with questioning surprise as she turned and saw them. 'Mammie?' called Angel. The men went pounding past. Ran out into the road. Angel grabbed Patience's hand. The two still leaned against the door, hanging on to the doorknob. One man stood, pointing down the road into the crowd of fleeing people. The other went down running. The man stood for a moment. Then he followed his companion, running too.

Angel and Patience walked on tiptoe out into the road. From down where the men had gone came the sound of shots. Screams. Patience's right hand grabbed Angel's left. Heads up, eyes staring, they walked up the hill, in the opposite direction. Up the hill towards the school where Patience taught – the convent which had been Angel's school. There they met screaming, frightened schoolchildren.

'Miss! Oh Gawd, Miss! Ah was inside de building!'

'Miss the police spray teargas, Miss!'

'Awright, awright! Calm down! Yes, ah know!'

'Miss, dey shoot, Miss. Ah see two men fall, Miss!'

'Me han get crush, Miss. Look! You could even see it still swell!'

'Miss, look eh, Miss! Ah din know meself!'

'Ah see a girl dive in de water by de carenage, Miss; she swimmin away an dey still shootin!'

'Woy! Woy-o-yoy eh!'

'Awright, awright! Take it easy!'

'Miss, ah sure eh, Miss, dat man Leader go dead wid e foot cock up in de air!'

'Something mus happen now,' Angel said to Patience. 'We go home.'

'But then what? We have to do something.'

'Like what? You have gun? You body could stop bullet? Go home, Angel. Lemme go an see if some o dese chilren know how dey reachin home!'

'But . . .'

And now Angel was in the market square. She wondered vaguely whether she would get a bus to take her home. She watched the looting as though in a dream. Men came out carrying fridges, televisions.

'Hois up dey!'

'Hol one en o dat!'

'Wey de truck?'

A policeman stood at the broken store window. He used his gun butt to control looters.

'One at a time, one at a time,' he shouted as they rushed by him. He pointed his weapon threateningly. He repeated, 'One at a time.' He let them through in single file.

Angel watched. She laughed. She cried. She wiped her face with her palm and laughed again. Further down, the sea crashed against the wall. The clouds bunched together. The policeman looked across at Angel. His gaze lingered uncertainly. He gestured with his weapon.

'Keep moving,' he said.

Angel moved. It started to drizzle. A fine driving sheet of rain. Angel wiped her face with her palm. A policeman came across the street. He watched a woman pushing a trolley filled with looted groceries. He turned back to look at Angel. She stood again to look.

'Move on!' the policeman shouted. 'Go home.'

'Why?'

'Because is the law.' Threateningly, he moved his weapon into position. Angel looked at the mouth of the weapon pointing in her direction. 'Go home.'

She went home.

If you pò djab, krapo smoke you pipe!

A car swung round the corner at the top of the hill and came hurtling down towards the woman. She glanced up at the policeman's profile outlined under the peaked cap. His white-gloved hand signalled robot-like to the cars. Angel hadn't seen his signal. She wasn't paying attention. She jumped across the drain to avoid the on-coming car. She skipped two at a time up the wide steps on the side. It was business as usual in town these days. She smiled absent-mindedly at the woman selling oranges and chenets on the step. She stopped. Searched in her pockets.

'Miss Constance, how much for the skin-up?'

'Two for five cents.'

'Hm . . . gimme four. Wey Cousin Eva today?'

'Ah don know, me chile.' Dragging the words in the way that said, 'Me? Ah better don talk dat, you hear.'

Miss Constance's hands moved the skin-up on the tray. She shifted the yellow oranges.

'Buy de skin-up, darlin! Buy de skin-up, lady! Two for five!'

'She din come today?'

'Hm?' Constance fanned her face with the straw hat. She loosened her headtie. 'Non. Non, chile. She din come today!'

Angel turned back down the steps. She stopped and turned. Looked at Miss Constance. The skin-up tasted sour. Behind Miss Constance was the solid structure of the bank. Miss Constance leaned against it.

'Buy de skin-up, darlin!'

'Ay! Angel, what you doin stan up dey lookin like you don know wey you goin?'

'Helen! Girl ah don know when ah see you! How you do?'

'So-so. You don married yet?'

'Chupes. Helen, you know de lady dat does sell skin-up on de step dey? She not dey today.'

'Who? Miss Clementine?'

'Non! Janice family dey!'

'Oh ho! Cousin Eva.'

217

'Yeh.'

'How ah don know Cousin Eva! We tief so much plum from er when she use to sell up by de school gate! You remember? Janice say was she cousin so we use to go an stan up by the tray an say "Ay-y! Cousin Eva!" all de time we tiefin de lady skin-up! We din good, non, girl.' Helen sucked her teeth. Looked back over her shoulder. 'Poor lady.' Helen lowered her voice. 'Ah hear dey pick er up!'

'What! Pick who up?'

'Ay! Ah thought you ask me because you hear something! Leader police pick er up day before yesterday for lootin!'

'For lootin? Don make joke! Cousin Eva could loot something too? Little weak Eva coulda compete wid who drog out dey fridge and dey washin-machine an what not else? What loot Eva could loot?'

Helen glanced around nervously. 'You better hush you mout youself before dey pick you up!'

'Jesus Chrise!'

'Wey he? He livin?'

Angel looked at Helen. In her mind, she was saying to her, but was youself dat use to curse me for not goin to chapel on campus. You sayin dat! But the shock of hearing about Eva just jumbled everything up in her head.

'Girl, don hurt you head too much. All dem so go learn de hard way. Eva bad for she Leader, you know. You caan say taaw against him for she to hear!'

'Ay-ay!'

'Anyway, don fall down in de road. Ah have to go to meet de bank open! We go see eh!'

Angel watched her friend walk up the steps. She watched her wave to Miss Constance. Miss Constance straightened the tray on her knees. She dipped down into her bosom, pulled out a cloth, untied it. Looked inside. Shook it. Took a dollar note from the tray on her knees. Put it in the cloth. Took out some change. Tied up the cloth. Put it back in her bosom.

'Buy de skin-up, darlin!'

It have more mad people outside dan inside . . . more tief too!

Eva was given a six-month sentence. Rupert and Angel went up one day to the prison to visit her. Rupert stood with his hands in his pockets looking up at the prison building. He turned his back to it and stood looking at the thick trunks of the nearby trees. He smelled something like stinkin-toe. There mus be a stinkin-toe tree around. He looked up into the trees. It was somewhere around. An armed guard escorted Eva to what looked like a small waiting area outside. When Eva saw them, she held her head down and cringed against one of the pillars in the covered area. She put her hand up and pulled the two ends of her headtie to tighten it on her head. She looked ashamed. She bit her lip. Her eyes filled. Rupert walked to her. He took her hands in his.

'You don have nutting to shame for, Eva. Don mine dat. Is not you fault. You din do nutting. You don have nutting to shame for.'

Angel put an arm around her shoulders. 'Mammie say howdy.'

'Doh stan up dey.' Rupert led her away from the pillar. 'Come an siddown by here.'

From a few paces away, the guard stood looking at them. Rupert looked at the youth. About my age, he thought. He hardly older. He turned the wooden stool so that he wouldn't have to watch the guard. Thought better of it and repositioned the bench so that he could see him.

'Ah glad to see youall. One set o chilren dat never forget me snowice an me skin-up!' Eva smiled. 'An through allyou you Mammie does even look for me in de market sometimes. What about you little brudder?'

'He not little again, non!'

'Yes. Dose chilren does get big quick.' And the tears were in Eva's eyes again.

'Don feel bad, Cousin Eva. You go come out jus now.'

'An is only because ah see everybody takin dat ah take a little someting too, you know.' She looked up, straightened a little. 'An nutting much, you know, ma'am. Nutting at all, non, chile. Jus a few poun o flour an sugar an rice. Look eh, ah carry it in me han!' striking the fist of her right hand against the palm of her left. 'Ah din even have to take trolley like some ah see!' With the edge of her headtie, Eva wiped away the tears that came down the groove in her cheeks. 'Even de judge say he sorry for me!'

'So why e din let you go?'

'Is really de fault of dose dat report me through envy, you know! De judge say dat he could see ah din take much, but he couldn let me go scot free an encourage oder people, you know.'

'Is de judge fault, too, Eva! He coulda let you go!'

'Well Ma, meself ah don know!'

Rupert looked down at his hands.

'Look! We bring some bread for you, with some cheese, and two oranges. Look. They check it at the gate arready. Is awright for you to take it.'

Eva glanced under her brows at the guard.

'They caan stop you,' said Rupert.

'Me chilren come wid someting, an dey din let dem through wid it, non! But perhaps dey go see more reason wid allyou.' Eva took the things hesitantly. 'Allyou could handle allyou self better, you know.'

Rupert stood up. Perhaps dey go see more reason wid allyou! 'If you need anything else, you mus tell us, Cousin Eva.'

'Non. Non, chile. Ah don want no trouble.'

'Is no trouble, Cousin Eva. People allowed to bring things for their friends and relatives here. If dey tell you different, is not true.'

'Ah really glad youall come! Ah glad to see someone! An to tink, eh!' Eva was crying again. 'In me ole age! Never in all me young life ah dey inside of a prison. Now when me hair grey arready. Fifty-eight years over me head wid two granchilren!' The tears were coming fast. 'To tink eh! In me ole age!'

'Okay! Never mind! Never mind!' The only consolation that fled through Angel's mind was 'God is good! God is good!' The automatic words fled in through one ear and out the other. Angel said nothing. Rupert held Eva's hands.

'Stay strong, Cousin Eva! Stay strong. Things not easy, but stay strong! At leas you learn how people stop! Stay strong, see?'

'Yes, me chile. Ah glad to see allyou.'

The guard walked forward.

'Ah smellin stinkin-toe!' said Rupert. 'It have a tree aroun here?'

The guard gestured.

'Jus under the hill by where ah was standin up dey! Is govament property!'

Rupert smiled.

'Ah did figure so!'

Eva, head down, walked ahead of the guard, back down the passage. Angel and Rupert stood watching them go.

Angel talked to her friend Jerry about Eva.

'Serve her right,' said Jerry.

'I sorry for her.'

'You sorryin for Leaderite? I not sorry for none o dem. Is all one ban o tief. Let them learn from each other.'

'But Eva only supportin Leader because is he alone she could remember from time doin anyting for her.'

'Le dem siddown dey an remember! Me! Ah gettin fed up! Ah not in no mood for psychology.'

She went sometimes to visit Eva's children during the six months. Doodsie smiled wryly at this.

'Ain't they lucky now! It good to see how in the struggle allyou talkin about you understand how people could get fooled an support people who not really workin for them!' Doodsie lifted the heavy wet khaki pants and knocked them against the stone. She started scrubbing them, her teeth biting into the lower lip. Her hands made that squelchy sound which as a child Angel had always tried to get hands to make when she washed. 'Is a pity you caan understand with you own father, though. Like somebody wrong somewey about where this charity ting does begin.'

Angel looked at her mother, and went out to make her visit. But the comment stayed somewhere at the back of her mind. She thought of her father's sister, Aunt Cristalene. When last had she visited her?

Eva's biggest grandchild, Tina, told Angel that it really wasn't Leader's fault. Some covetous people who lived next door and wanted to hide how much they had taken themselves, had told a lot of lies to Leader and that had put him in a funny position; he didn't want it to look as if he was encouraging bad things in the country.

Angel looked up at the framed Christ is the Head of this House. Christ ruled in Eva's house. Is like marriage, she thought suddenly. Ah wonder why ah tink about dat now? She searched her mind, looking for the link. Anyway, she thought, is jus the same way people always makin excuse for whoever they married!

When she left Eva's house, she walked along Melville Street.

221

She stood looking over the retaining wall, down at the sea. The sea rushed up at her, dashed itself against the wall, the spray touching her face with salty fingers. She put out her tongue to taste the salt. The waves gathered again in the distance, bunched together, planned their approach, and came dashing back towards her. In the distant blue, the horizon stretched, remote and peaceful. She suddenly thought of Kai. I might not have had to make so many excuses for him. She looked quickly over her shoulder, as though fearing someone might be close enough to hear the thought. She frowned down at the gurgling sea. She turned her back to the sea. The sea came forward more furiously, thundered against the wall. Automatically, Angel ducked. The water splashed up. She turned back to look down upon the rocks. Lifted her eyes to look at the horizon, a stubborn, unending line in the distant blue.

Ten

'Miss McAllister o-o-oh!'

'Woy! Who dat?'

'Is me, Victoria!'

'Oh is you? Doodsie up de hill dey under de nutmeg. If you shout loud she go hear you!'

'Is awright, becus . . .'

'Eh? Ah caan hear what you sayin. Lemme turn down de radio. Dese children does put on de radio so loud an den just walk out an leave it dey shoutin!' Shuffling her feet into the slippers, Jessie pushed the chair back. She hurried to the living-room, turned off the radio, opened the door.

In the big yard with its tall, untidy grass, Victoria waited. She moved from the middle of the yard. Came around to where Jessie stood at the front door. One hand on the doorjamb, her thin face looking lost beneath the thick hair, Jessie looked down the steps at Victoria.

'She up de hill. Jus behin de pigpen dey, under the nutmeg. If you shout er she would hear.'

Victoria turned. Looked uncertainly up towards the dirt track near to the pigpen. Jessie looked at her, looked at the thin figure in the grey shapeless dress, at the two plaits sticking out from under the straw hat.

'What you want? Anything ah could help you with?'

'No. Is nutting much, non! Ah will call back.' Victoria smiled shyly. Jessie didn't smile.

Dat girl face always talk an say someting different to she mout! Watch de eyes! Underneath like what! She caan look at nobody straight, as if somebody take her only clean-neck fowl!

223

Life meet er hard, anyway! She hundred per cent worse off dan us here!

Victoria had walked out to the grapefruit tree. Bending, she picked up her cutlass from the ground.

'Is jus something ah did want to talk to er about!'

'Oh ho! Well ah will tell er you pass!'

Victoria walked back to the bottom of the steps.

'Miss Jessie, what you hearin?'

'Eh?' Jessie was startled. Her hand dropped from the door-jamb. The heavy silver bracelets tinkled.

'It have a lot a lot of talk flyin aroun. You don hear nutting lately?'

'Me? Wey ah is inside here dey, what ah could hear?'

Jessie walked down the steps. 'What? What do? What happenin?'

Victoria lowered her head. She smiled what would be a shy smile if she didn't look up so you could see her eyes.

'Well ah hear is confusion wid dose boys an dem!'

'Who? You mean de Horizon boys?'

'Huh!'

'What happen? More demonstration?'

'Ah don know!' Victoria took off her hat. 'Ah hear . . .'

'Aye! Victoria, you awright?'

'Oh! Miss McAllister, is you? Ah din hear you come!'

'Doodsie, come non! Like Victoria have someting to say.'

'Wait! Ah comin! Wait, lemme put down dis bucket o nutmeg!'

Doodsie walked to the back, put the bucket down on the step behind the kitchen door, pulled the door open and placed her cutlass in the corner. She held on to the doorpost, pulled off the heavy boots, pushed her feet into the big shoes in front of the door. She hurried into the kitchen, opened the tap, sucked her teeth impatiently as it gurgled.

'Damn stupid pipe!'

Doodsie dipped a container into the bucket of water on the kitchen table. She poured some out, gulped; she gave a deep 'Ah'. She hurried outside and around to the front.

Victoria was looking up into the grapefruit tree and slapping the sandflies off her feet. Jessie sat on the stone at the bottom of the steps.

'What do?'

224

'Well, we waitin for you! Victoria jus saying dat it look as if someting happenin!'

'Someting like what? Wey?'

Victoria gave a half-smile.

'You so will hear about ting dat happenin before me, Miss McAllister.'

'Me?'

'You chilren right inside dey, thick thick wid dem!'

'Oh dey thick? Victoria, girl, in de kitchen wey you see ah is peelin bluggoe dey, if dey thick dey thick for deyself!'

Victoria smiled. Jessie got up, turned towards the steps.

'Well whatever it is, when it come we go see it.'

Victoria looked at Doodsie. 'So you don hear nutting in truth?'

Jessie turned back towards them. She stood with arms akimbo, looking at Victoria.

'What?' Doodsie opened her hands, palms upwards. 'What it is ah suppose to hear? Unravel de parable.'

'Well.' Victoria rubbed the side of her mouth. Moved closer. 'Ah hear all dose Horizon boys an dem in hidin!'

'In hidin? What? What happen?'

'Huh! Meself ah don know!'

'But Leader not even here,' said Jessie, her right hand up to her mouth, eyes wide.

'Ah doh know, non, ma'am!'

'Dat nastiness? He don have to be here to do he ting an dem. He jus order he henchmen an heself hide in de dark.'

Victoria picked up her cutlass. 'Well, ah better go.'

'Dat is one wolf dat not even in sheep clothing. Ah seein im loud an clear!'

Victoria dug her cutlass into the hard ground. 'But dose boys provokin too, you know!'

'Who more provokin dan he? He provoke us for twenty howmuch years, fullin up he pocket!'

'All o dem does full up dey pocket! Who you know reach up dey an ain full up pocket?'

'Victoria, open up you eyes an see!'

'Doodsie, what do youself? Dat is Victoria people! She support im, so . . .' Jessie turned away, lifted her hands slightly in a dismissive motion, started walking up the steps.

'Plenty people dat use to support im see de light! Plenty

225

people. Way you ever hear leader of country lootin? He dat suppose to protec people dey, senin he people an dem to beat up people an boastin on radio about how he recruitin who rough! Eh! Dat is leader too?'

Doodsie sucked her teeth. Victoria bent down, pulled a stalk of grass. She straightened and started picking at her teeth.

'Yeh!' said a man's voice from across the yard. They jumped. All eyes focused in that direction.

'Bon Jé!' Jessie put a hand to her mouth. 'Ah din even see im! Look how people could kill you, eh!'

Joseph walked across the yard, limping, forcing along his short leg. They called him Hop-an-Drop; he didn't seem to mind.

'Ah jus come to get some water, please. Ah stand up dey an ah hear what allyou sayin. Allyou so absorb! Anyway Miss Mac ah agree you hear! Dat is not no leader!'

Victoria eyed him. 'See how you ungrateful!'

'Ungrateful what? He suppose to grateful to me! We put im dey! Is through me he enjoyin de fat o de lan! An look how he beatin up we own chilren now!'

'Dose chilren shouldn follow bad company!'

'Is he dat is de bad company!' Doodsie's voice was a shout.

'Bon Jé, youself, you talkin too loud.'

Doodsie lowered her voice in answer to her sister. 'Is he dat is de bad company.'

'Ah support im until election before las, me an me whole family, but not again. He runnin de country to ruin!'

'Huh!'

'Is not huh, Victoria. Open up you eyes an see!'

'Miss Doodsa-a-ay!'

'Woy!'

'Dat soun like Melda.'

Hop-an-Drop peeped over the wall, down into the path below.

'Is she self.'

'Ay! Watch youself dey, Hop! Take care you fall, non!'

'Eh, what do youself, Victoria? Since ah small ah in dis Delicia yard here, on dis lan wid dis same short foot, is today ah go get stupid an trow meself down den?'

'Miss Doodsie dey, Hop?'

'Yeh! Come up Melda! Come up!'

226

'Lemme put down dis heavy basket.'

'You come out in de garden?'

'Uh-huh! Ah come out an dig de potato. It ready.'

'What you climbin dey for, girl? Why you don pass roun an come up de step?'

Melda sucked her teeth. 'Move lemme pass, non!' She hoisted herself into the yard. Hop playfully lifted his stick at her. Melda ducked, wiped the sweat from her face, took the kata off her head. She stood blowing hard and using it as a fan. She dropped to sit on the ground.

'Fu! What smellin so?' She rolled away. 'How is here dog could come an do dat dey!' Melda rolled again to get further away from the spot. She half-lay on the ground, supported on her elbow. 'Miss Doodsie how you do? Oh, God, ah tired! But allyou hear de news?'

'What?'

They moved slowly towards her. Stood looking down at her. Melda slowly sat up. Sat back, supporting herself on both hands. She threw back her head, looked up at the faces encircling her.

'Well ah hear Leader out o de country!'

'Yeh! De radio say dat.'

'An he leave orders.' She looked around at the four faces circling her. Four mouths partly opened to catch the news.

'E leave orders to wipe the whole Horizon outa de sky.'

'What!?'

'To wipe out dose boys?'

'Ay! You mean . . . you mean . . .' Jessie fumbled with the words.

'To kill dem?' Doodsie supplied.

'Dat self!'

'Oh dat is why dey in hidin!'

'Jesus Lord, what happenin in dis lan at all!' Jessie made the sign of the cross. Absent-mindedly, they all followed her. All except Melda. She remained in the same position, supported on her hands. 'Ah say ah din like de way how dose dog howlin howlin dese las few nights!'

'Ah understan dat somebody tip dem off,' continued Melda, 'an dey disappear in dey hole like manicou.'

'Huh!' Victoria looked up at the sky. 'Lord! Lemme go, you hear!'

'Yes.' Hop took up the bag he usually carried slung across his shoulder. 'Ah better make it home.'

Melda struggled to her feet. Victoria moved off. Melda moved closer to Doodsie. 'You better warn you two dey, eh! Especially Rupert. He organisin in de area an dey have dey eyes on him!'

'Jesus God!' Doodsie looked up at the smiling blue sky. She made the sign of the cross and turned slowly towards the steps.

When God caan come, he does send

Doodsie got up early as usual. The sound of movement awakened Jessie. She got off the bed, pulled out the tensil. Crouched there over the tensil, she glanced at the clock. What do er at all? she thought. Half past five, yes. Outside dark still! She doh have little chilren to sen to school again dat she ha to hurry for, non! Even Carl is big man now he could see after himself. What do er at all? Dat is what you call people dat caan res! Jessie climbed back into bed. She drifted off into a light sleep.

Doodsie took the radio off the living-room shelf and carried it out to the kitchen. Put the clock next to it. Six o'clock ah gon put it on, she decided. She liked to listen to the early morning prayer. She washed the pots that had been left to soak the night before. Allyou dis damn pot an dem so disgustin, she accused them, all how ah scrub you you lookin like you never see wash. Musbe de stupid coalpoat ah usin to save de gas dat burnin up all you bottom so. Damn disgustin! She hummed:

> 'The Lord is my shepherd
> I sha-a-all not want
> He ma-a-kes me down to lie
> In pa-a-stures green
> He lea-ea-deth me
> The qui-i-et waters by.'

Angel was staying that night with Jerry's sister, whom everyone knew as Sister, and her husband Martin. Angel and Jerry had been to a union meeting and had spent such long hours arguing

228

afterwards with Martin and Sister, that Sister had said, 'Stay non! Use the other room!'

Sister got up early. She wanted to get a bottle ready for Kwame. She glanced at the clock. Five-thirty. Ah mus put de radio on after six to hear de news, she decided. Angel heard her moving about in the kitchen. She turned, snuggled down, pulled up the covers.

'You awake?'

'Non. Sleepin!'

'Ah just caan sleep. Whole night, you know.'

'Hm-m-m!' Angel was drifting off to sleep.

'Leader gettin desperate!' Jerry cleared his throat. 'Ah had a hell of a row wid me ole man! For him Leader is like a god. He is Leader campaign organiser for nex election.'

'Ah know. Ah know.'

Doodsie turned on her radio at six o'clock. A buzzing sound. Uh, stupid, dey late again. She turned it down low. Five past six. The buzzing still there. What do dem at all today? Eight minutes past six. Low music. Ay! What do dem dis morning? Six-fifteen. *This is the voice of the free people!* Damn stupid plate break! What! Doodsie swung around. Stood staring at the radio. What was that? She frowned. *'I repeat, this is the voice of the free people of Grenada! The Leader government has been over-thrown! I repeat . . .'* Doodsie grabbed the radio, stared down at it, *'the Leader government has been overthrown!'*

'Allyou! Allyou come! Come! Allyou oy-y!'

'What? What do, Mammie?'

'You awright, Doodsie?'

'What all dis noise?'

'What happen, Mammie?'

'Allyou listen! Listen!'

They stood. They gazed at the radio in Doodsie's outstretched hands.

Sister put on her radio at six-ten. Ay! Music? Wey de news? Ah ain miss it? De clock musbe wrong!

'Martin! Come an iron dis ting here lemme make de breakfas! Martin!'

'Hm-m-m?'

'Boy get up! You too damn lazy!'

'What time it is? It six o'clock yet, non?'

'Long!'

Martin answered from the room. 'It jus gone six. What you get up so early for?' He snuggled down.

'Boy get up eh! You too damn lazy!' Sister went to the room; she pulled the covers away; ignored Martin's fretting. She went back out to the kitchen and turned up the radio.

'This is the voice of the free people!' Sister frowned. Who voice dat?

'I repeat . . . this is the voice of the free people of Grenada!' Sister stared at the radio. 'How dat soun like Apechu so?'

'I repeat . . .'

'Martin!'

'The Leader government has been overthrown!'

'Oh Gawd! Martin! Oh Gawd, oh Gawd! Martin! Angel! Jerry! Allyou come!'

'What do?'

'You awright?'

'What? Whappen?

From inside, Kwame screamed. Sister held Angel by the shoulder. Eyes wide, she pointed at the radio.

'Oh Gawd!' she said. 'Oh God, ah cole!'

'The Leader government has been overthrown!'

'Eh?'

'What?'

'Dey not serious?'

'Wait wait! Allyou listen!'

'The Leader government has been overthrown! People are asked to . . .'

'Ay! What de . . .'

'Wo-o-y! Blow shell!'

'An is de 13th, you know.' Jessie laughed. 'Never trus dat number at all. You never know what it will bring!'

'Well dis time it bring something good.'

'But for days you coulda feel something different in de air!'

'Ay-ay! ay-ay!' Allan's face wore an unbelieving sort of half-smile. His hands were stuck an awkward unrestful angle away from his body. 'Well what is dis at all? Ay-ay! Ay-ay!'

'Wait! Listen! Listen!'

All over the country, the streets were a mass of people shouting, waving sticks, beating pans. In Leader's home village, a few people stood at the sides of the road, arms folded, lips pouted, watching the joy in the impromptu carnival.

'Dey tink is so? It won go so, though! Is not so, non!'

'Dey playin dey don know bout ballot box? Is not so, non!'

In Hermitage, a crowd stood in Paren Comesee's yard. Maisie cradled her grandchild, thinking: Dis ting not good at all, non! How dey could do de man dat? Is true ting wasn always for de bes, but he did try! How dey could do de man dat? She watched her son leaning against the mango tree. He was blowing a conch shell. As she watched, he threw back his head and laughed. 'Is better times ahead!' he shouted. 'We slay de dragon wid we bare hands! Mammie girl, it go be better!' The people laughed, shifted their sticks, watching, waiting. They looked from him to Maisie.

'Allyou blow shell!' he shouted. 'Blow shell!' He put his mouth to the conch shell.

In the streets in the capital, some people were just standing still and shouting.

'Wey im? He gon away? Well let im stay wherever he is!'

'Non! Let im come back! We want im back! Let im come back an explain heself!'

'Woy! Makomè! We do it!'

'Ay!'

And they sang:

> 'Carry me over the wa-a-ter
> Carry me over de sea-ea-ea!
> Carry me over de wa-a-a-a-a-ter!'

Melda led a group chanting:

> 'Ah want to hear my African drumming
> Give me my African chant . . .'

It was a chant Melda had sung often in Carriacou where she had grown up.

Whistles blew.

231

'Allyou les head for de police station!' shouted Melda above the din. 'De radio say make dem put up white flag. Is dey we goin!'

We doin we own ting!

At a New York switchboard one April morning, Simon, doing the ten to five shift, was so engrossed in his letter that he hardly heard the greetings of those who passed by on their way to their rooms. He handed out keys with an impatient frown. What bee's in his bonnet today? they wondered. He's usually such a pleasant fellow.

> *Simon, you could imagine!* Angel had written. *It went something like: This is Radio Grenada. We repeat. The Leader Government has been overthrown. Then they asked the police stations to put out white flags and asked people to go out on to the streets to stop anyone trying to cause trouble. By the time I tell you dat, me an Jerry were dressing, pulling on things to go outside. And Sister self shouting, 'Wait! Wait! we don even know if is true.' Martin self shouting, 'How you mean if is true. You think them fellas in the radio station could make joke so unless they want they neck cut out?' And all Sister could do is laugh and keep on saying the same thing over and over. Simon, I can't even tell you in a sensible step by step fashion what really went on.*

Simon grinned. He had read the story umpteen times in different letters, and they all said the same thing: I can't even tell you in a sensible step by step fashion.

> *But you could imagine the feeling in the whole country that day. Look, eh, with that announcement is like the whole of Grenada was in the street going to get police stations to put up white flag an ting . . .*

'Woy o yoy!' Simon laughed, scratched his head, looked up at the clock.

> *You ever see that! Revolution directed by radio! Tout moun out*

232

*in the streets, Simon! Was like carnival. If people didn want
that change, eh, nutting coulda happen, because is people dat
go out an get dose police to put up white flag an ting! You
should see Melda! Remember Melda dat use to work under
Delicia cocoa! You shoulda see Melda leadin a side! Simon,
was something else! Mammie all right. When I went up by her,
she was actually crying real tears and saying, 'We win! We
win!' Boy she something else you know.'*

Simon scratched his head, bit his fingernail. He laughed
again.

'Letter from home?'

Simon looked up at the bearded white face.

'Yes. Room forty?'

'Yes, thank you.'

'It's in your country recently there was some sort of coup or
something, isn't it?'

'Er . . . yes.'

'Strange for that part of the world, isn't it?'

Simon nodded.

'It's close to the Virgin Islands, isn't it?'

'That region. But a long way off.'

'Oh! Well! See you later, then. No messages?'

'No.' Simon glanced at the box. Touched the cubby-hole.
'Nothing.'

The man walked off, nodding.

*Daddy self was jus repeating 'Woy! That is a serious move, you
know, a serious move.'*

'Woy! Oh, Gawd!' Simon grinned. Put his hand over his
mouth. Looked up. 'Lord! Ah forget wey ah is!'

*And he saying 'Ay-ay! ay-ay!' You know how he careful
arready. He and Leader hadn't been doing too well recently
and he been gettin some pressure, so I don't think he's too sorry
but I suppose he's kind of waiting to see what will happen and
then move with the breeze.*

'Huh!' Simon glanced at the clock.

But you know Mammie. She not waiting. She is the biggest revolutionary. You should hear her saying things like 'Is only forward now'. Boy, Simon, if you were here you would laugh too much. So that is it. Now you don't have to wonder what you will do when you are finished studying. We waiting for you. We need you for nation-building, you hear!

The phone rang. Simon picked it up automatically, his eyes still on the letter.

'Yes, sir. No, he hasn't been here yet, sir. I'll give you a tinkle when he arrives, sir!'

You should see your young(!) brother. No joke, Simon. There's nothing 'little' about Rupert. He's clearer on issues than I am. When I think how less than ten years ago, that boy didn't even know what Vietnam was, I have to laugh! You remember the Egg Nog? Even Carl talkin about 'we Revo'! Is a thing to see, not to tell. Is a new beginning, I tell you.

I'll tell you more next time. Meanwhile, all the best. And do mind that right hand, which seems to have been broken. Find yourself some paper and write me, you good for nothing. Hope you're very well. Take care of yourself and don't let them work you too hard up there. Lots of love.

Your dearest sister,
Angel.

Simon folded the letter. He leaned against the counter. Ah feel like goin home, boy! Imagin missin all of dat! Since dis ting happen, every day I jus feel like goin home!

Angel's excitement reverberated in faces and smiles and songs and drums and steelbands throughout the country. The cocoa trees rustled with unruly delight, the banana leaves moved in the breeze. The sea bashed itself up on the beaches. The sand glinted silvery white and welcomed the water into its depths.

Everybody puttin dey grain o salt!

'Miss Doodsa-a-ay!' Melda was shouting from where they always called 'below the road', under the wall by the grapefruit tree.

'Aye!'

'How tings? Wey me chile? Wey Angel? She dey?'

'Chile? Dat big ole horse is chile too den? What heavy bag you have on you head dey?'

'Some yam ah jus dig up!'

'Oh ho!'

'Not long ah plant de ting, non, an dey well good arready! Ah know you have some dat ready so ah won't offer you two.'

'Non. We get a good few this time.'

'Well I won't keep you.'

'What about your own dey? What about Micey?'

'Well she doin awright, yes. She teachin now, you know. In the school up the road.'

'Yes. Ah did hear dat. Since last September, non?'

'Uh-huh! An is so she hot up hot up in Revo jus like Angel and she age-partner dey. Rupert! How he an de army?'

'He awright. Dey strong, me chile!'

'Meself ah strong too, yes. I in all dose meetin ah hear what goin on. Well how! I want to know what doin wid we country, yes! You mus come!'

'Me? Dey don want me so, girl. Dat is young people ting.'

'What do you? What about me? Me teeth nearly fallin arready, yes. You mus come an hear ting goin!'

Doodsie laughed. 'You good, girl. Meself, from de corner here, ah givin dem every ounce o support ah could manage.'

'You frien Veronica an she people dey don please, non! Dey only grumblin an talkin about how nice Leader was!'

'Ah chuts! Dem livin in de stone age, wi!'

'Oh Gawd, look how Miss Doodsie makin me fall down here, non! She say stone age, wi! Don kill me here today, non!'

Doodsie sucked her teeth.

'Anyway, lemme leave you to prepare you husband food, you hear. Greet me daughter give me when you see er, eh!'

'When ah see er is right!'

'Is so it is, chile!'

Doodsie turned to go inside. Melda settled the weight better on her head. Her body moved to the tight rhythm enforced by the heavy bag as she went through the cocoa on her way home.

You tink was a easy lesson?

Teaching became more difficult. The students questioned, argued, listened to political speeches and asked all sort of questions about other countries. Angel was in a constant fever of excitement.

'Miss, you hear the US President's speech last night, Miss?'
'Yes.'

Angel looked around the class. Some faces were eager, some uninterested. Lisa pulled out her *Macbeth*. The fifth-form classroom was like a mini-theatre space. The long benches were high above her, sloping up towards the back. She put down *Macbeth*, leaned against the desk.

'You heard it, Miss!'
'Yes. I listened.'
'Woy! That was fire, yes, Miss.'
'Yeh, boy, big talk down de line!'
'Hear how de boy talkin bad, non!'

There were giggles around the classroom.

'So youself you talkin better den?' someone asked.

'He not talkin bad. He's speaking a different language, that's all. It's no better or no worse than English.'

'Is not dat Cambridge want though!'

'True! So we learn English, but it isn't better than our own language.'

'Miss, lewwe discuss de President speech today, Miss. Tomorrow we go do the *Macbeth*, Miss.'

'Miss, I don find that make sense, Miss. Don take dem on. He Jason always want to talk about politics. Dat caan help us pass the exams, Miss. Even self we usin de class for language, lewwe do the precis, eh, Miss.'

'Boy you really backward. That is about we, boy, about we life. What you talkin about precis? Miss, lewwe talk eh, Miss.'

'I find . . .'

'Okay! Okay! How about if we go ahead with the precis lesson? We have a double period today. We have the speech on tape and it has been transcribed. How about if I pass around copies and we do a precis of the American President's address to the Congress last week? I'll give you thirty minutes to read the address and do that. Then we could use it as the springboard for our discussion. Okay?'

236

A babble of sound. Lisa's voice emerges.

'Miss, I think we could just do the discussion and no precis.'

Jeremy: 'No, Miss. We have to do the precis.' Encouraged by a subdued buzz of agreement around him, Jeremy continues, 'And furthermore, Miss, I don't see what sense it make precising the President speech, Miss. Cambridge not goin to give us that for exams, Miss.'

'Aw, shut up! I never see a boy so . . .'

'I agree with Jeremy, Miss. When time come for exams, Miss...'

'Yes, Miss. It don't make sense doing that, Miss. We have enough past paper to revise, Miss.'

'Miss, let's not do no precis, Miss. As long as we could discuss and get a-a- what you always tell us, Miss, a – clear vision of concepts and ideas, Miss.'

There was some laughter, some jeers. Some students sucked their teeth.

'Concepts and ideas, what! You only want to follow you stupid brother wid he big talk! Go an tell Cambridge about concepts and ideas come June.'

'Okay! Okay! The important thing as far as your precis exam is concerned is understanding the *concept* of the precis and being able to apply it to your work, not only for the particular passage from Cambridge, but for any passage. So we'll do a precis of the President's speech.'

'But, Miss!'

'Great, Miss!'

'Miss!'

'Okay. Enough talk about it now. I . . . er . . . I've . . .'

'Ay! Miss, what you laughing at, Miss?'

'Aw! What do Miss all of a sudden?'

'Okay! Okay!' Angel tried to stifle her laughter. How to tell them that she was thinking of Rupert and Vietnam!

'Miss!'

'Yes. Erm . . . all right!' Angel held up her hands to get their attention. 'I've heard enough ideas on this. I've made a decision. If we begin now,' she looked up at the clock on the wall, 'we'll have time for discussion later.'

Murmurs. 'Dictatorship.' 'Aw-w-w-aw! Well, Miss!' 'You well right, Miss!' 'Good!' Lisa: 'Before time we use to well siddown an do we precis!' Jason: 'True. Is different times, girl!'

'Jason, this doesn't mean precis is at an end. It's a necessary skill. You're just learning to make it apply to what's going on in the world around you. Okay?'

'Yeh. I dey wid dat, Miss.'

Miss smiled.

In the staffroom the battle raged. Some of the teachers said that there was too much politics in the school these days. Angel said that politics was never out of the school, never had been. Some of the teachers said 'Ah chuts!'

'But before when Leader used to want to put politics in everything, we self used to complain.'

'But that was different, Brian. That time it was a case of if you not Leaderite, crapaud smoke you pipe. I mean, it wasn even so bad for those like us so who have little bit of education an could probably go somewhere else, even out of the country, but for people working on estates an ting, on roads . . .'

'So it different now?'

'Oh, gosh, Brian! You know it different. That is jus pure bias!'

'Okay! Okay! I know youall don't victimise people like Leader and plenty Leaderite still have job an ting, and a lot of things good.' Brian turned, shouted to someone near his desk. 'Close de blasted window, non! You doh see de rain drizzlin in on me books?'

'Awright! Awright! You jus like a blasted Papason!' Gale pulled away the stick that kept the window up, pulled down the heavy board window.

'Papason? Who is Papason?' Gifta laughed.

'You don know Papason? He livin up on de road by me, dey. Quarrelin from mornin till night! One time . . .' Gale giggled, unperturbed that she had disturbed the flow of the argument. They listened. 'One time, rain start to come while he up in de mountain. De ting so in he skin, he up dey thinkin how he sure Mamain – dat is he wife – will have the door shet so tight dat he won be able to take off he boots quick when he reach down an go inside an shelter. So he run down in a rage, boy.' Gale rushed half-way round the room. 'When he reach down the door part-way open, you know, she push a cloth to stick it little bit open so he won have no trouble. He so surprise that he stan up. Den he shout out . . .' Gale lifted her head high. 'Mamain! Main-o-o! Shet de door, shet de door, Papa wettin!'

238

Gale giggled. Collapsed against a desk. Some of the others chuckled. Some sucked their teeth.

'Ah chuts, Gale!'

'You too lie!'

'An . . .' Gale was still giggling. 'An . . . he leave runnin . . . he run back up in de mountain go an look for a place to shelter!'

'Gale you too stupid!'

'Bon Jé dis girl dotish yeh!'

Gale sat at her desk, her head down, holding her belly and giggling while the laughter roared around her.

Brian chuckled. Pursed his lips. He pulled his exercise books together. The laughter subsided gradually.

'I not in dis politics business,' continued Brian, 'but I'm not comfortable with all this hailing of Cuba and Nicaragua. Next thing we know we going communist.'

'I hear, eh, Angel, that in international conferences we even talkin more comfortably with countries like Zimbabwe and Mozambique than wid St Lucia that right next door.'

'So because they next door? You always agree with the opinions of you next door neighbour?'

'I mean, Zimbabwe an dem little better, because at least they black, but you caan trus them payul an dem in those Latin countries. They don like black people, you know.'

'But, Gifta, you caan look at it narrow as dat! Dey have endless racist attitudes, in truth. But why? Is because of the same damn history that have fair-skin people here still feeling dey high-up! White was right, and the nearer you been to white, the righter you was! But we have to fight against dat, an as long as people respect our right to choose wey we goin and what we doin, we could talk to dem – as black people with the particular experience of our own history!'

'Wo-o-o-y!' Gale looked at Angel with mock-admiration. She pushed the glasses higher on her nose. Arms akimbo, she stated, 'You mus run for election, girl! You have me vote firs ting!'

'Somebody put er outside gimme, please!'

Gale laughed. 'Dat is what you call silencin de opposition! Allyou see? Huh! It don easy, non! Ay-ay! An is not even opposition, you know! Ah supportin, yes! Well ah tell you! Dis is a hard life, boy!'

Angel opened her mouth to continue. Her right forefinger went up preparatory to emphasising some point.

'Awright, awright, Angel! Ah caan take it!' Gifta broke in. 'Allyou would never imagine me an dis woman go to same school at aroun same time! Believe me, girl, ah don know wey you get these ideas an dem! I even go university jus two years after she, you know!'

'Is true!' Gale looked at Angel with suspicion. 'Is true, you know! Allyou come outa de same water barrel, so to speak!'

'But we don stan up one place. We go on findin out what history is all about an why we been prayin!'

'I don need to know dat to know that communism is not what I want for Grenada.'

'So what is communism?'

'All of us hear about what does go on in Russia. People can't go to church, although I know that won't bother you dis, Angel, in these days.'

Gale chuckled. 'Ah not gettin into dat! Brian! Brian, hush you mout! De two o dem come out of de same crabhole. Dey accustom prayin together! Let dem sort out deyself!'

'If they even see you prayin, you in trouble. And nobody could really own anything!'

'Non,' said Gale, 'well dat is not me line at all.'

'For somebody who suppose to read a lot, Gifta, ah find you should at least want to investigate things people say. I find you should at least investigate. Where you get dat news from? You never feel sad that after we pray we never even try to look for books to find out what history is all about? We never even curious. We jus take what people tell us an say "Yes, Massa. Yes, Baas. Yes, Ma'am. You say so, so ah sure is so, Ma'am" '

'True.' Gale was suddenly serious. 'You damn right, dat is what we do. We always swallowin. Never makin de drink or even watchin how it make.'

'Right!' Angel stretched out her hands towards Gale. 'Eh? We never even try to find out more about what Russia is, if they policies good, if they bad, or even if we could really make a change and still do things different to them. Our education was so perfect that we never even try to find out what other people in the world do, who other people is, or nothing. We did just know bout Britain an we feel we British, so we great! Poor djab us!'

'But wait, non!' Gale stood in the middle of the room. 'It have more worl dan us an dem?'

The bell rang. Teachers shuffled papers. Chairs were scraped back. Brian straightened up from leaning against his desk. He shook his head. 'It not dat simple, girl! It not dat simple at all!'

Pwangad waya piké mwen!

During the run-up to elections for the teachers' union, most of the teachers from Angel's school campaigned, some secretly, others, like Brian and Gifta, openly, to ensure that Angel and those who shared her views did not get on to the executive. Gifta looked mutinous and kept away from Angel. Brian explained his position.

'Me? I fraid allyou, Angel. These ideas youall have dey not me style. Allyou talkin about bourgeois and reducing influence of big business an all kine o ting that soun like danger talk to me.'

At the union meeting, the old executives retained their leadership. Bitterly disappointed, Angel kept her eyes on the colours of the flag at the back of the room as she made an impassioned speech denouncing the prevalence of 'backward, reactionary ideas'. Feeling defeated, she went home.

'Lord, Mammie, some of those teachers so damn backward is a shame. You should hear Gifta! You remember Gifta that was in school wid me?'

'Hm. Backward how?'

'All de same old stupid ideas. No new thoughts of changing curriculum and having new approach to language an . . .well you know what ah mean! I did jus feel like heavin dem out de window!'

'So what dat would o do? Change dey ideas or mash up dey head? Look, somebody move dis cat outa me foot before ah throw it to kingdom come, eh!'

The cat moved against her legs. Frowning, Doodsie kicked out her feet.

'How come you have cat again?' Angel laughed at her.

'Not me. Allan an Jessie dat feel dey mus have cat becus dey hear two rat in de kitchen. Me? Ah prefer twenty rat-trap! Move, cat! If you come back here, you dead.'

'Leave de cat alone, non!'

'But I serious, you know, Angel. How allyou expect everybody to agree wid everyting one time? Me, I more revolutionary dan allyou.' The crochet needles clacked. 'Dammit! Look you make me drop a stitch!'

'Me!' Angel watched her mother look for the dropped stitch. 'Look! Look it dey!'

'Move you skin! Ah try me bes wid you but you caan crochet to save you life!'

Angel watched.

'Anyway, we well boo dem afterwards!'

'What!' Doodsie moved her head to look at her daughter's face. She sat back and pounded the arm of the chair, laughing. 'Well ah never hear more! You not serious? Allyou boo dem?'

'How?'

'Wey you ever hear you change people mine by booin dem down? Dey more dan allyou in dat group, dey winnin vote an you booin dem? Joke you makin!'

'Dey want improvement, but dey doh want tings to change.'

'Ah don say non, but . . .' Doodsie shrugged her shoulders.

'Mammie how you tink tings goin?'

'Well good. Well well good. We caan do everyting one time. You have to creep before you could walk. People sayin a lot o tings but we goin to make it. And the airport they buildin now is something we been waitin for for a long time. God is good.'

'They sayin a lot of things about the airport too.'

'Yes. Ah know. Jack sit down right here in this very yard, on the copper you see outside there, yesterday self, and tell me that the airport is base for Cuba and Russia. Ah say ah chuts, Ki bés sa? We need the b . . . a . . . sted airport . . .' Doodsie mumbled the word as she did any word that might be considered obscene, ' . . . they dey talkin stupidness.'

'But what happen to dem wid dis base idea at all?'

'Chile, you know what I tink? Look at us!' Doodsie threw her arms wide. The grey hair made a perfect fringe around her head. The home dress was clean, the faded brown flowers settling into the pale brown of the material. Every day she gettin to look more like Grannie, thought Angel. Same shape an everything. 'Eh? Look at us! We don even have one good airport. America musbe have about three hundred. So if all airport that size is base, America musbe have about three hundred or more. What do if we have one? An America lettin who dey want use their base, so because we poor we not folks too? What we do wid ours

242

is we business!'

'You don hear talk! Dat is revolutionary, wi!'

Angel stood at the window. She looked outside at the copper.

'Is not today dis copper self musbe dey, non!'

'Right out dey he siddown! Right out dey on de copper!'

'You was born arready when dey use to dance on cocoa in de copper?'

'Ay! How! Dat is yesterday ting, yes. Is a while now dey stop, but all de time I was little girl in those De Lisle people yard, people still dancing on the cocoa! In de yard in his Hermitage property, Mr De Lisle had a big one jus like the one you see outside dey. As a child ah could remember people inside dey wid headtie, holdin on to the rim of de copper in a circle so,' Doodsie put down her crochet, stood up. She leaned her body slightly forward, indicated a circle, and grasped the rim of an imaginary copper. 'Man an woman, man an woman, dancin on it so, so . . . an singin, girl:

'Manman o!
Manman o
Mwen wivé
Mwen wivé

Mama o
Mwen wivé
Pwangad waya piké mwen!

'An dey dancin, man, an it have others beatin drum an is dance, so, so.'

'Come! Come! Lemme do it, too!'

'Manman, o, mwen wivé!'

Doodsie laughed, sucking her teeth and sank back into her chair. 'Girl, ah too ole for dat, you hear! Move dey lemme do me work!'

The crochet needles clacked. Doodsie held the work closer to her eyes as she concentrated on the pattern. She stopped, her lips moving as she counted the stitches. She glanced at Angel.

'All you just keep allyou head. Dis is something powerful. Allyou don let it go, non. Ay! Huh! Secondary school free.

Education in swing! Where you ever hear dat in dis Grenada here? Huh! Chile, ah don believe allyou even know how much good allyou doin.' The crochet needles clacked. Doodsie whispered: 'One, two, three.' Angel's mind automatically registered 'Look at Mr Lee' and waited for 'Three, four, five.' 'Sometime ah tink ah woulda prefer to see you in far country workin for good money, but if is so dis ting is, an it helpin us, is so it is. All you jus keep allyou head!'

Doodsie looked up. 'One thing though, Angel. You mus go to church. Ah not sayin ah want to hear allyou shout God like how Leader used to do just before he go an do all he wickedness, but you mus at leas go to church, Angel. God not sleepin. An whether Chief an dem realise it or not, this government is God own. Chile, God works in mysterious ways!' The crochet needles clacked. 'So you mus go to church and give God de praise!'

'Hm.'

'What you mean hm?'

'Ah mean . . .' Angel scratched her head. 'Ah mean ah didn know God wake up. Ah really thought he did sleepin still.'

'Chupes.' Doodsie's elbow nudged her daughter gently off the arm of the chair. 'Girl move dey before ah throw you down eh!'

'Ay!' Angel fell with a louder thump than the gentle push warranted.

Doodsie sucked her teeth.

'What about Daddy, by de way?'

'Ay-ay! He talkin revolution too, yes.'

'You jokin!'

'Non, girl. He is revolutionary, yes. Well you know how he an Leader wasn doin too well? An now he like how de Revo movin wid agriculture, so he in line.'

'Ay!' Angel rolled about on the floor. 'Well é ben wi! Wid action like dat, no wonder God wakin up!' She sat up. 'Ah know dat, you know. He realise how much he go miss if he ain take a stretch an a yawn an see what goin on!'

Doodsie cut her eyes at her daughter. She sucked her teeth, and chuckled as Angel danced away singing, 'Pwangad waya piké mwen!'

Is a sure sign! Enemy in de bush

Angel dreamt about snakes. She had been walking along the

244

Delicia road on her way out to a meeting. She had thought of making a short cut through the track down the hill, then had decided not to. It had rained; the cocoa leaves would be slippery. She walked the long way. Just as she came to the spot where the short cut would have ended, she heard a sound. She paused, looked up at the hog-plum tree. A snake's head curled towards her from the bushes behind the trunk. Angel jumped back. The snake's head stretched out towards her, stretched, stretched, stretched, until the whole body was stretched right across the road and now the snake was a big kwibo. It turned its head and kept its eyes fixed upon Angel; they say a kwibo could wind itself round your body and break your bones. Angel screamed and woke up. Aunt Jessie said, 'Eh-h-e-h? Snake? Dat not good dream, non! You have some enemy somewey dat you don know about.' Rupert said, 'Dat okay, most of us ha dat!' Carl said, 'You should o call me, girl!' Allan said, 'Huh! dat don sound good!' Doodsie said, 'If you stuff youself wid green mango before you go an sleep, you don expec to dream about snake an kwibo?'

Someting boilin under de surface!

Grenada
June 1980

Jerry,

How you do? This is just a short letter. Things are a bit hot these days. There's all kinds of talk in the air. I'll tell you more about it some other time. I hope you can get back for the holidays. Will the scholarship cover that?

Yes. I know you're the one owing me a letter but I decided to write because of something awful that has happened. Perhaps by now you've heard of what happened a few days ago. Two people were killed in Chantimelle. One of them was Jason. Remember Jason who I taught? I was in Dominica when I got the news. He had written to me just a few days before excited about becoming a pilot, saying that he had hopes of getting a scholarship to go to Mexico. Do you remember him? He was always very talkative and excited; no big set of revolutionary, but really excited about the changes and the opportunities. He used to come down to meetings with me sometimes.

245

I'm not too sure what's boiling under the surface, but some people seem to be feeling things are going too fast, while others think they are going too slow. And there are those who just want to see the whole process stopped. The murders were apparently a part of the activity against the revolution. There's a big hunt on now for the murderers. I'll let you know what happens.

Take care of yourself. I don't need to tell you that the Revolution needs you. Your Mom sends her love. I think your Dad is still regretting that he didn't have the opportunity to campaign for Leader.

Lots of love,
Angel.

We runnin neck an neck wid you!

On the large billboard outside the new community centre, there was the image of three clenched fists. A woman's hand, a man's hand, crossed at the wrists, a child's hand coming up in between. The culmination, three fists clenched and powerful. The billboard held the words A PEOPLE UNITED. Inside, a zonal council meeting was in progress.

The youth chairing the meeting was Melda's son. He was a parish coordinator.

'Les bring the meeting to order, please! Les bring de meeting to order, please! Tonight we have wid us Mr Flanders, Head of the Water Commission and Mr Wellington from the Public Works Department. They will report on what they have done since the requests put to them at our last meeting and answer any further questions we have. But first of all we will start the evening with a skit from the area women's group and two poems – one from Sister Miona Spencer of the Literacy Programme and one from Brother Melvyn Chateau. We'll start with Sister Miona! Sister Miona!

'Yeh! Come on, Sister!

Whistles.

'Roll it, Sister.'

Sister Miona walked out onto the stage. She was a woman perhaps in her fifties, her headtie was in the red and black colours which symbolised the revolution. She wore a full black skirt and a bright red shirt. Sister Miona gave a clenched fist salute.

246

'Long live the struggle!' she shouted.

There was a scraping of chairs. People leapt to their feet.

'Long live!' came the answer. Fists went up into the air.

'Long live the struggle of the Nicaraguan people!'

'Long live!'

'Sisters and brothers, long live struggling peoples the world over!'

'Long live!'

'Awright, sisters and brothers!'

The people sat down.

'Sisters and brothers, this poem that I will do for you I write jus a few weeks ago when ah siddown an really tink bout wey we is today an wey we comin from! I have it in me pocket here, but de eyes not too good today, you know. I forget de glasses, so I hope I could remember it well. But ah sure ah could remember it.' Miona cleared her throat.

'Ay! Well we try it in '51!
We say come pa come
Ting bad for so
Take up we burden
We go help you go!
Pa take up we burden
He take up he purse
An when he purse get so heavy
He caan carry de burden
An hol on to purse
He throw down we burden
Down on de groun!
So we cant im over!'

The crowd roared. Miona walked across the stage. Made the canting motion with her hand again. Moved her body as though preparing to lift and cant over a heavy weight. Repeated: 'So we cant im over!'

'Woo-oo-oo!'

'Bow! Bow! Heavy, sister! Right on target!'

Whistles.

Sister Miona opened her mouth. 'Sh-h-h!' The people were silent, waiting to hear the rest.

'De Horizon come up
Pa star go down!
An we watchin de Horizon
Like is really a dream
Becus
Hear, non!'

Miona leaned confidentially towards her audience. Heads craned forward towards her.

'Me at me age ah in school again!
Wey you ever hear dat
In dis country here!
Me granchilren in secondary
Dey not payin a cent!
Ay! Wey you ever hear dat
In dis country here.'

'Uh-huh!'
'True!'

'So Horizon go on
We neck an neck wid you
Don throw down we burden, non!
We dependin on you
Don throw down we burden, non!
Ting too sweet for dat!'

Sister Miona bowed. Whistles.
'Wo-o-y!'
'The sister really good, you know.'
'Thank you, sisters and brothers!' Miona left the stage, walking back down into the audience. People turned, applauding her as she passed by, shaking her hand.
'You could give me a copy of it, sister?'
'It really good, sister.'
'Heavy, sister.'
'Yes. Thank you very much, Sister Miona. Sisters and brothers, that is the kind of talent that was there hidin all de

248

time, dat the revolution bringing to light. Yes! Yes! Awright, comrades! Les go on wid de programme! We have a lot to do tonight!'

When it was time to question the public officials, one or two people made their way from the back to try and find seats towards the front.

'Lemme get a good place where ah could hear what dey sayin about dis water business! Ah don want to miss nothing!'

'The roads! Ah want to hear good what happenin wid de road!'

'Now the position is this. In a situation such as the one in which we find ourselves, there are certain variables to be considered . . .'

'Mr Wellington!'

'Look me han up in de corner here!'

'Comrade!'

'Well, Comrade Chairman, do you job, non!'

'Okay! Okay! The brother over there in the green shirt! Ask you question, comrade!'

'Mr Wellington, ah jus want to say dat what you start to say dey ain make no sense, comrade. We want you to break it up! We don want you to wrap up nutting in big word so dat we caan understand. Is information we want, an we want it clear an simple!'

'Heavy! Da is it!'

'Non, is awright, ah don want to ask nutting again. Is de same ting ah was goin to say.'

'Yes, sister?'

'I jus want to say that I in the literacy programme. Not all of us did go to High School, through no fault o we own. So jus give us de ting straight an simple, like, an ting settle.'

'Okay. Thank you, sister. Anybody have a different point to make or . . . Awright! Comrade, you want to continue an answer the criticisms?'

'Yes. Yes. I accept that.' Mr Wellington laughed, passed his hand round the back of his head. 'We learnin too, you know. But you're right. You have a point there. I'll break it up. You see, we have to give more attention to the feeder roads, to fix those that farmers need to transport their bananas and cocoa an tings first. Especially the bananas. If the roads bad an de bananas get bruise, it mean de country lose money an we don even have to fix the rest of the roads. So we have to be – to be – to be talkin to the agricultural department all the time, to arrange with them for fixing up those roads first . . .'

'Yes, but how long dat going to take? You tell us dat since las year June, ah tink! A whole year, now.'

'We aimin to fix thirty miles of feeder roads; if we were a rich country with money, we could jus snap we fingers and do that quickly, but we have to take it bit by bit.'

'Ah don lyin non! Ah fed up, all ah know is dat is years now ah walkin dat road in de same condition, an ah tired get me foot juk up!'

'True, yes!'

'True, yes!'

'Comrades, I think we correct to be upset, but we have to be conscious, too, of the fact that a lot is being done in other areas and as de comrade say we not a rich country, so we have to wait a little bit for some things. We gettin free education now, houses gettin fixed, free milk for children an so on, and a lot of money spendin on airport which will bring money into the country. So we ha to take tings bit by bit.'

'True. But chair de meetin, comrade, an let de people give dey speech!'

'Hey! What do dat boy at all?'

'Well he chairin de meetin!'

'I have a question. Why it is that even now wid de new system we install, water in my area go for one whole day an a half jus las week?'

'I could explain that. It was last Tuesday and Wednesday morning. There was a particular problem with the pump. It wasn't pumping up the water as it should because something was wrong with the electricity in the equipment. It all right, now. We fix it, so you shouldn't have that problem again. Is teething pains, comrades.'

At the end, they decided it wasn't a bad meeting.

'Sister Miona poem was heavy, girl!'

'What they say was true, you know, is jus dat ah fed up wid de roads, man. Ah wish those other things would reach a good stage, so we could turn we attention to that.'

'True, true, but everything does take time, boy!'

'Uh-huh! We on the road, anyway! Is just to be vigilant.'

'You right, wi! Da is de watchword! Be vigilant!'

Eleven

A letter arrived from Janice in Brooklyn. She wrote it, she said, when she could tief a chance from the people work.

What the hell's happening? What is all this thing I hearing bout bomb and thing exploding under people where they sitting down? I hearing all kind of rumour about confusion at the top but at least I know that not true because those boys sticking together in spite of what people up this side wishing. But what the hell going on, Angel? You know me, I not in youall politics business, but it look to me like that thing going good, and people supporting it, so allyou stop gettin suspicious and stupid every time you hear some little piece of talk, because I hear that is what going on. So ah hear Rupert in the army? Carl still following he father in the agriculture?

She asked Angel to drop by and visit her mother, to find out if her little girl was still giving the grandmother trouble and 'acting like is devil child'.

And Angel, write and tell me what the hell going on in the country!

Then came a surprise letter. Everyone was making contact.

Dear Angel,
This isn't a missive from outer space. I still do exist in this arena. How are you? I'm writing now because someone mentioned that they'd met you during a visit to Grenada. I

251

*thought you were still somewhere out in the wider world. You
intended going somewhere when we lost touch. So you're part
of the process? How's it going? Are you finding the answers we
felt had to be found? Is it rewarding? Is it going somewhere?
Me? I'm still teaching. Trying to teach young people the joys of
Social Sciences and encouraging them to make a career in the
Social Sciences! Would you believe it! Actually, it's not too bad
now because I've discovered that I really do enjoy the subject. I
also do a course in Literature and I've discovered that there are
sides to people like Shelley that are really quite exciting and
thought-provoking, which is no doubt why they were never
introduced to me. So! I'm coping.*

*Barbara sends her love. Says she may visit you one day if
we're in that part of the Caribbean. Might be later in the year.
Or you should visit us if you're ever in Jamaica. Well, take it
easy. I hope the pinch of the protective power doesn't get to you
as it did to us. It's hell. Take care. We'll talk more some day.
No chance of my ever forgetting you, even when we lose touch
by mail.*

With deep love,
Kai

Papa-mèt oh!

Allan and Angel talked to each other more now. And now that
she talked to him, Angel was strangely surprised to find that he
listened, even when he didn't agree. He didn't always accept her
views and they sometimes had heated arguments. Still, they
continued communicating.

'Sometimes I don't understand your mother, you know.
Today she vex like hell, because ah can't find money for
something she want to do.'

'Well, I suppose she want money sometimes.'

'But, Angel, listen. Right now, eh, I have to pay four hundred
dollars a month on the land, manure this month cost me a hell of
a lot, the nutmeg bonus didn amount to nothing much, the
cocoa wasn too bad, but after ah pay out what I owe on that . . .'

'Daddy, ah not sayin no, but how much time you an Mammie
siddown and work out these things together an decide how much
spendin on what an how you go spend what over?'

252

'But, my God, Doodsie know how expensive tings is!'

'The thing is, eh, Daddy, you treatin her in a way like how you tell me the boss, Mr Peter, used to treat you. It even worse in a way. She workin on the land too, but she not even gettin paid because is you wife an she have no say in how the money spend. Mr Peter used to pay you an not consult you an act as if all decision suppose to be his an all the money you make is really his alone. She not even gettin paid!'

'Ay! So you mean I should be payin my wife, then? What . . .?'

'Daddy, is here alone Mammie workin! An ah not sayin give her a salary, but don act as if every cent she get is a favour you do her! Because she workin as hard as you. And I find you must talk with her about how money will spend because she is part of it. You know, if she wasn here all day, you would have to hire somebody to watch the land and other things; to pick up nutmeg, to take out de mace, to cook an ting. Or you would have to do it for youself. So . . .' Angel looked at him. Allan was looking skywards. 'You see what ah mean? I not tryin to jus criticise you or to tell you how to do things. I jus feel if you notice these things more . . .'

'Yes. I see. I see. But – but –' he thrust his hands in his pockets, put his right foot slightly forward, leaned back a little, turned sideways and whistlingly spat a thin strip of saliva through his top front teeth. He stood with his head back, looking up at the sky. 'Huh!' he said, 'huh! Is a hell of a ting. Is like . . . you talkin as if you mean I was exploitin! I never mean . . .'

'I know, Daddy. I don't think you siddown an say all right, I will exploit Doodsie in this way an that way, but you grow up to expect certain things and sometimes those things could be . . . could be exploitative, yes. You see what ah mean?'

'Huh!' He stood looking up at the cocoa trees on the hill. Picked up his cutlass. 'Okay. Uh-huh! I see what you sayin. I don know, non! Meself ah don know. I will try and talk to you mother, as you say. But I really don't know.'

They walked up the steps. They sat listening to the music on the radio for a while.

'So how the work goin?'

'So-so. What about the teaching?'

'Half an half. I get real fed up sometimes.'

'Is so with everything, chile. Everything.'

Angel nodded. Allan looked at his daughter. He remembered that day two or three weeks before when he had introduced her to the twin girls of fifteen who were his daughters. Doodsie, to whom he had always doubted their existence, had quietly told him one day that he should tell the boys about them, especially now that these last two so active wid the people around. He should tell them to avoid any 'shameful family mix-up'. He had told the boys and then decided that he had better tell Angel too. The boys had listened and nodded. Angel listened and said, 'Oh! I see!' One day, when he was in the car with her, he had pointed out the girls in the street and asked Angel hesitantly to stop. She did so, said 'Hi' to the girls, looked into the distance while he asked them some inane question about school. She had then driven on, talking to him about other things. She said nothing more on the subject. Allan sighed. He leaned his head back against the chair. Angel looked at him.

'You tired?'

'Little bit.'

'You workin too hard. When you holiday due?'

'In a few weeks.'

'You mus take it an rest.'

'Uh-huh! I must really do dat!'

Allan closed his eyes. He looked relaxed as he ran his hand across the back of his sparse, rapidly greying hair.

Secure allyou fowls! Galin in de area!

'Caw! Caw! Caw! Caw!'

The fowls lifted their heads at the sound. Some lifted one foot slowly, put it down, down, down, let it touch the ground. The hens clucked. The cocks kept their heads lifted, listening.

'Caw! Caw! Caw! Caw!'

'Woy!' Doodsie rushed out of the toilet, adjusting her clothes. 'All you watch out! Chicken-hawk!'

'Caw! Caw! Caw! Caw!'

The fowls clucked, scattered, ran every which way.

'No! Move! Go away!' Doodsie pushed the back door of the kitchen shouting.

The chicken-hawk had already swooped on a chicken running towards the pigpen. Doodsie stood in the yard near the copper and looked up with anguished eyes as the chicken-hawk rose higher and higher into the blue, clutching a chicken in its claws. The hens clucked in distress. The cocks crowed nervously.

'Youall so stupid!' Doodsie looked around at the yard empty of fowls which were hiding in the bushes, up on the steps, under the house. 'If youall would stay togedder, the chicken-hawk won come down an do nutting! Stupes!' She stamped her foot, distressed, shielded her eyes and looked skywards again. The chicken-hawk had disappeared. Slowly, the fowls began to regroup. 'Stupes!'

It have someting in de mortar besides de pestle!

It was October 1983. Doodsie, Allan and Carl were having breakfast.

'You want more toast, Mammie?' Carl headed for the kitchen.

'Yes. Jus one piece.'

They heard Angel's car outside. She entered quietly, greeted them and went to her room. Allan gestured, eyebrows raised. Doodsie shrugged.

'I don know. In one of her moods, I guess. Not so allyou is?'

Carl gave an amused 'Huh!' and looked at his father. Allan looked across at Doodsie. She was looking away over his head, ignoring his glance. Carl laughed more openly.

'What do you, boy? What you laughin at? Eh?' Allan's voice was sharing the amusement on his youngest son's face.

Carl looked at his mother from under his brows and laughed again. He rushed to the kitchen, came back with the toast. 'It nearly burn.' He put one piece on his mother's plate, the other on his. 'You din want any non?'

'No. No. I finish.'

'Mammie say Angel jus like you.'

'Look, boy, you hear me say anything?' Doodsie joined in her son's laughter.

Angel rested for a while, refused breakfast, went outside to pick some grapefruits. Then she stood in the kitchen watching as

Doodsie beat the cake mixture.

'You awright?'

'Uh-huh!'

'You father was worried about you.'

'That good. After one time is two time, eh!'

'Uh-huh! Some people does get sense late in life, but that better than never.'

Angel stayed all day. She sat on a chair in the living-room until midnight, listening to the radio.

No, thought Doodsie, she quiet for too long. Something wrong. Ah wonder if what those fellas say is true, Carl thought. Ah wonder if it really have confusion goin on in de Party. To hell wid dem an dey Party! As long as dey leave de Revolution alone! Stupid mood as usual, thought Allan.

The music stopped. There was an announcement. Chief's voice. Carl sat up on his bed. Something about a rumour. He heard the word investigation. Carl got off his bed. Switched on the light. Touched the doorknob. Angel exploded.

'What kine o ting is dat? What crap is that they sayin at all? Like they figure dis ting is theirs? What the ass he talkin about?'

Doodsie stopped ironing. She walked from her room out into the living-room.

'What is dat? What happen? Why you have to talk dat way? Was a announcement? It finish?'

Carl stood looking at her.

'Ah couldn't hear, Angel. What de radio say?'

'Something about rumour dey investigatin!'

'Dat is all? You could tell me dat! It come out on de radio, so is not news dat inside youall secret society!'

'What secret society? What you talkin about at all?'

'What out on de radio, is talk for everybody!'

'Yeh, but what you mean?'

'Well, it obvious something goin on. If it affect a few of you an is secret, right! If it affect the revolution, it ain belong to Chief or to assistant chief or to any government minister. All of us suppose to know!'

'Carl, all dat happen is dat Chief talk on de radio. He say dat a rumour goin roun an de security forces tryin to find out wey it come out! People should stay vigilant and not lissen to rumours. Dat is all!'

She got up. Headed for the door. Doodsie looked at Carl.

'Someting wrong, Carl?'

'I don know, Mammie. It look as if something in de air. Ah was jus tryin to find out if anything wrong!'

'What wrong, Angel?'

'Nothing, Mammie. Nothing wrong.'

'Where you goin this late hour?'

'It not so late. Wednesday night they have jazz an blues at the club. I jus goin an lissen for a while!'

Doodsie looked worried. Allan was standing at the bedroom door. He was stroking his cheek.

'Is nothing much, Mammie. Ah think they goin through some problems, but they goin work it out.'

'You mean Chief an them?'

'Yes. They have a difference of opinion at the top.'

'The same thing people use to say?'

'Yeh. But it not dat serious. Is jus Party business. Is nothing that go affect us.'

Doodsie made the sign of the cross.

'I don know what it is, but whatever it is, I pray God they work it out. Things lookin up so well an America jus waitin for us to fall for dem to laugh! Allyou jus work out whatever it is!'

'Yes. Is nutting serious.'

Angel opened the door. She looked at Carl.

'The car workin?' he asked.

'For a change, yes. I go see allyou, eh!'

As Angel drove by the corner before the river, she turned up the car window, smiling at the automatic reaction left over from childhood. She marvelled at the way it still felt very much a part of her own present reaction to the corner. She changed from third to second gear; the vehicle began the uphill climb. Under the stinking-toe tree, she stopped, put on the inside light. She turned the mirror towards her and just sat for a while looking at herself, intently, as though to make sure she was really there. The mirror came apart in her hand. This damn car, it fallin to pieces slowly. She struggled, trying to settle it back into the groove. The mirror held, at a different angle, but it held. Cautiously, Angel took her hands away. She put off the light and turned to look at the silent, watching blackness. She put the car into gear again.

Tout moun ca playwai!

'Miss Doodsie!' Melda came to the kitchen window. 'Miss Doodsie, you hearin? You hearin about tings?'

'Girl!' Doodsie wiped her hands on her skirt. She hurried through the kitchen door. The two stood near to the copper, talking.

'Girl, someting happenin for truth now! Angel in a worl o she own! She not sayin much! Rupert ah doesn see at all dese days because he always down in de camp. But someting goin on!'

'Dey not suppose to hide ting from us. Dey on top but is we dat make Revolution. Revolution counta make if weself din go out on de road and make Leader ban give up. Horizon din even have no big army as such! Is we dat do we ting! Widdout us, de Angel O, de Micey O, de Rupert O, de Chief O, an all other Co-Chief an who not else, none o dem din nutting! Like dey forgettin!'

'Girl, ah don even know what it is!'

'Girl, you see me talkin dey, but me head hot, you know! Huh! If ah tell yu what ah hear! It so bad dat is not even ting to tink about much less to say!'

Doodsie moved closer.

'What? What?'

'What Angel tell you? She don tell you nutting?'

'Well is de other night she hear a announcement on de radio an she get so vex dat ah ask er what happen.'

'Was de announcement about rumour?'

'Yes! What? What happen, Melda?'

'Girl,' Melda sat down on the rim of the copper. 'Jus down de road dey, ah meet some of dose women from the group an de talk is dat de quarrel between dose top man an dem reach it height! Burs open an smell up de whole place like dead crapaud.' She looked up. 'Chief under arres, dey say!'

'Wha-a-a-a-at!'

'Sh-h-h! Hush you mout!' Melda stood up; she looked over her shoulder, looked around the yard. 'Don talk loud. But dat is what ah hear! An is not talk people talkin easy!'

'Bon Jé!'

'Huh!' Melda sat down again, both hands gripping the copper on either side of her body. Doodsie stared wide-eyed at her, both hands to her mouth.

They hadn't even seen the rainclouds gathering behind the mountain. When they looked up questioningly at the sudden darkness, the curtain of blue sky was covered; the rain came tumbling down. Behind Doodsie, the dry clothes on the line flapped a protest in the rushing wind and rain. Doodsie stood there, hands to her mouth, staring at Melda.

None of us din born big!

Angel couldn't remember when else she had seen her mother cry. Once, a long time ago, she thought, trying to focus her mind. From the steps, the cocoa trees looked wet and bedraggled. Melda came by, said only, 'Where you Mammy?' Angel pointed towards the kitchen.

'Miss Doodsie, ah don know bout you, but me, ah goin in demonstration.'

'But Melda . . .'

'Dey jokin! Arres Chief! Dey sayin is Party business! To hell wid dem an dey Party!'

'But . . .'

'Micey vex wid me, you know. Tellin me ah should know better dan to say ah goin an demonstrate! What do dem at all! Sayin how Chief agree to something an den break he word! To hell wid dem!'

'But Angel say it have nutting to do wid who is Prime Minister. Is strictly Party business. Is who to lead Party dey talkin about!'

'Well dat is their business! If Party is dey secret den keep it secret. Don come an . . .'

'Well Angel say is Chief dat wrong to bring it out!'

'To hell wid de Angel, de Micey an all de res o dem in dey secret Party.'

'But if . . .'

'Look eh, ah don even doubtin Chief wrong to spread ting dat suppose to be in secret Party he agree to. He well wrong too! If dey Party ha to do wid we Revolution, den we suppose to know bout it! An don matter who bring ting out in de open, it dey now, an dey ha to deal wid dat! An what we sayin now is leggo Chief! You don sayin dat?'

'Ay! How ah don sayin dat dey? Ah shoutin dat!' Doodsie's

259

face crumpled as though she was about to cry. 'Ah shoutin dat!'

'Lewwe go in de demonstration, den!'

'Yes! Yes, ah go come! Ah don have you strength an ah mightn be able to walk much but ah go stan up on de side when ah tired! Yes, ah comin!'

'Angel an Micey go want to dead. But forget bout dem! Accordin to those schoolchilren, de only Party dey ever tell me bout is de one to do wid de disco an dose club an dem! Is we Revolution we know about an we education an we woman's meeting. Forget bout dey Party! Joke dey makin!'

When water more dan flour!

The crowds gathered. People had come from all over the island, walking through the narrow streets, singing, shouting.

> 'A people
> United
> Will never be defeated!'

Fucking hell, thought Angel. How we reach here? What the hell is this?

'We want Chief! We want Chief! Let im go!'

> 'A people
> United
> Will never be defeated!'

Shouts of: 'Let the masses decide!'

Some people stood at their windows, stood cramped on little balconies, looking down on the crowd. They looked down on fists, on blue and white uniforms, on green and white uniforms, on uniforms burgundy and white, on ribbons white, red and blue. Some people waved the red and black flag of the Revolution. On it there were words: UNITY IS STRENGTH! LET THE MASSES DECIDE! LONG LIVE THE REVOLUTION! THE PEOPLE WILL TRIUMPH! LET THE MASSES DECIDE!

The people marched, flowed, rushed, to the house on the hill.

'A people
United!'

Up on the hill, the front part of the crowd, propelled by the indignation within, and the pushing force of the bodies behind, rushed to the gate. The soldiers shifted their weapons and watched them come. Those at the front saw the soldiers shake the gate, ensuring that it was closed. They watched them test the lock. They didn't look too sure of themselves. But, oh God, if they shoot! The crowd slowed. The soldiers shifted their weapons. Dammit fut, they caan shoot! The soldiers shuffled their feet. Dem damn gun is we own, man! Dey caan shoot us! The crowd was surging forward. The soldiers fired. The people screamed. Retreated in a tumble. Allyou wait! Wait! Don run! Dey shootin in de air! Cautiously, the people turned back towards the gate. The soldiers fired into the air.

'Dey caan shoot us, man! Is we gun!'

The soldiers aimed their weapons at the crowd. The people stopped. Watched. Waited. Linked hands and started singing.

'We marchin!
We marchin!
We marchin for we rights!
The masses know
that the masses strong
an de masses won give up!

We marchin!
We marchin!'

Someone shouted: 'Long live the Revolution!'
The answer was a roar. 'Long live!'
'Long live the struggle for justice!'
'Long live!'
'Down with colonialism!'
'Down wid it!'

'We marchin!
We marchin . . .'

The crowd moved again. One step. Two. Slowly. A little faster. The soldiers aimed. Fired into the air.

'Dey firing in de air!'

'Dey caan shoot we!'

'Is we dat buy dat!'

'Demself know dey caan shoot us!'

The crowd advanced. They could see the soldiers' faces clearly now. The soldiers could identify people in the crowd. They shifted uncertainly. A few people rushed to the gate, pushed the guns aside, confronted the soldiers with arms akimbo. There were supportive shouts as others rushed forward.

'Allyou playin allyou bad? Do someting, non!'

'What do dem so?'

Some soldiers shrugged, grinned sheepishly, held their guns pointing into the air, allowed themselves to be pushed aside. If the people say . . . The guns of the Revolution, their training had said, were not to be used against the people. Melda looked closely at one soldier. In the din, her voice did not quite reach him but others heard her. She shouted.

'You too? You my cousin boy dey, you guardin gate too? Ay-ay! Well look at me crosses, non!' She turned, looking for Doodsie, who had been walking with her. She couldn't find her. 'Ay-ay!' Melda stood with arms akimbo, ignoring the jostling crowd, looking at the soldier. 'Dat is Hop-o nephew-in-law, me cousin little son, dey, yes, dat stan up dey wid gun guardin gate, yes! Ay!'

The crowd propelled her towards the steps of the house, through the house, stumbling. The doors burst open. Chief was swept into the air.

'We get we Chief!'

Outside, there was the sound of a shell. Further down the hill, there was the sound of another shell.

'It look like dey get im out, yes!'

The sound of conch shells reverberated through the town. Holding Chief high in the air, they swarmed back into the yard. Through the gate. Down the hill. Half-way down the hill, they stood him up on the ground. Someone scooped him up again like a baby. Chief looked bewildered. He kept repeating, 'I will explain, I will explain!' Melda, who had found herself in the circle right around him, said, almost threateningly, 'Yes. You go

262

do dat. You better believe you go do dat! What de hell allyou tink it is at all?'

Doodsie, standing at the roadside cheering with some of the crowd, pointed as she saw Melda standing on the back of the open truck in the front of which Chief drove.

'Ay!' she shouted to no one in particular. 'Look, Melda, yes!'

People, whether they knew Melda or not, looked in the direction indicated.

'We go save we education!' shouted Melda. 'We go save we airport!' And she started the refrain of an old Sparrow calypso on education.

'Is a good ting me head was duncie-e-e-!' Melda shouted above the din. 'Otherwise today ah woulda be a damn fool!'

The truck went on down the road. Doodsie stared open-mouted at the person standing on the truck next to Melda. It was Veronica's second daughter. What she doin dey, wondered Doodsie. A rabid Leaderite, dat girl is, yes! The young woman was laughing and shouting. 'O for opposition to Chief! O for out wid communism! C for crap! C for communism!' Ay-ay! Doodsie marvelled. Ah don like dis ting. It have bad in dis ting. Lemme walk up de road an see if ah could fine a bus. We have to fight but some people usin dis for dey own gain! Pò djab-o! Is so life is arready! Ay-ay! Veronica girl! On truck supportin Chief? What ting is dis at all? Dat is what you call wolf in sheep clothing! They not dey to help! Dey dere to hinder! Uh-uh! Uh-u-u-h! Uh-uh!

The Bush-gram busy

Throughout the Caribbean, people listened to their radio. It was the first time that, outside of a West Indies Test Match, people stayed so glued to their radios.

'What do dem at all? How dey could arres de man?'

'Ah hear dat man talk. He good, boy!'

'Grenada jokin! Dey caan do dat, non! We only hope in dis region so far. Allyou do someting good, wi! All eyes on you!'

'Is not communism arready? Ah sure Cuba ha someting to do wid it!'

'Don be stupid! Is de first ting de Americans always sayin! So you have to say it too den? Cuba keepin deyself well out o dat!'

On the campuses, students waited.

'Grenada is our biggest hope so far! Dey caan do this!'

'Somebody gone down dey to try an mediate!'

'I hope those comrades realise dat dis ting is all o we own, you know!'

'It go have plenty governments right in dis region here dat go glad to see dem fall!'

'Well dat ain no surprise! Plenty of dem feel Grenada too small an too fast to talk as loud as they does talk!'

'Dey fraid anybody dat challengin America!'

'Oh God, ah hope ting work out!'

'Well in the final analysis, is the masses that will decide, eh!'

Never say never!

The crowd saw them coming, these trundling tanks. Some people shouted. They gave clenched-fist salutes to the soldiers. The tanks trundled on. The people stood on the sides. Some people leaned on cars just outside the entrance to the fort; arms folded, they watched the tanks come. Some people shouted at the soldiers. What they were saying wasn't clear. The tanks trundled on.

'Lewee go down de road, eh, boy!' Carl touched his friend on the shoulder. 'Lewwe go an stan up on top by de bank. We go see better.'

They walked away down the hill.

Inside the fort, Melda froze.

'Chief! Chief, dey comin wid big machine, yes!'

'They won't use the guns. They won't use them against the people!'

The sound of shots. People screamed.

Chief shouted some advice that was lost in the noise. Some people put their weapons down. Melda hastily put the weapon she was holding flat on the floor.

More shots. Now there were screams. Loud. Louder. Heavy firing. Jesus, dey usin the ting! The people hadn't moved until the very end. They knew for sure that the soldiers wouldn't shoot them. Until the shots came.

'Lie flat!'

Inside the fort, they lay there.

Outside, they were screaming and jumping every which way.
'Woy!'
'Dey shootin!'
'Oh Gawd, ah go dead! Lemme pass!'
'Wo-o-o-y! Me mudder!'
'Jesus!' said Melda. 'Wey Micey?' She started to scramble to her feet.
'Down!' A hand pulled her down.
In the corner, Melda gazed at a mass of blood and crumpled flesh. Veronica, she thought. Veronica girl! But how come she here too? Veronica girl!
Upstairs at the bank, Carl and his friend stared towards the fort. 'You seein? You seein?'
'Oh, Gawd! Oh, Gaw-aw-aw-d! Watch people jump dat high wall!'
Melda looked across at Chief, lying there with others on the floor. His face had a startled look, as if, suddenly, he saw his whole life story flashed before him, but had missed a bit that he was straining forward to catch. A few feet from him lay a soldier with whom he had been arguing a few minutes before. A soldier who opposed his point of view. The young soldier's face had that same startled look. The firing seemed to increase. The windows shattered. They kept their heads low. Bullets ricocheted against the wall. Melda leapt to her feet.
'Down!' someone shouted.
Melda came down, holding her stomach, dancing gracefully down.
For a while, Carl and his friends, looking from the top of the bank, stared out into the sudden silence. No sound of shots, that is. On the road below, people rushed by, screaming, hurtling along the road, bending forward, glancing back, mouths parted, eyes wide in faces frozen into silent masks of unbelieving terror.
Carl stood there looking out. His mouth was slightly parted. He couldn't say anything. There was the sound of shots again. He looked at the fort.
'Lewwe go home! Lewwe go home, Carl! We ha to get out o de road! Lewwe go home!'
People rushed home, fell inside their houses; they stood there and sat there shaking and sobbing and shaking their hands and moving their feet and looking over their shoulders as if to be sure the horror hadn't followed them home.

Angel hadn't gone to the demonstration. On the street, she stopped a running figure. She had heard the shots. She had heard the confusion.

'What happen? What happen?'

'Ah don know! Dey shoot! Dey shoot!'

Eyes wild with terror, the young girl in the blue school uniform put her hand to her head.

'Wey me brudder? Wey me brudder?' she asked. 'Wey im? He was wid me. An wey im?'

The child looked over her shoulder. Started to run again. Angel went home.

There was no wind, no whisper in the trees. The air was still, silent, listening. Angel's eyes darted from one side of the road to the other. One two three, she counted. One two three! Oh God! One two three.

She sat bent over double in the chair, cradling her shoulders from the cold inside, still, listening to Doodsie's sobs. Aunt Jessie paced. Allan turned around in one spot. Moved. Returned. Cleared his throat. Moved. Turned. Came back to the same spot and stood clearing his throat, his hand occasionally going up to touch the back of his head; he stood as if listening for something. Carl stood in the corner by the sewing-machine. He held the scissors; he was methodically snipping a bit of cloth on top of the machine. No one said anything.

Carl's mind went in a fast rewind over the events of earlier in the day. He was in the demonstration. The crowd, running down the hill with Chief.

A people! United!

Veronica's girl on the truck with Melda. Let go we Leader! C for crap! C for communism! A people! United!

The guns!

The guns!

Carl snipped away at the cloth.

A people! United!

Lewwe go down de road by de bank! We could see from up dey!

A people! United!

The tanks! The people! Clenched fists! A people! United! The screams! The screams! The screams!

He flung down the scissors. He stood in front of his sister. 'What do allyou, eh? Allyou damn mad or something?'

Angel looked up at Carl. Went back to rocking herself. Carl went to his room. Angel rocked. Just the day before, Doodsie had said to her: 'But they mus listen, Angel. I not sayin is not a confusion in the Party that they know best how to solve but they mus listen to what all of us down here sayin!'

'Is not a question of who down an who up, Mammie.'

'Yes, me chile. Whether you want to see it or not, is always a question of that. Because now what happen? Look eh, when ting just start all of us been speaking with one voice, so was all right then. Was all right because practically everybody was on same side. Now mos people on same side again, saying leggo Chief, but now some of allyou who fight wid us self sayin is because we stupid an we caan see de truth! Perhaps. I not sayin so. But den that is how it is. If a few of you see it an de res of us don see it, what you go do, tie us down? Is not so it is, Angel. Dat is not what we fight for. We moving together or if not, we jus not moving, ah suppose. Oh, Gawd, what is dis at all?'

'Hm!'

'Hm! Is not hm! If you know anybody that go listen, say someting, you know. Because allyou caan spoil we ting jus so. Oh, God, if I say ah don disappointed, ah lie. I believe in dis ting too much for this stupidness to happen. Oh, God! Look we airport! Look we education! Look everything! Look how we movin nice! Lawd! No!'

Angel had just stood helplessly by. Doodsie sobbed. Angel stood staring.

'Mammie,' she had said, 'we go work it out.'

'Yes, me chile, ah hope so.'

Doodsie had got up and moved away. Angel was suddenly seeing her grandmother again; Ma Ettie, tired, disappointed, leaving to walk back to Hermitage.

'Mammie!' she called after her, suddenly afraid. But when Doodsie turned back, all Angel could say with a feeling of almost angry helplessness was: 'We go work it out, ah tell you.'

Sense make befoh book

They put on the radio; they listened. Jessie stood at the door looking out. A cat went slinking by underneath the grapefruit tree. The moon above, a deep confident yellow. Jessie looked

up. Full moon. A star pitched. Jessie watched its swift movement downwards. She shivered. Turned away. As she pushed
the door behind her, an owl hooted in the grapefruit tree. Bon
Jant, Jessie murmured.

It came as a 'special announcement'. Jessie sat down; she put
her hands over her ears. She didn't want to hear. She pushed her
fore-fingers into her ears. She watched the faces. Shock. Un-
belief. Carl was pounding the door with his fist. Angel was
staring straight ahead. It looked like she was making a sobbing
sound. Doodsie – Doodsie . . . She better watch it, yeh! She
know de pressure high, arready! Jessie took her fingers away
from her ears.

'The people died because they were in the line of fire in a time
of crisis at the army headquarters! The fort is not a civilian
institution! In order to avoid further distress, we hereby declare
a dusk to dawn curfew . . .'

'*No!*' Doodsie held on to the back of a chair.

'Ay-ay! Ay-ay! Ay! Ay!' Allan looked as if he had been hit.

'Wo-o-o-y!' Jessie's eyes had an uncomprehending look.
'What dey say? Dey dead in truth, den? Dey dead? Carl, who
dead?'

'Is like dey say, Auntie. Chief dead, an a lotta other people
who support im dead. People in de crowd dead, ah suppose,
although we don hear! Ministers who support im dead! Dey jus
dead!'

Angel was making a strangled, sobbing sound.

Doodsie looked at her. 'Angel, where Rupert?'

Angel said nothing.

Then Doodsie was shaking her. 'Where me chile?' she
shouted. 'Wey im? Allyou dey wid allyou mout close until de
end! Wey im?'

'I don know, Mammie.'

'How de hell you mean you don know? Who to know? Me? Is
not allyou blasted Revolution? Where is *my son?*'

'Awright, Doodsie. Awright. Awright. You didn see im
today, Angel?'

'No, Daddy.'

They didn't ask Carl. He didn't say that he had seen Rupert
during the day, after Chief had been released, organising to get
a loudspeaker so that Chief could speak to the crowd. He had
gone with his brother to a house. The equipment was there. It

had broken down. He stood by and watched while Rupert fiddled with the equipment, trying to get it to work. They had left the house together, but then gone their separate ways. Carl had gone back to the demonstration. He didn't talk about this. No need to worry people further. He didn't know what had happened to his brother.

Angel had seen Rupert. He had not reported back to base a week ago, had given up his weapon and declared himself no part of the confusion. But she knew that today, when Chief had been released, Rupert was on the fort with a weapon. One of the soldiers had told her. He had been having a rough time over the last few days, because his girlfriend Janine and his best friend Dick were both bitter about Chief; they said Chief was being dishonest and flouting all decisions, because he knew that the people loved him. Rupert told them that was talk for another time and another place. Right now they had to deal with what people thought, and people supported Chief. Angel and Rupert had had a real tearing down time just yesterday. She had been down to his friend's house, where he was. She told Rupert that he should get Chief to see that a fight would be bad for both sides.

'Civil war is blood, Rupert.'

'Which side you on, Angel?'

'I not on no blasted side. Side talk is war talk.'

'That is rubbish. That opportunist nonsense could only mean you not on the side of the people. Why you don take a stan? The ting that frighten me about you is dat you able to support everybody. You always balancin! That is pure opportunism! Dammit to hell, Angel! Follow you mind! Come down on one side!'

'Opportunism, hell! So it not possible to see dat both sides have some truth in it, that both sides wrong, that they doin shit!'

'Yes. Yes. That possible. But in the final analysis, you still have to have a opinion about the treatment of the people. The *people* you siddown in you ivory tower an say you fightin for, dey know who side dey on! Fight for youself, eh, sis, because dem don have your problem. They know where they stand!'

'Rupert, you know for youself dat you have a lot of information dat people don have! People caan see de truth, perhaps, as clear as you.'

269

'Den dat would be *my* problem! If I in de ivory tower too an dem outside without information, dat would be my problem! What dotishness you talkin? More information hell! How you suddenly want people to judge on information you never give dem? Why any government should siddown dey an expec people to tink that they rulin so dey musbe right? An what de hell information you talkin about anyway? Me? I don have no special information!'

'Ah don feel we could solve nothing by going out there an shooting up each other! The Party . . .!'

'To blasted hell was de Party! Any Party dat in Mars while people on earth is not no party we want to know about anyway! Let it stay to ass in Mars!'

Angel said nothing. Rupert turned away. Turned back. Angel thought of him putting brick upon brick upon brick.

'Look eh, Sis. When you find out how to solve it, give me a shout, eh.' He walked away, turned back. 'I not lyin, Angel. Ah disappointed. I always use to feel I learnin from you. All of a sudden is like wasn you talkin.'

'Look, Rupert, the issues are clear . . .'

'Don give me no lecture. They clear to me, too. But you siddown dey wid you clarity. If you clear an everybody else unclear, what you go do? Go an siddown in the museum?'

Angel didn't answer.

'See you, Sis.'

Rupert walked away. Came back. He stood silent for a few moments. He walked back into the house, kicking down a house of play-bricks that a child had built on the step.

It have more ting is dis world dan what we know about

Angel had a dream that she used to have often, when, as a child, she slept on the bedding right in front of her parents' bed. She used to pull the cover right over her head and curl up in the corner when she couldn't sleep and the shadows came at her even if she closed her eyes.

'Mammie,' she used to call. 'Mammie!'

'What?' impatiently.

'Nutting. I just wan to see if you sleepin arready.'

'Look, chile. Shut you damn mout an sleep an stop disturbin me, eh!'

But when Angel knew that her mother was still awake, she felt better and could drift off to sleep. Often, on those nights, she would dream that someone had come up out of the old cane mill by the river, out of the old large stones on the right-hand side just after the bend by the river, right under the hill, the place where she had been told the slaves used to grind the sugar-cane in the water mill on the old Delicia estate.

The figure, clothed in a long, flowing white gown, walked the half mile up through the cocoa into the yard. It walked to the pipe in the yard, opened it; it stooped down there by the pipe watching as a bucket was filled up. It had a pipe now, smoking, smoking. A pipe like the one her father's mother used to smoke sometimes. But who was it really? Was it she? Or was it Ma Ettie? Angel went to the window and stood there peeping outside. The figure moved its head, the coloured headtie shifted backwards; the woman looked straight up at Angel. She couldn't remember the face. The woman removed the pipe from her mouth; her lips moved. She was saying something. She was – saying – something. Angel strained forward, unable to hear.

One night, as she was straining forward to hear, she woke up, screamed. Doodsie woke up; Allan grunted impatiently in his sleep.

'Somebody in de yard, Mammie.'

'How you know dat wey you like down dey? What do you? What happen?'

'Somebody in de yard, Mammie.'

'You hear someting?'

'Non. Non. Ah jus feel so.'

'Dammit, chile. What wrong wid you? You want to go an see who it is? Well go, non! Nobody holdin you foot.'

But Doodsie had got up and put a match to the small lamp. She moved about quietly, using the pail, touching to see if Angel and Simon had wet the bed, moving quietly about until, reassured, Angel had dropped off to sleep again.

That dream hadn't come for a long time now. But now it came again. When Angel looked outside, the figure stood up and started gesticulating angrily, moving her lips furiously, talking, talking, shouting everything . . . shouting . . . shouting . . . shouting without sound. As she talked and shouted silently,

271

more people came from up under the cocoa and passed quickly behind her back. Some carried buckets. Some carried bags. A bent old man with what looked like a full bag of cocoa on his back looked sideways at Angel. He looked like Hop-o. He lifted a hand and wiped his streaming face. He continued to support the cocoa bag with the other hand. Two women passed by wearing bright red skirts, faces concentrated, one hand up behind their heads to steady the heavy baskets of cocoa. Their knees were bent slightly forward to keep the bodies steady. Children ran alongside, urging on sheep, cows, goats. One cow was watching her bad eye . . . watching her bad eye . . . watching her bad eye. Angel whimpered in her sleep. Some people carried bundles of sugar-cane on their heads, holding them tightly, walking quickly, glancing back sometimes over their shoulders, almost running . . . running . . . running. The cane tilted. They approached the fields at the bottom. The swaying cane trees . . . the swaying . . . no, it wasn't cane trees. It was water. The people were filing into a boat. The boat moved restlessly on the blue sea. The people ran! They pushed. They surged forward. The line was suddenly a mass of people in a panic. They turned to shout at those behind them.

'Run!'

'Come on!'

'Hurry up! De boat leavin!'

'Run! Run! Ru-u-u-u-u-u-u . . .'

Angel jumped up; she was sweating. Somebody . . . somebody . . . somebody . . . She breathed hard; she felt as if she had been running. She lay down again, pulled the covers over her head like she used to do; this time she covered her ears, squeezed her eyes shut. Run! run! r-u-u-u- She slept in fits and starts.

Today for policeman, tomorrow for tief

People closed their doors. They stole quietly out to nearby gardens. Occasionally, a vehicle sped past. People looked out from behind curtains. A jeep. It looked like an army jeep. One of them, the people thought. Anybody speedin by in vehicle now is one o dem! Huh!

Someone went to Delicia asking for Rupert. Someone in an

army jeep. Carl looked out from behind his window curtains. Angel stayed inside. Doodsie talked to them. They left.

'What goin on, Angel? Why they want Rupert?'

'I don know, Mammie.'

A car came to pick up Angel. She went out. She told them she was going to 'a meeting to sort things out'. 'Meeting! You jokin!' Carl hissed at her from the door of his room, low, so that no one outside would hear. 'You would go to meetin now wid dem?'

'We have to talk, Carl! We still mus talk! Ah not on de fence! Ah definitely against what happen! Nothing justify it! Nothing! Nothing! But I at least have to hear what they want me for!'

It was nothing, she reported later. A meeting to plan a meeting. She wouldn't be going to the meeting planned.

Nen Ezra, who had been home on holiday earlier in the year but had returned to the Virgin Islands, called.

Yes, said Doodsie quietly, things were all right.

Aunt Emma called from New York.

'I've been trying to get through for days, yes. What happenin to all you down dey? How tings?'

'We all right, yes, Emma. We all right!'

'How you mean allyou awright? Is now I tryin to get through, then? An all this ting we hearin, we seein on TV and everyting. Ah see people jumpin an all ting, and I so frighten, eh! I tinkin about allyou, ah tinkin about those chilren . . .'

'Don say nothing on de phone dey, you know, Mammie.'

'De chilren all right, Doodsie?'

'Yes. Yes. All of us okay.'

'You don want to talk! Nothing don happen, I hope. How is Simon?'

'No. We okay in truth. Since Simon come back last month, he up there workin in Grenville, so that's where he is. He in a firm up there, you know. He all right!'

'You sure?'

'Yes. Yes. He call up this evening self. He all right! He up there, so he not in the centre, you know.'

'An Rupert an Angel an Carl an Allan an Jessie?'

'They okay! Look Angel sittin down here by me right now! Talk to her! Hol on, eh!'

Yes, said Angel. Everything was okay. Caan talk too much. No problem. Everybody fine, though. No problem, Auntie

273

Emma, don't worry. We okay.

People kept close to their radios. Music. In times like these, the announcer said, people should be vigilant. There were reports, the radio said, of intended American aggression. Ambassadors and country representatives, the radio said, were visiting. The Interim Army Council was assuring everyone that residents were safe. People should go back out to work now, the radio said. Our crisis had come to an unfortunate end. Let us pull together to build the pieces. It was a tragic time for us all, the radio said. People should pull together. The country should concentrate on rebuilding, on putting the revolution back on course. Go back to work. Go back to school. Put the revolution back on course.

People went back to work. People went back to school. Soldiers smiled at people. They smiled at the tops of people's heads. People kept their heads down and hurried past. People worked one day. They hurried home and kept their curtains tightly drawn. That night, the radio announcer sounded excited. An aggression was being planned, he said. The masses should be vigilant. Doodsie made the sign of the cross. They sat there throught the night, grouped around the radio, dozing, listening. Come out, militia members, this is the time to defend your country! The time gone, muttered Carl, an allyou sen us inside! Is allyou country! We don goin no damn place! Angel looked at him.

'Is our country still, Carl. We wrong. We do real stupidness. But nobody don have a right to invade. We doesn invade dem when dey killin black people in their country. We caan invade dem because we small. But anybody at all invade dem is war. We caan let nobody jus invade we country.'

Carl said nothing.

Jessie went to her room. They heard her praying: 'Our father, who art in heaven . . .'

Carl sucked his teeth. He went to the door and opened it. He stood, hands in pockets, looking out at the darkness.

An invasion is imminent, the radio announced. They are here. They are trying to land already.

'You not goin anywhere you know, Angel. We bring this on weself. We beg for it. We buy it cash. You not going anywhere, I say.'

The voice of fear. It was years since Doodsie had ordered her to do or not to do anything. Angel paced.

'We musbe buy Horizon death cash, Mammie. Me ain know. But we ain buy invasion. Nobody have a right to do that.'

'But at this point now we just ha to say thanks, wi!' said Allan. 'How else we go get outa dis?'

'We go get out o it, Daddy. We get outa Leader. People march to get Chief free. We did fight for weself in '51! Dese same people dat comin to "save" us now did only too anxious to kill us yesterday! They don like us! They don like Chief! They jus tryin to control us. But slavery days done!'

'Angel, chile, is de only way I see to get out of dis.'

'Mammie, what you sayin?'

'Is true, Mammie.' Carl closed the door. 'They don like us. They don like no black people that tryin to do something. They like to see us grin teeth.'

'But somebody have to do something.'

'Vengeance is mine, saith the Lord.'

'Yes, Auntie, even dat better than sayin let them wreak vengeance.'

Doodsie looked at her daughter. 'Well you gettin religion in you ole age,' she said.

They sat; they listened to the radio.

'If they don come, Angel, how you figure we go make it? What go happen to us?'

'We go make it. We have to figure a way to make it. Is only us black people that does suppose some great white father suppose to come inside we country an put things right, you know. We learn so good how to be inferior, we forget how to be anything else. You tink dem like us better than who here like us? You think they like us better than we like weself?'

'But, Angel, chile, the way ting happen . . .'

'Yes. I know. We wrong. But that don make dem right.'

'All militia personnel, please report to your nearest unit head-quarters!'

Doodsie frowned, flung her hand dismissively at the radio. Angel suddenly remembered her grandmother, Ma Ettie, walking with determination towards the radio, a glass of water in her hand. De man inside dey only talkin, talkin . . . ! Angel chuckled. Doodsie looked at her in surprise.

'Well I suppose it good somebody could fine something to laugh at!'

275

It was five-fifteen in the early morning. The planes came. Carl stood on the steps and watched one of them. Hands in his pockets, he stood there and was without fear. What they doin here? What the hell they doin here?

Jessie made the sign of the cross. 'Thank God they come, you hear! Because ah don know what goin on at all!'

'Thank God!' echoed Doodsie. Allan went to the door.

'If Carl want to play stupid an stay outside dey, Allan, leave im. He big. He won listen. But what you self goin an do outside dey, eh?'

'Woy! Wo-o-o-y!' Allan looked up into the sky. 'Look at it! Look at it! Well low, you know.'

'Daddy, les go inside!'

Jessie looked at the door. 'So he not frighten then?'

She leaned against her room door.

'He rememberin his war days.' Doodsie was calm now. Lord, she kept saying to herself. 'Wey me chile?'

Allan came inside.

'Allan, wey you tink Rupert is?'

'Take it easy, non, Doodsie.'

Angel came from the kitchen.

'You mother don sleep las night, you know. Headache whole night.'

'Is the pressure. Since she small growin up is so tings does affect her. Is the pressure! She does beat up sheself too much, an get too excited!'

Carl and Angel looked at each other. They knew they were thinking the same thing. And she don even know Melda dead yet!

A plane swooped. Droned. Allan rushed to the door.

It was about midday when Rupert came to the yard in uniform, hurrying, looking hunted, sweating.

'Rupert! My chile!'

'Yes, Mammie.'

He looked at her, at the hands outstretched to him.

'I all right, Mammie. Nothing don do me. I jus couldn't get to you before. But I all right. Angel, les go.'

Doodsie looked startled. Angel looked at him. Carl looked at his brother.

'You fightin, Rupert? After what they do you fightin with them?'

'I not fightin *for* dem, Carl. I fightin for us, because nobody suppose to be in we country. After ah fight wid dem, ah could fight against dem, because that fight still have to go on. If they coulda fine me befoh invasion start, ah mightn have been here today. But is a different fight for the present. People won want to fight because of how it happen, but we have to fight!'

'Me ain know, non,' said Carl. 'I see what you sayin, but ah couldn fight with them!'

Rupert held his brother's hand. 'The country bigger dan dem, Carl. What we country is bigger dan dem. That fight still in front.'

'Angel?'

'Ah frighten.'

Rupert laughed. 'You gettin big, sis. You startin to speak you mind. To tell you de truth, ah well frighten too.'

'Allyou stay here.' Doodsie pleaded.

Rupert went out to the kitchen. Doodsie followed him. Angel dressed. Doodsie was crying when they left. Carl was crying too. Allan sat on the steps with his head in his hands. Jessie stood near to her room door and made the sign of the cross.

They stopped at Louise's house in the cocoa. Rupert knocked. Louise had moved down the hill after falling out with her children's father; with the help of her big children, she had built herself a two-roomed house in the cocoa. The blind went up. Louise's face appeared at the window. A long, thin, severe face. A long nose. Little curls around the head. Louise was part Asian. The blind went down. Silence. They waited. Rupert knocked again. Louise came to the door.

'What? What allyou want?'

'Myrna an John there?'

'No, Rupert, they not there.'

'Let me come in.'

'No, dammit. Myrna an John not there an they not goin nowey. Allyou mash up de ting; fix it. Nobody not goin noway!'

The door slammed shut. Louise went back inside muttering.

'Ah know dose chilren like me own. I give all o dem masanto to light dey way through this very cocoa. So help me God ah don want to see nothing happen to dem, but if they know what good for dem, dey better go back in Mr McAllister house.'

Look how trouble could come right inside people house an meet dem eh!

For two days, Doodsie rushed to the door every time she heard a sound. She kept looking out for Rupert and Angel. Veronica came by.

'Mr McAllister, sir, allyou should pack. Everybody down de road takin what dey could an movin out!'

'What!'

'What happen?'

'Why?'

'People say dey plannin to bomb the woods in the area. They lookin for Cubans, you know!'

A helicopter hovered overhead. A voice was shouting something.

'Dey tellin us to move? Dey tellin us to move?'

'No,' said Carl. 'Dey talkin in Spanish. They askin de Cubans to come out an give up deyself!'

'It don have no Cubans roun here!'

'Dey say you never know!'

'Since when Cuban become devil?'

'Dey was good before, but dey say dey been fightin down de airport, you know!'

'If somebody attack you, Veronica, you go stan up like a chupid-i an don fight back?'

'Ah don know. Meself ah don know!'

'Who say dey go bomb, Veronica?'

'People get the news! They say is that they sayin in de plane when they pass!'

'Is not that they sayin!' Carl was speaking with the authority of his O-level Spanish. 'Is not that they sayin at all! But me ain know if people get it somewey else.'

'If they wanted to tell us that,' decided Allan, 'same way they talkin now, they would announce it.'

'So what youall gon do? You go take de chance?'

'Yes,' Doodsie was thinking of the children.

Jessie was nervous. 'Well if is that youall decide!'

'Thanks, Veronica.'

'Thanks, you hear, Veronica. It was good of you to come all

up here an tell us.'

'Thanks, Veronica.'

They tensed each time they heard a sound. The helicopters flew over. They came back. They circled. They came lower. In the distance, dogs barked.

Rupert returned barefeet, in civilian clothes. No one asked him anything about the battle.

'You hungry?'

'No.'

'What happen?'

'The fightin more or less done. The invaders in control.'

'Angel? Where . . . Angel?'

'She din come home? She not here?'

'She . . . she . . . no.'

Rupert's hands hung loosely at his sides. Doodsie gestured helplessly. She looked around, wished she could offer him some building bricks. Wey Angel? Oh God, wey Angel? She born St Michael and all angels day! St Michael, pray for her.

'Mammie. Mammie, Janine dead.'

'Janine? You – you – ' Doodsie always found it difficult to say words like 'girlfriend' and 'boyfriend'. Even now. 'Janine?'

Rupert looked at his mother. He looked as if he hoped she would contradict him. 'I see her. She was the gunner in the fort. I was dey de first time dey bomb. We run to the caves an lie down. The bombing – the bombing . . .' Rupert covered his head. 'They bomb an they come back again, tryin to slip de bombs into the caves to make sure they flush us out! The bombs – the . . . They din bomb for a long time. We thought they was attacking the other fort. She was on the top, Mammie. She was the gunner. I did jus leave de fort when dey bomb it again. Oh Gawd, she dead, Mammie! She dead!' Hands together, stretched down straight in front of him, Rupert cried. He threw his head back, opened his mouth and cried.

'Awright, Rupert! Awright!' The tears were running slowly down Doodsie's cheek. She wanted to ask him what he meant when he said he had seen her. Had he seen her just before they bombed? Had he seen her body. She couldn't frame the words. She searched her mind for something to say.

'John,' she said. Why ah sayin dat, she wondered. Ahm . . .

'John? John Miss Louise?'

'Yes. Yes. Louise come up here bawlin. Somebody tell er dey

see he body on de side of de road in Beausejour.'

'Oh Gawd! Oh Gawd!'

'Louise din even know he go! He leave widout her knowin!'

The invaders searched. The invaders took people for questioning. They talked about 'the communists'. People did what Rupert called 'jump off one dream to go for a ride on another'. The invading forces took Rupert for questioning.

'Were you a member of the army?'

Rupert didn't answer.

'Are you a communist?'

'Are you a capitalist?'

'We'll make you talk, boy!'

'I'm not a boy!'

'Got a fast tongue, eh?'

While they held Rupert, they went to the house in Delicia. Only Doodsie and Jessie were there when they visited. In Rupert's room they picked up a book called *The Story of Communism*.

'Ah ha!'

The white soldier looked at Doodsie.

'Does this belong to the communist teacher who lives here?'

'I don't know any communist teachers, sir!'

They didn't keep Rupert for long. They released him. He smiled when Doodsie told him about the book. 'They so fraid the name it make dem bazoodee! Dat book is written by one of their own. It explains what good Americans must look out for. Let dem keep it! It might help them!'

The invaders searched cars, too.

'Any Cubans in your trunk?'

The soldier stretched out his hand for the keys. They opened the door, walked back with the keys, watched him open the trunk.

'None that I could see,' he grinned engagingly, handed back the keys to the woman at the wheel. His eyes searched the inside of the car.

'Check under the mat,' she invited him. 'They're kind of small, you know.'

'Move on, baby!'

'Baby, you – !' the woman raged, the words coming quickly to her lips. She stopped, raging to herself, not wanting to submit even *his* mother to that indignity.

280

'Oh God, wey Angel?' Doodsie asked repeatedly. To herself she said, Me chile alive. Nothing don happen to her. Nothing doh happen to her non, God!

'A lot of people hidin still, Mammie! I been lookin all around for her. She musbe by one of her friends.'

Rupert found his sister. A friend took him to the hospital. There, in the open ward, Angel lay with a screen round her bed. Her whole head seemed to be wrapped in bandages. Bandages covered her eyes.

'It's her eyes,' the nurse said. 'They leave it late to bring her in. Somebody brought her in last night!' Rupert looked at the nurse. He recognised her. She lowered her voice. 'One of the comrades brought her in. She had been in his house for a few days. She was hurt fighting, it look. Something musbe go through her eyes! It's bad. She's been sedated. We don really have what we need to treat her. Ah sure youall would have to bring her away somewhere!'

Rupert was crying. He didn't seem able to stop the tears these days.

'She – she – she might have to lose the eye.'

Rupert kept his head lowered.

'There's another sister in the other room. She's in a bad way. Her family organising for her to go to America for treatment!'

'To their country!?'

'We don't have a choice, comrade. They have the money. They have the treatment.'

Rupert's tears couldn't stop. He wiped his face and immediately it was wet again.

Doodsie stared at him, hardly understanding.

'Take it easy. Take it easy, Doodsie! She coulda been dead. We jus glad she alive!'

'Praise the Lord!' said Jessie.

'Look, Mammie. Look! Drink this. Where de pressure tablets de doctor give er, Auntie?'

'Is awright. Is awright. Ah take them arready.'

Rupert spoke to Auntie Ezra on the telephone.

'Oh Jesus Chrise!' she said. 'Ah know something was wrong! Oh God! Is she self ah did fraid for!'

'Mammie want to talk to you, Auntie Ezra.'

'Ezra, de hospital will be expensive. We will try to get a loan from the insurance! We don have that kine o money!'

281

'Make up what you could over there! This side we will do all we can! We go get her over!'

'We have to call Emma, too. An Allan sister in England.'

'Yes, but whatever it is, even self we have to owe self, go ahead.'

In cow-belly crossways!

From the United States they called regularly. Angel had arrived. Angel was in hospital. The bandages had been removed. The bandages had been replaced. Ezra called to say that Angel had to have another operation.

'Ah not too sure, but they say it's to remove something from de eye.'

'An . . . an . . .'

'Don worry! She awright otherwise! She talk to me today!'

'She talk? She talk to you?'

'Yes. She was conscious an we tell her what happen an wey she is and everything.'

'What she say?'

'She was jus laughin like. She say to tell you she awright.'

'As usual. She always awright.'

'She was kine o groggy, you know! But okay.'

'Hol on, eh! Talk to Ezra!'

'What! De line not so good!'

'Ezra! Talk to Ezra!'

'Ezra dey? I thought she went back.'

'She come back las night.'

'Hello. Hello?'

'Ezra? Girl ah glad to hear you!'

'You don worry about nothing over dey!'

'Ah know all o dis costin a fortune!'

'Jus relax youself over dey! We go all put together, an what we caan pay now, we go pay later.'

'Girl, look trouble, eh!'

'Girl, leave it in de hands of de Lord!'

'The Lord?' said Rupert when Doodsie told him. 'Oho! Lord Ezra and Lord Emma! Dey get knighthood! No joke. They deserve it in truth! One ting wid de Lord, when you see you put im in countries like dese without facilities, he doesn perform to the bes at all!'

Don look to see who behind you! Look in front to make sure you see wey you goin!

Doodsie sat knitting in the living-room. Allan had his glass of mountain-dew. On the small table in the corner were large photographs of the four children.

'Ah don know how allyou lookin at it, non!' Allan knocked back the mountain-dew. 'But for me is Crown Colony, you know. Crown Colony is de bes!'

'Hm! Tings bad, yes. But ah still caan say dat. Crown Colony! What do youself, boy!'

'Ah don know, you know, but . . . Hm!' He put his head back, stayed there looking up at the ceiling.

'Meself,' said Jessie, 'as far as ah concern, is six o one, half a dozen o de other!'

'Crown Colony!' came Carl's voice from his room. 'That is plain imperialism, Daddy.'

'What word is dat dis boy know arready dey?'

'Is not so de worl come now?' Jessie laughed. 'Is what in dey head.'

'You caan want dat, Daddy.' Carl was decisive. 'Is like sayin other people better than you an they know better than you what you want.'

'Well, perhaps they know how to rule.'

'They just have the habit of rulin! But we caan say we like it!'

'These young people these days won let that happen!'

'Is true,' said Doodsie, 'is why they did never want the slaves to learn. Because they didn't want people to find out how they doin dey ting!'

'Dat's right! So now that all like Carl an dem so dat comin up could stand up on dey own foot, dey not lookin for nobody else to rule dem!

'Huh! Well, ah suppose is to see!'

Allan twirled the empty glass. He walked to the door and stood looking at the distant darkness blotting out the horizon.

The phone rang.

'Doodsie! Doodsie! Is Angel!'

'What? On de phone!'

283

'Yes. Yes. Come quick. How you, then? Eh heh? Eh heh? Good. That good. Yes?' Allan laughed. 'Well look, talk to you mother. It really good to hear you!'

'Angel?'

'Yes, Mammie.'

'Chile, how you?'

'Much better now. I alive, so I okay!'

'You soundin bright!'

'Yeh!'

'Ah really glad. God be praised!'

'Auntie Ezra here. She goin back to the Virgin Islands tomorrow!'

'Thank the Lord for Ezra, eh!'

'Uh! I know!'

'So how – how the eye?'

'It awright! Me face lookin awright. You wouldn even know!'

'So you seein okay?

'Yeh! I have to wear dark glasses still an go back some days still for check up an ting, but it okay!'

'So how it lookin really? You – you – ?'

Angel laughed gently. 'No. I not disfigured. Is jus a glass. Unless you know, you wouldn't really stare at me.'

Doodsie heaved a sigh.

'I all right, Mammie. I okay! Ah coulda been dead!'

'Auntie Jessie here. Jus say a word to her.'

'Okay. What about Rupert?'

'He not here now. But he pullin things together, you know. He was thinkin of tryin to make a move outside the country. But for the present I hear him talkin to he father about he an Carl startin a agriculture project wid some other young people dat out of work. So I not sure how they will make out!'

'Oh!'

'Yes. I would like him to go an study.'

'Well is what he decide ah suppose.'

'Chile, ah really glad to hear you, soundin so good. Anyway, talk to Jessie, eh! Let me not take up all de talk! Keep good, eh! An ah would like to talk to Ezra afterwards!'

Jessie didn't talk for long. She was really pleased to hear Angel, she said. 'Yes, child. Yes. Take care, you hear! Take care of yourself. We thinking of you.'

'Ezra, well we caan thank you enough!'

Ezra reminded her that the child was hers, too.

'The priest thought you din sufficient, though. Allan siddown dey laughin now!'

'Ask im if he have de pries number. We could ring im an ask im to contribute a little something! Anyway, you should see you daughter soon!'

'Ay-ay! She din tell me! She comin back?'

'Ay! Ah musbe sayin ting ah shouldn say then? No, I think she jus didn tell you that one yet. But all the madam head is for Grenada, yes.'

You not no egg, girl!
You caan break so easy!

Doodsie, Allan, Jessie, Carl, Rupert, Simon, all watched as Angel walked down the steps of the small aircraft.

'She get thin,' said Doodsie.

'She wearin shades,' said Allan.

Simon bit his nails.

'Huh! She doh lookin bad,' said Jessie.

'Look me sister, yes!' said Carl.

Rupert stood with arms folded, looking at her.

'Angel!' Carl shouted.

Angel turned in their direction. She waved. Rupert wondered if she saw them clearly.

They waited. Rupert went back to the car he had borrowed. Angel's car seemed to have disappeared. Had probably been bombed out somewhere. Through the driving mirror, he watched them approach. Simon was saying something to his sister and laughing. Doodsie walked on her other side, looking occasionally at Angel, laughing too. Allan carried the suitcase. Carl was walking backwards, looking at his sister. Jessie held a small bag. Angel's hands were in the pocket of her light blue jacket.

Simon had to go back to work. He would come down later. He was not travelling with them.

'Go in front.' He opened the door. 'You an Carl could siddown there an de rest in de back.'

Angel got in. She sat there looking at Rupert. Carl reached across and took off the dark glasses. Rupert stared at her. He held her hands hard. He still hadn't learnt how to control the tears.

'Ah know Janine dead,' she said. 'Ah know.'

He nodded.

'The eye not lookin bad,' he said. 'You wouldn't know.'

Doodsie stared at the unmoving eye, her throat filling.

'It not hurting?' Carl asked.

'No. It used to feel strange, but I gettin accustomed to it.'

'It could open an close.'

Angel demonstrated.

'They mus make one that could see now!'

'An make you not have anything to invent?' Rupert laughed.

Rupert suddenly slapped his sister on the shoulder.

'Boy what happen to you? Dat is a shoulder you know!'

'Well, sis, dey say blind people does develop a keen sixth sense, you know!'

'Rupert! Aw-w-w-!'

Allan laughed. 'Leave dem. Leave dem.'

'Well everyting in place,' pronounced Jessie. 'Once you hear confusion start, everyting awright again.'

So far so good, thought Doodsie. But she quiet. She really quiet.

We never get more dan we can handle!

'Well, it all over now.'

'We caan jus wipe the slate, Mammie. It not easy as that.' Rupert's voice was low.

'You should start goin to church, Angel.'

Angel said nothing.

'Look at the fingers of you han, chile. Some long, some short. You can't change the Lord world!'

'If you are the long finger, you could afford to look down and tell the others they suppose to be down there.' Rupert glanced at his sister. Angel sat with her head back, eyes closed.

'But people theyself perhaps not askin for nothing really different.'

'Is the same thing they used to say about the slaves. Happy contented niggers. They not askin for nothing different. They talk to one or two slaves who grin an say "Yes, Massa" becus they learn so well dey forget how to say anything else, an they figure that prove the point.'

They sat in silence. The clock ticked loudly. Angel counted. One. Two. Three. One. Two. Three. One. Two. Three.

'Mammie, how come angels always so white?'

Doodsie looked startled. She remembered Martin all those years ago in Hermitage.

'I mean those that drop out of the sky to come and save us.'

Jessie cleared her throat. She shouted from her room.

'It have black ones that come with them too, you know.'

Allan, in the dining-room, lifted his head from his letter. 'Saint Martin de Porres.'

'How he reach in dat?' Angel wanted to know. She meant this Saint Martin, but Carl, lying in his room reading, thought otherwise.

'Yes,' he said. 'He always fas in people business!'

'Well dis boy don have no respect for he father at all!' laughed Jessie.

'Meself ah not putting me mouth!' said Doodsie.

Allan laughed. 'Ay-ay! Who dis boy tink he talkin to at all? But seriously, you know, Saint Martin is one.'

Doodsie sucked her teeth. 'Don take God heaven an make allyou stupidness, eh!'

They laughed at her; she sat there frowning lightly, relaxed in the warmth of companionship.

'Angel,' she said quietly, 'Auntie Ezra tell me about a young man from Jamaica that come over there to be with you while you sick. Who is that?'

'Oh! A friend. A very good friend.'

'Hm-m-m! Tell me about him, non!'

'It don have nothing to tell, Mammie. We close. I like him very much. But neither one of us thinkin of marriage or anything like that. I like him a lot, though, but that is all.'

'What about Jerry?'

'Me an Jerry not the same kind of people. We grow apart, I think.'

'What is dis young man name?'

'Kai. Kai. If ah gon to married or live wid anybody, it gon be somebody like him!'

'But not him?'

'I don know! It mightn be possible!'

'You should be thinkin in terms of marriage, Angel. Not livin wid! What is dat! Livin wid!'

Angel chuckled, the first sound of fun they had heard since her return. Doodsie smiled.

'Ah don know where you chilren get you ideas from at all!'

Twelve

High up, the chicken-hawk circled.

Doodsie heard it. She threw open the kitchen window. She called the fowls, whistling loudly to attract their attention. She threw out a handful of corn. The fowls gathered. They came running.

'Caw! caw! caw!' High up, the chicken-hawk circled.

Doodsie threw more corn. 'Allyou stay togedder!' she shouted. Some of the fowls lifted one foot, kept their heads up, listening.

'Don study it, you stupes!' Doodsie threw more corn. 'It jus tryin to frighten allyou for you to scatter so that it could swoop down when allyou frighten an grab a chicken. Come! Come! Come!' Doodsie went out into the yard, gathering the fowls around her. She looked up. The chicken-hawk seemed to be disappearing in the distance. She waited. The fowls ate. There were no more calls from the chicken-hawk. I mus tell those children to fix that coop an keep the chickens inside. 'Allyou self too stupid,' she said to the fowls. 'Don run when they try to frighten you. Stay together an dey caan get none!'

Doodsie, Angel and Carl stood at the window; they watched the rain; it came pelting down. It was like a mini-storm. The tender plants just shooting out of the ground bent and broke under the force of the wind and the weight of the water. Somewhere behind the mountain, thunder grumbled. The carrot seeds that they had sprinkled in the back garden would be completely washed away. They would have to plant again.

Later, when the land remained washed and waiting, and a pale hesitant sun peeped over the hill next morning, Angel walked down the road.

Inside, Doodsie went out to the kitchen and opened the window. A bird jumped down from the drainpipe and started picking daintily on the windowsill. Doodsie lifted her hand from the sink; the bird flew off. Doodsie's eyes followed it. Suddenly she remained still, her mouth open. Her mind did a somersault in time to come up again years back, standing on the deck as the ship came in from Aruba. She remembered the birds, white birds dipping and graceful over a beautiful blue sea. Doodsie had stood transfixed, seeing this view of the land for the first time and suddenly understanding what the white people she worked for meant when they said to her that her island was 'extraordinarily beautiful, with the most fantastic harbour'. Even as they talked to her and she focused her mind on her country, her only real memory had been of the nutmeg trees, of her hurting back, of the white people's kitchens; but she had smiled sympathetically when they said it, feeling vaguely pleased. Seeing it from the boat, she had understood and agreed. The bird flew off to the golden apple tree.

Angel stopped at the corner just before the river. She jumped across the drain and walked to the walls that used to surround the old watermill. She watched the bamboo trees shooting out through the top, in the middle of those walls. She wondered how far down the roots went. Angel stood back a little and turned her head fully so that her good right eye could look to the left. Someone had put up a house now that that bit of land had been sold out, like so much of it around here now. All the old workers on Delicia estate, including her father, were buying spots. Delicia estate was no more. And spirits don like to live same place wid people, said Doodsie. Jus now, you go see! Delicia gon lose it reputation for spirits!

She looked around quickly, guiltily, feeling a little bit stupid about what she was about to do. Seeing no one, she swiftly pulled the candle and matches out of her shirt pocket. She put the lighted match to the wick, watched the lighted candle and waited. In her mind, she sang the song they always sang at wakes.

Chandinel kléwé-é-é!
Chandinel kléwé-é-é!
Chandinel kléwé-é-é!
O cièl!

In her mind's eye, she could see the figures circling the room, singing, the candles bobbing. 'Light the way for us!' She looked at the flame. She smiled as it remained steady in the still, cool morning. Well, she said quietly to the Sunday school teacher, dead now these ten years. The spirits gone, you know. The candle not goin out. They either gone, or they sympathetic. Nothing to fraid.

She jumped back across the drain, walked around the corner and stood looking at the tumbling muddy waters of the Delicia river, so calm before the rains, rushing down now to rid itself of the tumbling dirt.

Glossary

alé to go

bakra béké white boss
bazoodee stupidity, evil
boli calabash, a large round fruit (a word of African – Wolof
    – origin)
Bon Jé Good God

caraho an expression of annoyance, perhaps of Spanish origin
chabin fair-skinned
Chandinel kléwé light the candle (from a song: **chandel,**
    candle, and **kléwé,** to light)
chupid-i stupid person (**i,** he, she)
cièl heavens

dékatjé destroy, crush, mash up
Do Do petit popo   Sleep little one
Maman go in La Bay Mama has gone to La Bay
    (From a lullaby. **La Bay,** the sea or the bay, is the name by
    which Grenville, Grenada's second town, is known.)

é ben wi well, yes!

gadé bèt-la look at that beast
gadé mizè mwen non look at my trouble

hefe chief (from Spanish **jefe,** probably absorbed into the Gren-
    adian language through workers at the Panama Canal).

Ka dammit fut expletive (probably a mixture of progressive
  Patwa **ka,** English **dammit** and Patwa **fout,** damn)
kata wrap worn on the head to carry heavy loads (a word of
  African – Twi – origin)
ki bés sa? what base is that?
krapo frog (from French **crapaud,** often figured in folk say-
  ings)

lougarou a being resembling a ball of fire, into which humans
  can reputedly transform themselves to feed on the blood
  of their victims, though not usually harming them

Makomè familiar terms of address to woman friend (literally,
  godmother)
Manman o   O Mother
Mwen wivé   I have arrived
Pwangad waya piké mwen Take care lest the wire pricks me
  (song)
maman mother, mama
matité rude, used also to mean womanish
mawun an event organised to provide assistance for a member
  of the community in the carrying out of a specific task –
  moving house, cutting a cane crop, etc. (Pronounced
  maroon, the word possibly originates from the communal
  activities of the Maroons, African slaves who ran away
  from the estates.)
mwen I, me

nyam up de ital eat up your food (Jamaican)

one day one day congoté some day it will happen / did happen
  (but usually infers it never did or will)

palé Patwa speak Patwa
papa mèt exclamation (literally, my father)
payul white people (usually refers to Spaniards)
pèctus stately, proper
pli mal it gets worse and worse
pò djab o poor devil
poupa father
pwangad be careful

sa ki fè'w? what's happening?

saracca ritual feast of African origin, held for a healing
purpose, to bring good spirits to the neighbourhood

se kon sa nonk-li yé that's what his uncle is like

se kon sa tout nom an famni-a yé all the men in the family are
like that

tout moun ca playwai everyone is crying

vini ou kai vini, ou kai wè you are coming, you will see

vyé nèg old nigger (from **vyé,** old, and **nèg,** black)

wi yes

Joan Riley
Waiting in the Twilight

When Adella, a talented seamstress, moves to Kingston, Jamaica, life seems to promise much: a respectable career and the chance of professional status. Instead she falls for a young policeman who leaves her with two children. She is befriended and married by Stanton, a carpenter, and sails for England to join him. But Stanton too deserts her, for Gladys, Adella's own cousin.

She resolves to buy a home of her own, but is forced into sub-standard housing; in the end even this is taken from her by the council.

Now a grandmother crippled by a stroke, Adella waits patiently for her husband to return. Haunted by memories of the past, she assesses what has been achieved. Her life, apparently bleak, is sustained by her own generous love, and the warmth of her children.

This is the moving story of a woman's struggle for dignity against a background of urban racism. Riley pulls no punches in her effort to portray 'the forgotten and unglamorous section of my people' within a system which 'openly and systematically discriminates' against them.

Joan Riley's first novel, *The Unbelonging,* was published by The Women's Press in 1985.

Fiction   £3.95
ISBN: 0 7043 4023 2

Rhonda Cobham
& Merle Collins, editors
Watchers and Seekers

Creative Writing by Black Women

Here at last is a major anthology of some of the most exciting
creative writing coming from Black writers living in Britain.
These are poems and short stories by African and Asian
women exploring their identity as Black; common to all is a
glorying in the creative potential of language to illumine and
exhilarate. The collection as a whole casts an incisive eye on
social and political issues affecting Black women and on racism
in Britain today.

Rhonda Cobham teaches English and creative writing at
Amherst College, Massachusetts.

Merle Collins is a poet whose published work includes *Because
the Dawn Breaks* and poems in the anthologies *Callaloo* and
Words Unchained.

Poetry/Creative Writing £3.95
ISBN: 0 7043 4024 0

Jump Op ! Kiss Me
Nellie Payne